FORGIVE ME NOT

JENNIFER BAKER

Nancy Paulsen Books

Nancy Paulsen Books
An imprint of Penguin Random House LLC, New York

First published in the United States of America by Nancy Paulsen Books,
an imprint of Penguin Random House LLC, 2023

Visit us online at PenguinRandomHouse.com.

Library of Congress Cataloging-in-Publication Data
Names: Baker, Jennifer, 1981– author. | Title: Forgive me not / Jennifer Baker.
Description: New York: Nancy Paulsen Books, 2023. | Summary: Set in an alternate version
of Queens, N.Y., fifteen-year-old Violetta must participate in the Trials, a series of tests
meant to push her to the edge, to atone for her sister's death.
Identifiers: LCCN 2023019092 (print) | LCCN 2023019093 (ebook) |
ISBN 9780593406847 (hardcover) | ISBN 9780593406861 (ebook)
Subjects: CYAC: Grief—Fiction. | Forgiveness—Fiction. | Justice, Administration of—
Fiction. | African Americans—Fiction. | LCGFT: Novels.
Classification: LCC PZ7.1.B3513 Fo 2023 (print) | LCC PZ7.1.B3513 (ebook) |
DDC [Fic]—dc23 | LC record available at https://lccn.loc.gov/2023019092
LC ebook record available at https://lccn.loc.gov/2023019093

Printed in the United States of America

ISBN 9780593406847 (hardcover)
ISBN 9780593698044 (international edition)
1st Printing
LSCH

Edited by Stacey Barney
Design by Eileen Savage | Text set in Adobe Caslon Pro

FORGIVE ME NOT

PART I

The Sentence

CHAPTER 1
VIOLETTA

Days in detention: 22

~~LHT~~ ~~LHT~~ ~~LHT~~ ~~LHT~~ II

Right in front of me is a TV with my crying face on it. In the here and now, I'm pretty sure I'm all out of tears. I'm over my eyes itching and having a chapped nose after constantly wiping it with paper towels from the detention center bathroom. (Holding a tissue, I'm reminded how soft something can be.) I'm dried out, but the me on-screen isn't. *That* Violetta's covered in snot, salty tears, and guilt. I don't turn away or move. I watch myself on the monitor because my family's watching me too.

My counselor, Susan, grabs another tissue from the table on her side of the couch. She offers it to me and says under her breath, "If you need a break, I can turn this off for a moment."

"I wish it were me!" screeches from the video. I force myself to keep my chin up. In the video, I make wishes out loud while more echo in my head: I wish I'd listened. I wish I'd stopped myself. I wish I hadn't invited Pascal over that night. I wish . . . a lot.

I stop fiddling with the top of the jumpsuit Corrections gave me. The sports bra underneath pinches, and the pants irritate my skin from the starch. They don't fold much when I move. I'm hoping I look better now. But for a second, I wonder if I *should* look like the messy Violetta.

Three weeks earlier, my mom and dad stared at me as the ER doctor revealed that their number of kids had gone from three to two. *I* was okay. Scratches, a sore chest, and a mild concussion were my only injuries from the impact of the steering wheel before the airbag inflated. But my little sister was dead. Because of me.

On the TV, Violetta rubs her sleeve across her eyes, swelling the skin around them even more. My own brown eyes bore into me. She's sincere. Violetta on-screen clutches her hands together. She, *me*, asks to be forgiven for everything, not just the night of the accident, but the months before it. I regret my entire freshman year of high school, including the evening I woke up in the hospital. The Violetta in front of me apologizes for all of it.

In a way, this video is me fighting for my place in my family. Do I get to be forgiven and go home without a criminal record? Or do I serve time in confinement or . . . the other option?

Every night that I've been at the facility, I've practiced how to explain to my family what had happened. Two weeks ago, a guard sat me down and Counselor Susan explained that this was my last chance to make my case before sentencing. Just me in a room—really, a gray box—begging for forgiveness from the victims of my crime: my family. They would get to see my video, then "bestow judgment"—Counselor Susan's words, not mine. After explaining, she set up a camera as little as a match-book and said, "You may begin your plea."

I was going to be calm in the video. It was time for a plan, not a meltdown. There wasn't much else to do in detention, so why not mull over and over how to ask your family to forgive you for being a horrible daughter. A couple other detained girls gave me advice during meals: Don't be too serious, one said. Be *super* serious, someone else said. Bring up stories to remind your family how much they love you. Show you learned your lesson, that you don't need to be taught one. Be funny. Be remorseful. No matter what: Don't lose it!

But as soon as the camera beeped and the blinking light turned solid to record my plea, I dissolved into the screaming girl on display right now.

I can't take my eyes off the Violetta on-screen. How different she is from me now: She had hope.

"I'm sorry—sorry for everything. And I swear I'll listen and make better decisions. I promise." On the TV, I finish my plea. "*Please* let me come home" is the last thing I say, through sniffles and more snot.

The screen darkens as the fluorescents come back to life. I blink to adjust to the light. The sentencing room is stifling. One wall has a window with black glass while the others are painted indigo. A light bulb is above the TV. And the door next to the screen makes a horrible *ca-chink* when the bar to unlock it opens. My reflection reveals nothing once my face fades from the screen. My eyes look shrunken and dim, as if there's nothing behind them. Who could forgive me?

Because of the lights and the itchiness of my clothes, it's tough to keep my shoulders back or my head lifted. All I want to do is curl into a ball and rest.

Beside me on the couch, Counselor Susan looks like a professional in a blazer and heels, her hair in a bun, her super-thin legs crossed. She smiles at me, with ruby lips and blushed cheeks, as if there may be good news on the way. She didn't see my parents after my sister's death three weeks ago, the disgust that clouded their faces, how quickly they turned away from me. I shiver and mumble how cold it is, even though it's not with the lights beaming down on me.

I jump at her hand on my shoulder.

"Violetta," my counselor says, "I asked if you were ready."

I stare at her for a moment before it hits me. My trimmed nails dig into my skin. I think I nod.

"Okay." She smiles again, but it's strained. "Would you like me to explain things once more? About what will happen next?"

I think I shake my head no. I think I blink. I think I breathe. But I have no idea, because all of this feels unreal, like I'm watching myself again. My little sister is dead. I'm here waiting to know if I'll be forgiven or not, under juvenile law. I'm one of *those* kids. The type who needs to face justice before they can rejoin society.

I've heard about juvenile offenders. My parents tsk-tsked whenever news about them came on. "Don't be like them. Be *better*," Mom or Dad said before changing the channel from the news to a cooking show or a sitcom. A click of the remote erased someone else's reality in favor of something with a happier ending. Always "be better," they encouraged. Be better than the terrified teen who didn't want their parents to find out they were pregnant, so they hid their growing belly, then threw the newborn out like trash. The ones who got in fights that went wrong way too fast, resulting in casualties. The ones who carried weapons that accidentally went off in school or in someone's hands at home—or, worse, those who used them purposely on others. Supposedly, those teens were a whole other group. Not *me*. Not *my* family. Yet here I am. One of "*those* kids" who screwed up so badly I need to be made an example of.

I must have given her some kind of signal, because Counselor Susan says, "If the light is blue, you're forgiven and you can go back to your family. If it's red . . ." She lowers her head to indicate what I should and do already know.

My chest swells, and my heart beats faster. I grip the armrest because I can almost see a flicker of blue in the bulb. I could be forgiven. We could start over. I can be better, because I'm their daughter. I could be pardoned. I—

Red.

My hand flies to my mouth. I suck in air, needing to cough it out at the same time.

The screen crackles, and a new face blinks into view. I expect to see my parents, hear them say I'll be sent away and locked up forever, that I can go to hell, for all they care. Instead, it's my older brother, Vin, who has the same eyes as me, Mom, and my sister. His tawny skin is shiny, and he bites the corner of his lip, a gesture he makes before he says something I don't want to hear. He did the same when I asked him if he liked my boyfriend, Pascal, or if he'd please take me to one of his junior hangouts. He'd chew the corner of his lip, and right away I knew I wouldn't like his answer.

"Letta," my brother begins, "I'm sure you saw the red light." His words come in quick bursts, all jumbled, like he wants to toss them out as fast as he can. "You know what that means. However, while we as a family don't yet forgive you . . ." He hesitates. "While as a family we don't yet forgive you, we want to give you the opportunity to learn from this incident. We don't want Viv's death to be for nothing. We need you to"—he clears his throat—"repent."

These aren't *his* words. He'd never say *repent*.

"So . . ." He stops. My brother swallows hard. When he opens his mouth, he doesn't speak.

Just say it, Vin. Say it!

"We think it best that you participate in the Trials so that you may understand the severity of this matter. But you know you don't have to take this option."

Of course I don't *have* to, but the other option for no forgiveness—confinement at an upstate juvenile facility—isn't any better. *Is it, Vin?*

"Should you take this option, your first Trial will occur in the next week." Vin leans in, his face large and imposing. His eyes reflect as much pain as I feel right now. All kinds of rumbling moves through me as he speaks. "We do love you. You know that, right?"

The video cuts off, and my brother disappears.

I push my palms into my eyelids. I want to undo everything that's happened. But there's no going back.

We do love you. You know that, right? is the only part of the message that sounded like Vin. The only part where I could feel him pull me into a side hug after a fight, after I'd stomped away from his questions about why I was acting differently now that I was in high school. Why did I laugh at everything Pascal and his friends said, even when it wasn't funny? (Because my brother knew what made me laugh, and making fun of other people wasn't it.) He'd say this after catching me stumbling into my room after a night with Pascal. After I had my first, then second, then third tastes of hard lemonades or beer. After splashing water on my face and putting me to bed, Vin would say, "You know I still love you, right? Even though you're acting like an idiot."

It would've been a little better if he hadn't been the one on the video. If he hadn't had that disappointed look I can't erase, reminding me of my parents' faces after the accident.

My counselor is speaking. Her words seep in slowly as she asks the question I dread: "Violetta Chen-Samuels, do you accept participation in the Trials?"

My hands are wet. Guess I wasn't done crying after all.

CHAPTER 2

VINCE

Days since the decision: 22

Since the accident, our home has been a revolving door of people working for the city or the state. The morning after the crash, two officers stopped by asking all types of questions: How exactly did my fifteen-year-old sister procure alcohol? Why did my parents leave the car keys where a non-licensed driver could get them? Was Violetta prone to this type of behavior? Every question was a judgment of "How did you let this happen?" All that led to the decision for Violetta to go to detention. About a week ago, the rep from Detention Services became a constant presence in our home. Our assigned judicator prodded them, encouraged them that the next steps had to happen sooner than later. Last week was also when we watched Letta's plea, and it wasn't pretty. (It isn't pretty to rewatch either, if I'm being honest.)

Letta was a hot mess on-screen. Her face was greasy and wet. She screeched apologies and regret. Watching her breakdown was the longest five minutes of my life. Didn't help when the judicator arrived right after, saying we had to make a choice about sentencing.

"You have three choices," the judicator said, all monotone. "You can forgive the offender so she can come home. You can *not* forgive her so we can formally confine her in an Albany facility and determine the length of sentence based on her crimes. Or you can assign her rehabilitation through the Trials; this way she'll remain detained in the city."

The judicator tugged at his striped necktie and smiled. His grin did not put anyone at ease, even if it seemed like he was trying to. "There's no sense in delaying the inevitable. You have to inform your daughter of your latest decision," he said.

Mom couldn't keep still. She went from rubbing an ear against her shoulder to rolling or unrolling the sleeves of her robe. Dad tried to hold her, but she didn't want to be held. The judicator glanced at me and said, "Why not have Vincent record your decree?"

Every day since the accident brought up the question of whether Letta should come home or not. How this would be handled. And Detention Services wanted an answer, preferably right then and there.

"Would you prefer she go upstate?" the judicator asked.

"We don't want to send her upstate or away, we just . . ." Mom couldn't finish and Dad didn't take up the end of her sentence like he usually did. Mom concluded with, "We want her to be okay."

The judicator had a tablet in his hand, prepped and ready. "If you choose rehabilitation, which has shown excellent results"—he held up the screen to back up his statement— "then she can potentially return home sooner. It may be the best option for a case of underage drinking. You do want your daughter to get better, don't you?"

And that was that. In the end, I just couldn't say no to the video.

So several days ago, I sat in front of a camera on a tripod, with a slate backdrop behind me and my parents in front of me. I read the words my family was encouraged by our judicator to recite. The camera zoomed in on my face, so no one else saw how much my right *and* left legs jiggled.

Today is sentencing day. And right now we're watching my sister watch me on-screen. In the video, I glisten from sweat, but it doesn't seem like there are other signs of nerves. My parents are in the corner seated at a metal table, farthest away from the glass separating our viewing room from Violetta's judgment location. By our door stands a guard dressed in a navy uniform. Where we are is slightly larger and just as sparse as the room my sister sits in.

I'm standing at the two-way mirror with folded arms. My breath makes clouds on the surface of the glass. Violetta resembles a mannequin, the way she stares at the TV, at me telling her what's what. She doesn't seem to be breathing or blinking, or awake at all. I press against the glass, waiting for any movement.

There's another reason I agreed to the video:

A week after the accident, literally the day before Viv's funeral, I passed Viv's empty room and peeked inside. Everything was how she left it, but Viv wasn't there. I stepped into her bedroom, and I swear I almost saw Viv tumbling past, asking if I wanted to play. But she was never, ever gonna be there again.

That realization brought me to my knees. The urge to grab my jacket and head out to get lit one more time was so strong. I mean, I could just start fresh the next day, right? Could've called my teammate Byron and asked him to hook me up like usual instead of going to his source.

Pain pricked my chest so bad it made me realize I'd be no better than Letta if I started clean later. It didn't matter how many times Mom and Dad asked to meet Pascal but Letta refused. Didn't matter that I could *smell* the sour alcohol on Letta's breath some weekends and warned her this could get worse, quick. Didn't matter that Letta was grounded the night of the accident because earlier that week she'd come home close to midnight and mouthed off to Mom and Dad that she wanted to be left alone—more of Pascal's influence, I'm sure. Since September, Letta said things with Pascal weren't out of control, that she was having *fun* letting loose. I'd said the same thing about the pills I'd swallowed, insisting they were only for when I needed it—finals, big games, anytime I need to be *on*— nothing more than that.

A week after my sister died, I took in everything of hers. A typical seven-year-old's room, with cartoon posters covering teal walls. The half-open drawers under her bed that oozed clothes, puzzle pieces, and toy food stations. A hanging corkboard, with the red envelopes Viv saved after every Chinese New Year and some pictures of our family tacked up.

I sat back on my heels and took a deep breath. That moment

in Viv's room was when I knew the sister that remained needed my help.

When my video started, I squinted to see Violetta sitting on her hands in the darkened room. Now she has the couch in a death grip and no emotion on her face. Is she about to cry? Is she thinking about Viv? Is she hating us, hating *me*?

"We think it best that you participate in the Trials so that you may understand the severity of this matter. But you know you don't have to take this option," I hear myself say. My nails dig deep enough into my biceps to draw blood.

The video ends. I fade away from sight. In our room, my parents hold each other. My mom's eyes gleam in the subtle lights above us. Violetta looks like both of them: Dad's brown skin and wide brow with Mom's lidded eyes and round nose.

The counselor asks Letta if she accepts the Trials. That's when one tear, then another, drops down my sister's face.

My mother grabs Dad's wrist and starts rambling off questions. "Do you think this is a good idea, Albert? Maybe we should've waited? She looks too skinny. I don't—"

"Annie, our daughter needs *help*," Dad says gently. "We have to believe this will be what helps her see things have gone too far."

In the hospital, I held Violetta's hand while she took ragged breaths. Viv was dead. Thrown against the windshield when Letta braked too hard and swerved off the road. The passenger airbag deployed too late. I was so goddamn mad. I'd had the urge to shake Letta and yell, *What the hell were you doing driving?* Thankfully, I didn't do that. I sat back in the chair next to Letta's hospital bed, wondering what we'd do. Wondering if I'd be found out for my wrongs like Violetta had been for hers.

Right now, I expect Letta to try and escape. To curse or scream or apologize some more. The glass is an unwanted barrier, but it's there, and I kick the wall under it, hard, feeling the sting through my sneaker into my big toe. I haven't felt much besides the withdrawal. This is good, this basic jab of pain.

"Hey!" the guard warns. He takes a few steps toward me.

I kick it again, hoping Violetta can hear me.

The jolt to my shoulders confirms he's not kidding. "What did I say?" The guard's spit trickles inside my ear as he twists my arms behind my back. The stale scent of the coffee he had earlier wafts to my nose.

"Get off my son!" my dad roars.

"Vincent!" my mother yells.

I don't look away from my sister. I don't shout at her not to accept, and I don't tell her to accept. I can't take my eyes off Letta, even as the scrape of the table and chairs thunders behind me.

My sister wipes her face and says, "I'll do whatever it takes." That's when I go limp in the guard's grip. His hold loosens, and I'm on the ground. The throb in my limbs pounds through my bones, all the way to my temples.

Mom and Dad don't move to help me. They're watching Letta too.

We know that "whatever it takes" is gonna be hell.

CHAPTER 3
VIOLETTA

Days in detention: 22

~~|||| |||| |||| ||||~~ ||

The air feels heavier right after sentencing. It makes me drag my feet on the rocky path from the sentencing building to the girls' main facility. The girls' and boys' detention centers are like a row of broken teeth. Spirals of wire glint on top of the gates sealing us in. On the left is the girls' center. Past these gates and security mounts sits the boys' facility— larger and just as dreadful. Both facilities have athletic fields and sheds where inmates can garden year-round. The visitors' parking lot is practically two city blocks away from the girls' detention center, but it's visible from our athletic field. The staff parking lot is closer to the boys' field. I can already see guards arriving in pairs for their shifts. With their uniforms draped over their shoulders, they walk by inmates without a word or glance. Must be nice to know you can clock out of a place like this.

We barely ever see or hear anyone on the boys' side. Not until days like today, when the boys are also in lines, waiting for judgment. We all exit sentencing after learning if we're forgiven, doing time upstate, or doing Trials, then we split up to deal with whatever else is scheduled for us that day.

Piedmont Facility is in a part of Queens I'd never been to before. Someone said we could be an island, a forgotten one. That's exactly how it feels. Endless roads and patchy fields, oak and maple trees; the Little Neck Bay divides us from the residential neighborhoods. From my cell, the trees are so far away I can only dream of touching them.

Outdoors, some of the sounds are familiar: The police sirens. The squeak of buses parking, and the *beep beep* when they lower to let off visitors. Even the shouts of inmates on the concrete basketball court is something I cling to, thinking about the times my brother, sister, and I visited the Westbridge playground or went to one of my brother's lacrosse games. Then there are the other sounds specific to this place: The clank of every door, the static and buzz from electrified fences. The clomping of guards' boots. The jingle of keys chained to their belts, and the click of their security cards on the same chain.

The frost and weight of the air is nothing compared to how it feels being sentenced to the Trials. I'm in a loose line with six other girls and guards in front and behind us. We're led out of one building and toward another. I'm nudged from behind.

"It's too cold for daydreaming," Eve says. Dried tears are two chalky lines down her dark-brown skin. A knit hat covers her ears and her pixie cut. Apparently, none of us are ever going to stop crying.

Serena gives Eve a quick pat on the back before stuffing her hands into her assigned coat. Serena's neon-pink dreadlocks are tied back into two pigtails on either side of her head. With her coat collar pulled up, I can't see the lilac tattoo on Serena's neck. Its colors usually stand out on her beige and freckled skin.

When we came out of our sentencing rooms, Eve shrugged at me. "Nothing yet," she mumbled once we got back in line. "The *victims*"—she didn't hide her dislike for the word— "requested more time deciding if they forgive me or not."

I didn't know what to say. What *is* there to say?

But Serena was able to figure my news out. "It's written all over your face," she said. "Trials?"

A wipe of my nose was all it took to confirm it for her.

"Same, girl. Good times," Serena said with a suck of her teeth. She twirled a finger in the air in mock celebration.

Some of the other girls around me look younger, some older, and most are taller than me and Eve—including Serena, who's said she's the shortest one in her family at five-eleven. The facilities house juveniles age thirteen to seventeen. Eighteen means you're an adult and, when charged with a crime, you do actual time at the upstate prison. If you're younger than thirteen, you go through a "process" where officials determine if you're old enough to be considered a juvenile. I'm fifteen. Everyone insists I'm old enough to understand what I did and that I need to take responsibility.

And I will. *Whatever it takes.*

Twenty-two days ago, Eve and I arrived at the facility on the same day in the same white bus. Serena came a week after that. Her cell is in Eve's dorm. Most of March has flown by with me anxious about what's next. Even with a kind of answer, I'm still all nerves, wondering what I'll have to do to see my family again. While Serena and I wait to hear what our Trials are, Eve will be back here next Saturday, sentencing day, hoping for an answer. Not knowing your sentence is its own kind of punishment. The chill doesn't leave me once I'm inside the facility. It's just different now that I know I'll be here a bit longer. We're patted down to make sure nothing was brought over from the sentencing building, but it's quick—a relief, considering how these checks can go. I'm taken to my dorm while Eve, Serena, and the other girls split off with guards to theirs. Guards escort inmates to and from our dorm whenever we want, or need, to go somewhere else in the facility. No one can go anywhere alone in case, as Counselor Susan told me, "something happens." She didn't explain what that meant; she didn't have to.

My "dorm" is a corridor with cells above and below. There's a kind of common area filled with rectangular metal tables with stools connected to them. Concrete walls and military-green doors separate inmates from everything. Pipes are exposed in the ceilings. Holes appear in random places. Dents are messily filled with putty where the wall and floor meet.

My home these past weeks is quiet. Nerves and nothingness keep most of us mute in the dorm area. Some girls play cards, others sit on the floor to read by the window, and others stare outside. From here our view shows us the entry and exit of the facility, and who gets bused in and out. Right now, I see a van bringing in more girls. Even from inside, I can hear the burr of the gates opening. Since everything is limited, from TV to the internet, I can see why watching the ins and outs of the facility is its own entertainment. What we have in real time is the makeshift garden where some girls farm in a hut filled with heat lamps and blankets of dirt. We do have designated TV time. The movies we watch are usually cartoons or family-friendly stuff—lots of talking animals and happily ever afters.

Outside of the guard station near my corridor's entrance—literally a booth where two guards sit—are fourteen cells. Seven are on the floor level and seven on the next level. More than half of them are in use. Glancing out the big window at the new arrivals, I wonder how many more cells are in this monster of a building waiting to be filled.

"Violet!"

Petra calls out to me from the top of the stairs. She hangs over the railing, waving both arms so she's practically a windmill. The guard escorting me is already halfway up the stairs. Petra's cell is tucked in a corner by mine.

As soon as I take the last step, Petra wraps me in a hug. "Tell me your news," she whispers, "and I'll tell you mine."

She's buzzing; she can't be contained. She pulls away so I can see how rosy her cheeks are. Her smile reveals the slight gap between her top teeth. From day one, I noticed how pretty she is. Tall and curvy, even in the loose bottoms and top we're assigned. Her brown hair covers her face whenever she takes it out of the mandatory ponytail. We either have short hair, just past our ears, like mine now, or we tie it back.

Seeing me up close, her head falls to the side. "Oh," she

says, losing a bit of her light. I must have *Trials* scribbled on my forehead.

"We coming or going?" the guard asks with a shake of the keys to unlock my door. I keep pace with him, and now Petra is by my side on our way to my cell.

"I . . . I," my voice gurgles. I swallow down what wants to come up and say, "Trials."

"Oh, Violet," Petra breathes.

The creaking sound my cell door makes when it opens or shuts makes me jumpy. I should be used to it by now. But I don't want to get used to all this. The guard leaves without a word. The minute I step inside my cell, the smell of mold and old blankets hits me. There's a thin mattress, a barred window the size of textbook, a shelf lodged against the wall for a handful of things, mostly trial-size soap and shampoo and conditioner, a small sink, where I can balance a composition notebook on the edge, and the toilet in the corner, which I don't use until after dark, if possible.

Petra stands in the doorway scratching her arm. From the day I met her, she's worn only long sleeves under her uniform. But today she has short sleeves and her arms are out. I can see pink and red scars from her wrists going past her elbows. I try not to stare. The first thing I noticed about her were her arms. Day one inside, I was led to my cell holding my provisions— clean uniform, toiletries, underwear, and socks. And there was Petra, arms straight out in front of her like a zombie, her skin wrapped in gauze.

She usually went to the nurse to tend to her wounds after her Trial. At the time, she didn't say much about what she had to do. Only that she had an Endurance Trial. Sometimes she'd say, "A lot of thorns today" before settling into bed, arms crossed over her chest like she was being laid to rest.

I'd wondered if her Trial was to hurt herself. I got the courage to ask her that on my second day. Everyone in our dorm was in line, headed to breakfast. She laughed at my question, but it sounded more like she thought I was stupid.

"*I* don't have to hurt myself," she said to me. "That's what the Trials are for."

We didn't speak again for a few days. By the end of my first week, Petra heard me crying in my room. That's when she asked my name. When I told her, she said, "Nice. It's different."

Those first few days inside, I kept to myself. Mostly spoke to Eve when we saw each other at meals, class, or recreation. Eve and I relied on the frail bond of arriving together before Serena joined us. No one else had spoken to me until Petra did. When she saw me crying, I'd expected her to laugh or say something mean. She didn't do either. Recreation period had just been announced for our dorm, and she asked if I wanted to go for a walk.

Petra didn't wait for my reply, and she didn't ask if I needed time. She sauntered out of my cell and expected me to follow. Which I eventually did.

Five days in detention, and I had a friend.

Seeing Petra like she is now isn't normal for in here. Trials take place Monday through Friday, same as mandatory classes.

It's Saturday morning, and Petra is not bandaged or sad. I'm glad she's not recovering or upset, but right now I want to be in my feelings.

"You know," Petra begins, "it may not be that bad. Plus, it is your family. That may help."

A spring inside the mattress bites my thigh as I plop on the bed. "How?" I lie down, hearing the rustle of letters under my pillow. Four letters total from Grams and my aunt Mae. Three from Pascal, one for each week I've been in here. I haven't responded to any of them, because what's there to say? How do I explain the biggest mistake of my life to my family? Pascal wants me to know he's thinking of me. But what I get from him are letters that read more forced than friendly, like someone made him write to me. Every time I start to think of what to say, to Pascal or my aunt or Grams, it never feels like enough.

"Well, your family may have more sympathy, for one," Petra says. "My victim's *family* actually sentenced me to my Trial, because he wasn't able to speak for himself. The guy's parents, well, let's just say they were not kind to me." It may be a tic when she rubs her right arm, tracing one of the longer scars. Petra tilts her head to the other side, and her ponytail droops. "But that's part of what I wanted to tell you!"

When I turn to Petra, the papers under my pillow crinkle again. "You're—"

"Getting out of here! Next weekend!" She sways her hips with each sentence. *"Finally forgiven!"* Her voice echoes in our corridor.

I squeeze my eyes shut, because I need a moment. I'm not mad. *I'm not.* But why couldn't we both have been forgiven today?

I'm not sure if she can read my silence for what it is: jealousy. If there's one thing I've learned about Petra, it's that she likes to fill the quiet.

"Forgiveness *does* happen. All the time, Violet. Some other girl I knew here got like a two-week Comprehension Trial as rehabilitation for stealing and totaling a car. All she had to do was roadside cleanup every day. Someone else did like a one-day Trial of garbage detail in a landfill for breaking and entering at the mall. So maybe yours will be similar. Nothing too bad, you know?"

"I didn't only wreck a car or break into a mall, Petra." I don't mean to snap at her, but it comes out like that anyway.

"Oh, I know, Violet." She squats in front of me, remorseful. "Well, there was another girl? A month of changing bedpans after abusing her grandmother, who she was supposed to help. That girl got *way nicer* after that Trial." She puts on a big, goofy grin, with tongue out, to make me laugh.

It almost works. *Almost.*

"I'm so sorry," she says. "I just want to make you feel better, and I'm failing."

"I failed at being a good daughter, so we're in the same club. Do we get stickers?"

"Letta, I know what happened is bad."

"Bad?" I respond. "Don't you mean the worst thing ever?"

There's no getting around what I did: underage drinking,

drunk driving, and vehicular manslaughter. At my first meeting with Counselor Susan, she read off *manslaughter* as one of the charges, and I wanted to vomit. I think my counselor thought she was helping when she said "manslaughter" was better than "murder," since murder means harm was intentional. They both mean the same thing: My sister is dead. Because of me. How could I have ever thought forgiveness was an option?

I try lying down again, but the view of my ceiling isn't soothing. Peeling paint threatens to fall to the floor. The other inmates, who stayed inside all day, have their doors open, so I can see there's no difference in how little we're given: flaking gray walls, shabby beds, old smells. I want to be alone, but at the same time, I like Petra. She's been through a lot and earned her release. Her smile almost makes me feel optimistic. *Almost.*

"It's bad. Yeah. But you're not the only person to accidentally—" She thinks better of finishing. As if *not* saying it will make all this hurt less.

Petra and I know what each other has done. Once we became friends, I heard about her assault; it made me angry and terrified at the same time. As usual, she was in my cell trying to cheer me up, but got lost in her own memories. Describing the night of made her relive it. She told me about the guy she thought genuinely liked her pushing her down on his bed; her torn blouse; scrambling to find something, *anything*, to get him off her; clutching a pair of scissors from his desk so tightly it made an imprint in her palm; and how much of his blood soaked his sheets. While Petra told her story, her cheeks were ablaze. She rolled her neck over and over in an attempt to erase what happened. So yes, I am happy for her forgiveness. I really, really am.

The happier Petra squatting in front of me this very moment deserves to heal in a real way.

I tell her, "Counselor Susan said to think of my Trials as 'an opportunity,' not a sentence."

Petra's laugh sounds like a sneeze. "Ugh. She's my counselor too. The hell does she know?"

"So, it can get bad?" I search her face. "Really bad?" I want to know what's possible, what options my family may have for me. Petra named some minor offenses and Trials just now. But her scars aren't from garbage duty and bedpans. Hers are from field work that she may never forget.

Petra doesn't say anything at first. She rubs her arm as if she's cold, bringing back my earlier chill.

"Be strong, girl. Sometimes people need time to forgive, like, really forgive."

"How much time did yours take?"

She slides in next to me on the mattress to show me the backs of her hands. I take in the raised skin, marks of her journey. She holds up her fingernails; they're the color of sapphire. "I can't control much of what's out there. All I can control is me, right? This is what I did for myself. My family sent it to me so I could do something to remind me I'm . . . me. Day after day for nine months."

Nine months!

"That's thirty-six weeks of *one* Trial. All those damn weeks of rosebushes and greenbrier. *All* those thorns I had to wade through, *all* those spiky branches and prickles I had to crouch down in, to clear a field. And for *what*?" Petra's fingers zigzag up and down the opposite arm, like she's counting the days with every bump.

"Did you know there's actually a plant called 'crown of thorns'?" She doesn't wait for me to answer. "Every day, I waited to hear if I finally passed and showed my endurance. And now I can go home. Forgiveness is worth fighting for, Violet. It means no record for your offense. That's worth it to me because *I* did nothing wrong when I defended myself." She lifts my chin so her brown eyes lock on to mine. "I almost kissed Counselor Susan when she told me."

"But—"

"Doesn't matter. You'll rock this."

Petra and my cell—my home for who knows how long—get blurry.

"You're gonna have bad times. I did all the time. But I figured, at least if I could be forgiven, if at some point his family could understand why what happened *happened*, well . . . things might get better. I held on to that instead of quitting and choosing time upstate with a record. The Trials are how some of us get out of here free and clear," she says. "You'll be next. And then I'll see you on the outside, okay?"

Everything about her is so strong and certain, the exact opposite of how I feel.

"I guess."

"No guessing!" she shouts in my face.

"Do you want to get us in trouble?"

"Say it! Say it with me, or I'll get louder."

I try to shush her, but there's no shushing Petra. Her energy is too big for this whole place, let alone my cramped cell. She's so much of what I'm not.

"I'll get out of here," I mumble.

"I can't *hear* you!" Petra blocks my door. There's nowhere to run. "Say. It."

"Fine. I'll get out of here! Happy?"

"Yes!" Her grin is so big I almost smile back.

She disappears. I think this means I can take a nap before lunch, but she's back from her cell in an instant with something in her hand.

"Here you go, pretty Violet. A gift from me to you."

She holds what looks like a pen; the gel inside it is something between pink and orange. I'm surprised, since we're not allowed anything more than a golf pencil in here, but when I take it to look closely, I see it's all soft plastic. Once I take off the cap, the smell is powerful, familiar.

When I squeeze the pen, polish drips from the tiny brush tip. A drop lands on the floor, adding a bit of color to my cell.

I twirl the polish pen between my fingers. It's soothing to hold something from outside, something to remind me of home.

"We're both getting out of here. And that's that." She claps her hands.

My biggest hope is that I'll start to believe her.

CHAPTER 4
VINCE

Days since the decision: 22

I'm on my third bag of red licorice. This is becoming a problem. Whenever I move, the wrappers near the gas and brake pedals remind me of my gorge fest. After Letta's sentencing this morning, I decided I needed time alone, and some serious sugar.

Outside the 24/7 Mart, the smell of gas is heavy. The mart is a glass cube with neon lights advertising dollar deals and low (for this part of the city) gas prices. You can see the orange-and-green awning from any nearby roadway, especially once it gets dark. I'm on an afternoon sugar high that I hope settles enough for me to sleep. The mart parking lot is a nice place to be alone, though. Just me, some strawberry twists, and the slight thrum of the car's heater to combat the winds outside; hopefully, these weeks will be the last of the chill as we head into spring.

From here, it's a ten-minute ride on the expressway to Main Street and the dim sum spots my family used to go to on Sundays. There's also a jiggly pancake stall on one of the side streets that Viv dragged me and Letta to, where we wolfed down fluffy, sweet stacks. It's a few minutes more to Citi Field, where Dad got dugout seats for the Mets game. Us praying for the minivan's AC to work faster when our bare legs touched the leather seats that had been boiling in the sun during the game. And there's the sculpture park further west of Flushing, where Viv played around the new art installations while Mom and Dad took pictures and me and Letta lounged on the grass, staring at our phones as an East River breeze passed over us. Mom and Dad offered a ferry ride, and though Letta and I begged off, Viv was willing. And sometimes there was a longer drive to visit Dad's family in St. Albans, Viv and Letta gardening with Grams and Aunt Mae, then all of us hitting up the best spot for beef patties. Scorching days brought the ice cream truck and the jingle that made Viv brush the dirt from her knees and rush out of the garden for a cone. I wasn't far behind, because who doesn't love some soft serve? Every part of my borough brings good memories turned sour, so I take another bite of licorice to try and get the bad taste out.

Scrolling through my phone, I'm reminded why I've been a ghost online. Mom says social media is the devil; I'm inclined to agree. My profile page welcomes me with posts of condolences and a crapload of emojis.

DUDE, I'm sorry about your lil sis!

This is so sad, man. 😵 Does this mean you're out for the season? 🙁

What about track championships? Vince is our ace!

RIP to an angel 👼 is under a family photo from last summer. There's also the judgy ones:

If it were me I'd let Violetta rot in detention.

Vince's sis was always so quiet, who knew she was a party animal?

The comments under those aren't any better. People agreeing that Letta should be in a cell forever or face serious consequences: **I lost my brother to drunk driving. She deserves punishment!**

I get angrier the more I scroll. None of them ask how me or my family are doing; they want to gossip. Mostly declarations, not questions. But I can't blame them. I'd be the same way if I were on the outside looking in.

There are also the daily texts from my friends Janice and Jorge. *They* ask how I am. Outside of "Okay," I haven't known how to answer either of them since I saw them at the funeral.

Then there's the texts from the guys from track and lacrosse. My teammate Byron is the most insistent, saying he's happy to connect me with Ross or just stop by with something to "mellow me out." It's how he shows support. I delete Byron's messages as fast as they come. I don't even reply with a **No, thanks,** afraid I'll type the opposite and slide right back into a hazy abyss.

Be better than that, Vin. Be what Mom and Dad and your team need you to be right now: a rock.

Levi's messages, on the other hand, go unread. Me caring versus pretending not to care about him is a battle I wage daily. This is another reason I need more licorice. Nothing cures heartbreak better than candy. Hell, maybe I'll throw in some peanut butter cups to get this pity party to its height.

I toss my phone to the passenger seat. I'm planning on going in for a fourth (fifth?) bag of licorice and water, and possibly chocolate, when a customer inside catches my eye. Really, his brown leather jacket with the fur collar does. The shine and soft look of it, plus the length, can only mean it's Ross. There are three rows of food—all junk—some beer, lots of scratch lottery tickets, and a big ole Icee machine near the entryway. Ross ducks to get something on the bottom shelf in the middle of the mart, and when he pops up again, I see his face. I don't think he can see me. But if I turn on the ignition, he'll catch me immediately, thanks to the way this junk car shrieks. Mine is one of six cars in the lot, including two at the gas pumps fifty feet away.

I'd been hoping I could avoid Ross a while longer. At least until I knew I could kick pills for sure on my own. My thumb drums against the wheel, then my right leg starts shaking. I can almost feel the pills he and Byron used to give me working their way through me, making my mind and body lighter, almost like I was floating.

The chime of classical music makes me jolt. My phone vibrates, and the screen lights up the inside of my car. I've lost track of Ross.

A new message reads, **Good to see you.**

"Huh?"

A knock on the driver's-side window startles me.

Damn it, Ross.

He motions for me to roll the window down. My car is a tuned-up older Ford that Dad gave me for being a good student.

A good son. Even when I saw its dents and rusty edges, I told him I was grateful. It was all he and Mom could afford.

I offer Ross the same fake grin I did to Dad. "Hey! How's it going?"

Ross extends a fist. I bump it. He rests his arms in the window, positioning himself in my space. Late winter frost lingers and seeps in, along with the heavy woody scent of his cologne.

"Hey," he says. He's a mass of teeth, nose, and eyes. All of his features fit perfectly on his long, pale face. He glances at my back seat, then gives me the same judgmental look everyone else does. I see what he sees in my rearview mirror: the empty energy drink cans, the lacrosse helmet, the track shoes, the mound of clothes, including my Track & Field jacket. My costume of All-American Son in full effect.

I repeat a "Hey," wishing I had a curtain to hide that part of my life from everyone.

"Been a while." His words form clouds in the cold.

I shiver and zip up my coat. "A few weeks. Because of . . . stuff."

"Yeah, everyone at school's been talking about it."

I keep my hands on the steering wheel, hoping he doesn't see my body tremble. My foot slips under the brake.

"Really sorry about Vivian, Vince. Really." He slaps a hand on my shoulder before folding it back into his jacket pocket.

"Violetta won't be back at school for a bit," is all I say.

"Figured." He sniffs the air, looks dead at me, sniffs some more. His face gets close to my lips. I open my mouth to ask what he's doing when he says, "Ah, cheap licorice high. I know it well."

The lights from the mart spotlight him: The crispness of his leather jacket. The way his thin dirty-blond hair is mussed. I can't see his shoes but know they're nicer than nice, more than likely the newest Nike collector brand. Ross wears his family's money well. I look around for his Mustang that has an engine that roars, a painted wing, and a coat and taillights that'll blind you.

"I told you—"

"Yeah, yeah. You *told* me you were going 'straight.'" He lightly punches me and laughs. "But I get it. Life sucks right now."

He grabs the shoulder he just punched. He massages gently, then digs in, his fingers pressing through my down coat. Ross bends so his breath hits the side of my face. "You know I'm here when you need me, and even when you think you don't." His fingers work their way to the back of my neck. They're cold to the touch, which sends another shudder through me.

The night everything went to hell, Ross was close, just like he is now. The night he offered me his latest, I was dejected and rejected, thanks to Levi. I thought Levi and me were together, officially together, since we'd been *doing stuff* for weeks. My lips couldn't get enough of his, and vice versa. So imagine my surprise when the night of the accident Levi broke things off with me at Westbridge Peak. I didn't wait to hear anything after Levi said, "I can't be with you, Vin. Not the way you want." I raced into the cold, not even bothering to slam his car door shut. That's when I ran right into Ross. The ridge along the water had a great view across from the lit-up tip of LaGuardia. Our ears rang from the zoom of the planes overhead. Ross led me to his Mustang. Told me to take a seat on the hood. "I got something. Just for you," he'd said. I stared at his empty hands. He smiled, all teeth, and opened his mouth. On his tongue was a yellow capsule. The pill's colors bled into his mouth.

"This is guaranteed to mellow you out," Ross had said with a lisp, making sure not to swallow the product.

The wind whipped through me. And I'm pretty sure that's the moment Letta's car crash happened. I ignored the feeling, though. Instead, I'd tilted my head, leaned in, and kissed him. Ross's lips were soft, but that's not what I cared about. The pill went down easy and blurred the world around me quickly. That's what I wanted, to forget the pain.

In the here and now, I gently take Ross's hand off me. This is what got me in trouble in the first place.

"I see." He knocks on the side of the door, thrusts a small packet into my lap.

"Ross . . ."

Already backing off, he says, "Take it. Don't take it. It's there if you need it. Plus, I'm only a phone call away."

It's easier to take it and go, so I do. The engine coughs and belches smoke as I reach around the headrest to back out. I try not to think about him, or his gift, as I speed off.

Once I'm in our duplex, I kick off my sneakers and rush past the kitchen and up the stairs to flush the pills down the toilet. No way I can leave them in the car with Mom or Dad occasionally driving it now that their van is totaled. I stop mid-step when I hear, "You can't do this to her!" I stuff the Ziploc in my pocket before thundering back down to the kitchen to see Letta's best friend all frantic. Callie waves her arms while moving around my parents at the dining table.

"Callie?" I say.

"Vince!" She wraps her arms around my neck so tight the charms on her plastic bracelet press into my skin.

"Callie," I cough.

"They just told me about sentencing! Tell them they can't do this to her!" She lets go of me and rushes back to the table, brown hair flying, hoop earrings jiggling. I try to hold on to her so she can tell me what's happening, what she thinks she's doing. But she's short and slippery. Callie was always the more hyper of the Letta-Callie duo.

Dad's head is propped on his hand, and Mom focuses on her slice of pizza. Two large pies and a bunch of soda cans are spread on the kitchen table alongside sympathy cards. The cheese and green peppers make me both hungry and not. I'm so tired of pizza. We've had it a dozen times in the past few weeks. Mom keeps ordering like all five of us are home to devour it, like before. She hasn't cooked since Vivian died. Viv used to follow Mom around the kitchen, helping her make cashew chicken, fried Shanghai noodles, Chinese broccoli in oyster sauce. Dad's parents, my aunts (mostly Aunt Mae and her wife, Sonali), neighbors, and friends occasionally bring food. Their dishes help spice things up from all the takeout.

Callie bends so she's in Dad's face. I hold my breath at her boldness. "It was an *accident*. She's sorry," Callie screams. "You can't make her go through the Trials."

Dad's lips disappear. He's straining to stay composed, everything about his face is tight. He hasn't shaved his head or his face in a few days; gray strands pop up along his chin, super obvious against his dark skin.

Mom looks like she'll blow at any moment. I rush over to Callie and snatch her away by both arms to give my parents some air.

"They've been through enough today," I whisper to her.

Callie turns to me; her hazel eyes are so penetrating I almost have to look away.

"Violetta's been through a lot too!" She looks at my parents. "Have you even seen the holding area for them?" Her voice is as shrill as an alarm. "If you *did* you'd consider forgiving her so she can come home."

"You're not exactly innocent in this, Callie." Dad's voice is low, but there's danger in it. "We had no idea the extent of things, but *you* did. Why didn't you tell us? Or try to stop Letta? Huh?" When Dad's expectant "Huh?" comes it's usually a sign to watch out, but this time it's wobbly. He's tired. Same as Mom, and me. My hulk of a dad is a lump of sadness. He's been wearing his sweatshirt with the colored alphabet of each subway line stretched across his stomach. The sweatshirt and black sweatpants have been a constant wardrobe choice since Letta went to detention. You can tell from the cereal and coffee stains. Mom's grieving uniform is a silk robe she wears over everything. The green and gold fabric covers the blouse and pants she wore to sentencing earlier. Mom's ivory hand is on Dad's back. We all wait for Callie's reply.

Callie and Letta are *tight*, practically twins. Back in February, I found them both hungover, hidden under bedcovers trying to block out the sun. The two of them were in Letta's bed, dry mouthed, hair smooshed to a side, remnants of lipstick and eye shadow slashed across their faces like they were in a circus. A freshman-year mess. That was a total 180 from the Callie and Letta I knew, who were giggly together and shy in front of others. Callie was always more talkative. She grew into the voice that's demanding my parents to explain themselves.

Callie's chest heaves steadily as she calms. "I'm sorry. I really am. But . . . she's hurting," she says.

I tug Callie to the other end of the table, away from Dad, and point for her to sit. I stand behind her, with my hands on the back of the chair. My hold on it wobbles, the usual tremors. Callie's jittery too. I can't tell if she's liable to jump across the table or not. Better to be on the safe side.

Mom wears the same gloomy face she's had on since Viv died. Practically everything droops from her eyes to her mouth permanently slanted in a frown. "We're *all* hurting, Callie. I know you're her friend—"

"Best friend," Callie says.

"*Closest* friend," Mom agrees. "Yes." She reaches between the gap of pizza boxes to squeeze Callie's hand. Their hands in each other's are so small. Callie is tanner, her fingers longer as she clenches Mom's. Callie sniffles a little, and Mom joins in.

"Callie," Mom says gently, "you have to understand that this is a family matter."

"This is the consequence of her actions. As much as we love her, she doesn't get to escape that. If we'd done something sooner . . ." Dad adds.

Mom gestures at the pizza, urges Callie to eat. "It'll make you feel better," she says.

"Eating isn't the cure to all ills, Mom," I say, to no response. It used to make her laugh when I said that.

Callie waves the food away. "It's fine. I'm fine. I'm sorry. I wish—"

"Things could go back to the way they were," I finish for her. I'm pretty sure we're all thinking it.

Like he's noticing them for the first time, Dad brushes at his belly and the stains on his sweatshirt. "There's no changing what happened," he says. "And life certainly isn't fair," he grunts like he wants to throw his hands in the air at everything happening around him, not just the spots on his shirt. "But everyone should be held responsible when they mess up. That's why we chose the Trials. It's not to torture her, it's to help her learn. You don't drink as a teenager. You don't drink and drive. You *don't* do what Letta did and evade the consequences. Vince would *never* have done this."

I gulp at my name.

Mom nods, and some hairs from her topknot fall into her face. When she speaks, she sounds kinda like our judicator. "This method of juvenile detention has been effective since before you were born, Callie. And," she adds, "Violetta is *our* daughter. We believe rehabilitation is what's best for her since she . . ." Mom struggles on the next words but manages to utter, "She has a problem."

Callie swallows whatever she was going to say. Instead, she asks, "Can I have some water?" I'm about to get Callie a glass when she says she knows where things are. "I practically lived here, remember?" She heads for the cupboard and picks out a mug, then fills it at the sink.

Once she's seated again, I figure it's safe for me to sit too. Except Mom gasps, and Dad starts in on a coughing fit.

One side of Callie's mug is solid yellow, so she doesn't see it. From our viewpoint, VIV is scrawled in big purple letters, along with my sister's drawing of a sun. It's a mug she made on a family trip to Virginia. Viv loved mugs and shot glasses. She'd decorated this one with a marker that wasn't supposed to fade but did. Still, it reminds us of who isn't here.

Callie's face creases in confusion. Then she turns the mug to see what we see. She drops the cup as if it's poison. It falls on the table, spilling water, then rolls off the edge. I try to catch it, but it cracks and shatters against the floor.

Mom dives for the mug, getting her knees wet from the water dripping off the sides of the table. Her robe fans out around her as she scoops up bits to save. "Maybe I can glue it . . ." My mom's words dissolve into sobs. Dad rubs his face, scratching at all the hairs sprouting across his chin and cheeks. I just stand up looking at the mess. A big damn mess.

Callie's speaking, but I'm not listening. I yank her out of

the kitchen, into the hallway, to the front door to get her shoes before she goes.

"I'm sorry. I'm so, so sorry." She sounds like Letta did in her video.

"Go," I say.

Callie clings to my shirt, trying to get me to listen.

"I'm tired of hearing 'Sorry' from people," I say. "Sorry this, sorry that." The night everything happened, Levi had said, *Sorry, I can't be with you, Vin.*

I'm so *sick* of "Sorry."

"I didn't mean to make things worse," Callie says. "I just wanted to . . . Violetta doesn't have anyone on her side. *None* of you visit her."

I repeat my parents' words: "This is a family matter."

"I thought—"

"You thought what, Callie? That you'd stride in here and be Letta's defender? She's made shitty decisions. We've all made shitty decisions and this is the result."

Callie's grip on my shirt falters. "I thought," she says, "I was family."

I cover her hands with mine and, gently, make her let go.

"Callie. Leave."

I know Callie doesn't deserve this. Letta messed up. Letta did all this. But she isn't here. What Callie can do now is leave us be for a while. Hopefully even carry my message to my sister, so we can all move forward.

CHAPTER 5
VIOLETTA

Days in detention: 23

~~卌 卌 卌 卌~~ |||

The day after sentencing, I get a crash course in the Trials—the beginning, the triumphs, the expected outcomes. Me, Serena, and another girl newly sentenced to Trials listen to my counselor give us the rundown. We're in the room used for our mandatory schooling during the week. Counselor Susan stands at the front. A whiteboard is behind her, with a projection of her presentation: "What You Need to Know about the Trials." My eyes dart from the board to the notebook Counselor Susan gifted me at our first meeting. We're not allowed to bring the study books to our cells. This offering from Counselor Susan is the only extra thing I have since I haven't received commissary funds. Petra gave me a couple of her colored golf pencils—one blue and one red. Combined they make purple, my favorite color. This helped me color-code my thoughts, including what my counselor will say about the Trials.

I was always good at taking notes in school. Only this time it's my life, not a quiz. I want to make sure I remember everything she tells us. Apparently, I'm the only one writing all this down. The girl sitting up front and Serena stare ahead, waiting for this to be over.

This room is pretty tight for instruction, not like Claremont High School, where desks are spaced out and the walls are painted beige so it feels roomier. Here, three wide bookcases line dull green walls and block all except for a sliver of the windows. Tattered textbooks and donated paperbacks, some worn and some in pretty good condition, fill the shelves, along with student workbooks. Our school notebooks are stacked based on the group we're in. Detention holds two sets of classes Monday through Friday, where our instructor stuffs math, history, composition, and earth science into three and a half hours. Serena is part of the morning group, from nine to twelve thirty, before lunch. I'm in the afternoon batch with Petra and Eve, from one thirty to five, before dinner, at six.

If I thought the moldy smell was a lot in my dorm, it's nothing compared to how musty this room is. A ceiling fan barely circulates the air, plus the lone radiator near the door is covered in cobwebs; every so often it clangs to signal its attempt to work. I rarely feel any heat in class, so I make sure to wear a thicker undershirt beneath my jumpsuit. We sit at slim, unsteady picnic tables and on dusty fold-out chairs. There are four rows with three tables, each with scratches, markings, and old gum decorating them. During class, all the seats are filled, but today the three of us are spread out. The table I'm at jiggles when you lean on it. After it threatens to tilt over one too many times, I stuff a folded page from my notebook under a leg.

Counselor Susan raises her voice in an attempt to make

her presentation interesting. With a laser pointer in hand, she moves from one side of the board to the other, letting the dot emphasize what she's saying. She seems nervous. She keeps tugging at her pencil skirt or the edge of her black blazer when she talks. I'm not a fan of public speaking either. Yet another strike against me whenever I'm compared to my older brother. The world is Vin's stage, for track, for debate, for lacrosse. You name it. But Counselor Susan's cheeks flush when she stumbles or when she clicks on the computer to move the slide forward but it goes backward. It reminds me of how much I fidget when called up to read a report in class or when I had to be onstage for more than a second to pick up a certificate. Her fear makes her more real and less like an authority figure.

Serena sits at the end of my row and raises her hand a few minutes in. I try not to stare at her. The lilac tattoo peeking out from under her jumpsuit top always catches my eye. How bright the purple and white flowers are on her freckled skin. She's chewing gum, a luxury in here, and each smack punctuates her question. "Sooo what you're saying is this all started because someone killed a kid by accident? That's why I gotta deal with this bullcrap?"

"Well," Counselor Susan begins, "yes and no. It started with an understanding that something more needed to happen to encourage a decline in recidivism for offending youths."

"Resida-what?" the girl in the front row, biting her nails, asks. From the traces of blood I see on her pale fingers, she's chewing them raw.

"Recidivism," my counselor says. "It means repeat offenses. We want to limit that."

An index finger in her mouth, the girl is a little hard to understand when she responds, "So why not just say 'repeat offenses,' then?"

"How about I get through this and then you can ask questions, all right?" Counselor Susan smiles so wide it takes up her whole face.

Counselor Susan brings up a slide with a timeline of the history. The Trials started twenty-five years ago because a seven-year-old Black girl was killed by her thirteen-year-old cousin when he wrestled with her. I almost drop my pencil and have to hold back a sob hearing how a kid younger than me also hurt someone in his family. And my sister is, *was*, seven too.

The boy's name is LeVaughn Harrison. Even at his age, he was considered developmentally sound enough to understand what he did was wrong, and a grand jury decided he should be tried for murder. This caused an uproar. Some argued he hadn't been vindictive, that it was an accident, while others insisted the girl's medical examination revealed injuries worse than an accident would account for. A year after her death, when LeVaughn was fourteen, a jury sentenced him to life in prison.

My counselor clicks to images from news clippings. The side-by-side photos of LeVaughn and his cousin are black-and-white photocopies, making their skin even darker, so some of their features are hidden. But I can still see how young they are. The seven-year-old girl has four puffy braids sticking up from her head. Her eyes are dark orbs staring straight ahead. The boy has pouty lips and his nose is a rounded nub at the end, like mine and my mom's. The photos feel like mug shots. They don't look like children; they look like ghosts.

My counselor plays a one-minute video of people encouraging government officials to take cases like this more seriously.

In the video, a woman dressed as professionally as Counselor Susan leans into a microphone. "Reform needs to happen," she says. "Real reform. How do we know a kid at this age can understand the repercussions of their actions when sent to prison for murder? Studies show . . ." And so on and so on. Appeals were made by the boy's family members all the way up to federal courts. The boy's life sentence held, but people in office agreed something needed to change.

Per Counselor Susan, "When an investigation was conducted by the Federal Department of Corrections in conjunction with the Bureau of Detention Services, they saw how much money was spent simply to house inmates for years on end, on top of all the time spent in courts. All this was brought to Congress, who helped create this new form of juvenile justice nationwide."

"Is that how most decisions are made in this country?" Serena asks.

Counselor Susan doesn't answer. She goes to the next slide, with a list titled CONSIDERATIONS. I scribble this down too.

Before the Trials, she says, many juveniles couldn't afford legal representation and got assigned public defenders or dealt with bias in the court system, especially Black and Brown kids.

Serena and I glance at each other in recognition of what's been obvious from the moment we got here. I've noticed how many more girls who are inmates look like me, compared to how many guards and counselors look like Counselor Susan and dictate our every move.

Counselor Susan tells us that juvenile reform programs weren't given enough funding to survive or work on a wider scale. There were no guarantees that repeat offenses wouldn't happen. And at the same time, there was the question of how juvenile inmates could support the economy. Trials were developed as a way to try and respond to these needs.

"The goals are less kids on the street doing harm, so they don't grow into adults who cause harm."

Serena pops a small bubble before asking, "Okay, so where do the victims come into play?" Her arms are crossed. She looks skeptical and I can't blame her. This is a lot of information. I've filled up two pages with history, considerations, LeVaughn and his cousin, speeches for and against how LeVaughn would live his life. Mostly, it sounds like adults pushing what they think we need to hear, rather than talking to us.

"I'm glad you asked, Serena." Her next slide says VICTIMS at the very top. "Think of what we do now as similar to a court but not. Say the victim is pressing charges against you, the offender."

"Thanks for that," Serena says.

"Sorry. *An* offender. The victim decides to press charges, and you—I mean, the offender—is taken into custody." The red dot circles the word CUSTODY. "Then a judicator serves as a kind of liaison assisting the victims, helping them understand what options are available to them. That means three choices." Counselor Susan uses the laser to underline TRIALS, CONFINE-MENT, FORGIVENESS. "From there, the victims make a decision on what fits the situation, and then you—I'm so sorry, I mean, *the offender*—is sentenced to one of those three options.

"For confinement, the judicator and the Bureau will decide a fitting time at a long-term facility, and will work with the victims to ensure that's acceptable based on the offense. In the case of Trials, the victims pick the category, there are several. However, I won't be getting into all that. Then a judicator, with the help of the Bureau, creates the Trial in conjunction with the victims, based on the category and the offense. Us counselors could be considered your defense team, because we're here for you. The victims make all decisions alongside their assigned judicator. This includes how your Trials are measured."

"Do people ever get forgiven?"

The red dot lands on the nail biter's face. "All the time!" Counselor Susan says a little too enthusiastically. Petra is the only person I know who's been forgiven, yet that wasn't from the start. It was a hard-won forgiveness.

"Speaking of forgiveness." The board gleams with so YOU'VE BEEN FORGIVEN, along with a yellow smiley face. "This is the good news for you. As I said, forgiveness happens all the time. Your Trials are pass or fail, and it depends on how many you have. It could be one." She holds up a finger to illustrate, as if we can't count single digits. "Or it could be several. Your job is to show your dedication to forgiveness."

"Forgiveness" is the biggest word on my page. It's in all caps and I underline it twice. I linger on the word and the possibility. It's not impossible. Petra said so. This is what I'll have to cling to. And maybe Counselor Susan can help me make this a reality.

"Yeah, okay, but how brutal are the Trials?" Serena chimes in.

"Girls, that's not what this is about. The Trials aren't meant to be brutal *at all*. Remember that being here"—my counselor's pointer stops on each wall to the ceiling to the whiteboard behind her—"is not about incarceration; it's about *rehabilitation*, a reset. Consider the Trials a do-over.

"Crimes have been committed. And comprehension of why these things happened as well as ensuring no offenses happen again is the goal here. And with that—" A pie chart fills the whiteboard: 89 percent success rate in reducing juvenile recidivism throughout the country since the initiation of the Trials. This stat brings a grin to my counselor's face that isn't forced, the whole front row of her teeth show and they're as white as her blouse. Another adjustment of her blazer, and she says she's done.

"Any other questions?"

A pop of gum and a raised hand signal Serena's latest question. "Sooo, what happens if you don't finish the Trial. Like . . ." Serena chews before finishing as if this helps her think. It's just like the *click click click* of my counselor's pens whenever she pauses before answering during our meetings. "Like if you quit the Trial. Then what?"

The upper half of Counselor Susan's body does a little shake before she points at Serena, almost like she's won a prize. "I'm so glad you asked that!"

We wait for a new slide, but Counselor Susan doesn't click for one. The laser pointer doesn't highlight something else we need to know beyond the success statistics lit up in front of us.

"Quitting a Trial means the victims, along with their judicator, decide if they'd like to forgive you regardless and expunge any record of your crime after a short probation. Or pursue confinement. Unfortunately, confinement means—"

I rest my golf pencil and repeat Petra's words from yesterday to myself: *You have a criminal record.*

My nail digs at a leftover patch of old gum. Probably one from Serena from another day. "What happened to the little boy?" I ask.

"What little boy, Violetta?"

"LeVaughn. The one who started all this." It's hard to believe a seven-year-old girl's death forced a whole new way of "justice." I know kids have helped initiate change before. But this boy was only two years younger than me. By now, he's a grown man. Does he get to live out his life like normal, or as normal as life could be after you've killed someone? Did his family ever forgive him for roughhousing, or is he still sentenced in prison? What I really want to know is: Is he okay?

"I'm sorry to say he died."

Serena whistles. "Damn, that's a sinister mic drop."

I almost pound the table. "*Died!* Of what?"

"I don't know. He passed away about twenty years ago. I believe he was eighteen at the time."

Shutting off the projector, Counselor Susan stands a bit more confidently, with her thin arms at her sides, or maybe she's just relieved to be done. The red glow of her laser pen disappears when she announces, "Ladies, your respective Trials will be during the time you usually have free. And you'll still have to attend class in preparation for testing in June." Counselor Susan almost scolds us with a wag of her finger. "Just because you have Trials doesn't mean you don't get an education. It's incredibly important."

Picking up the nub of my pencil, I circle LeVaughn's name over and over. I have to find out what happened to him. I just have to.

The Trials were born as an *option*. I know my sister's death is my fault. There's no arguing that. The question is: What comes next? Because she's not here, my family gets to decide. And they've decided I need to be reformed.

CHAPTER 6

VINCE

Days since the decision: 24

When I enter the kitchen, there's a half dozen boiled eggs in a bowl on the dining room table. I make some toast with butter and jelly for a breakfast of champions. Before sitting down to eat, I peek over Mom's shoulder and catch a glimpse of all the tabs open on her computer for the electricity bill, car insurance, mortgage payment, and whatever's left of Viv's burial costs. She was cursing up a storm about "liability insurance" until she noticed me. Mom didn't minimize the windows fast enough. I saw the numbers, some in red, with OWED right next to the sum total. Apparently, bills are also the devil. Thankfully, uniforms and sports fees were paid in full in September. Grams and Gramps helped cover the costs of the SATs, plus the college prep classes I took last summer. I'm pretty good at math, so it doesn't take long to tally up how much all this is. How these amounts, especially after the accident, mean I shouldn't ask for anything outside of what's absolutely necessary. Dad's job as an electrician and Mom's job at a city college mean we're not starving. We're fine, but it's not like we're rolling in dough or anything. As a kid, whenever I asked for a toy or device I saw on TV or in a store, Dad explained, in detail, that money was something people earned. It didn't suddenly appear like the cool images enticing me on a screen.

Thanks to birthday, Christmas, and Chinese New Year money, I've saved enough for what I'll need for my car—as long as nothing else goes wrong. If things keep going well with track and we make it to the championships, I may actually land a scholarship. It's what we've been betting on since freshman year. It means my parents won't have to take on another burden.

I've been out of school for almost a month. Same goes for Mom with work. She took a paid leave of absence. With the accident, planning Viv's funeral, the sentencing video, and having Viv's funeral, it's a wonder I even know what day it is. So why not add another three weeks off? Hell, maybe the whole school year outside of sports. What does school matter anyway when everything sucks?

Since the accident, I've managed virtually. Teachers set me up with remote classes. I emailed them my homework and even did coursework on the web boards our teachers created at the beginning of the year. I'm pretty much all caught up, so why do I have to *go* to the actual building? Can't I just do track meets and stay home?

As per usual, Mom's hair is tied up on top of her head, and her face reads tired. The creamy skin around her eyes has deepened into wrinkles, so have the lines around her mouth. She's in her daily uniform of the green silken robe with a golden print of a dragon and lilies on it. It's so big it pretty much swallows her up.

I gulp down a "Can I . . ." What surprises me is Mom notices. For three weeks, we've been so out of tune with each other. She used to know what I would say before *I* knew what I was going to say. When you're hiding stuff, the last thing you need is the paranoia that your parents can read your mind. That's part of why I don't want to go to classes. Performing at top levels is my thing. But I don't think I have it in me for eight periods straight today. As quiet and tense as it is at home, when my parents are off in their sad world, I get a little break from being who everyone thinks I am.

Mom's scrolling, but her eyes briefly meet mine. She leans over, kisses the top of my head, and says, "I know this is not easy for you, honey. But hiding out makes it worse. Believe me."

I make a *Yeah, okay* face.

She's been able to escape her co-workers' mournful looks and comments about our family. Sure, folks stop by with food and well wishes on occasion. But she's been able to avoid them. I want to ask: Why can't I do the same?

"Oh, you don't believe me?" Her fingers work the keyboard as she talks. "In high school, some girl—I don't remember her name, but she was mean, so let's leave it at that. Really mean." Mom shakes off the memory. "I don't know if she didn't like me because I was popular or because I'm Chinese. She made up horrible rumors about me and some boys. She said— You know what? It doesn't matter."

Mom shuts her laptop. I'm all hers. She tightens the belt of her robe before moving to sit next to me and stealing one of my toast crusts. I'm enjoying having her to myself—it almost feels like things are normal.

"I know I'm asking a lot." Wiping crumbs from her finger-tips, she cups both my cheeks, forces me to really see and hear her. "Vince, you have it in you to push through. The minute you hear from scouts about that scholarship, you'll look back and know *no one* can take anything from you that you don't want to be taken."

I haven't forgotten how important this scholarship is. How could I? Everyone, and I mean *everyone*, in our family has drilled home how crucial it is for us to get a higher education. And that meant serious financial help. Because, as Mom says, "You deserve the best. You've worked too hard."

Sit with the Chen-Samuels extended family for a holiday dinner and you'll learn a whole lot about family members who worked in laundromats, as bus drivers, for call centers—a thing they had back in the day—or as nurses. Listen in on how family on both Mom's and Dad's side scraped by or made do through luck, goodwill, and a hard work ethic.

"Save your pennies," Grams and Gramps always said.

"Your education will be what gets you to the top!" Sonali and Aunt Mae often added.

Dad went to community college and got a job as an elec-trician immediately. Mom got a scholarship at the same city university she's an administrator at. Their work hours can be unpredictable at times, but my parents insist they're happy.

They also repeat how much they wanted us to never limit ourselves or let the world limit us.

"Just like your grandparents wanted for their unborn child when they immigrated to New York in the sixties," Mom recites, mid-chew, like it's a song. One I know the lyrics to very well after seventeen years on Earth.

I'm prepared to counter, just like in debate class, because I'm a jack of all trades. Mom's cell phone interrupts me, though.

Mom blows me a kiss and picks up the phone vibrating in the center of the table. One glance at the screen makes her hesitate. In the end she answers with a soft "Hello?"

Mom's whole expression darkens. Eyes closed, her head falls forward as she mumbles, "Yes, yes. I understand" to whoever is on the other line.

"We'll have that paid off in a month. I promise. I know I've missed several calls—"

It sucks to see my mom revert to a kid right in front of me. A bill collector shaming them for forgetting a payment when our whole world is upside-down. At any point in time Mom's mood can be up like it was with me for all of three minutes or brought right back down to reality with someone mentioning a missed payment or bringing up how sad they are for us.

I scarf down another couple of eggs and leave without saying goodbye.

The short hallway to the front door is cluttered with salt-covered shoes from storms past, along with bags from drop-offs of flowers or food or books on grief & loss, and a bin full of empty bottles we have yet to recycle. As soon as we got home that dreadful night, Mom stormed into the kitchen, tearing through the cabinets in search of wine she saved for special occasions. She emptied everything into the sink before chucking bottle after bottle into a garbage pail, mumbling through tears with each crash of glass that our family wasn't a bad family. Right beside all this mess is the table where we put our keys; it's littered with unopened mail that's mostly junk and lots of sympathy cards. After the first week, none of us had the stomach to keep reading them.

The day is windy, which means cold, which means I underdressed again. I sprint down the stairs. I'm trying hard to convince myself to be good ole charming Vince on my first day back at school.

My car is on the other side of the parking lot, under one of the maple trees. It's still weird to see the empty spot where the family van usually is. Now that I'm going to school, Mom and Dad said they'll take the express bus into the city for work so I don't have to worry about bumming rides. I feel kinda guilty, then again, I'm relieved to have these moments to myself. Driving is the easiest way to get to school since there aren't any subways this far north in Queens and the closest bus stop is almost a mile away.

Twigs are bunched under the wipers. But the sticks and condensation from the night before aren't the only things I see. My best friend Janice calls out to me from her slumped position on my hood.

Patting my pockets for my keys, I say, "Listen, I haven't been feeling well."

She pushes her glasses up, then shields her eyes from the sun with a hand. Her rainbow-colored braids are thin like spaghetti and go all the way down her back. A quick breeze blows some of the braids over her shoulder and sends the flaps of my jacket sailing back like the cape of a superhero.

"You've been avoiding all of us. I get why you're ignoring Levi."

"What do you mean?"

I'm impressed she doesn't roll her eyes. "Levi feels like crap for breaking your heart. *Womp womp.* I'm worried about *you*, period. And your family. How . . ." The strength of her voice fades back to the sympathetic tone it had when she first heard the news, when she wanted to know if me and Violetta were okay.

"I can't really talk about it, Jan." Meaning *I don't* want *to talk about it, Jan.*

"We can talk about other stuff. I don't know if you heard about a recruiter coming this week? To see the team. But we know who they're here for."

Damn it. Of course it's this week of all weeks.

"Let's talk later." The last thing I need is a Mom 2.0 reminder about what's expected of me. My hand is on the door, but Janice stops me.

"BS. You haven't even answered a text—from me *or* the group." She ticks off each method of communication on her fingers. "Chat message or any post to your page. I get you didn't want to talk right when it happened. But it hurts you wouldn't think I'd be here for you."

I overestimate Jan; everyone does. Like she can take any-thing and everything. But she's a mushball inside, just like me. None of this is fair, and I sure haven't been fair to her either. She takes her seat on the hood again and pulls her braids to one side, a habit whenever she has extensions. Her hickory-toned skin glows thanks to the hint of glitter on her cheeks and eye-lids. I sidle over next to her. "I'm sorry."

A pat on my shoulder tells me all is forgiven.

"You don't have to talk about it. But, Vin, seriously, you *can* talk to me."

We stare at the smattering of cars around the lot. Many of them much nicer and newer than mine.

"Viv was one of a kind," I say.

Janice laughs. "She was a trip! She could've run a marathon every day for the rest of her life. That girl was on batteries."

The feeling starts at my stomach and rumbles up until it erupts. Legit laughter at remembering how much energy Viv had. How she literally ran circles around us and tired every-one out.

"I know things suck big-time."

I lock in on the barely there bruise above and below Janice's eyebrow, where she had a piercing for all of two minutes. "That's an understatement."

"How are your parents?"

I glance at the door to our duplex, wondering if Mom is still on the line with someone asking her for something she can't give right now. "Not great."

We hang side by side, not saying anything else. I wish it

was the comfortable silence we used to have. Now it's forced, because we don't know what to say. I've seen the messages from Janice. **Just checking,** she keeps saying every night at ten o'clock on the dot. She tries to make conversation too. Sometimes complaining about taking the Q115 to and from school instead of riding with me each morning: **Believe it or not, I miss riding with you in that hotbox on wheels.** Her braids flick against me as they blow in the wind.

When I'm alone, I think too much. I almost say this, but I keep quiet. I'm worried everything will come out if I begin with a portion of the truth. It's funny how things can be with friends. How you can say almost anything that comes to mind and not worry about repercussions. When Janice found out Levi and I were messing around at the start of junior year, she didn't say anything at first. She eventually *did* give her thoughts on the matter. It was just the two of us in my car, the AC choking its last breath on an unreasonably humid September day. Her ready to curse me out (unfairly, I might add), since her hair was blown out and curled at the time.

Janice had swatted me with a magazine. "You should focus on studies and track. All it takes is one guy to screw you up during the school year. Trust me, I know."

"Maybe the straight boys."

"All *boys*, Vin."

I'd insisted I knew what I wanted. And I did. It was Levi who ended up changing his mind.

I felt her knowing *Yeah, okay* glare. "You don't lack confidence. That's for sure," she said.

"It's the Blasian in me," I'd replied with a confident smile. *Stupid me.*

The last thing Jan said on the matter was she hoped I didn't get hurt. Another thing I wish? That I'd listened to her.

Even now my best friend's trying to guess at what I'm holding back. Janice intertwines our fingers, brings them to her heart. "As much as you're a pain in my butt, you're also one of the people I love most in this world. I'm here for you, always, just like you've been there for me."

I kiss her glittery cheek. "Thanks."

She declares the warm-and-fuzzy moment over. "Now open the door and take us to school, please. I'm cold."

"Bossy much?"

"Hopefully, your heat works, since your air doesn't."

A series of clicks echo around us when I hit the remote. "Love you too, Jan."

Students stream into school. Janice pauses when I send her ahead and insist I'm on my way. Before she goes inside, I tell her I just need to ready myself. I have eleven minutes before the first-period bell rings for attendance. And there aren't too many stragglers on the front lawn or the steps.

"Now or never," I say.

I tuck my chin inside my jacket, planning to get in and out of each class with as little socializing as possible. There's a buzz in my back pocket once I'm at the steps.

You okay? pops on the screen. This is the only thing Levi can say since we last saw each other at Viv's funeral? I'm tempted to go elementary and type, *What do you care?* Instead, I respond, **Yeah, fine. You?**

I'm grateful for the wave of heat that hits me once I'm indoors. Classmates, teachers, and security fill the main hallway. I slip into the mass and head for the stairwell, not glancing at the trophy display of back-to-back track championships I helped solidify. Weaving down the hall, I nod at people. Some open their mouths to speak, but I brush past them with only a "Hey." There are a few arm squeezes I don't acknowledge. Every two seconds, I turn my phone over to see if it'll glow with a response.

I make it to the third floor and take an immediate right to my row of lockers. I stop at 175, slip my phone into my pocket—not without another glance—and tap in my combo. There's a jab in my lower back. I twist around, ready to lay a punch, but come face-to-face with Jorge, their bushy black eyebrows inverted, concern written all over their face. They hesitate, like they're considering if it's okay to come in for a hug or not. Jorge teeters toward me on the balls of their feet, clad in really nice velvet heels.

I hope the smile I send Jorge looks real. "What's going on?" I turn back to my locker, rushing to get everything I need. Notebooks, pens, highlighters, my scientific calc. Anything I can think of, even a pencil sharpener, since it's there.

Jorge's voice is low and sad when they say my name.

I squeeze my eyes shut. *Please don't ask.*

"How's life?" they say.

I open my mouth to tell them I gotta head out, I gotta go

now, when a palm mushes the side of my face so hard I almost kiss my locker door.

"Long time no see, man." Byron's been texting and calling ever since Letta and Viv were taken to the hospital.

I'm stuck between the two of them. They're my friends. I've known them for years. But being around them right now, the concern and questions behind their eyes, is stifling. I press my back against the locker. The air feels thick.

"I haven't heard from you," Byron announces, as if I didn't know. His blond hair's gotten longer, to the point it covers his gray-blue eyes. He blows his bangs away, occasionally revealing the line of pimples on his forehead. "We're getting killed by the Centurions in the meets." His words are another weight I don't need right now.

Jorge pushes Byron, not as playfully as usual. "We *understand* you need your space, though," they say. Jorge lines up next to Byron and I could see them jabbing Byron with their heel if it came to it.

"*What?* I speak truth," Byron says. "We're getting creamed by the next Usain Bolt right now, and I'm tired of his smug ass at meets. Maybe Vin wants to think about something else. Right, Vin?" Byron dips his head at me, his way of asking without asking if I need anything, preferably in pill form—the only way he knows how to offer help or how to help himself. After all, Byron is who introduced me to Ross, and what he doles out.

Byron's and Jorge's faces are so close they look similar to sideshow mirrors, warped and comical, but right now there's nothing funny about my friends. My chest tightens. This would be a time I popped something in my mouth. My hand searches my pockets for the slight bulge of a pill, and my mind goes to Ross the other day.

When I say, "Hey, it's almost . . . I have to . . ." I'm wheezing.

"Jorge," Byron starts in, "some of us have to think about the future. Scholarships. Full rides. *Some* of us need the team to do well—"

Jorge holds up a hand to stop Byron midcomplaint. Their nail polish is stop-sign red, a warning to Byron to shut it. "You act like I was born with diamond teeth."

While my friends get into it, a new feeling starts in my chest and travels between my eyes. *Thump, thump, thump.* Blood coursing. Racing. Too damn fast. I claw my way past Jorge and Byron. I don't close my locker. The warning bell sounds. We have sixty seconds to get where we need to be. My whole body is on fire. I open my jacket, needing more air, sweat dotting my brow.

"Vince!" Jorge shouts, but I don't look back. I rush toward the boys' room, squeezing myself through more people— hearing my name thrown at me in ways that sound angry and hurt. My back pocket vibrates. I reach for it and get jostled by everyone rushing to class. A shoulder rams into mine, sending me backward. My phone drops and skids along the floor. It glows at the same time a thick-heeled boot cracks the screen.

"Hey, asshole!" I shout, but the person is already walking away from the damage. My face burns as I stare at the corpse of my phone. Another thing I can't afford to lose. *Screw it.* I chase after him.

When I catch up, I spin him around. Pascal's mouth is slanted in a shy look of amusement.

"You crushed my phone!"

Pascal glances over my shoulder to the remains on the floor. "Oh," is all he says. "Didn't see it."

I smack his chest. A rush surges through me at the startled look on his face. I push him a few more times until he slams against a classroom door. Every damn thing about Pascal pisses me off. From the sheen of his super tight curls to the dimples that would be cute if he weren't such a douchebag, right down to the knit checkered scarf around his neck.

"You don't care about anything or anyone, do you?"

"Geez, man, if it's that important I'll buy you a new one."

I shove him again so his body bangs against the door, making the window quake. "Stop it!" the girl beside him shouts. I sense the crowd around me, everyone holding their breath.

"It's so easy for you to swap one thing for another, isn't it?" I nod to the girl. "Get a new version, right, Pascal?"

His muscles are thicker than mine. But Pascal's also shorter, so he has to look up at me.

"This about Violetta?" he asks.

My voice becomes harsher. Just like the guard at Letta's verdict, I'm close and practically spitting on him. "You don't give a damn about my sister, so don't say her name."

"How can you say that?" he asks with a pout.

"What's going on here!" thunders down the hall. The only thing keeping me from completely pounding Pascal's face in is Mr. Nelson, the AP World History teacher—and my debate teacher.

"Vincent," Nelson says, "I think you need to take a walk."

"But he—"

Nelson bends slightly so we're more eye to eye. "You need to cool off. Walk. I'll see you third period."

Fine. Pascal's not worth it anyway. Soon enough, I'm down the stairs and out the door to fresh air so I can breathe. Mom actually thought I could return to what? Normal? Not even.

Pressure on my shoulder sends me spinning with arms raised again.

"Whoa!" Levi holds his hands up, ready to block. "You okay?" he says.

"What do you care?"

I stomp off, kicking at the grass and dirt. *Your parents already have one kid inside,* I tell myself. *No need to assault someone to add to their stress.*

"Wait a second! You almost pummeled Pascal in there. Do you know—"

"Yes, I know!" I roar in Levi's face. Have to admit it feels good.

Levi reaches for me, and I'm already backing off. "Don't."

"I don't want us to be like this, Vin. I was hoping we could talk, uh . . ."

Whenever Levi's unsure, he doesn't finish his sentences. It used to be cute; now it's plain annoying. He takes my hand in both of his, and I let him. Shutting my eyes, I lean into him. This is how stuff started between us. Levi was always the person I reached out to when I was stressed, with school or sports or *anything*. My mind was always on what had to be done to keep me a perfect student and a good son. I didn't think about dating seriously. When would I have time for that, with everything I was piling on since freshman year? The occasional hookup? Sure, why not? But nothing serious, that is until Levi. This moment right here is when I get close enough for him to take me in his arms. All he has to do is open them, which he does.

No Levi. No pills. And a family barely holding together.

"Hey," he says, pulling me closer, just like I wanted. "I'm your friend. No matter what."

"Friend." That word jolts me back to life. I break away from him, because Levi is the one I can't have.

"What makes you think I want, or need, you right now, Levi? Especially after dumping me."

His whole face sours, the same way it did at Westbridge Peak. That's when I had to admit I thought what we were doing meant we were a couple.

Levi's the lead photographer at the school—for the paper, yearbook, occasional social media posts, you name it. It's a given he'll be at if not every meet or game, as many as possible. There's not a chance to miss him if I wanted to. His gorgeous, goofy face with the lopsided grin will be in the stands or on the edges of the field, a digital camera held up, ready to shoot. This time of year, most hats don't fit his high-top cut, making it even easier to spot him. He's over six feet, but his hair gives him even more height. And when he's working, he cheers for me—"Vin wins!"—win or lose.

God, I miss leaning in to kiss him, him kissing me back, in my car, his room, a shady corner of the school basement. His fingers in my loose curls, mine on the back of his neck, where the fade started to grow back in. Another kiss, another, and another. My lips trailing over his mouth, neck, chest. Me, smiling each time. Me, happy the person I had known so long, who had listened to me whine and moan and be a ball of nerves, was as into me as I was him.

But we never *talked* about us being official, I just assumed, wrongly. And then there was the Peak. Us in his car. Me, putting my hand on his thigh. Me, moving in for yet another kiss. How I couldn't wait to press my lips against his. Him, stopping me cold, his gaze out the window, the back of his head, the shine of his dark-brown skin against the moonlight. The *whoosh* of a plane taking off above, and his words: "I can't do this anymore, Vin. Not the way you want." I didn't stay in the car long after his announcement. Turns out my life would change in more than one way the night Levi broke up with me. In that moment with Levi, I was as big an idiot as Letta was with Pascal.

I shut my eyes so tight I see stars. There's no need to be reminded. Levi made things clear weeks ago. I swat his touch away like a fly. "I don't want to see you right now."

Do not look at him, I tell myself. Or the scar on his hand from being bitten by a goat at the petting zoo as a kid, his freshly trimmed goatee, the shape of his torso under the fur-trimmed denim jacket he's wearing. None of it is going to help. Not today.

"Vin," he says, but I don't budge.

After a few minutes, he leaves and I'm not as shaky. But my mouth becomes a desert at the thought of going back inside. Ross's gift burns a hole in my mind. I can almost taste the gel coating on my tongue. I know exactly where the pills are in my room. If I go home, if I'm alone, I have a nagging feeling they won't end up in the toilet.

CHAPTER 7
VIOLETTA

Days in detention: 24

~~IIII~~ ~~IIII~~ ~~IIII~~ ~~IIII~~ IIII

My first week here, Counselor Susan handed me a thin composition notebook. She told me this was "to record my thoughts."

"This notebook is for you mostly. But sometimes I hope you'll share it with me."

Unlike everything else I was provided in detention—clean uniforms, socks and underwear, mini comb and brush, soap—this notebook felt like it was for me. Something that wasn't miniature-size, like my toothbrush and toothpaste, or didn't fit, like my clothes much of the time. I didn't usually write in notebooks outside of homework, but this was something that looked exactly like what I'd have back at home.

Pressing the notebook to my stomach, I'd nodded and said, "Sure." I didn't mind sharing what I wrote with her.

Counselor Susan also recommended I write people back and try to get my feelings out, in case it could help with my video for sentencing. I never got up the nerve, and now it's the Trials for me. I'm attempting to take my counselor's advice, especially after yesterday's Trials orientation.

The first page of the notebook has a line down the middle, separating my current daily schedule from the list of things I would be doing if I weren't in detention.

It's 5:18 p.m. on Monday and I'm in my cell waiting for dinnertime to start. If this were a couple months ago, I'd be at home eagerly waiting for Pascal's face to appear on my phone screen. Or maybe I'd be with him, sitting in his lap at a coffee shop or a school game while I wrapped his soft curls around my finger. Either way, I wouldn't be doing what I was supposed to: homework. I wasn't doing any of the chores Mom and Dad had listed on the kitchen dry-erase board, like washing dishes or rinsing off rice to put in the rice cooker. I certainly wasn't helping my sister with her homework if I wasn't doing my own. I probably wasn't doing errands for Grams or Gramps, even though I had my permit and could drive as long as someone with a license was in the car with me. I definitely wasn't at home looking at my sister's CooKids or karate advancement certificates posted on the fridge along with my lone honor roll one. I also didn't have to see the trophies collecting on a bookshelf of Vin's winning lacrosse season in the fall.

After school, I'd be ready and waiting for Pascal to pick me up, call, or text. At the dinner table, Mom would lightly smack my hand, telling me to put my phone away while we ate together.

"Your sister and I made a whole meal, a meal *you* were supposed to help with, and you're on your phone. I swear, Letta, if I did half of what you get away with, my parents would have . . ."

I tuned out most of what Mom said. Dad was no help, he

simply turned to Vin to ask how his latest meet was or if his time was improving on the field enough to be competitive. My little sister happily chewed her shrimp fried rice or whatever she and Mom had bonded over. Me? I sat there counting the minutes until I could be out of my mother's line of fire.

When Pascal did videocalls, he brought the phone so close to his face I could only see half of it, but I did see his dimples. "Jolie!" he'd say. "When are you coming over?"

Whenever he asked that, I'd say, "Soon." I wasn't ready to be alone with him, not yet. Being in his car or with others was less pressure, sort of.

We could kiss. He'd pull me into his arms so I could feel how tight his grip was around my waist. His nose would rub my cheek until his breath was against my neck. But as much as I enjoyed the feeling and the attention, the fear of expectation froze me enough for him to ask if everything was okay.

The only way I can call someone in detention is collect. Maybe hearing Pascal's voice would make me feel closer to him than his letters. His voice is distant in my mind, but it's always amplified in my memories. How deep he could make it whenever he flirted or whenever he wanted something from me. How high his voice became, almost like he was trying to sing a note, when he laughed or told the end of a joke.

My schedule before was Pascal. His name is written in a whole block of time, along with kissing, necking, his hands under my shirt, against my belly or under my skirt, resting on my knee or thigh. Watching TV and kissing. Drinking, partying, and more kissing. And laughing. I don't remember the laughing as much now, but I know we did. I know I didn't feel like Vin's sister with Pascal. I didn't quite know who I was with him. What was important was I knew who I *wasn't*.

I glance at my scribbled detention schedule. Staring at the lines reminds me that weeks pass slowly, like months. My new reality is I'm currently on a springy bed in my cell, waiting on a visitor.

To pass the time, I also read the letters I've received over and over. A new one is like a present. My grams's writing is big and loopy. A few lines take up a whole page. She sends her and Gramps's love. Says they're praying for me and the whole family. Says they love me and they hope I get better.

Get better is what I focus on every time. As if I'm sick and not a fifteen-year-old who messed up beyond belief.

Aunt Mae's letters tell me the details of her day, how she, her wife, Sonali, and Sonali's little girls are doing. I can picture my aunt's headscarves, sometimes yellow, sometimes neon green, tied around her forehead, holding her thick afro back while she works on flower arrangements. My hair matches hers and what's left of Dad's. Along with her letters, my aunt sent me the best conditioners—they smelled like honey or lavender—to keep my coils up. She also made sure to send a couple bonnets so I didn't have to keep wrapping my hair in T-shirts before lights-out.

Aunt Mae owns a flower shop and runs a community garden in southern Queens, where the kids and adults learn to farm and "bring more color to *our* spots." She kept telling us it's important to support other Black and Brown folks. In her letters, she praises the gardens and occasionally complains about the customers. *I understand not everyone knows what hydrangeas are, but saying "the poofy flower that's kinda like a bouquet . . . you know the one" isn't helpful. The internet is our friend,* she writes. I make a note to ask her about the crown of thorns Petra mentioned. I'm curious if they look like their name or something worse.

My aunt tells me her stepdaughters miss me. That I'm not so sure of, since they're around my sister's age and always played with her. My aunt tells me things will get brighter even through the darkness. She ends each letter with *Stay strong, Flower Child,* because she helped name me after her favorite flower.

The first letter I'd attempted to her only has *Dear Aunt Mae* written at the top. I'm a blank on how to continue. I want to tell her I'm trying to stay strong, or about our days, the rigid schedules and the announcements of every move we make. She probably knows about my sentencing. The family grapevine is speedy. Nothing feels right to put down on paper. I'd rather talk about anything except my Trials. That's the unknown.

Pascal's letters are the ones I'm confused by. At first, I was eager to open them. I was hoping for something sweet and sympathetic. But as I read them, he sounded not like him, almost bored.

> Dear Jolie: (That sounds like him, always calling me pretty.)
>
> How are things? Or is that a dumb question? I don't know what to write, but I think about you a lot. School

is school. People are disappointing. Life is life. You know you always made me smile, and maybe me writing you makes you smile too. Write me back if you want. No pressure.

Miss you,
Pascal

My attempts to respond to Pascal are even messier. I think I need to see him, because of everything that happened the day of the accident, this whole school year, leading up to where I am now. He asked how I am, but I can't get further than *I'm*. I just stare at the lined pages, wishing the same thing I do every day—that everything was different.

After what feels like way too many minutes trying to write, I rip a sheet out and spread the paper on my thigh. Gripping the end of the blue miniature pencil, tip flattened, I start a new letter. This one isn't for anyone who's written me. Surprisingly, the words come easier. Writing along the curve of my leg makes my words sloppy, but I don't stop until I fill out the last blank line.

A shadow appears in my doorway. "Visitor," the guard says. I fold the letters into their envelopes. The letter I actually finished I tuck under my mattress, not wanting to hear it beneath my head at night.

The guard punches a code into a panel beside the door, then leads me away from my dorm. The numbers blink. We enter a short passage. He has to punch in codes again and again. The halls become longer, and after many blinks, clinks, and counting steps, we arrive at the visitation area. Light seeps through the barred windows in here, but it doesn't help how dreary it looks and feels. The constant outline of the bars on the floors makes things even gloomier. Heading for a table closest to the windows, I figure I'll take what light I can get.

There aren't many others here. Weekend visiting hours are usually busy, but weekday evenings mean fewer people, and often it's the same ones week to week. The visitation room has round tables spread out enough to fool us into thinking we have privacy, even with guards stationed at every door. I can hear bits of the conversations around me. Two visitors wait in line for the vending machine in the far corner, right next to the water fountain and a counter where a microwave and paper cups are available for use. With a credit card in hand, a man taps on the glass of the machine, trying to figure out if he wants chips, nachos, cheese-and-peanut-butter crackers, or maybe instant ramen.

I catch sight of a girl I've seen in the cafeteria. She has her forehead on a table while an older woman talks to her, extending her fingers as if counting. The girl groans the more the woman talks.

I thank the guard as I take a seat. He gives me a two-finger salute.

I'm glad no one I know is around. It's weird when the outside and inside mix. To overhear parts of conversations where people reveal their biggest fears or, worse, hide how scared they really are.

A buzzer sounds on the opposite side of the room as the door opens.

Callie bounds in—not quite at a run, but she moves fast, and her chestnut hair bounces with each step. The jagged edges and streaks of emerald in her hair bring out the brown specks in her eyes. She never disappoints in her signature style: jeans and button-down shirt under a plaid vest. Her skin glows gold, and more color is on her wrist from the charm bracelet she always wears. It has a cross, a star, and a violin.

Compared to her, I look shabby. My skin is *so* dry. If Grams and Gramps saw me, they'd be ashamed at the ash on my elbows and in between my fingers. I'd clean toilets in here— yes, toilets—for cocoa butter. Still, I decide against asking Aunt Mae. What would I write?

Hey, Aunt Mae,

Thanks for the letters! How am I? Oh, I'm scared I'm going to be labeled a murderer forever and never see the outside of detention. But can you pretty please send a few jars of cocoa butter so I can be miserable and moisturized?

Love,
Letta

Callie gives me a tight hug. She lets me go after a couple minutes. "You okay?" she asks.

"Do I look okay?"

Callie opens her mouth.

"Lie to me," I say.

"You look fantastic!" She opens her arms wide, like she wants to welcome me into the lie.

"Thanks, darling." I flick my hair back, a Petra gesture. I forgot my hair isn't as long or thick as before, so it doesn't have the same effect. "I'd do anything for some moisturizer, actually. All they give us is watery lotion."

Callie dares the briefest touch to my cheek. "Yikes. Consider me on it."

As much as there's a list of rules for us inmates, there's also one for visitors. Anything brought inside that isn't food—that's been searched—is considered contraband. The options are commissary or mailing or nothing.

The minute we sit, Callie folds her fingers together, as if in a thumb war with herself.

"They're not coming, are they?" I ask.

Last week, Callie swore she could convince my parents and Vin to visit before my sentencing. I haven't seen them since they walked away from me in silence at the hospital. A day or so later, I was told they wanted me held. Every day inside, I've hoped they'd come see me. I've prayed they'd let me explain face-to-face what I can't seem to put to paper and what I didn't get right in the video. There's a handful of people on the guest list: Callie, her mother and father, and my family. Callie and her mom are the only ones I've seen. I was told, and maybe my family was too, it's better to keep our distance with me in detention.

I fold my hands in my lap and stare out the window, unable to take the sadness in Callie's hazel eyes. If my video couldn't convince them I was sorry, I don't know why I thought Callie would have a better chance.

"They hate me."

"No! They don't hate you," Callie says. "On our way here, my mom was saying, you know, parenting is tough. 'Qué triste,' she said over and over again. Everything is so sad to her these days. We can't watch the news, because there's not enough happy stories. 'Qué triste.'"

Knowing Callie's mom is outside waiting makes me sad too. I wish I could hug her. Mrs. Castillo gives great hugs.

"Vince misses you."

"Then why doesn't he come see me?"

Callie's eyes go wide. "There's just . . . a lot."

Aunt Mae's and Grams's letters haven't said they'd come visit me either, only that they are worried and love me and hope I find peace soon. I wish *someone* in my family would come by or let me know what's going on. All I have are the reruns of the worst night of my life and the fear that I'm all alone.

I also have LeVaughn Harrison's name in my head. How vicious it was for a jury to label him a murderer. If that was the case for him years ago at fourteen, before the Trials, what does that mean for me now when it comes to my own family?

"I know they hate me," I say, in defeat. "Everyone does."

"They don't!" Callie's hand is warm and kind of sweaty, but she takes mine and doesn't let go. I feel like I'm going cold inside. Almost like I'm one of the undead, my best friend is part of the living, and our kind should never mix.

Callie's hugs and her touch are the small mercies I get when she's able to visit. The reminder that Violetta exists outside of what landed me here. Petra tries to cheer me up, and

Counselor Susan wants me to acknowledge not just the night of but how I'm feeling each time we meet. But it's different with Callie, because she knows me from before all this. If she can forgive me for manslaughter—I cringe even thinking the word—then maybe, just *maybe*, my family may not hate me forever.

Grateful for these brief visits with my friend, I squeeze her hand back. "Let's talk about something else. How's school?"

"Augh, as boring as ever," she says. "Do you really miss quizzes, and the history of the three branches of government, and geometry?"

I laugh. "We have a routine, but, I don't know . . ." I shrug and stare out the window. "Sometimes it's easier in here." There's Petra, walking with another girl on the track. She's laughing, with her head thrown back, her ponytail swinging.

"You won't be here for long," Callie says. "I miss you."

"You're the only one."

"I'm not."

"Who else?"

Callie fiddles with the plastic cross on her bracelet. She's had it since she was tiny. I gave her the star pendant, because, even now, she shines.

"Well, *Vince*. I know your parents do. Just . . . Uh, Cora in gym was asking about you, because she misses the fact that you were the slowest to run track and now she is."

I'm shocked at how big the laugh is that comes out of me. I bounce in my seat.

Callie grins. "Mr. Allen was asking about you, because . . ."

She makes kissy noises, knowing he was my favorite teacher and I was one of his best students.

I ask her to name others. She names names, but not the one we both know I'm wondering about.

"Is he dating anyone?" I ask, even though I don't want to know the answer.

As far as Callie's concerned, I should burn all of Pascal's letters. I told her burning stuff wasn't an option in detention.

"What do you care?" she says.

"Just curious."

"He's been hanging around Monique. Has he mentioned *that* to you?"

Monique is curvy and confident, like Petra. The difference is Monique is conceited.

When he and I were together, Pascal's eyes stayed on me. His gaze was an X-ray machine. It was like he saw every part of me. It made me edgy and excited. I couldn't stop grinning that first day he motioned me to his locker saying I was "jolie." I felt wanted and seen. And, most importantly, I wasn't alone. At school, he'd sling his arm around me, pull me close, while we walked the halls side by side, and people actually moved to give us room. This was Letta not in the shadow of her superstar older brother, not a girl who got bumped into or overlooked. At home, I was the whiny one compared to my little sister, who did what she wanted, who was encouraged when she spoke loud or stood on chairs to get everyone's attention. But I never had that kind of voice. And apparently, being quiet doesn't get you much. Pascal saw through the silence to me.

As nervous as I was to start high school, Pascal made it, made *me*, feel like I didn't have to be behind anyone. I could be part of something. And who isn't mesmerized by Pascal? The dimples dotting his face whether he's grinning or frowning, his skin that shines as golden as Callie's, or how I thought he could protect me from the world whenever he wrapped me in his thick arms. He isn't into doing sports, but likes to weight train. Plus, he can talk about anything, whether he knows about it or not. People listen to him. I wanted that confidence to rub off on me. When I was with Pascal and his friends, I lost track of everything except maintaining our connection, because with him I wasn't an afterthought. And afterward . . . I'm not too proud of what happened after.

I ask, "Monique parle français, oui?"

"She's in Honors French."

"Slut."

"Listen," Callie says, getting so serious she releases my hand. "You have more important things to worry about. Like this Trial. Your parents told me about it. And . . . I can't believe you're doing it, Letta."

"Wait. Wait." A little hope sprouts up. "Did they tell you what my Trial will be?"

"Oh, no. Nothing like that."

I deflate on the spot, but I manage to regroup, just a bit. I tap into the hope Counselor Susan and Petra insist I'll need. "The Trials are like tests," I say. "I can pass a test."

"Okay, so right after I left your place on Saturday, I started digging into them online. I told my dad it's for a report when he checked the internet history, but he didn't believe me. As of this morning, we have internet curfews and firewalls. My brother is pissed he can't game at night anymore." She sighs. Still, I can't blame her parents for being overprotective, considering where I am and how close Callie and I are. "But what I did find was stuff like endurance tests and physical tests, and tests of mental capacity. This is kind of an intense experience. 'Rehab' is the word I kept reading."

"Yeah, that's the word they keep using here. That and 'reform.' But what do you mean, 'intense'?"

Because juvenile offenders' crimes are kept confidential out of respect for us being minors and the family, what's available to Callie is from hours of internet searches, reported features on the juvenile justice system, and a ton of conspiracy vlog posts. Callie rubs the cross charm as she takes a breath and fills me in on what turned up:

A seventeen-year-old charged with grand larceny by victims of the robbery. He did a Comprehension Trial, working for hours a day in a freezer at a market, doing inventory. The point was for him to understand how much hard work others did. This one didn't sound so bad, but Callie says, "Wait, there's more."

Of course there is.

Callie mentions an Accountability Trial where a girl had to parade—"That's what it actually said online, Letta, 'parade.' Like women don't have issues owning our bodies without men—"

"Focus, Callie."

"Sorry," she says, continuing. At church services, the girl

had to walk around in the skimpiest outfit ever. Her crime was online bullying because she shared seminude photos of another girl at her school. The victim of the crime was a classmate, and the Trial was meant to show her how it felt.

This one definitely didn't sound okay.

There's also a woman who did the Trials almost ten years ago, when she was my age. She's now a public advocate *against* this form of rehabilitation. Callie says the woman claims her Volition Trial was so manipulative she was in therapy for years due to PTSD. Competing reports noted that since her crime was a violent offense, who was she to say that rehab had caused her trauma and not committing the crime?

I stop Callie, my head spinning at the possibilities. Despite what my counselor told me yesterday about Trials being a better option, this doesn't sound better. Supposedly crime is down, but at what cost? Petra comes to mind when I look out the window again.

"See that girl out there with the ponytail?" It's been hammered into me that it's rude to point, but I do anyway. Callie gazes out the window at the same time Petra's approached by a guard in the center of the track. Petra's smile dwindles. In an instant, she's rushing into the main building, with the guard following her. *Wonder what's going on there?*

"She's my dorm mate," I continue. "She's been doing an, I think, Endurance Trial for nine months."

Callie doesn't hide her gasp; she covers her mouth for full effect. It's all very Callie. "Oh my God. That's how long it takes to, you know, carry a baby, Letta."

"Yeah. I'm not sure what her Trial was. She has a bunch of scars and told me she works in a field of thornbushes. Do you think . . . ?" I can't finish the thought. My arms tingle from imaginary scrapes.

Callie jerks to attention in her seat with a "Hell no!" which is way too loud for the visiting area. Irritated stares from the guards, and other visitors, land on us.

"Sorry!" my best friend says just as loud, not helping the situation.

To me, she continues almost at a whisper. "There's no way your family would, what, torture you like that. Besides, maybe—sorry to say—that girl deserved it?"

Her comment shocks me mute. "I accidentally killed my sister. What do I deserve?"

"Shoot. Sorry. Shoot." Callie grasps for my hands, pulling them close, near her heart. "I didn't mean it like that. I don't know her, but you're my best friend. I just want you to be okay. Like I said, you're horrible at track."

I get up from my chair, then sit down again. Standing means the guards will think I'm ready to go, and I'm not. My head pounds; my best friend doesn't believe I can get through the Trials. I meant it when I said I'd do whatever it takes. I ignore the rippling in my stomach, because I *have to* get through it.

"You don't believe in me?" I ask.

Callie's mouth drops open. "I didn't mean that. I just mean, considering what you said and what I read, plus you're . . ."

"I'm *what*?" I don't control my voice.

"Don't be mad. I'm scared for you. That's all. This should've never happened."

"Yeah, I *know* this should've never happened. But it did. I got drunk and I said she could ride with me, and I crashed and she died, and I'm here paying for it. So that's it. If I have to go through the Trials, I will. I can handle it," I say. "But I need you to believe in me. I have to think my parents want me to get through this. That Vin does. That *she* would if she were alive. I need every bit of that to make it through, Callie. Okay?"

"Okay," Callie says.

"Can you do me a favor, though?"

Perking up, she says, "Anything!"

"Could you look up what happened to LeVaughn Harrison?"

A scrunched-up face means Callie is all questions. She scratches her head before tucking brown and green strands behind an ear like she needs to hear me more clearly. "Who?"

I say his name again, slowly. "He's the reason the Trials started, or at least he's kind of part of it. I want to know what happened to him. Could you do a search for anything about LeVaughn and let me know what you find?"

Thumbs-up from Callie. "Done and done."

"Chen-Samuels, time!" startles us both.

Callie's bright eyes go moist. "It's never enough time." She says the same thing every visit once the announcement comes. And it never is. Not for the person I'd stay up all night with talking to or singing to karaoke videos during our sleepovers. We'd always laugh whenever we couldn't hit a high note. I'd give anything to have those moments back.

Callie gets up and rushes around the table to hug me. "Mom said to tell you we'll be praying for you."

"Tell her thanks. But you don't have to."

Callie fingers her cross again. "Letta," she says, "we're Catholic. We pray for everyone."

I watch Callie leave, listening for the clunk of another door closing on everything I used to know.

I count the steps as the guard and I return to my row. It's not as quiet as it usually is in the evening time before dinner. I can hear wailing coming from upstairs, right near my cell. The guard rushes up the stairs, with me not far behind. From Petra's doorway, the guard and I watch my normally composed friend become a bawling mound on her cell floor, arms over her head.

Here, you don't ask questions. But Petra has always asked me how I was. "How's your day, pretty Violet?" she'd say during meals.

I ask if she's okay, the way Callie asked me, even though I know she isn't.

All that comes out is hiccupped sobs.

"Petra?" I say.

The guard doesn't urge me to my cell next door. He doesn't leave my side either.

"Petra?" My voice squeaks. I kneel in front of her and ask, "Petra, what happened?" Everything about her is the opposite of the past couple days; it doesn't make sense.

Her words come one hiccup at a time. "For-give-ness. Re-voked. I have to continue my Trial."

There's nothing to say and so much to say. All I can do is watch my friend, a puddle on the floor.

"But they . . . they *said* they forgave you!" It all flashes through my mind, how happy she was to get the verdict of forgiveness on Saturday. Her, all smiles, telling me how long she's been at this. I grab her shoulders. I need to know how this happened, how this could happen to *her*.

She wipes her face through her sobs. "Well," she manages to say, voice as dead as her eyes, "seems like forgiveness doesn't always last."

CHAPTER 8
VINCE
Days since the decision: 24

At the end of the day, Janice is smart enough not to stop me from going straight home or ask if I want to talk. She says she'll get a ride home with Jorge or Levi, since they're all staying after for yearbook. While Janice can always take a hint—hell, she's able to predict my mood at times—Byron is not as skilled. I find him by my car, scrolling through his phone. Seeing him with his reminds me I have to figure out if I have enough saved to get a new phone without telling Mom and Dad.

"Hey," I say, already unlocking the car to chuck my bookbag into the back seat. It lands on my track spikes, sending up dust.

"Can you give me a ride?" He's already opening the passenger-side door. That's Byron for you, ready for the yes before it even comes.

"It's been a long day, man. Can you ask Jorge? They'll be done in an hour. Or maybe someone from the team?"

"Why would I wait an hour when you're right here?" Byron isn't dumb or a jerk, just oblivious. I catch how he doesn't stay still; he's shifting from one foot to another, a kind of limited dance. And I know exactly what that means.

Me getting inside without a word signals him to do the same. As soon as our doors are closed, I ask, "What are you on?"

Blowing hair out of his eyes, he says "Huh?" all innocent-like. His phone's stuffed in his jacket pocket, so now his hands are empty. He taps his fingers on my dash to a rhythm only he can hear. Since he's wearing shorts and a hooded sweatshirt, I can see how white his legs are and the gashes from falls and tackles we've shared during lacrosse season last fall. He mirrors my own reactions when I'm on. If you get the uppers, you are *up*, a whole bundle of energy that needs to be released. Being confined won't help; you gotta move. My engine revs to a cough. Placing my arm on his headrest, I check to make sure I can back out easily. That's when I catch a whiff of Byron. He's super sweaty. I can practically smell the salt coming out of him.

I got to see and know more of Byron halfway through freshman year whenever I drove him home after our games. He'd try to hide the holes in his sneakers in winter. Or he couldn't always afford uniforms on the due dates. It became clearer how some of us are given a lot and others not so much. I could relate, since my parents didn't always have what I needed. Like I said, my parents make do. We're never hungry and have what we need. Thing is, Gramps and Grams helped more than Dad would've liked when it came to school activities—cleats, lacrosse gear, a trip to a debate meet out of state. Being me isn't cheap. Byron and I bonded over the need to perform well, because there was no safety net for him, and for me no guarantees of college without taking some serious loans. He wants to go to a school where there's no reminders of what he doesn't have. I need to get away to figure out who I really am.

"I'm taking you home so you can sleep it off, I guess?" I know the way to his place by now. Byron usually gets a school MetroCard to take the buses, but at this point everyone on the team has given him a ride at least once. Usually, the job falls on me since we don't live too far from each other in Westbridge. Plus, there's an ease in how things are between us. No expectations outside of the field. So we ride in silence, mostly.

His stomach gurgles; mine does too. That's a sign we should hit up the Burger Barn, load up on protein and fries, after burning off calories in practice. But I'm not in the mood to be out longer than I have to be. I do ask, though, since it's part of our routine, and whether Byron admits it or not, he may have missed it while I was out. Byron motions for me to take a turn that's not toward his apartment or the Burger Barn.

"Here?" I point to the upcoming left turn that goes to a part of the burbs I'm not too familiar with.

"Yup."

"What's there?" Or who. "A guy?"

"Yes." He turns to his window so I can't see his face outside of his reflection. "But not like you're thinking."

"Any prospects?"

"You know I'm focused this year. No distractions."

"Now you sound like Janice."

"She's a smart woman."

His tapping on the dash ramps up: less rhythm, more frantic energy.

"I can turn on the radio if you need a beat."

"No, thanks," he says. "Quiet is good."

"Is it?" I ask, thinking being alone with my thoughts would be way too much. How I crave and don't want it at the same time. Once I get home, what'll I do? Veg out on some videos? Go watch some track clips for form? Try and fill my mind with outside noise and refocus.

"Next stop sign, make a right. It's a one-way."

I do what he says. "You gonna tell me where we're going?"

"Do you really want to know?"

"Answering a question with a question is suspect, Byron. Where am I going?"

"From what he told me, you didn't want to know."

He? My thoughts immediately go to Levi, but this isn't where he lives. Where we are now is getting, well, fancy. I'm seeing the McMansions of Jamaica Estates up here, except they're not on hills. Wide houses with pillars and some serious layers. Stone walkways and barely any lawns. Places that look new and shiny, with remnants of construction scattered around in slate slabs and concrete bags. It's not that Westbridge doesn't have fancy areas, but this? These homes set people apart, maybe by choice. My duplex and the two-bedroom Byron shares with his parents and brother are tucked into residential areas off the main boulevards. Where he and I live, we can walk a couple blocks to the supermarket or a coffee shop or takeout Thai food or the 99-cent store. We're not isolated from the things that remind you you're in a major city. When homes are clustered together, farther away from the stores and whatnot, it makes me think the people there don't want to be found.

"Up the block. That big house."

That big house isn't super descriptive, considering the massive homes I'm looking at. I know what he means, though, especially when you compare this place to the ones around it. The one he's talking about is an enormous box with terraces attached to the top two floors. The whole house looks like it's been lined with sandpaper, rough to the touch. I pull up, and the front door is open. *Who the hell keeps their door open?*

From what I can see inside, the floor has to be marble, so smooth you could skate on it. And, okay, seriously, am I seeing a winding staircase in a house in Queens?

"Byron, where the hell—"

That's when I see the person in the doorway beckoning us in.

He's barefoot, in jeans and a loose-fitting sweater with long sleeves. Ross's hair is styled just so, with a nice wave. His Mustang isn't parked anywhere on the street.

"Dude, what are we doing here?"

Byron mashes his hands together in circles, like he wants to keep them warm even though it's not chilly in my car. Whenever I confront him, Byron doesn't look at me. I'm not mad, but I'm also not *not* mad. Yeah, Byron introduced me to this stuff—and to Ross. Thing is, I didn't decline anything I was given when sophomore year got rough and the pressure was on. When it sunk in that my family was hard-working but not drowning in dollars. Byron tries to help. But again, it's that misplaced kind of help.

Byron's already halfway out my door. I manage to grab him by his hood, tug him back inside. "I'm not trying to control your life. But I've been off almost a month, and I'm okay." That's not the truth; it's also not a complete lie. Life sucks, and the cravings continue to come. I have to believe I've kicked them at least.

Byron pulls away with a force that impresses me.

"I'm not a total asshole, Vince. I know you have a lot to deal with. It's why I'm not expecting anything besides the ride." He's out much quicker this time. The door slams in my face when I try to yell at him to come back.

"Damn it." I park on the street and follow. I'm at a jog right behind him. If I let him go by himself, he could do a taste test, and then he'd be here all night. At least if I keep an eye on him, I can get us out in minutes.

Yup, this house is just as elegant as I thought. Like a museum, where you're scared to touch anything. This is literally how I imagined rich people lived. Leave it to Ross to blow your mind with and without pills. Photos framed in silver line the walls in the main hallway. The pictures are black-and-white, labeled with famous landscapes around the world—the Eiffel Tower (Paris), Sydney Opera House (Australia), the Colosseum (Rome)—and are as big as the HD TV in our living room.

My sneakers squeak on the blush-colored marble. I should

probably stay put so I don't leave streaks. I'd take my shoes off if I intended to stay.

Byron gives Ross a one-armed hug, and he's already up the staircase, leading the way. My friend is way too familiar with this place for my liking.

"Make it quick!" I shout at his back.

"Yeah, yeah," Byron says.

Ross hangs out at the bottom of the stairs. "You wanna come up? We can play something on my new system. No one's home to bother us."

Outside of what he wears and the Mustang he drives, I've always thought he was spoiled. Turns out my instincts were right. It's not like his family has any pictures of themselves around, or any of Ross. In our duplex, you can't make a move without a photo of me, Letta, or Viv at any given age in frames Mom was gifted or got on sale. Our walls are painted different colors, mostly earth tones, Mom's favorite, but it feels like a family lives where we are, thanks to worn furniture, a spotty carpet, stacks of mail or pots or clothes depending on the room you're in, and stained countertops. There's no color or life to this place, just a display of money in steel, rose, and white furniture with sharp edges; everything appears hard to the touch.

I take a step, only one, to the open room nearest the entryway. It's the dining room, but it looks untouched. There's a ridiculously long table, probably also marble, with high-backed chairs around it. A crystal vase sits in the middle without any flowers in it. There's no bowl of browning fruit or pizza boxes or water spots anywhere to be found.

"Ross!" Byron calls. Since Ross's place is pretty empty, Byron's voice carries easily.

Ross moves up only a step. His gaze is a bit intense. Come to think of it, every time his eyes are on me, I feel like he's sizing me up. Not in a bad way, but like he's trying to figure me out.

"Must be boatloads of fun," I say, "having all this to yourself."

"Mom and Dad traveling for business was fun, at first," Ross says, ignoring Byron. "Summers my sisters and I go with them. After two years it's been nonstop deals so kinda lost its flavor." I can hear the hint of disappointment in his voice, but he rebounds fairly quickly, smiling that perfect smile of his. *"Anyways*, lemme not bore you with that stuff."

Ross's whole body language is chill. He leans on the stairwell like someone's directed him to pose with not a care in the world. His blue eyes are relaxed and still penetrating; his pink lips are pinched like he's holding a secret. "Gotta make my own fun during junior year."

It's obvious Ross doesn't need whatever he gets from what he doles out. Byron and I aren't rolling in anything but grass and dirt during lacrosse games compared to all the luxury Ross gets to sleep in. Bet he isn't worried about scholarships or recruiters, or things like the "liability insurance" my mom was cursing about this morning.

I wonder if Ross can hear my thoughts, because, like a kid caught, he focuses on his toes and digs them into the rug covering the staircase. Ross cranes his neck once he hears his name again. He makes a move to go but turns to me, kind of a question of whether I want to follow.

"The sooner you give him what he wants, the sooner we can get out of here," I tell him.

Jogging up the stairs, Ross throws a smile my way. "Maybe I don't want you to leave!"

Every passing minute, I get more irritated, and I have to pee. But it's not like I can check email or anything, thanks to no phone. I could leave Byron. Know what? I really should leave him here. If he wants to get lit, let him. Why should I care? Funny enough, I can't get mad at Byron. Not when I know he's hurting for different reasons than I am.

More time passes that I can't ignore that I have to use the bathroom. I hesitate on the first step, but nature calls. At the first landing I can hear a faint *boom-crash* that reminds me of the latest level of the game *Hollow*. It's one of the new military ones, almost like a real simulation. Of course Ross would have it. Instead of heading toward the noise, I figure a bathroom must be nearby. After passing several closed doors I find one that's slightly ajar. And from what I can see there's a sink. *Jackpot.* As soon as I open the door, Byron's "ouch" follows.

The hell? I push again so it fully opens to see my teammate clutching at the edge of a sink full of pill bottles. The medicine cabinet is wide open and also has double-sided glass so we can see each other.

If the house is a museum, then this cabinet is a full-on pharmacy.

I grab a bottle out of Byron's hand.

"Vince, come on," he says, trying, and failing, to snatch it back. It's barely a struggle because his knees are bent and shaky. I smack his hand away. Byron topples over when he tries to stand up. I drop the bottle and urge him to sit on the toilet between the sink and the glass shower door. The name "Celine Allen" is on most of the bottle labels. I don't know the names for the pills. They could be for illnesses. Even though I don't know the names, one bottle has capsules I recognize. Yellow gel, easily melts on the tongue. The same thing Ross offered me the day Viv died. I drop that bottle like it's scalded me.

"Come on," I yell at Byron. I try to pull him up but he's sludge. His pupils are so big I can barely see the blue of his eyes, and his skin feels hot.

"Byron! Get. Up." Hooking my arms under him is no use when he can't move. He's definitely on the downers and there's no coming back from this without some help or a long rest.

Rushing out of the bathroom, I run straight into Ross.

"Hey," he says, glancing behind me to Byron, who uses the edge of the sink as a pillow. "See you found the stash."

"Won't your parents be pissed?"

"I told you, my parents are barely ever home. Deals in Dubai, ventures in Venice. My sisters check in when they can but they're dealing with their own stuff at Yale or with kids. It's just me most of the time." Ross walks past me to check on Byron, just a quick look. Satisfied, he rolls up his sleeves and leans against the bathroom doorframe, eyeing me.

"How long is he gonna be like this?" I ask.

The way Ross shrugs, like my teammate being passed out

in his bathroom is no big deal, makes me want to punch him. Why should I expect anything? This is what he does. This is what I used to come to him for, to be as blissed out as Byron is right now. And I hate, I really hate, to admit my teammate looks peaceful and I kinda envy him.

Ross shakes a bottle that rolled onto the ground and into the hallway. I'm backing away trying not to bump into anything on my way out.

"If you want it, just take it. On the house like usual." He smiles, all teeth and confidence. And why wouldn't he be? He has smooth skin, a big house to himself, and gets to spend junior year free and clear of any pain with all these pills at the ready.

Ross tosses it to me. The bottle hits my chest before rattling back to the floor. "Trust me. They don't miss the stuff," he says. "And I'm helping my fellow student at the same time."

Times like this, I wish I was stronger. Strong enough not to be tempted at all. I can't even look at the bottle rolling past my feet, because I'm afraid I'll scoop it up and run.

Damn it, Byron.

I can't and won't be here for this. I tell Ross, "He's your problem now. Get him home safely or it's your ass."

On my way out, I make sure to shut the front door behind me loud enough for them to know I'm gone.

CHAPTER 9

Hey Viv,

Where I am now, we only get shoes you can fasten with snaps or Velcro. No shoelaces because— You don't need to know why. Every time I bend over to put my shoes on, I think about how long it took me to figure out how to tie them in the first place. Vin showed me how when I was five. He did rabbit ears. You learned super quick at that age. Not rabbit ears. You did the "one string, two strings, fold, and new string" way. I thought I could help you with that—turns out you didn't need me. I don't know why I'm talking about this. It just came to me when I was putting my shoes back on while I wait for Callie to visit.

You know what I always admired about you? That you never showed fear. When I was seven, I was sort of afraid of all the things. At amusement parks, Dad carried me toward rides until I screamed so hard I almost burst an eardrum. The most I could do was the teacups or the merry-go-rounds. Nothing in the air. But you, you were right at the height line for some of the smaller roller coasters, and you sped through to sit in front so you could see every hill or drop as it happened. On roller coasters, I kept my eyes shut, feeling the rise and fall right in my belly. I was always thankful when they were over, while you went back for more.

You weren't afraid to fail either. We all took swimming lessons together, and you couldn't get your legs and arms to move in the water at the same time. That was surprisingly one of the few things I caught on to quicker than you. Maybe the only thing. Being in the water made me feel free to "relax and let go." My whole body floated right to the top. Underwater, I could see some of the things that sank to the bottom of the pool—like Band-Aids and balls of hair. Even the smell of chlorine helped me relax. I'd look over while floating or doing froggy kick or freestyle to see you struggling in your favorite cow-print bathing suit and matching swim cap. Getting your hands to slip in & out of the water but not splashing your legs hard enough to move forward. I watched the instructors watch you, how they grabbed you when your arms flailed and held you up when you had trouble keeping your body afloat. And sometimes—I'm so sorry to say this—I was glad to see you fail. At the same time I admired you for trying. It made me feel better to know there was something, even <u>one thing</u>, you couldn't master that I did. You nailed Mandarin, cooking with Mom, making all the friends wherever you went.

In the pool, you never cried, though you got frustrated—a lot. You'd stomp up the kiddie stairs from the pool to the floor, making sure everyone heard the smack of your wet feet against the tile.

"Next time," I'd tell you in the car on our way home. Mom or Dad would treat us to ice cream while our skin dried from the chlorine, the smell of it clinging to us.

Looking back, I realize I didn't offer to help you. The instructors tried, but even when they held you, you couldn't get it. Nowadays, I wonder if maybe the words of a big sister would've helped. If I'd showed you on your bedroom floor or in the bathtub, or even in that senior center pool we visited twice a week in summer. I think about things like this a lot. I wonder if I was a good big sister to you while you were here. I'd like to believe I was. Then again, I wouldn't be where I am if that was the case. Would I?

I'll try to write again soon,
Letta

CHAPTER 10

VINCE

Days since the decision: 24

I'm home in minutes. Which is good, because I'd like to wash away every bit of Ross's temptations, including flushing the pills still in my room. But there's a car in the spot reserved for mine. This one is compact and sleek, in a metallic color that makes me think of money—like Ross's Mustang. On the side, I see a faint decal of the American flag and the words DETENTION SERVICES.

I was already tense, but I'm practically granite the whole walk to our duplex entrance. This visit could mean Violetta did something to herself. It could mean my parents changed their mind. Maybe Callie's visit helped, or even seeing Viv's mug set them to forgive Violetta. I hit the steps to our landing, and dread settles in, because they could have changed their decision in either direction, maybe sent Violetta upstate to serve time.

When I first met our judicator, he asked me my opinion, said it was good to decide things as a family unit. But I stayed quiet about the sentencing decision. I wanted my family together, but was I certain Letta should be forgiven outright when everything about Viv was now a memory? I wasn't so sure.

Voices come from the kitchen. I linger in the doorway as I kick off my sneakers. My parents stare at papers spread across the dining table. And there's Randall, a ridiculously tall and lean guy, hovering over them. Dad's bulk and height are usually intimidating, but Randall constantly looks down at you. He wears a gray suit with a tie as metallic as his car. He has skin so white you can see veins, slicked-back auburn hair, and eyes that sink into his head. He also carries himself like he owns the place and has a tablet permanently tucked under his armpit.

He stares at me for an uncomfortable amount of time before saying, "Hello, Vincent. I'm Randall. Remember me?" He offers a hand. I ignore it.

Dad raises his head to talk to the judicator and suddenly notices me. "Vince? Aren't you home early?"

"I only had debate today," I say. "What's going on?"

I ask my parents, but it's the judicator who answers. "We're discussing the details of Violetta's Trials."

"Without me?"

Dad grimaces. Mom picks up one piece of paper in each hand. They've cleaned up for Randall. Dad's in a button-down with a red sweater over it. His head and face are clean-shaven. In fact, the top of his head gleams, so you can't see any grays. Mom's hair is still in a topknot, but at least she's out of the robe and in a flowy red skirt and a matching floral blouse. She even has a bit of makeup on. My parents look ready to go to a school recital, not decide the fate of their imprisoned daughter.

"This is for Endurance?" Mom says, her face clear, eyes squinting.

"Yes," Randall replies. "Remember, there are various choices. Endurance. Volition. Comprehension. Benevolence. Humility. Accountability." As he names each one, he points to a colored folder. My eyes slide to the rainbow of options for rehabilitation.

"What do people usually choose in these situations?" Dad asks.

"Depends on the crime . . . uh, incident," Randall says, correcting himself. "You want to make sure your choice fits what has transpired. If the offender committed an offense against your morals, you may choose a Benevolence Trial. This helps her prove she retains the values she was raised with. Many choose Endurance or Accountability Trials for teens, because then they'll never forget what they went through. Ultimately leading to a lower chance of recurrence. They are particularly helpful for those with addiction problems like Violetta."

I gulp at "addiction." I don't want to believe Letta was drinking that much. Sure, I saw it a couple times—just like I've taken pills—does that make me, or my sister, an addict?

Randall continues, "Comprehension is often applied to the younger sect, as is Volition. Those last two ensure juveniles truly understand the circumstances, and why they need rehabilitation. Volition often ensures juveniles make better choices."

Better choices.

Randall doesn't stop. "Benevolence can be assigned to bullies and those who inflicted harm on others. We've found Benevolence Trials help the offender experience a form of their crime from the other side."

Mom picks up a purple folder and shows Dad what's written inside. He grunts at it and leans closer.

Taking in what Mom and Dad are reading, Randall nods and says, "I've seen excellent results in those Trials."

"Really?" Dad asks. He looks up at Randall, hopeful.

I cross the room and end up ripping the purple folder in half. My mom holds one half, and the other is flat under my palm on the table.

I ask Randall, "Why are you here? This is a family thing to decide. You're not family."

"Look what you did!" Mom attempts to salvage the half I'm holding on to. "Sorry," she says to Randall. "It's been a rough time."

"I can imagine," Randall says.

"Vincent!" Dad's irritation echoes. "This *is* a family matter. *However*, these particulars are up to your mother and me. You need to respect what we say when we tell you we know what's best for Violetta."

"Are you serious? I'm seventeen. I'm her brother and your son. We said—"

"When you start acting like an adult, we'll treat you like one." Dad's knuckles prop him up as he rises, transforming into the giant I've feared and loved my whole life. His eyes hold mine when he says, "We already had one kid fall through the cracks, and we're rectifying that as best we can. You do not have to be here for that. Understand?"

My eyes slide from Dad to the judicator to Mom, now flipping through items in a yellow folder marked HUMILITY.

"Yeah. We understand each other."

"We'll talk later," he says, his voice softening slightly. But he's still upset. The pinch of his mouth tells me that.

I back out of the room. When I turn around, I catch the judicator staring at me like he knows something about me. I swallow hard. I start up the stairs, but stop midway so I can still hear some of their conversation.

Mom asks, "How many Trials do people choose?"

"As I said, it depends on the incident. You know," Randall says, "if Vincent is upset, perhaps we should do this another day."

"He'll be fine," Mom says, like she's waving his idea away. "How soon does this begin once we make a decision? I'd like to get this all over with so my daughter can get the help she needs."

"A couple of days to a week to set up . . . depending on the Trial itself."

"We want our daughter to succeed, but we need her to understand," Dad says. "I . . . will we know she's okay?"

Mom chimes in. "Yes, will we get updates on how she's doing? She's okay, right? She looked healed from the accident."

A pause happens, stirring up my nerves even more. Does that mean Letta *isn't* okay or—

"Hmm," Randall hums until he has an answer. Probably from that tablet he carries around. The man literally never leaves home without it. "No bruising. She's fine. No sign of relapse or alcohol dependency. There's no way for her to access alcohol in detention, so that hasn't been an issue for any offenders if that makes you feel better. And I see your daughter is cleared physically to participate in a Trial if that's your concern."

"Our concern is her getting better so she can come home. We need to know this won't happen again and we don't—" Mom sniffles once, twice. From the slight choking of her next words, I can tell she's full-on crying, again. "We couldn't help her. We couldn't even prevent this from happening!"

"Listen, we love our daughter. We do," Dad insists, like he's the one being judged instead of Letta. I can picture him wrapping Mom in a hug, protecting her like he always tries to do.

"No one thinks otherwise, Mr. and Mrs. Chen-Samuels. I'm here to help take on the harder decisions. This way, neither of you have to. If you give us the Trial category, the Bureau of Corrections will develop the specifics of what this Trial will entail and update you when we're ready to begin.

"I'd also be happy to connect you with parents of offenders who have encountered this dilemma. They can tell you how their children have benefitted from the system." Even when Randall attempts to be accommodating, he sounds like a damn robot. No feeling, just facts. As though my sister can be calculated in such and such way.

I'm tempted to swoop right back into the kitchen just to scream Violetta's name in Randall's face: *She has a name, and it's not "offender."*

"Maybe that will help. Annie?" Dad asks Mom. From how muffled his voice is, he's probably kissing her head to calm her.

"Okay," Mom squeaks.

"Alright. I'll make a note to do that. Circling back to the Trials, perhaps you'd like to do a few?" Randall suggests.

Sometimes, you can hear a person smile when they're talking. I could whenever Levi and I spoke over the phone. When he was shy, saying "Aw, Vin," after I complimented him. I could just tell he was grinning that goofy grin, and it made me smile too. But this guy Randall? Something is off, almost like he enjoys this part. It's enough to make me want to rip up a few more folders.

Mom stretches out another "Okay" before adding, "Augh, all this is giving me another migraine." I can picture her massaging her temples, attempting to ward off the pressure in her head and the pressure from Randall.

"Yeah. I mean, *yes*," Dad says. There's a pause. "Um, this one and this one. Annie?"

Silence—until Randall says, "Is that a directive?" It ticks me off to hear how robotic he sounds. "And this one too?"

"I guess . . . if necessary," Dad mumbles after another pause.

"So that's three Trials in total," the judicator says. "That's a good number to set up for her."

More silence, which means nods or some form of silent agreement from my parents. Every time Randall explains something, my fingers clench into fists because he's not being comforting, at all. But apparently, to my parents, he's the guide they've been searching for on how to fix a broken child.

What do they think Violetta making amends should look like? That's what scares me most, but at the same time I'm relieved it's not me facing this punishment. The last part confirms I've earned a shirt with I SUCK AS A BIG BROTHER on it.

"Will they be okay for her? Are they"—Mom coughs—"effective?"

More shuffling and crinkling of papers. Then the judicator's voice ends the meeting with a promise: "Don't worry. I'll take care of everything."

CHAPTER 11
VIOLETTA

Days in detention: 25

~~卌 卌 卌 卌 卌~~

Every morning, I wait on my bed for the door to be unlocked. At seven thirty, the first trip of the day for everyone in my dorm is the bathroom. Towel, a block of soap the color of a paper bag, miniature toothpaste and toothbrush, plus a plastic hairbrush are bundled in my arms. Some girls make a sack out of their pants to hold what they need. We walk single file.

Petra is not with our group today. Her cell door was closed when I went to meet our guard escort. I'm worried about her. She wouldn't talk to me after we found her crying in her cell last night.

My sandals slide against the floor as we march to the bathroom. Two female guards wait at the entrance—there's no door. I enter; another girl exits. The whole place is damp brick, warm in temperature but not in feeling. A few girls hang around the sinks, some chatting, with towels tucked tight around their chests.

I'm glad the guards leave us alone. Morning showers mean a little privacy, even though we can hear them talking to one another and feel their eyes when they peek inside to ask if we're almost done. When we first arrived at Piedmont, our bodies were put on display: our hair checked for lice, our legs spread for pat-downs performed by a woman behind a curtain, clothing removed to confirm there's no contraband.

The showers are cement blocks, one after the other, inscribed with names of other inmates. The drains are clogged with hair of all lengths and colors. I step into an empty stall with my sandals on to undress. I stand a foot away from the showerhead, angling it so the water covers me. I don't wash my hair today. I scrub myself with a cloth before the pleasure of hot water turns into a shocking cold blast.

As soon as I'm done, I get dressed in a hurry. My undershirt and jumpsuit stick to my skin; my face is still wet. So are patches of my hair. My sandals slap against the floor, leaving a trail of water on the way back to my cell.

The shoes they gave me are half a size too large. I stuff them with paper towels and wear two pairs of socks so they don't rub against my heels too much. I tighten the Velcro straps as much as I can so they don't slip off. All set and dressed in dry clothes, I wait. It's April 1st. Beginning of the month means dispensary day of designated items. Anyone with commissary funds can buy something extra. After the bathroom, my dorm is guided to the commissary, to the end of another line of girls fidgeting along a wall. A girl wearing a sweatshirt tied around her waist leans on the counter where items are handed out.

"How many?" a gruff voice asks.

"A lot," the girl says, tugging at her ponytail. She slips a few strands of hair into her mouth. "It's one of *those* days."

"I need a number." The voice comes slightly harder, more demanding.

"Just tell her so the rest of us can get going, huh?" the girl ahead of me snaps.

"If you had something beyond the cheap ones, I would! I need"—here, the girl whispers, spitting the hair out from between her lips—"something substantial, 'cause Aunt Flo is movin' fast." She tugs at the sleeves of the sweatshirt. It shifts enough for me to see the edge of a rust-colored stain on her inner thigh.

After a minute, and some intense bargaining, the girl is offered a box of pads. She scoops it up, grinning as she passes us with her winnings. The others respond faster to the same question.

When it's my turn, I have to think, though I've had minutes to do so. Today's dorm guard waits nearby. *How many will I need, for how long?*

"How many?" the same voice asks, their face masked and split by the wire separating us.

I throw out a number to end this show. The person in the box of the dispensary is surrounded by shampoo, conditioner, soap, maxi pads, candy, deodorant, and anything else you'd find in a pharmacy, but with way less variety.

I hold my items close, ashamed that I have to ask for what I need in front of an audience, and wait for them to parcel it out as though that's all I deserve. I also ask for shampoo, and I beg for hair grease and moisturizer. But all I get is watery lotion that smells like coconut and does nothing for my dry skin.

Next stop is the mailroom. More grating separates me from the person on the other side. The adults wear gloves and hold letter openers, the only sharp tool in sight. A pile of envelopes are sliced open, letters unfolded and opened. Except for the morning bathroom run, which has a time limit, there's no privacy here. Not even in the letters or packages we receive. Everything's checked and split open by the time it gets to us.

"Chen-Samuels. Inmate number 965829."

"All we need is the number," the woman says, typing into her computer. "Nothing today. Anything to send off?"

"No, not today."

There's still no sign of Petra when we come back from our commissary spree. It's become force of habit to look at her cell when I pass by. Her door is shut, but her bed is made, and her stuff is there. I'm guessing she got up early to talk to someone about a possible appeal. It's been three days since I heard about my sentence and almost a day since Petra's forgiveness was revoked.

Once I've put my things down, I stand outside my cell again for the next trip.

"Everyone accounted for! Let's move," the guard shouts.

We follow security from our cells. Two floors down we're lined up for breakfast in the cafeteria. I spot Eve and Serena at one of the center rows of tables—closest to the food, in case there's extra left. Serena's shocking-pink dreadlocks are fading at the roots to their original onyx color. Petra's not with them either.

Oatmeal is slapped into one partition of my tray; a fruit cup, into another. A small carton of milk has its place, so does a slightly burnt slice of toast. The food has no real taste, not like what Mom cooks back home. No dishes rich with soy and oyster sauce. No meats crusted with cornstarch or flour. No eggs with savory spices. A pound of salt or pepper or sugar wouldn't improve the taste of things here by much.

"Thanks," I tell the person behind the counter sludging out our food.

I keep my head low on my way to the table. Eve and Serena are gobbling up everything on their trays. The two of them scrape at the syrup from their fruit cups, then bring them to their lips. After several weeks, Eve and Serena are almost mirror images in the way they huddle together and dive into their food. There's not a trace of ash or bumps on Eve's brown- and Serena's sandy-toned skin. Plus, Eve's short black hair is bone straight and actually shines. I'm jealous. Someone must send them the good stuff.

Serena watches me poke at my oatmeal. "You don't eat it, you lose it," she says. "You know that's the rule, sitting with me."

"I know. I know," I say, putting a protective arm around my tray. "Funny, considering you always complain about the food."

"I'm a growing girl," Serena says. When I first met Serena, I asked if she played sports, since she's so tall. She sucked her teeth so hard I thought I'd offended her. "I'm a mathlete, if that counts," was her reply.

Eve speaks while chewing, so I can see the bits of oatmeal in her braces. "It's like I'm hate-eating in here. What else is there to do until that sorry excuse for school this afternoon?"

"Have either of you seen Petra today?" I say. "The last time I saw her she was—"

"Devastated?" Eve offers. She looks to Serena for agreement, but Serena is negotiating with one of the servers for another fruit cup.

The sounds of the cafeteria grow from a murmur to a chorus of booming voices as more people arrive for breakfast. I scoot closer so I can hear Eve, and vice versa.

Thinking back to Callie's visit, there are so many things I wished we'd had time to talk about. "But the Trials and everything," I say to Eve. "You can't just switch a decision."

Counselor Susan didn't say anything about *reversing* forgiveness. She made it sound like a done deal. That Congress and everyone had this all figured out. "This justice system is supposed to be fair and . . ." I stop, noticing Eve shaking her head.

"Fair?" Eve stabs her spork at a remaining chunk of peach. More fruit ends up in the brackets of her braces. "No offense to you all with Trials, but the waiting on at least a decision of what's next is the worst part."

I must look confused and disappointed, but Eve goes on. "I'm here because of some kid I used to tease." Eve's high cheekbones and constant frown make her appear always in deep thought. But right now, even though her short cut is sleek, perfectly styled, she looks anything but together. As she goes on, she practically fades into her seat. "Apparently, what I did was online bullying. I'm waiting to hear whether or not I have to do Trials."

The way Eve sulks keeps me from asking why the girl can't make up her mind.

Eve continues, "The girl's parents are probably waiting for her to wake up from her accident to hand down a sentence. My counselor calls me in, saying a decision's been made, then her parents change their mind but I never know *why*. It's stressing my mom *out*. She's starting to lose her hair. My dad is already bald."

I hold my head, trying to get this all straight in my mind. "People can keep you in limbo?"

"For me they are, and . . . maybe Petra? She's also dealing with the parents of her 'victim' making decisions. If they're designated, they may be making every decision on their own or talking to him." Eve chews so quickly she almost chokes. After some hacking sounds, she takes a sip of milk and continues as if nothing happened. "I dunno the details for Petra. And it's not like my counselor tells me everything the victims are thinking. I hear what I'm 'allowed to.'" Eve does air quotes on the last two words.

Serena returns with a fruit cup. "What'd I miss?"

"Trial stuff."

"Oh, *that*. I got enough of it from orientation." Serena slurps at the fruit and syrup while asking me, "Didn't you, Letta?"

"There's more I'm trying to figure out. I mean, they can forgive you and take it back when they want?"

"From what my counselor tells me"—the word *counselor* is heavy in Eve's mouth—"the victims *can* change their mind about forgiveness while you're inside. Once you're all signed out and back at home, no takebacks."

Serena starts to slowly drag my tray her way. "I'm eating, I'm *eating*," I say. "Counselor Susan never said anything about—"

"She didn't say a lot about *a lot*, Letta." Serena sucks her teeth again, but this time it might be to get food out of her teeth. Every time she does, the tattoo on her neck flexes, as if the flowers are blowing in a breeze.

"What do you—"

"Listen." Serena interrupts me again, which is getting annoying. "You can trust the counselors in here all you want. To me, the counselor's just another adult making me jump through hoops for stealing. No one cares *why* I stole the things I did, just that I did it . . . a lot. That's what I don't like about all this. It's not that different from before, from what my grandparents tell me."

Eve crushes her milk box. "*Yup.* My dad talked my head off when it came to laws and procedures, following the rules. He *still* expects me to go to law school."

I thought orientation was a lot to digest, but I'm having a hard time swallowing what the girls are telling me too. Eve bullied someone into a coma. Serena stole *a lot*. Petra did something that apparently can't be forgiven. And my sister is dead. But three out of four of us have Trials, with forgiveness as a possibility, even though now it feels farther off than it was before.

There's a faint "Hey." I'm so thankful to see Petra holding a tray. I slide over so she has room to sit. She doesn't look like herself. The thin skin around her eyes is puffy with blue veins. Her ponytail is loose and off to the side instead of tight. She's also wearing long sleeves again under the jumpsuit.

I ask if she's okay.

"I'll be all right. Things will get settled," she says, but she sounds weak.

"Hear anything about them reversing the decision?" Serena asks.

Petra shakes her head as she takes a bite of toast.

"I'm so, so sorry, Petra," I say. I wait to see if Serena is going to try and take anything from her tray. Petra continues to chew for a minute or so, leaving the rest untouched. The girls have solemn looks on their faces.

"Counselor Susan said the victim's parents had a change of heart due to circumstances they didn't want to disclose right now."

Petra takes a deep breath. She rolls up her sleeve, showing the full scale of what none of us speak of. The patchwork of scars goes all the way up her arm into her armpit. They vary in size and shape, but they're threaded together, a full scene.

"Nine months of trying to find a needle in a haystack, except it's cleaning up garbage in a field of endlessly thorny bushes off the interstate. I swear they have the biggest spines you've ever seen." She presses her fingers to the marks, pink or red and angry, along her forearm. "It's not just my arms. Face shields cover our faces at least. In the colder months I can wear a coat to cover most of my body or swamp boots. Nine months of balm, lots of pain, just . . . all over. I thought I was done. I really thought . . ." She pushes her tray away, slumps onto the table.

Serena waits a bit before taking claim. When Petra nudges her tray over, Serena enjoys the spoils.

"Who picks a Trial like that as Endurance? It's so vindictive," Petra cries.

"Can't your family help talk to them?"

"My parents tried. Just so happens, I got assaulted by the son of a rising council member running for borough president. They said I cut so close to the spine that the damage is permanent. But *I'm* a threat when guys like him—"

"Is there a problem?" Petra's voice has risen so much a guard stationed at the wall comes by.

"No," she tells the guard. Petra ruffles her mass of hair out of her ponytail as if shaking out her thoughts. She rolls down her sleeves, an end to her story.

"It is what it is," she says. "I told the investigators, the guy's parents, Counselor Susan, *everyone*, that I was protecting myself. If anything, *I* wanted to charge *him*. They don't see it that way because he landed in the ICU that night and, in the guy's parents' words, I got away 'unharmed.'" Quieter but still with force, Petra adds, "Whatever. I only wish—" Her voice breaks.

I ease over to put a hand on her lower back. She smells like I do: soap and paper towels.

"I love my family," she says. "My mom, my sisters, my aunts. They all tried so hard to help. And the guy—that jerk . . . He gets to call himself a victim, but not me. I had to prove I was hurt."

When her tears come, I hug her. It's the only thing I can offer. My stomach growls, not from hunger, but unease.

Petra wipes her face with the back of her hands, making her cheeks redder and wetter. She gives a broken laugh. "I'll be fine. I'll figure it out." She pats the side of my face. "And you, Pretty Little Violet, will get through your Trials, because you also deserve to be forgiven." Acknowledging Serena feasting on her oatmeal, she adds, "You too." Serena smiles, and chews, in appreciation.

"Chen-Samuels!" is shouted, drawing the attention of half the cafeteria. The guard who escorted me here makes his way through the rows of girls. "Up. Now." I rise, stumbling between the table and the bench.

"Meeting with your counselor. ASAP." The guard motions for me to start walking.

It's like all the color in the world has seeped away and pooled onto the floor. My arms go slack. I look back at Eve, Serena, and Petra. Their faces shaped by one thing: deep concern.

CHAPTER 12
VINCE

Days since the decision: 25

Because April couldn't start without getting its kicks in, the ground is covered by a thin layer of frost, so every step is wet and hard. This is the second time we've been to the cemetery since Viv's burial. Mom leads the way on the hilly path while Dad hangs back with Aunt Mae, who drove us here. I hang even farther back.

Queens has a dozen cemeteries, and this one is a short drive south for us through Flushing. It sits right across from a couple high schools. (That's gotta be a pretty sight while waiting for the bus.)

Viv's headstone is new, so it hasn't sunken into the dirt yet. Took a couple weeks to make. Viv was buried a week after the accident, and the mound from the funeral has mostly flattened into a five-foot patch of dirt. She's right beside my grandparents, Pa and Ma Chen. And by the look of the potted flowers lined up, Aunt Mae and Sonali were here before today's visit. Even though the ivory lilies and butter-yellow chrysanthemums are wilting, the petals are littered around my baby sister's plot like confetti, bringing some beauty to a spare spot. Aunt Mae is armed with new life this time too. Mom asked her to bring a few white flowers from her shop for today. The Qingming festival is in a few days, but we decided to come today so it'd be just us. Mom's carrying individually wrapped sesame cookies, Viv's favorite treat.

Viv's stone is as small as she looked the day of the burial. Swear to God, it must've been the coldest day on record. At the funeral, Viv was made up to look like she was sleeping, but all I could see was the face we had to identify at the hospital. When her maple-brown skin was washed-out, almost unrecognizable, and a sheet covered her from neck to toes. At the funeral it didn't matter that my baby sister was in her pink lace dress. Didn't matter that her eyes were shut, half her face patched up from the accident. Didn't matter that her wavy hair was pulled back in barrettes and her cheeks were way rosy, like she was a doll made up for show. All I could see was broken Viv, and I hated having that visual stuck in my head.

My suit was too tight. I'd had issues tying my tie, and Dad wasn't much help because he was too busy being a rock for Mom, who couldn't decide what to wear. She changed into a navy dress, then an olive-green one, then a black one, and repeated the cycle until Dad said we needed to go because the limo was here. Our three-person procession met our family in the living room. Scanning my family's faces, I could tell everyone was trying to hold in their grief. Sonali clutched Aunt Mae, who held on to Gram, who wouldn't let go of Gramps, who was leaning on his cane. Our great-uncle Rog offered my mom her coat, one arm at a time, while Dad kept wiping away tears and maybe the whole nightmare of the day.

My friends and teammates, even Coach and Mr. Nelson, were all at the service. The worst thing was standing in the receiving line taking on everyone's tears, condolences, prayers. There were so many hugs, lots of people patting my cheeks, a ridiculous amount of people I didn't know squeezing my left shoulder to the point it was sore by the end of the day. Throughout the services I was pretty much empty. I couldn't tell how I looked or what people saw. Was I also a rock or a reflection of everyone else's grief?

By the time Levi approached me in the receiving line, he hugged me for so long the hurt of his breakup almost melted away. I got to bury my face in his chest and just be held. As quiet as I'd been with everyone after the accident, I was so thankful to have my friends there. Jorge managed to make me laugh after they kissed me on the cheek and said, "Only for Vivian would I wear all black. You know it does nothing for me." I told them they rocked the fitted suit and sparkly black boots, and that Viv would've appreciated it.

After that, a string of black cars took us to the repast at Grams and Gramps's house in St. Albans. There, we entered a sea of dark outfits and awkwardness since no one knew what to say to any of us beyond the stock "So sorry for your loss" and "Please let us know if you need anything." Even if they didn't know what to say to us, people did talk. Like our neighbor Mrs.

Bennett and great-uncle Rog. I could turn a corner and talk suddenly stopped around the cold cuts platter. Mom retreated to Grams and Gramps's bedroom after overhearing a sympathizer say, "Could you imagine being a parent to that kind of child? I'd be devastated." Who knows what was said when we weren't around.

Mom, Dad, and I rode home in a rental limo that was with us all day since their van was totaled and part of a crime scene. The seats beside and between us were packed with Tupperware leftovers. Some of them still warm. I'm pretty sure we were all in a daze as we unpacked the funeral limo, took everything inside, squeezed what we could in the fridge and whatever else in the freezer. Then lights out. The next day was a rude awakening. Funeral flyers with Viv's face on the coffee table in the living room. The bounty of sympathy cards and eats. On top of that was a seriously hollow feeling without both my sisters.

Every Qingming, Mom touches her fingers to her lips before pressing them against the names on each gravestone. It's like her own special greeting. That's what she does as she crouches down to Viv's stone now. As low as she speaks, we all hear her: "My baby."

My cheeks, nose, and fingers are the first to feel the chill. My fingernails go purple. There's no time limit to how long we stay here. It's eerie to stare at endless rows of rocks marked with spare details and spiritual quotes of who the dead were.

Aunt Mae cleans up the dying plants, then sets down a pot of white petunias. The first in front of Viv's headstone, which is half the size of Pa and Ma Chen's. My grandparents share a pretty large tombstone, with their names on either side and cemetery pictures adhered to the granite.

Pa Chen died when I was a toddler, Ma Chen several years after Letta was born. I know Mom's parents from stories, not as many concrete memories. Sometimes I imagine them holding hands underground, like they're united forever in the afterlife. It's a nicer way to think about it. Wish I could think the same for Viv.

We're usually surrounded by other families burning incense and other offerings for the annual Qingming festival in spring. On those days, Viv would read one of her favorite stories to Pa and Ma Chen while the rest of us cleaned any debris around the tombstones in silence. We'd make our paper offerings to the deceased, have some conversations with other families, and sometimes, on our way to our cars, exchange leftovers. If someone had matcha cake, Letta and I were all over it.

Mom's palm lands on the granite. A squeak comes out before sobs rack her body like she's having an attack while crying "My baby" over and over. Dad's tears fall after, and my own after that. Tightening the belt on her wool coat, Aunt Mae stands beside me letting us feel all the feelings. Her afro is tucked into a fluffy green hat that matches her coat. The way she stands is so much like Dad: chest out, hands in front of her, like a soldier. I'm sitting on the nearest tombstone.

It's not right. Viv should not be here.

Each time we visit her gravesite, my thoughts become a mental movie reel of me and Viv, us and Viv.

One night Viv asked me, "Would you protect me from dinosaurs?"

"*What?*"

I was on the edge of her bed, reading from my tablet. The glow of the screen made us look like we had ghost heads, shiny and shadowed. She preferred the dark, was never afraid of it.

From the glare of the tablet, I could see her eyes roll. "*Dinosaurs*, Vin. Like in this book." She tapped the screen. "The big sister protects her little brother from dinos. Soooo . . ."

"Of course I'd protect you. A T. rex may be a deal breaker."

She laid her head on my arm, which was already falling asleep. "They're scary. But you're *supposed* to say, 'Yes, Vivian, I will protect you. No. Matter. What.'"

"It's obvious I would, though." I tapped the side of the screen to flip to the next page.

Viv touched the other side to go back to the previous one. "Not finished."

"Sorry."

"You're forgiven," she said.

I can't place when this was. How far or near in time. It's one of those memories you don't think of until it's all you can think of. One of those moments that was not a big deal until it is a big deal, since it can't ever happen again. Me scratching at my wrist and elbow when her hair brushed against my skin, in fear something was crawling on me. The smell of flaming nachos whenever she spoke, which meant Viv hadn't brushed her teeth like she'd said she did.

Before saying good night, Viv would pull us into some kind

of conversation or activity. We'd read together or talk or play cards until she fell asleep. It was peaceful and easy, and I don't know why I didn't do it more than once in a blue moon. Why my seven-year-old sister had to beg me to spend time with her when it wasn't that hard.

At this memory, a cramp hits my thigh and calf at the same freaking time. Neither of my parents notice me slap the pain out of my legs as I slide off the stone I was on to the cold, damp ground. Every so often, these cramps would creep up and Ross would give me something to numb the pain.

The days go by in a haze until something comes in full and focused, like that memory with Viv. Me promising to protect her and me breaking that promise because—

Damn it! I clutch my right calf, trying to contain another spasm. Why wasn't I home with Viv or helping to kick Letta's butt into gear? Those questions make my tears return. Not just because of the lightning bolts shooting up my leg.

"Damn it," I say under my breath. Dad's head tilts my way, and I mouth, *Nothing*. He focuses back on Mom.

"I just want you to know, baby," Mom says, "your sister will get the help she needs soon. I promise."

"Letta doesn't need help," Aunt Mae begins, but Dad raises a hand that magically cuts her off. Clearly, that means now isn't the time or the place. Considering Randall was at our home just yesterday, what comes next may help Letta or—I'm scared to think—be a heck of a rude awakening.

Maybe my sister doesn't need help, but looking down at this gravesite and the mound where Viv lives now doesn't make me think she doesn't need *something*. We all do. Aunt Mae has been more a counsel than a judge or jury about all this, insisting Letta messed up but not that she deserved to be locked up. Though the times she's brought that up haven't been pretty, and usually end in a brother-sister sparring match between her and Dad. Aunt Mae exuding older sister vibes when she cuts him off and Dad insisting that she couldn't understand. In the end Grams made them make amends by respecting my parents' wishes first and remembering family supports family, no matter the hardship.

After I'm certain the spasms are done and my legs won't give way, I'm up. The knees of my jeans are wet from tears and the mud. Mom's face is streaked. She's stopped wearing makeup for this reason. The first time we came here, she had raccoon eyes from the eyeliner and mascara. She'd mustered a laugh when she'd wiped her cheeks and, examining the evidence, said, "I should email the company and let them know it's not waterproof."

Grunting as he bends, Dad offers a hand to help Mom to her feet.

"We'll be back again soon, sweetheart," Mom promises.

"With your favorite roses," Aunt Mae says.

"See you later, baby girl," Dad adds, taking a big sniff of air. They're already headed back the way we came.

"Mom, Dad, give us a minute," I say. *Us.* As if Viv and I are going to have a chat.

Dad glances at the burial plot, then me. "Take all the time you need, Vince."

"Vince," Aunt Mae asks, "you want me to stay behind too?"

I dunno if what I offer my aunt is a smile, exactly, but she takes the hint. She tucks one of the lilies she collected into the pocket of my coat before following my parents.

Even though the grave photo is absolutely Viv—her smile with the missing front tooth, a braid bun on either side of her head, Mom's eyes—it isn't *my* Viv. This isn't the girl who fought for attention or helped make dinner while proclaiming she did most of the work. My tears aren't silent anymore. My moan rings through the cemetery.

"I'm sorry, Viv. I'm so sorry."

"You're supposed to say 'Yes, Vivian, I will protect you. No. Matter. What.'"

I didn't protect Vivian. I wasn't there.

Letta will go through door number one soon. I wonder what her Trial is and if it will make any of us feel better.

"It's obvious I would, though."

I can't see or find Letta in that memory. Is that because she doesn't exist anymore for our family or for me?

Of course I'd protect you, I'd told Viv. The more I think on it, the more I wonder if Letta's the one who needs protecting.

CHAPTER 13

VIOLETTA

Days in detention: 25

𝕀𝕀𝕀 𝕀𝕀𝕀 𝕀𝕀𝕀 𝕀𝕀𝕀 𝕀𝕀𝕀

My counselor's framed diplomas are the only thing on her walls. One's lopsided, but the rest are perfectly straight. One university is in Iowa, where she studied psychology; the other, Michigan for social work. Her office is as pristine as she is every day. Her black hair is gelled to sleek perfection. There's not a wrinkle in her starched pantsuit or her face, thanks to her blank stares. And no makeup today to alter her creamy skin. Without makeup I can see the one thing that stands out about her: a mole on her upper lip.

Even her desk is clean of everything but her computer, keyboard, and mouse; a cup of pens that *click, click, click*; and a bunch of folders neatly stacked under her hands. Mine isn't very thick. It has multicolored stickies peeking out the edges. There are no pictures of her or anyone else. No insight into the type of life she has or who she is beyond what's in front of me. It's unfair when she has a file of my mistakes, the worst parts of me.

I watch my counselor closely as she reads. "Violetta, your first Trial takes place tomorrow morning. It's a Comprehension Trial."

She closes the folder. I wait for more, but we end up in a standoff of sorts. For a minute or so, no words are spoken between us.

I finally break. "Anything else?"

"I'm afraid that's all I can tell you at this moment. You'll be told the details of your Trial once it begins. Then you'll meet with me afterward and we can talk about it. As much or as little as you like. You've been assigned two Trials, with an option for a third Trial."

I pick at a hole in the arm of my chair, widening it more as every minute passes.

"I'm scared." I didn't mean to actually say this, but I can't take it back.

"That makes sense. This is all so scary," my counselor says. "We're all on your side here. And I am absolutely rooting for you. We want to see you move forward, not back."

I nod, choking on the tears pushing through and the mucus rushing down my throat.

"Hey, hey." Counselor Susan urges me to meet her eyes. "You still have the notebook I gave you?"

I garble out a "Yeah."

My counselor can make her voice as soft as cotton. It's what I imagined fairy princesses sound like, light and airy, to put you at ease. "Make sure to write in that. What's going on. Then we can talk about how you're feeling. It doesn't have to be about the Trials or what happened. It can be about what you wish for."

"Okay," is all I can manage.

"You're not your worst mistake, Violetta. Please remember that. The last time I read your notebook I saw you mentioned a boy, Pascal. Was he your boyfriend?"

"Yes." *Yes he* was.

Click of the pen. "And what happened there?" Her hand is ready to write something down. It makes me clam up for a minute. Should I tell her? She's already read about him. My finger digs deeper into the arm of my chair, and all I feel is a scratchy film around my fingertip.

"He . . . he was a guy I tried to impress." I try to put Pascal and me into words as she scribbles my stammering. "I don't know what I thought anymore. But he was a guy and I got to be kind of free with him. Or I thought . . ." I thought *so many* things that don't feel real anymore. Almost like a dream, no, a nightmare.

When I first arrived and spoke to Counselor Susan, she asked me to explain what happened. The most I could say was the actual things like the accident and the drinking and the pain I walked around with every day because of it. But I couldn't totally explain *how* I got there outside of a series of bad decisions that seem so obvious now. The day I invited Pascal over, even though I was grounded, I was angry. *So angry* that my parents took away something I thought I wanted. Sure, I came home late, but they weren't scared something happened to me.

The night I got grounded, before I could close the door, a

gust of freezing air blew in with me. Immediately, the hallway lights came on and my mom appeared. She didn't ask if I was okay or what was wrong when I stumbled in still reeling a little from the beers Pascal's older brother got for me and his friends. Mom clutched her silk robe and eyed me like I was a stranger, or worse, a disappointment.

"Letta, I really wish you were a different person. I do not know the girl standing in front of me."

"You never knew me!" I shouted, pushing her.

I didn't mean to do it hard, but I did, and Dad came bounding down the stairs. "What is all the noise about?"

I tried to get by him, but there's no getting by Dad. He's tall and round and most of the time cuddly. But neither of my parents were cuddly that night I came home late. They joined forces in how upset they were at me.

"You're grounded for at least two weeks. Now go upstairs and get yourself together, young lady!" my mother shouted, while my dad settled in by her side.

It was so hot in the hallway. I had to rip my scarf and jacket off because it felt like a sauna. I didn't look back at my parents. By the time I got upstairs, Vin was rubbing crust out of his eyes asking what was going on. I didn't answer. I slammed the door closed wanting to shut everyone out. I didn't want to be around any of them.

Whenever I think of the day that led to the accident, I know what happened in the moment, but all twenty-five days in detention have been me trying to understand *how* I got here. Could that be part of tomorrow's Trial?

In desperation to change the subject, I ask if Counselor Susan has a partner, or someone she tried to impress. Maybe that would help her understand.

"I don't. But let's not dig too deeply into my personal life. I'm here for you and every kid in here like you. That's why I do this job. To help."

Glancing at the frames behind her, I say, "Is that what you learned in school?"

"Yes and no. Some of it is on-the-job training," she admits, putting her pen down and resting her hands on top of my folder. She looks unbreakable and, if my brother were here, he'd probably say bland. "Not everything is in a textbook. I know you were a good student. You still are, Violetta. You have a life to figure out. It just turned out, shall we say, not great."

I sputter a laugh. "Not great sounds like an understatement."

I focus on the one new detail I see on my counselor as she offers me not just a smile, but words to hold on to in here. "Remember what I said, you're not your worst mistake, Violetta."

I don't get to respond any further. Not that I could. My counselor buzzes for the guard to escort me back to my cell. Just like that, she tucks my folder back in a pile, as if it's that easy to move on to the next girl. "My door is always open," she says before shutting it closed behind me.

By 9 p.m., we're all locked in our cells. Soon after lockdown comes Petra's snores. Her snoring has a sawing rhythm, rough and constant. It helps me get to sleep. My sister used to snore, but not as loud and not as ragged.

I drift off to a dripping faucet, the footsteps of guards, and Petra. I dream about my little sister. The night of. The worst parts. The loud crunch and the shatter. The blood pooled like strawberry syrup. The dream is black-and-white, but the blood is always red.

It starts with Pascal. He's heavy. That's the first thing. That, and me in a bra-and-undie set I bought with Callie at one of those clothing stores that smells like perfume.

Technically, I was grounded. It was supposed to be just me and my sister. Everyone else was out and I was stuck babysitting. So, Pascal and I weren't alone. He wasn't supposed to be there. It'd been a week since I'd seen him and I needed the reminder someone liked the person I was right then.

I bribe my sister with a weekend trip to her favorite arcade if she doesn't say anything.

"As soon as my punishment is over, we'll go and play for hours. My treat," I promise her. She sinks into our sectional and kicks her stockinged feet in excitement as though she is in control.

"Anything I want?" she says.

"Anything. As long as you don't say a word." I stick my pinky out for her to do the same. The pinky promise is like a sibling contract. Even at seven she knows how important trust is between us. Her pinky gripping mine seals the deal.

I don't wonder if I am corrupting her with my lie. I don't think I'll get caught. And even if my parents find out, all they can do is extend how long I have to stay home. (I wasn't thinking too much in those days.) In the dream my grounding isn't fair. I keep my grades and appearances up. Just because I came home past curfew a couple of times doesn't mean I shouldn't be allowed to see my boyfriend, especially if I want him to stay my boyfriend.

As soon as Pascal arrives, I tell my little sister we're going to my room. "Don't bother us unless the house is on fire."

"Only a fire?" she says, jumping up and down on the couch.

"Yes."

She calls out other disasters as we rush upstairs. "An explosion? A flood? Zombies?"

Whenever Pascal is amused, a corner of his lip ticks up and he sticks the end of his tongue out. "Where does your sister get this stuff?"

I can't answer. If I open my mouth, I'll call off the whole thing. I thread my fingers through his hair, give him a quick kiss instead.

Our fingers are knotted together. Every step makes me jittery. Earlier, I set up a picnic in my room, with crackers and the cheese that comes in small plastic rounds you have to rip off. Alcohol always appears at the parties Pascal takes me to, like magic. That night was no different since I found a bottle of red wine a co-worker gave to my mother over Christmas.

A flannel sheet is on the floor, the candle app on my phone flickers, and the light in my room is dimmed like we're outside at sundown.

Is this what sexy is? I wonder, looking at my picnic display. Pascal barely notices, though. He tosses his jacket off and lifts me up, trampling the crackers under his feet before plopping me on my bed.

It isn't romantic; it's rushed. Pascal does the work, because my fingers tremble on his shirt. His skin is soft. He has thin patches of hair on his chest.

It's been six months since I met him that first week, when he told me, "You are so hot." It's been two weeks since I thought I could handle taking things further after winter break. I bite my lip to keep from making a sound as he kisses my neck, then the space in the middle of my bra with the gold heart. He says, "You like this?"

I moan, or whimper, "Yes."

That's when he suggests a drink, a big one, to ease my nerves. Whenever he thinks I'm being too quiet, he suggests a drink, to "bring out the real Letta." I don't know if the real me comes with the alcohol, but it definitely isn't the same me. The bottle opener sits beside the wine and Pascal immediately opens it to loosen things up. He fills a glass near the top, then tilts it to my lips. The fruity, woody taste goes down like a river. The bottle goes from full to almost empty. My lips and teeth, stained maroon, are gray in the dream.

Pascal is heavy. I can't move.

My arms around him are tingly and warm. His thighs press mine open. Air comes in gulps. I keep my eyes closed.

"You really like me, right?" he says.

"Uh-huh."

"And you want me, right?"

My lips are numb, but "Mm-hmm" seeps through. I open my eyes. His raised eyebrow lets me know I'm not convincing him, or myself. "You're lying."

"N-no, I'm not," I say.

I feel stupid, dizzy. I'm losing focus. Usually, what I drink is sweet, like lemonade, and fizzy going down. It makes me giggle, and the world seems not as hard, not as big. But the wine isn't sweet like Pascal promised. This night, Pascal, all of it is heavy.

"Let-ta!" comes from the stairs, but it's as loud as if Viv is standing outside my door. "It's not a fire, but where's the microwave popcorn?"

I turn my face from Pascal, toward the door, and yell, "Above the fridge!"

One corner of Pascal's mouth lifts, revealing his dimples, as he places my hand on his belt loop. "Letta, you want to do this?"

The wooziness begins to fade, but my tongue is fuzzy, as if mold has grown on it. His other hand lifts my thighs.

I gasp. My sister is staring at us in the doorway. I cover myself with the sheet and scream at the door, scream at her, embarrassed but also thankful for the interruption.

Pascal is on his feet; he won't even look at me. "I should've never messed with a freshman," he says, adjusting his shirt. "You're too young."

"What?"

"You can't do this. You can't do that," he says. He shakes his head. "It's been months, Letta. I've been patient."

"I'm trying. Can't you see I'm trying?" I point to the spread and the crushed crackers. The itchy lace underwear I have on.

I think he's listening, but he only shakes his head and takes off. I rush after him, clutching his arm. None of it slows him down. Then he's gone.

My little sister is at the top of the stairs, her mouth a small O, her hair all over the place. She made me look immature. I could've settled myself if she hadn't interrupted. I stare at my clothes: The crop top and lacy bra, with the stupid gold heart hanging between the cups that I paid for with New Year money.

Pascal was supposed to feed me cheese and crackers. Tonight was supposed to be classy, because we were mature.

I return to my room to drink the rest of the wine, let it burn, and wait, hoping I'll feel lighter. That's when the idea hits me. I grab my coat from the hook, slip on my sneakers by the door, and take Dad's minivan keys from the bowl on the table. I only have my permit, but I need to find Pascal and settle this. Viv follows me all the way to the parking lot. My seven-year-old sister jumps into the passenger side, asking me to take her along because she doesn't want to be alone.

"Can we get popcorn?" she says. "We're out."

I start the engine, and all the locks click shut around us. "You wanna ride?" I burp. "We'll ride."

We veer forward when I mean to go backward. Hitting the curb, we bounce. Viv's head slams against her seat. I think I tell her to put on her seat belt, but that gets lost in the dreamscape. The outer rim of my vision is blurry, but I can see the center. It feels like I have a hold on the car, even though the traffic lines disappear and reappear. I could have sworn the roads weren't still patchy with ice and snow from last week's storm.

My sister is so quiet in the front seat. Quiet as I swerve, realizing too late I missed the turn for Pascal's house.

At this point, my head is not woozy. My mouth isn't dry. It's clear this was a bad idea. But knowing doesn't keep me from jerking the wheel toward blocks set up for construction. It doesn't keep me from panicking and hitting the gas instead of the brake as the barrier comes closer. It doesn't stop me from slamming into it. It doesn't put a seat belt on Viv. And it doesn't alert the passenger airbag to go off until seconds after impact.

When I wake up, I still see my sister's face, but I don't cry. Instead, I reach under my mattress for the only letter I've managed to write so far. It begins: *Hey Viv.* I can barely read my words with the room cloaked in darkness. Holding the letter in my hands, I sit up on my bed in my drafty cell and brace myself for what I deserve.

PART II

The Trials

CHAPTER 14
VIOLETTA

Days in detention: 26

卌 卌 卌 卌 卌 /

This route isn't familiar. The signs say we're headed west. At first, trees line my vision, then it's low-level buildings clustered together: donut shops, delis, and discount shops where you can get anything from laundry detergent to light bulbs. After that come department stores and restaurants for tacos or Italian food and a bakery with three-layer cakes decorating the windows. All this is followed by a space full of private houses and abandoned storefronts. The guards are up front with a grate blocking them from us inmates, or as they like to say, "protecting" them. Seated in the van are me, Petra, and two other girls. Petra is directly behind me, slumped and quiet, her hands zip-tied together in her lap. She hasn't moved or spoken since we left the compound. When we started out, there were eight girls. Of those eight, I didn't see either Serena or the nail biter from Sunday's presentation. Half of the inmates were dropped off first for their Trials. Each one left without a word. Just held out their arms for the zip ties to be cut, then slid out of the van into a building, a field, or, in one case, someplace that looked like a big parking lot with a dozen car skeletons scattered all around. When the girls' backs disappeared from view, the van drove off.

I'm having a hard time staying awake. I want to see the outside for the first time in weeks, but I was so anxious about my Trial I didn't sleep well last night. I dozed in and out, the whole time holding my letter to my sister.

I've tried not to imagine the grimmest scenario. But then I wondered if what I was imagining wasn't bad enough. Petra with her thornbushes. The two girls Callie told me about. It's never a good thing when people get hurt, but thankfully in their cases, no one died. And then there's LeVaughn; his mistake changed so much.

Despite the discomfort of the ties around my wrists, I fade in and out of sleep. The other two girls manage to nap through most of the ride. But Petra's eyes are open, staring ahead.

"You okay?" I ask her. She doesn't respond, just keeps gazing out the windshield.

Now we're passing through the quieter part of northern Queens; it reminds me more of home, with the 99-cent stores, the coffee shops, and a rotisserie chicken spot. The farther we go, the more buildings spread out, land separating them like we're headed upstate. I can almost see the orchard where my family picked apples and pumpkins. At the start of my high school year, we all piled into the minivan: my parents up front, my little sister, Vin, and his best friend, Levi, in the middle, and me in back. When we got there, my sister practically jumped out of the van.

"It's lovely here," Dad had said. "Smells good too."

"That's the apples!" my sister said, darting straight for the open field of trees. If she ever did stay still, I can't remember. Every time she comes to mind, she's excited. Smiling. Ready to conquer the world. Vin looked like he was bored already, which was why he brought Levi with him. But Levi's enthusiasm kind of spread to Vin. God, was this all in October, less than six months ago? Everyone got their sacks, and we were directed to the picking area.

"Meet in thirty minutes for cider doughnuts," Mom said, already out of breath from my sister tugging her to the trees labeled MCINTOSH. Vin and Levi went their own way toward a row of baby apples.

That left me and Dad. "Let's make sure we get a perfect carving pumpkin. Sound good, Letta?"

I shrugged. "I guess."

He put an arm around me. His aftershave smelled perfect for the occasion, a mix of cinnamon and allspice, just like apple pie. "Still mad Pascal couldn't come?"

"Yes," he said at the same time I said, "No." It wasn't that Pascal *couldn't* come. He didn't want to. He thought apple and pumpkin picking sounded kind of kiddie.

Pascal had suggested I spend the day with him while my family was out. Or, "better yet," that he come to my place while everyone was gone. *Alone?* I'd thought, pushing my panic down. He'd been pressing more alone time after we made things official. By Indigenous Peoples' Day, everyone knew I was Pascal's girl. Not everyone liked it—Vin first and foremost.

Mom and Dad balked at the idea of me ditching a family outing to spend the day with Pascal. I let it go, but that didn't mean I wasn't irritated.

"I don't see why he couldn't join us," Dad said to me. "At some point, we need to meet this boy, Letta."

"You will," I swore.

Dad and I stopped in the pumpkin patch. Searched around for pumpkins big enough for the two of us to carve for Halloween.

"You like him. And we love you. That means we want to get to know him. If you're a 'thing.' Is that what you all say now, 'a thing'?"

"Something like that, Dad."

Dad groaned as he bent down to examine one of the slimmer pumpkins. "Well, if you two are together, then we need to meet the guy. Same for Vince. Any boy he likes, he knows we get to inspect him first. Make sure they're good enough." My dad was joking and not. I'd seen how Dad talked to the guys Vin said he liked. Our dad is the tallest in our family, with a bit of a belly and hands that swallow you when you put yours into them. Most people are intimidated by him before he opens his mouth. Mom says he's a teddy bear, and he is.

"See! I knew you'd interrogate him." The last thing I needed was Pascal to think my parents' approval was out of reach.

"You're my little girl . . ."

"God, Dad, who wants to be a little girl forever? I'm in high school now."

Dad grunted as he stood. "High school doesn't mean grown-up. So don't think because you have a boyfriend you're grown, okay?" He lifted my chin. "You most certainly are not."

"Yes, sir," was all I said.

Dad exhaled like someone releasing the air out of a balloon a bit at a time.

"Is something wrong, Letta? Something about Pascal?"

"It's not him, Dad. Not really."

"Then what is it?"

Pascal was nice but, at the same time, older, and didn't older boys expect certain things? School was . . . okay. Classes were hard, especially AP English and World History—the surprise quizzes were never-ending and I wasn't confident passing them. Vin's lacrosse games meant more wins and maybe more trophies and definitely college scholarships. My sister had advanced beyond a white belt in karate. And me? I was hanging on for an honor roll certificate that might sit beside my brother's and sister's achievements. That piece of paper would be a reminder that I existed alongside them.

In the pumpkin patch, I saw my teddy bear dad, not the guy who asked how much things cost or backed Mom up whenever she nitpicked me for not doing something my brother or sister did. Teddy Bear Dad complained about his body aches more than bills and gave me his full attention, because no one else was around.

What I wanted to say was a jumbled mess in my mind. Nothing made sense, and it made me question myself. Instead of talking to the teddy bear who stood in front of me, ready to listen, I clammed up. I picked up a cute pumpkin, not too heavy, and said, "This one is good."

When we all met up, Levi and Vin carried a huge pumpkin between them. Mom and my sister came back with their own pumpkin, something skinny and yellow. My sister said it looked "so cool." I held my pumpkin, nothing like my sister's or my brother's, small and unnoticeable, just like me.

"Chen-Samuels, we're here!" The driver wakes me from my daydream. "What's wrong?" she asks. "You hurt?"

"Huh?" My fingertips come away from my cheek wet.

"Letta?" Petra says, coming out of her trance. "I'll see you after." She winks. A Petra gesture. I force a smile. We're both pretending in a way. She wants the best for me, and I really hope she gets through the day.

"See you," I say as the van door closes, separating us.

My ties are cut before a woman escorts me inside a place that makes me think of a hospital. But it's so . . . ordinary. Nothing on the walls. Unlike the juvenile facility, it's bright. There's so much white. My shoes squeak against the floor it's so clean.

A woman, also in white—skin, scrubs, thick-soled sneakers—leads me to a room with the words PREPARATION etched on a textured glass window.

"You'll be working in here for three hours every morning during the week until we receive word you've passed. I'll take you to meet Miles. He knows what he's doing and will guide you day to day."

"O-o-okay."

The woman tilts her head. "Do you have any questions? It looks like you have a question."

"Well, what am I doing? What's the Comprehension part of all this?"

"Oh, that'll all come to light once you're inside. Violetta, is it? Miles is helpful. Been doing this Trial a few weeks now. Any questions he can't answer, feel free to ring me. I'm Tess. There's a phone inside that buzzes straight to the main station on this floor. I'll be here the remainder of the day."

She makes an about-face and leaves without another word.

Clasping the door handle, I whisper, "One. Two. Go."

Antiseptic and scrub cleanser hit me so hard I cover my nose and mouth. Someone is already inside, wearing a smock and thick plastic apron. When he lowers the mask covering half his face, I see he's about my age, maybe, and darker than me, with a head the shape of a peanut and a barely-there mustache.

My thumb and index finger pinch my nose; the rest of my hand covers my mouth. I sound like a squeaky toy when I ask, "Are you Miles?"

His face is blank. "Yes."

"I'm Violetta."

"Okay."

Before I take my hand away, I prep myself for the fumes. The shine of the fluorescents makes everything crystal clear. Two wheeled beds are in the middle of the room. On one I see feet the color of dust poking out from under a sheet.

I take several steps back until I crash into the door. The fumes seem to get worse now that I realize what's going on. "I'm in a—"

"Yup," he says. "Let's get to work."

"Wait. Huh?" We're islands away. Miles's wide eyes bore into mine.

This can't be right. This can't be what's in store for me.

"We dress and prepare. They've been washed." He removes the sheet as if he's about to do a magic trick.

The person revealed is, *was*, a woman. She looks like a toy waiting to be dressed. *Oh: dress and prepare.*

"How many do we have to . . ." I can't stop staring at this woman, no longer here but right in front of me. She's as still as Petra was in the van.

Head lowered, Miles makes a quick sign of a cross before replying, "About four a day? This is a service spot before the bodies head to funerals. Some don't even get that, when they're unnamed or cash-strapped." He shrugs. "You'll follow my lead today, and maybe tomorrow, depending."

"What's her name?"

"Name?" The way Miles speaks, acts, looks at me is annoying, and it hasn't been five minutes.

"Yes." She's young and pretty, with full lips. All I can think of is what her end was like. I'm feeling so much tightness in my chest my heart has to have stopped.

With a curl of his finger, Miles urges me to come closer to see the tag on her toe. His finger points but never touches her. "Her name is Luisa."

"Thank you."

He gives another shrug and positions himself to one side, gets in close, focusing on her cheeks. A tray with makeup is within his reach: brushes, swabs, a whole color palette.

"There's a manual on that desk by the door. It's not long. When you're done reading, you'll watch me apply her makeup"—he motions at Luisa—"then help me work on someone else, then take one for yourself. Get it?"

I nod, unable to form words, worried nothing will come out but my breakfast.

He looks at me for a minute. "Are you gonna puke, like the last one?"

"I'm o-okay." My fingers are barely able to grip the manual, *Preparing the Dead for Viewing*. It's thin, only a few dozen pages, like something made on a copier. The edges are folded and frayed.

"Take a seat. First day doesn't have to be about touching them. If you need water, the fountain is down the hall. Gotta stay hydrated or you'll get woozy."

"Okay. Thanks."

"You can take a ten-minute break every hour before you leave. Time flies here, so it won't be too bad."

The document is list upon list of what should happen, and in what order, from when I first step through the doors. Lists of how to help prep a body for viewing after it's been embalmed. Bullet points telling me that the bodies—they're always referred to as *bodies* or *the deceased*—should be respected. Instructions on how to clean and dress the bodies, how to apply cosmetics to bring back their natural tone, how to add wigs. You can also spray—yes, spray—makeup on, in case it's hard to spread liquid with cotton. Sometimes you can use spray paint to fill in bald spots. We're to cover up as much skin as possible, because no one wants to see any marks from how the deceased died or where the blood was removed and the embalming needle went in.

The words blur the more I read.

This is the result of my actions—all of it, but *especially* this. I crumple the manual in my hands. My heart pounds so fast I can hear it in my ears. My dreams are about to get worse.

CHAPTER 15

VINCE

Days since the decision: 26

"Vinny!" The breeze carries Jorge's scream all the way from where they sit down to the track. Jorge and Jan prove once again they're the best cheerleaders, plus they often match. Between Jan's multicolored braids and the colors Jorge wears—today Jorge's decked out in their trademark fuchsia boots, aqua flare pants, and a loose yellow top with matching scarf—you couldn't miss them if you tried.

These past few days it's been nice being outside instead of indoors for track. Ribbons and banners of black and gold border the stands. The banners proclaim our record in New York, two back-to-back state championships in track. One for every year I've been on the team. It's been a minute since the lacrosse or football teams landed a trophy, but those folks are also gunning for championships. Everyone is hungry for glory. Most of the team hasn't shut up about it since September.

"Y'all screaming for Vince. What about me?" Byron shouts to our friends. He's spread-eagle on the ground, midstretch. He's got a headband on to keep the bangs out of his eyes. Today, the two of us are pretending like going to Ross's didn't happen. It's been easier that way. When we saw each other on the track, Byron looked at me expectantly. Like maybe I might scold him on the spot. I held out a fist; he bumped it. All good.

Jorge cups their hands around their mouth. "Yeah, I guess you too!"

Byron mutters, "Everyone loves Golden Boy Vince."

Not everyone. I cut my eyes at Levi, stationed in his usual spot right by the track team's benches. A camera with an attachable lens hangs around his neck, so I know he's ready to catch shots of us at the starting line.

Today is practice, not a formal meet. That doesn't stop a couple college scouts from showing up. Scouts are easy to spot. It's like they have a designated uniform. For one, they're prepared for the weather. Maybe in a windbreaker or sweatshirt or coat with a college insignia on a breast pocket, a baseball cap, holding up their phone. They never take their eyes off what's happening, and their eyes are everywhere. We're supposed to act like this is run-of-the-mill stuff. Like we're not being inspected and judged.

The two scouts present sit one below the other in the stands. The guy on the lower row of the bleachers keeps his neck craned to where all the runners are huddled. Occasionally, he tugs his cap down or raises it to see better. The one sitting above him is all bent over, elbows on knees, taking mental notes before sitting up to take real ones on his phone. I might even catch one of them snapping a pic or a video record of our speed.

"Go, Vin!" my friends scream. Jorge gives a thumbs-up and a

big-ass grin, as if this show will improve my chances with the recruiters.

The crowd is sparse. Some people are watching; some are scrolling on their phones. Parents who are a bit too intense about this stuff try to make conversation with the scouts— they're not supposed to, doesn't stop them. I know from experience that Ross is probably selling under the bleachers or nearby, along with the students vaping. I don't need to think about that either. I have fresh air today since we're moving back outdoors for meets after a stone-cold winter running on indoor tracks. It just wasn't the same inside; there was no gravel, no wind, no freedom. *This* is where I'm best. I kick Byron's sneaker, code for he's stretched enough.

"Let's get to our lanes and see who's golden."

Feet in the blocks, I wait for the *crack* in the air telling me to hustle, or the beep if one of us makes an error at the start. Then we're off! My thighs are ready for the quick jump. The sear in my lungs and the scratch in my throat as I clear hurdle after hurdle are exactly what I need. I tune out everything. I'm almost at a gallop, with ten hurdles set up in front of me. Today, I won't crash and burn.

I'm practically heaving when I conquer the last one, speeding past the finish first. My legs are in that springy form before I seize, so I shake them out to stay bouncy.

"Good job, Vince!" comes from the sidelines. My teammates blow by me in a burst of wind. I give my back to the stands, not wanting to see the scouts. Byron insists the crowd's reactions give him a boost during practice. For me, it's just more people I have to play pretend to.

My teammate Cameron gives a quick wave to the bleachers before he flops to the ground, body spread like he's about to make snow angels. "Damn, Vince. Out how long and still whooping ass?"

"Secret weapon for the relay!" Byron says, slapping my back. I'm walking in circles, hands on hips, ready to do this again if it can wipe yesterday's cemetery visit from my mind. To keep the cramps at bay, I have to stay moving. Stillness also leads to thinking, which is the last thing I need.

So I say, "Let's go again."

Cameron huffs from the ground. "Gimme an hour."

"Whatever. I'm ready," Byron says. "You and me, Vince?"

"Let's do it." I jog to the start.

"Glad you're back. Team hasn't been the same without you."

"Thanks, man. It's good to be back." I take the first lane, and Byron, the third. Says that one gives him luck.

From the looks of it, our team is already in top shape. Nothing much needs to be said since everyone wants a three-peat championship as much as I do. I took my place beside Coach during starting drills. For every one of Coach's orders—"Pick up your knees!"—I responded with a compliment—"Nice break out the block." People showed good form, automatically paired up for sprints, or did weights in rotation. It was all seamless, like clockwork.

I peek at the recruiters. Scholarships. College taken care of. Getting away from home. A guy can dream, after all.

Crouching down, eyes forward, I tell Byron, "Less talking, more running." He obliges and gets in position. Another *crack* pierces the air, and we're off.

Each hurdle is me trying to escape something or someone. My parents. Byron using. Janice's and Jorge's sad looks. Letta's Trials. The pills I craved, which also make me nauseous at the memory of them. My next jump feels off. I nearly clip a hurdle when I leap, but I clear it. The last one is the worst. That's when Viv's face flashes in front of me. Next thing I know, my jump is too late. My front leg clears, barely, but my back leg is too low. The toe of my cleats brings the hurdle with me, and I crash, hard. My forearms and elbows hit the ground first. The hurdle's thrown forward while I roll like a tire.

My team crowds around me, and Byron offers a hand, yet it's Levi who lifts me up.

"Let's get you inside. Have them check you out." I'm too shaken to push him away.

For the most part, I think I'm okay. The scariest part is the reminder there's too much I can't control. Levi puts my arm around his shoulders, holds me up around the waist. I'm limping, but the kinks mostly work themselves out the more I move.

"You sure you're okay?" Byron calls after me.

"Yeah," I call back. I catch the worry on everyone's faces and a slow shake of the head from one of the scouts.

Levi's camera bounces against his chest with every step. I ignore the occasional pokes in my chest from his long lens.

"You show off too much," he says.

"Go big or go home. Them's the rules."

As soon as we pass through the locker room doors, Levi's nose scrunches up at the odor, but I love the smell. Evidence of what we're pushing toward: winning, unity, leaving a mark with our names on it.

I tell him not to make a face. "It's my sanctuary. You know that."

"Well, it certainly doesn't smell like one."

He leads me to the bench in front of my locker.

"Can you walk to the nurse? Or, better yet, I can bring her here?" Levi twists his body to go but then turns back, unsure. It's nice when he shows how much he cares.

I flex my arms. I'm sore but okay. I tell Levi as much.

"You're always good, Vin. But I know you're not."

"I'm fine," I insist. "I am!"

Levi's camera swings from his neck with every move he makes. He mocks me with a couple nasally "I'm fines."

Levi doesn't wear a jacket when he's working because he says he has to move quickly, that layers slow him down. Right now, I have a close-up view of how he fills out his shirt, from his shoulders to the slight bulge of his biceps. His shirt is emblazoned with a camera and the words CATCH ME IF YOU CAN. It's bad enough Levi broke my heart. Do his clothes have to mock me too?

"Lemme see your arms," he says. "Hold 'em up."

I do, reluctantly. He bends down in front of me to get a good look at the red skid marks on either elbow. He squats and I see his high-top is as clean and straight as ever. Levi traces my scrapes, from right to left. I do everything possible not to react. It's difficult, though. Whenever he used to trace my jaw, I'd melt into his arms, kissing him hard and deep as we tangled together in my bedroom or my car, wherever we had privacy. I want what we had, even if it was just the two of us in a bubble.

"Hmm," he says with a pout. "Not as pretty as the rest of you, I'm afraid."

The minute his touch is gone hurts.

"I have to get back out there," I say. "Thanks for your help, but I'm good."

I hiss in pain the minute I try to get up. The shock to my ankle means I may have pulled something and that I need to go easy.

My butt is back on the bench. I roll my ankle a few times, feel the ache smooth little by little. *Damn it.* The last thing I need is an injury right now.

"So that's it?" he asks, stepping closer. "You're not gonna give a brother a chance to explain himself?"

"Seriously? Every time I hear from you, all you want to talk about is that night. In case you didn't notice, it turned out to be the worst day of my life. You have the shittiest timing on everything," I mumble.

"You know what . . ." Levi rubs the back of his neck. He's cute when he does that too. "You got me there."

What is there to say? I'm angry he broke up with me, yeah. I'm also angry he's standing in front of me trying to explain himself while I'm figuring out if I can finish the season first day back. Levi standing above me feels like he's got some kind of power: me injured, him taking in all my misery. I go easy when I rise again.

Nope. Still too soon, because now every inch of my body is throbbing. My elbows, knees, even my heels.

"But, *man*," Levi says, "what am I supposed to do when you run away from me like I'm diseased or something? I'm trying to talk to you, especially about what's going on. When you're stressed, you . . . you do things that aren't good for you."

My jaw is open, ready with some kind of lie. Usually I'm on the ball with lying, but Levi's liquid brown eyes melt me as much as his kisses did.

"You know what I mean. I'm not gonna . . ." He stops to look over his shoulder, like he also wants to keep my secret. "I found, *you know*, in your car. Maybe you forgot it was there, but . . ."

"Is that why you didn't want to be with me? You were ashamed?"

There goes the lip biting, meaning yes. Would it make a difference if he knew I haven't touched anything for weeks?

Finally, Levi says, "I'm not ashamed. I'm *worried*." Everything about him is discomfort, from the lip biting to the neck rubbing to him paying intense attention to his sneakers.

I need to stop wanting what I can't and shouldn't have. I shouldn't have pills, and I can't be with Levi right now. So what else is there? *Focus on what's important at this moment.* If I can bounce back, I can probably make the scouts forget about my fall. Remind them I'm "golden," just like Byron said. I can show my team I'm back, and just as good as before.

I'm fairly certain I'm not the only one relieved when my team filters in, meaning there's no do-over today. Cameron and others check how I'm doing. I throw out more of "I'm fine"/"I'm good." They gather around me, crowding Levi out. Levi doesn't fight it, though. What else is there for us to say? Him, his camera, his high-top, all disappear from sight. Byron edges himself through the line of guys in front of me. I don't need to ask; the frown painted on his face says it all.

He slaps me on the shoulder. I don't flinch. "There'll be other scouts on meet day," he promises.

"Did it look as bad as it felt?"

"Depends," Byron says, already ripping his tank off. "How are you feeling?"

My grin is automatic and fake. "I'm all right."

"Vincent?" Coach appears.

Everyone else is at their lockers. The usual talk begins, with the complaints (about today's performance) and worries (about another championship win), there's swearing of all kinds—curses and promises.

Coach looks me up and down, searching for marks. "Let's talk." He doesn't wait for me to respond, because my job is to follow. I limp a little, trying to loosen up the more I walk. "Push through the pain" is our mantra. Wouldn't say it's a good one, but it's what this team goes by.

Coach's office is a shrine to his favorite NYC teams. Teams

whose glory days happened before I was born, from when Coach was a kid watching at Shea or MSG or Giants Stadium. And players I hadn't heard of until Coach schooled the team, not that any of us asked. Beginning of the season, he plunked us down to preach about what greatness looks like. His cheeks always got red under his red beard the more he talked about watching the Giants' Super Bowl or Rangers' Stanley Cup wins in real time. He'd run a hand over his freckled bald head before putting his cap back on. Adults like to get real nostalgic.

"Lost your focus out there," he says before I take a seat. My ankle is still wonky, and my elbow is sore. It all feels fixable, though, not a total threat to the remainder of the season.

"I got distracted. Won't happen again, I promise."

Coach sits behind his desk and peers at me a second before saying, "Can't happen again, Vincent, scouts are busy people. NCAA is as competitive as it gets. You're on their radar because we win. The minute you fumble, they have doubts. We all start to have doubts."

"Coach, it's been a bad day."

"I know. It's been a bad year for you. I'm not saying you can't have a bad day, Vincent. I know what you're going through."

Pfft, no one knows. That's the problem.

"The minute you step on the track and your legs lock in place, it's about those hurdles and those markers. You're setting the example for everyone. In lacrosse, the minute your cleats get on the grass, once your net is in hand, it's about hitting those marks, getting goal after goal." He makes sure to smack fist to palm on each *goal*.

Cap off, he swipes the sweat from his head like he's the one under pressure, not me. "Remember what I told you about the '86 Mets?"

Here we go. I'm not in the mood for this sort of pep talk, inspired by something that happened in a whole other century, but he's already on a tangent.

The minute Mom, Dad, and I learned recruiters were a thing and, more importantly, that they were interested in *me*, it became full speed ahead. After wins in the 110-meter and 300-meter hurdles sophomore year, I became the guy to watch. And people were watching, constantly watching. Packets for colleges came in the mail, emails were sent to my parents, Coach got surprise visits and inquiries about "that fast guy from Queens." I was in the *Queens Courier.* That feature of me smiling with my state championship medal for the 300-meter hurdles is framed behind Coach. Every time I walk in or out of the school's main entrance I pass by our 4×200 relay trophies for the year and the proclamation that Vincent Chen-Samuels is a star, complete with shiny star stickers around my name. He doesn't need to spell it out. Today's fall shook things up, and not in a good way. I wish for once someone would say it's okay to fall. Even when Dad says it's okay to make mistakes, there's something under his words that lets me know it's not *really* okay. Even with everything going on this year, the well wishes from strangers and friends, some practically damning my sister in a facility . . . At the end of the day people still expect Vince to push through it all and win.

My knees shake. An escape would be nice. That's not an

option right now, because—I glance at the clock on Coach's wall—I have debate.

Coach sits back in his chair, filling the whole seat as he takes me in. "You're one of the best, Vincent. I know you can do this. Make sure you block everything out the next time you're on my field. Got it?"

As usual, my grin is automatic. "Of course."

By the time I stand again, the physical pain is gone, replaced by something else entirely. I don't push myself to a run, but it's a brisk walk out of Coach's office, out of the boys' locker room, and to the nearest empty bathroom on the basement floor. No one's at the urinals, and the only stall is unoccupied. Thankful the rim is clean, I take a seat. At first, I lightly push the door shut. Next thing I know, I'm slamming it. Every hit is a small relief. Bunching my jersey into my mouth, I scream as loud as I can, hoping no one and everyone can hear me.

CHAPTER 16

VIOLETTA

Days in detention: 26

~~LHT~~ ~~LHT~~ ~~LHT~~ ~~LHT~~ ~~LHT~~ I

First day done. As soon as the Trial is over, I meet my guard outside the mortuary. The moment the van doors open, I hold my arms out to get cuffed. Six other girls are in the van, wrists already bound in zip ties. I search for the missing person.

"Where's Petra?"

The driver looks at me through the wire separating us. "She quit before her Trial started. We circled back to drop her off."

"Oh." She'll probably want to be left alone. I'll get her something from the cafeteria for lunch. A banana or whatever sweet thing is offered.

The other girls in the van look exhausted. One's hair is half in and out of a ponytail. Another smacks at her arms—a new spot each time—like she's crushing bugs. A third girl keeps her gaze on the dirty floor. The ride is as quiet coming back as it was leaving the compound. On the final curve, another van, this one black, edges along beside us. The windows are tinted, but I can tell this is the van for the boys' facility. It has the same city seal, with CORRECTIONS in navy-blue lettering.

I didn't have to touch any of the bodies today, mainly

watched Miles do what he does. He moved from person to person; he didn't think twice about dressing them or the embalming scars on their backs. It was all routine to Miles.

In the parking lot, our vans split up. Boys one way, girls another.

Our driver announces, "Body checks as soon as you're all back inside."

We stumble out of the van and stay in a straight line. As soon as we're in the building, the ties are cut and the commands start—to take off my clothes behind *that* door, to stand *this* way until told otherwise. They shake out my clothes to make sure I didn't bring anything from the outside. They pat my arms, legs, and thighs. Urge me to bend, open my mouth—wider, *wider*— and stick their fingers in my hair. (My mom and Aunt Mae would lose it if they ever saw how the guards touched my hair.)

After my body check, a new guard says they'll escort me back to the cafeteria. But I want to see Petra first. Normally, I keep my requests to guards at a minimum. I've learned to stay in line, do what I'm told. But I ask before I can scoop it back into my mouth.

"Okay, a few minutes only. No tardiness for classes," the guard replies. My mood lifts at this small kindness.

My escort's walkie crackles with jumbled words that sound urgent, even though I can't understand them. "Everything okay?" the guard asks whoever is on the other line. It takes a minute or so for a *bleep*, followed by a voice responding. The walkie sounds fade in and out from static. Numbers are said. The guard's rosy face drains of color.

"Is something—"

She pushes past me. Not hard, but I'm so shocked I stumble, clutching at the wall to keep my balance. She's shouting for someone to unlock the dorm door before she crashes through it. I stand and wait for a second before understanding I should follow. Then I'm in the dorm and upstairs, where my guard plus a couple others are clustered at the cell next to mine.

Next comes a loud, shrill sound. I realize it's coming from me when another guard blocks my view of a girl under a white sheet, just like the bodies at the morgue. Petra's knuckles drag across the floor as she's lifted onto a stretcher.

"Stand back!" my guard calls to the girls looking on. More guards march upstairs.

Petra's fingernails are still painted blue. A gift to herself when she thought she was leaving. She was certain I'd be next.

A medic arrives. It all happens so fast. Someone tugs on my arm, but I snatch it back.

"We need you in the cell. Please." The guard doesn't touch me, but her hands hover over my shoulders as a silent request.

Everyone surrounds Petra. "I got a pulse!" the medic screams. "Let's get her to the infirmary. *Now!*"

The guard whispers to me, "You don't need to be here for this."

The group breaks up enough for me to see the top of Petra's head as they wheel her away. My friend, someone in here who believes in me.

Another guard shouts at a growing crowd of girls at the bottom of the stairs. "Go to your cells. *Immediately!* We will drag you there if necessary." This is yelled more than once until the inmates scatter.

As fast as the other girls appeared, they're gone. It's just me. My guard steers me to my room. She unlocks the door and holds it open until I step through.

"Is she—"

The door slams shut, cutting off my question, leaving me more alone than ever.

CHAPTER 17

VINCE

Once I'm through the front door of our duplex, my energy level drops. The day has been reminder on top of reminder of what I can't do and what I must. My elbows and forearm are patched with ointment and bandages, to minimize the damage from my fall. My shoes are the only ones on the doormat, meaning Mom and Dad probably aren't home. A part of me feels freer knowing I can sulk in peace.

I head straight to the kitchen for a quart of juice and to make a sandwich, then it's upstairs to my room. I figure I'll stay there for the rest of the day and turn in early. Once Mom and Dad get home, there's no need to bother them about the recruiter visit, my fall, anything really. Juice, check. Ham sandwich with a good amount of Swiss cheese, check.

I kick the fridge door shut and a couple of papers and pictures fall to the floor. The fridge door is full of Chen-Samuels Greatest Hits. When Letta and I were kids it was all our drawings and some certificates from elementary like Best Speller or Best Napper. Nowadays there's still a few of Viv's drawings, but it's mostly a wall of achievement. And, sadly, a mark of what our life is now with Letta's Trials and papers from the Bureau of Corrections.

I take a bite of my sandwich while scooping up the fallen magnet and papers that dropped with a free hand. One is a handwritten letter from the University of North Carolina—they have a great Track & Field program. The head of their athletics department wrote in sharp black letters, "Vincent would make a grand addition to an all-star team. We can't wait to see him develop." Dad made sure to post that right on the fridge. For him it was a source of pride, for me it's a constant reminder.

Whenever someone came to visit—family, neighbors, friends—Dad made sure to point at the UNC letter as proof I'd make it.

Along with the letter from UNC, I pick up a notice from the Bureau of Detention Services. It says that Letta is due for two, maybe three Trials—Comprehension, Accountability, and possibly Endurance. And—hold up.

"Hold up," I repeat to myself. "Violetta's Trial started *today*, and no one told me!"

Ham and cheese be damned—my appetite is instantly gone. I'd slam my sandwich on the floor, but it wouldn't even make a satisfying sound, just a *splat*.

Almost like I summoned my parents into being, I hear their keys in the front door. I'm in the hallway to meet them as they enter. My parents are huddled in the doorway slipping off their sneakers.

I don't try to keep my voice down. "What is this?"

"What's what, sweetheart?" Mom asks, shrugging off her coat. Dad has his arm out ready to take it and stuff their jackets in the hallway closet. From where I stand, I can see all the hangers and the handle of a vacuum peeking out.

I almost want to stomp my feet like a child. I can't believe they'd keep another thing from me. "Letta's Trial started today and no one told me!"

My parents jolt like they've been caught doing something dirty. Dad approaches, ready to explain.

"Vince, we weren't trying to keep this from you," he swears. Looking to Mom, he pauses before admitting, "I guess we just forgot. Today was our first meeting for counseling with parents of youth who are incarcerated. Plus, your mother had to go and settle some accounts so we could get extensions."

"Not to mention I had to talk to our insurance company *again*—" Mom adds.

"Then there was the bank loan and—"

My parents are back to finishing each other's sentences but not in a good, loving way. It's all tasks and responsibilities building into an impossible to-do list. Mom touches Dad's shoulder and he has his hand on her back; each touch is a signal of what else they had to do and what got left behind. Most of it's tied to money. Some of it is tied to time because they have to rely on public transportation since they can't afford a new car until the insurance check arrives. But, because Letta was involved in a bad accident as an underage driver, it's caused hiccups on that end too.

The more I hear, the more I see the grays peeking out of

Dad's unshaven jaw or that Mom's shirt is actually inside out and the floral design is faded rather than clear. I shouldn't be so mad, not at them. But I *am* mad about all of this. My fingers squeeze my sandwich into mush.

"Let's sit down," Mom offers. We all move into the living room. We take our usual place on the sectional by the front windows. Mom opens the blinds, allowing the room to be filled with sunlight. Like the rest of our home, the living room is a bit of a mess. Not too much cleaning has happened and there's a bunch of half-filled cups on the side tables and some unread magazines Mom subscribed to stacked on the coffee table.

The flat-screen is mounted to the wall above a mock fireplace with a mantel covered in framed family photos. Our smiling faces stare back at me, a testament to another time.

"Is her Trial happening right now? Where is she? What the hell, you guys?" The questions pour out, so does my anger.

"This isn't easy, Vince," Dad says, his voice pitched low to calm everyone. "None of it is. We don't want you to worry. You've got school—"

"And practice. Plus the recruiters," Mom says, as if I don't know. "You shouldn't be bogged down by all this too. We don't want you to have to worry about certain things."

"Not worry! My whole year has been worry!" The sandwich falls between my legs straight to the carpet, and, yup, the sound is too soft to convey my frustration.

"First, don't take that tone. Second"—Mom is quick to wave a tissue—"you're cleaning that up."

I'm already scooping up bread and fillings. "Sorry," I mutter, more to the floor than to my parents.

Me, Mom, and Dad sit with so much tension in the air it's prickling my skin. Neither of them say anything about my bandaged arms. This is the type of quiet I hate. Not the easy kind with Janice. This is the kind where you're waiting for anything to happen and confirm or deny your fears.

Mom brings both her feet up, so she sits the way a kid does listening to storytime. She pulls her hair up into her trademark messy knot and I can see all the sadness and lines etched around her mouth and eyes.

"You should come with us to counseling next time. It was good for us to hear from parents who have gone through this. How tough this is for *everyone*. And"—Mom reaches for Dad—"it reminds you that we're not damaged. Letta just needs help. I've had friends who had problems and they needed something more than the people who loved them could give. That's what this is."

"That's what they told you?" I say, skeptical. I want Letta to learn. I'm angry and love my sister. It's a hell of an emotional roller coaster, but at least I'm kinda used to the ride.

"Vince, one of the worst feelings is knowing I can't protect my family," Dad says. His words are heavy. He rubs his face so hard it's like he's trying to smooth away all the wrinkles that've formed over the past month. "I couldn't protect Vivian from what happened. I didn't protect Violetta from the bad influences entering her life. And"—he takes such a deep breath it alters his voice—"I can't protect you from this. Neither of us can. But you can trust that we're acting on what's best for you right now."

Mom pulls me in for a kiss on the cheek. Between that and what Dad said, my resolve fades. My parents love all of us. This is supposed to be for the best, right? For Letta's healing as much as ours. So I take it down a notch. Relax my fingers so they're no longer fists resting on my thighs. I let my body sink into the sectional's blue leather.

In seconds, Dad's on my other side, hugging me so tight I can't catch a breath at first. "We're a family. We can do this as a family," he tells me. I don't hesitate to return the hug.

"So, what's the Trial?" I ask.

Mom gives Dad the *Your turn* face. He explains as much as he can. "Randall and the Bureau organized the specifics. We chose the categories. But your mother and I didn't know what the Trial would be until today." Every few sentences, Dad stops to check if I'm with him.

Letta's first Trial is Comprehension. The goal is for her to recognize the impact of her actions on others . . . in a mortuary. My parents, along with input from Letta's counselor and Randall—I manage not to groan at the mention of the judicator—will decide if, and when, she's understood the severity of what can happen when you drink and drive.

Dad explains, "We'll be able to watch her Trial because of an app that streams footage from Detention Services."

"Sooo, this is happening now?"

"We were told it took place this morning," Mom says.

"Randall said we can see the feed whenever we like. Either live or at a later time or day."

"And some people choose not to look at all," Dad concludes with a shrug.

"I want to be part of this. I mean . . ." Truth is I do and I don't. My stomach, hell, everything in me rumbles whenever something is about to go wrong.

More questions pour out of me like "Are you going to watch?" and "How long do you think this Trial will be?"

Mom's wringing her hands. Dad returns to her side and holds her hands in his lap while rubbing her back. Every sentence from here on out begins with "Randall said." My parents were encouraged by Randall not to watch at first, but perhaps at the end of the first week. He told my parents "it depends" how long a Trial can go. He mentioned the family should take deep consideration of Letta's counselor's assessments on what she's learning. Randall suggested they base my sister's progress on how she approaches working at the mortuary. None of this sounds like concrete answers to me, more hypotheticals from a guy who doesn't know my sister, at all. Mom's dark eyes are glassy and Dad's voice catches on every hopeful note Randall gave them about Violetta's road to healing. Honestly, hearing how much faith my parents put into the system is almost as scary as whatever my sister may be going through.

CHAPTER 18

VIOLETTA

Days in detention: 28

~~HHT HHT HHT HHT HHT~~ III

It's day three of my Trial. It's also day three of me not getting a full night's sleep. The guards have been knocking on the doors up and down my dorm to make sure we're not hurting ourselves after lights-out. Ever since Petra's accident, they come every few hours, like clockwork. I try to ignore them or pull my bonnet low over my eyes to block the light, but it's no use. A flashlight is shined in each of our faces until we yell our name. I don't know much about how Petra is doing except, thankfully, she's alive. That's as much as Counselor Susan told me. My counselor clicked her pen several times, then mentioned my dorm would be monitored at night. Not in a bad way, she assured me. "Just to make sure," she said.

This is why I'm yawning as I pull up my stool to work on the first body of the day.

"Bored?" Miles asks after a bit.

"Sorry. Haven't gotten much sleep."

"Nightmares?"

"Kind of."

The dreams of my sister haven't gone away. Not exactly.

They've become an awful blend of the day of the crash plus Petra under a sheet. Petra's now off-site, "under observation" at a hospital. My sister is dead. And I'm in a morgue.

"Miles, do you get nightmares working in here?"

"Who wouldn't?"

"Is that a yes?"

Instead of responding, he does his cross gesture—chin tucked, right hand up, down, then left to right like a prayer. It's his habit. If we weren't in detention and allowed jewelry, I imagine he'd be like Callie and touch a cross around his neck before working on the next person. Miles concentrates on the man in front of him. That's the signal for me to concentrate on the woman in front of me. Miles told me about the previous inmate assigned beside him, another girl, who didn't take this Trial very well. He said she threw up every time a body came in for preparation. After two days, Miles commended me on not vomiting on anything or anyone. That made me smile before I realized how pitiful it was how much his comment meant to me. I haven't heard many good things about myself in a month.

This is just a job once you get used to it. I can't say when I got used to it or the smell, but these bodies aren't the ones haunting me at night. So far today, I've made up this woman's face. Because everyone comes in pasty, the goal is to not make them look too cartoonish. Or so the manual says. Everything I've used, from the spray foundation to the eye shadow, is a subtle rose—to make her look at rest.

Miles is in his zone. He starts quietly beatboxing to himself. Whenever I try to make conversation, he gives me one- or two-word answers. The man he's working on now is clothed from the waist down, his hairy chest exposed.

Before all this, I don't remember ever seeing a dead body. Mom shared her memories of Pa and Ma Chen. Pa died before I was born and Ma passed when I was a baby. Mom said she brought me and Vin to Ma Chen's funeral. In the photos on our mantel, Ma had a broad nose, and a few silver strands in her hair. Every photo of her shows her wearing a ruby headband; apparently, that was her favorite color. Mom looks so much like her. Pa Chen's head had a fluff of hair on either side and some sprouting from his ears. Tan spots covered his hands and the bald part of his head.

The photo of them that I love the most hangs in our hallway, right by the kitchen entrance. They sit side by side. Pa Chen looks shorter than Ma, just by a few inches. They're squeezed close together, their faces etched in wrinkles and smiles. Something about how happy and warm they appear in the photo makes me imagine them as the type of grandparents who gifted the best sweets—mochi, mini chocolates, or pineapple buns—whenever they came to visit. I imagine that they're people who didn't scold and who'd embrace you for so long you felt immediately better in their arms.

Despite that picture, Mom said her dad was a reserved man. "But," she added, "I always knew he loved me. You don't always have to go kissing faces and boo-boos to show that." On some basic level, I always knew Mom loved me, but I really felt it after she said that.

I yawn again. To help pass the time, I make silent bets in my head whenever someone new is wheeled in. Will they be elderly, college-aged, somewhere in between? I never know how they died. I could make up stories, but I don't. Miles says it's easier to disconnect; it makes the work go faster. This is how he speeds through his days.

What's next on the list? Oh, right. Nails. First thing is to check under them. The hands are viewed as closely as the face. Especially when the deceased doesn't wear gloves. (They encourage dress gloves in the manual.) Viewers tend to touch the deceased's hands or cheeks.

My latest is a woman, older than Mom, younger than Grams. Her hands will be on top of her stomach. No gloves, so her nails will be visible in the coffin. I sit on my stool and hook my foot onto the underside of the wheel-y tray to bring it to my side. The dirt under her fingernails isn't bad. Cutting nails when they're long like hers is a chore. From what I've read so far, it's harder to get a clean cut, because they're brittle. And filing is a test in patience. If you get to them soon after death, the nails are workable, but too long and the protein that fed the nails decays. I guess I'll paint them to help, and hope the polish covers the jagged edges.

It's like I'm a nurse for a super calm patient. She doesn't complain or stare or judge. It's kind of freeing. The woman will be in an oversized floral print dress. I'll have to pin her sleeves around her biceps, cinch the bulging fabric around her waist, and give her more color on the neck.

Once I'm all set, I place a work order on her sheet for pickup. The wheels of my stool skid and squeak, one of the few sounds in the room.

Today marks the end of my first week. No Trials on weekends. Will I be doing this another week, or month? Is this my new normal, like it was for Petra? How can I pass this Trial? Counselor Susan isn't too much help with these questions. She tells me to "take my time" and to "keep track of what I'm learning each day." She constantly asks if I'm writing in the notebook she gave me. Showing her what I've written means I don't have to admit out loud what's going on in my head.

In yesterday's meeting, my counselor skirted the topic of Petra, circling back to me.

"This time is reserved for you and me, Violetta. Let's focus on that. Now . . ." *Click click click* went her pen. "Would you like to share your notebook with me?"

Aside from the schedules and my notes from her presentation on the Trials, the notebook is a jumble of thoughts and memories, almost a diary. I'm down to only the red golf pencil. The tip is so flat it looks like I'm writing with a crayon. Oh, maybe that's something they'll allow me to have to write with.

My counselor flipped through the pages, her eyes scanning each one while she hummed. I wasn't sure if it was in approval or acknowledgment. Halfway through, she held the book open for me. I had a whole page labeled REGRETS. Right under the top line, I'd scribbled *Pascal?* I anticipated a question about him, one I didn't really want to answer.

"I see there's some ripped pages. Why's that?"

"Oh, those were pages I spilled stuff on," I lied.

"It's okay to share whatever you write with me, Violetta. No need to hide anything."

Hoping my voice didn't betray the way I felt, I swore I wasn't hiding anything. But why couldn't I have one thing for myself? My letters are opened by the mailroom. My body and hair are searched each time I reenter detention. My classwork and this notebook are read by adults. My letters to my sister are the one thing I'm not ready to share. It's not a small thing to want to keep this for myself.

Counselor Susan smiled as she handed my book back to me. "Thank you for sharing. Please keep writing."

I move on to the next gurney. Another yawn happens as I uncover my next body—a young girl. The minute I see how tiny she is, I yell out. The little girl's cheeks are full. Her hair's a halo around her head, and there's a mole in the center of her left eyelid. Her hands are already folded on her stomach under the sheets. And her skin is a slight mahogany, pasty like everyone else's, with her lips tinted blue. At first, I think it's my sister; her face flashes right in front of me, just like in my dreams.

I back away so fast I don't notice the tray beside me. There's a crash. The clatter of combs/brushes is a symphony in my head. Miles jumps up from his station, and I bump into him next.

Her details are different the more I look at the little girl. I think my sister's name, but I can't say it out loud. I just can't. This isn't her. But it could be. This girl is even younger. She takes up only half the pallet she's lying on. This child shouldn't be in here.

I killed my sister pounds in my head so much it hurts. Miles asks if I need a break.

"How do you think she died?" I ask, snapping off my mask to use it as a tissue.

"We're not supposed to ask."

"Can we find out?"

"Maybe. But . . ."

"Not part of the Trial?"

Miles asks if I'm sure about not needing a minute.

I need way more than one, I tell him.

"Hit the bathroom," he says, already back to the guy he's working on. "Take as long as you need."

The bright lights in the bathroom show me how different I look now. I trace the pieces of me that were also her. The eyes that guys have told me are "exotic." The nose, rounded at the end. The skin, a mix of Mom and Dad. And the forehead that is all Dad. All this was her, is me.

I take a breath. There's work to do, and this little girl deserves to look good before her burial.

When I come back, Miles is on his stool, arms at his sides, like he's contemplating the state of the world, or at least the man he's halfway done dressing. I go to the sink to wash my hands, dry them, and put on a new pair of gloves.

Miles slides his mask down so it hangs under his chin. I can see his face and thickening mustache, and not just his eyes. "Thirty-six days," he says.

"Excuse me?"

"You want to know how long I've been doing this Trial? Thirty-six days."

I don't want to believe it. It seems—

"Harsh," I say.

"These folks thought I should do a bit of time in here. I'm guessing this is a Comprehension Trial for you too?"

"Yeah. I—"

"Whatever happened with you is not my business. I know what I did, and I'm just here to make amends, you know? Say a prayer for those passing on and pay my dues like God intended."

Appreciation that Miles hasn't asked about my crime keeps me from asking about his. I'm still curious, though. If this is about him understanding death, a very real *the end* for people, could he have accidentally killed someone too? I try not to stare at him as he rolls the man onto his side to slide a shirtsleeve on. Miles seems so . . . focused and steady. Not the type of guy who'd be sentenced for anything, let alone anything really bad. Then again, I sigh, here I am. Nothing in how he moves appears scared or hesitant.

"You're at the Piedmont Facility too? Boys' division?" I ask.

"Yeah."

"Is this your first Trial?"

"Nah, this is my fourth Trial."

"Fourth? How?"

"Do the crime, do the time."

"This is my first. I have one more after."

Miles sizes me up for a good minute before sliding his mask

over his nose. "Good for you," he says. "Two isn't bad. None is great. But two? Not bad. Hopefully, yours won't be too long. So far, none of mine have gone more than eight weeks. Folks like to be petty and drag out that last Trial. Or at least," he says, "that's what I've heard."

"Is this your last one?"

"Yup. After this, I'm praying I'll finally be forgiven. It's been about six months."

I try to hold back a shudder when I turn to the little girl. Petra at nine months, Miles at several. Eve spending almost a month awaiting judgment. Our lives are all numbers and measurements. It's not really living; it's a countdown. The common denominator between Petra, Eve, and me is that, unfortunately, we've hurt people physically. I fold the sheet and tuck it under the girl's arms. Some of us have hurt people in the worst way possible. For Miles's sake, and his victim's, I really hope that isn't the case for him too.

"So, what do you do?" I ask him. "To not, you know, lose it?"

"These days, I leave it up to God. My family, the Good Book, all that helps me stay strong when it's really hard. I know I'm not a terrible person because of what I did. Plus, I'm not the guy I was almost a year ago. My mom and brothers' visits remind me of that. We pray together, for peace, for the victims, and for me." He looks off for a bit, seeing something in the distance; maybe it's the finish line or maybe it's another hurdle. "You know how it is with family."

"Yeah," I say, lifting a new mask over my nose. "I know how it is."

AT NIGHT, THEY check on us, but during the day the guards don't mention what happened to Petra. It doesn't matter who I ask; guards steer me from place to place in silence. Nothing is in Petra's cell, because they've erased her. Her uniform and shoes, even the elastic bands for her hair, were removed. So were the sheets. The mattress is rolled up, ready for someone new. They locked her door as if nothing happened.

"Making sure everyone's accounted for," the night guard says every evening after waking me up. It's a different voice each night. But they're not counting the person I care about most.

Outside of my Trial, counselor check-ins, and classes, I've asked to stay in my room as much as possible—for sleep but also because I'd prefer not to walk past Petra's room very often. Even after they've scrubbed Petra away, there are still too many reminders.

In my cell, I hold the latest letter from Aunt Mae in one hand and the remaining pencil Petra lent me in the other.

Dearest Letta:

The indoor garden is going strong, and soon more of the warmer time veggies will bloom, because it's heating up outside. Girl, I'll get these kids to eat squash if it's the last thing I do!

On a serious note: I don't know what it's like for you in there. I won't pretend I do. But I'd love to hear back from you. Let me know you're okay, please? I worry. Your Aunt Sonali worries too. So do your cousins. We <u>all</u> worry. And we all make mistakes, Letta. But we aren't defined by them. Believe me. My mistakes made me who I am today. In fact, one of my mistakes is how I met Sonali. (I'll tell you about that later, because it's a grown folks' story.) And your daddy's had a few doozies himself, but he wouldn't want me to get into all that. Anyways, people heal like wounds. Don't pick at them. Allow them to breathe.

One last thing I want you to know is, Viv knows you love her. Each time I visit her grave, I leave flowers on the plot from you. Please stay strong, Flower Child.

Lots of Love,
Aunt Mae

I fold and tuck her latest into my pillowcase with the rest. She sounds like Miles: Who he is shouldn't be defined by what he's done. Deep down, I know I should hold on to that, but that little girl today scared me. The last time I saw my sister, she was curled up in the passenger seat begging me to slow down. After the crash, all I remember is the crack in the windshield, like a spiderweb with a hole in it. I didn't get to see my sister again. The last thing I remember before I woke up in the hospital was the swirling red and blue lights from police before they arrived.

Earlier today, I took my time making the little girl as pretty as possible. I hope whoever worked on my sister put in the same effort, because she deserved to look good on her final day.

I have to pinch the lead tight between my fingers to keep my writing steady. The letters to my sister are mounting and I scribble out one more. Once I'm done, I stuff it under my mattress, alongside the ragged edges of the others.

Everything has its place in here, even in a cramped space. I return my notebook and pencils to the slim shelf above my sink, accidentally knocking Petra's nail polish pen to the floor.

Coral polish is not something I'd usually go for, but I decide to open it. There's the tiny *clack* when I shake the pen and the sharp smell of rubbing alcohol that hits me as soon as I unscrew the cap.

"Might as well." I keep still as I apply the first coat on my big toe. Sticking my foot out, I examine it before I move on to the rest. I grin at my feet.

It's like seeing a single flower sprout from concrete. All this drab, and here a pinch of color. When I think of the empty cell next to me, I know that getting through today is a triumph. No matter what I've done. I'm still here.

CHAPTER 19

VINCE

Days since the decision: 28

There's a hum in my body. Like the rumble of a subway under your feet, alerting you it's about to crash through the station. Breaking through the quiet and shattering the peace. That's the feeling before a race or game. Right before I take the lacrosse field or the moment I crouch on the track. It's time to ignore everything else and get to it. The crowd is lively, but you block them out too. You have to, right down to the last second.

Hyperspeed. Split-second decisions. Sudden movement; I'm going, going, gone. I get lost in all this.

We have a handful more track meets this school year, and we're not about to lose. My teammates and the students from other schools are spread out in their respective blocks. There's no pain from my fall at practice. And I'm eyeing the other black uniforms with gold lettering to know who's on my side.

I rush past person after person. Almost like I'm levitating. What I do know is this, this right here, is when I feel most alive. I can feel the guys on my tail. I can hear the grunts of the other runners trying to catch up. Someone is right beside me, just outside my line of vision. *Focus on what's in front of you, Vin. Focus.* My arms are in perfect form. Every huff is another meter cleared. Going. Going. *Past the finish!*

I raise my arms to the sky and scream. This is the good part. The energy, the high of the win, the teamwork that got us to this moment.

Byron's not far behind me. "Hell yeah!" he shouts in my ear when he lifts me up. His adrenaline must be off the charts because he's never been able to lift me before. "You did it! Vince is *back*!"

The cheers of the fans slowly hit my ears. The chant of "Semis, semis, semis" is a current throughout the field. A herd of my teammates mob me, hugging me from all sides. "You were a beast out there, man. *A beast!*"

I'm grinning. The crowd roars. Friday night events mean a bigger audience, so classmates, parents, Claremont High staff, along with neighborhood folks invested in the school win for bragging rights, fill every row. My parents are somewhere in the stands. Usually, I can spot my family right off the bat. They'd all wear a signature color like yellow or lime green or red so they'd be an easy-to-spot cluster. But today Mom and Dad wore dark colors, like they're always mourning, though Mom said white can also be associated with death.

Even though every row is filled to the brim it's like there's a gap. What's missing is Letta and Callie cheering with their hands cupped around their mouths, Viv raising one of my old jerseys like a flag. All of them too jazzed to sit so they're standing on their seats. The roar hits my ears and their voices are absent. But you know what? I won't let anything take this moment from me.

All us runners look to the board to see me and Byron took the top two spots with someone from Stuyvesant nabbing the third for the 100-meter. If there are any recruiters in the stands, they'll see I beat my best time. That's right, everyone, Vincent Chen-Samuels kicked ass tonight.

My team marches as one back to the lockers. Arms reach down from the bleachers for high fives. I spot Ross's and give his a quick dap. A weird peace surges through me, knowing that I ditched his gift and still dominated today. I didn't need him or any pills for courage on the field. I race along with my team. We've smacked so many palms mine stings. I'm not paying as much attention as I should when I turn a corner to head inside.

"Sorry, I wasn't loo—"

"Not a problem." Levi's hands steady me, but his voice doesn't. It's like I'm noticing new things about him every time I see him, since we haven't been together every day. The stache above his goatee is growing more defined around his lips, less drawn-on and more realistic. "You all were . . ." His arms are wide, like he's trying to take in the world. "Wow. Man, you were fire out there! I'm so proud of you." He holds up his camera as proof. "I made sure to catch every second. Check this out." By now, my teammates have mostly filtered inside. But I stay with Levi as he sorts through a few scenes. It's like he was actually next to each of us, not on the sidelines clicking away.

He zooms in on one shot of me with my arms raised to the darkening sky, screaming my lungs out. I'm damn fierce in the photo. Like no one could touch me. Like the world isn't shattering, and I'm on top of it.

"Whoa, I'm—"

"Fire, man! I *told* you!" He plays at blowing on his finger after he points to my chest.

I think on what he said. *Proud.* I haven't heard that from someone in a while. "Thanks, Levi."

Maybe it's my postgame adrenaline talking, but it kinda feels like Levi and I could start over. He bumps my shoulder on our way toward the locker room. I'm not limping this time, but I wouldn't mind being in his arms again. He's filled out his shirt completely, no fur-trimmed denim, just his broad shoulders and dark-brown arms swinging by my side.

If I'm being honest, I really wanted to shine. I needed this win to block the world out, and I love that Levi captured these scenes. I'm a whirring ball of emotions. I haven't had a chance to get a new phone yet. And I want to tell him everything, let loose, release what's wound up inside me. Because why not? Of course, that's the same moment several teammates come back for me.

"C'mon, Vince! Celebration time!" Byron shouts. He's already torn off his top. His chest is as patchy and red as his face. Could be winners' high, could be something else.

"Well," Levi tries to say above the noise, "I'll see you later. Great job again, Vin!"

His hug is short-lived. Another guy on my team blocks me from him. My teammates' faces are close and excited. They practically carry me backward to the locker room.

Our stench is strong once we're all piled inside. Sweat

and earth, with a sprinkle of BO. The smell of victory, if you know it.

"Great job, guys! Every damn one of you. And *you*." Coach's finger is directed right at me. "You goddamn miracle!"

"A beast!" Byron repeats, sending spit flying.

Time for the usual speech. I step up on the bench, screaming for everyone to shut up for a minute. Cupping my hands over my mouth, I ask, "Who got this?"

My teammates growl back at me, "We got this!"

"Who got this?" I say louder now.

"We got this!"

"Damn right," Coach adds to the mix.

We're so amped we don't notice the visitor at first. Someone who doesn't match the room in his khaki pants, skinny tie, dry face, and composure as he takes tender steps around my teammates. The assistant principal's head kind of startles to and fro as we jostle one another around. Assistant Principal Orlando finally makes it to Coach and whispers something in his ear.

"Are you shitting me, Dante?" Coach says, silencing the whole room.

"Language, Carmine."

"Language? We're in the *semis*. I don't want to lose anyone on the team because of whatever stupidity they do at a party."

"I understand. And congrats, team!" The assistant principal's fist pump is pretty weak. "However, this isn't my decision. And it's not something I want to be working overtime on. I know we've got good kids. Point is, we have to be decisive here. We have to fall in line with everyone else, because—"

Someone clears their throat, and it's like suddenly the adults realize there are other people here. Reminds me of home.

One of the other hurdlers asks, "What's up?"

The assistant principal throws a look to Coach. Coach shakes his head as if to say, *This is on you, man.*

"Well." Assistant Principal Orlando clasps his hands, widens his stance. We're holding our breath at what he's about to say. Reminds me of home.

"Earlier today, the school board heard some concerns about drug use throughout the district."

My blood goes still. I'm surprised I keep my head from snapping to Byron.

"Of course, there's scrutiny when it comes to sports teams in particular. Your rival Clinton Tech had some students test positive for drugs, some known to enhance performance. Several students were caught partying and underage drinking was reported." I may be imagining it, but I swear AP Orlando gives me pity eyes at the words *underage drinking.* "This means," he continues, "the entire division is testing every active athlete before semis. From there, they'll continue with random drug tests for those entering the championships. Anyone who tests positive for anything that is illegal and/or known to enhance performance will be suspended and removed from the team immediately."

The responses tumble out: *"For real?"* "I'm cool with it." "What kind of drugs exactly? I have ADHD. My parents will off me if I stop taking my meds again." "Why are we being punished for Clinton's mistakes?"

I've been clean for about a month. I'll be fine, I think. Telling myself this doesn't keep my legs still. If I had a new phone, this is one of those moments my fingers would be flying with a message to my friends. "Guess what Coach is flipping out about now?"

"I know you all are good students," the AP repeats. "Things happen. You're allowed to have fun. But I hope everyone is being safe and smart about how they handle themselves. Don't endanger yourself or bring your team down because you want to be reckless. We're also alerting your parents about this."

The AP and Coach talk some more. Coach doesn't hide his irritation over this new rule.

He eyes us all with a clear threat. "I swear if any one of you messes up, it'll be your heads. You understand me?"

"Carmine," the AP warns again.

"That's how I get them motivated!"

At some point, the two of them go into Coach's office, filled with paper clippings of past wins, and hopefully more to come.

"Can you believe this?" my teammates ask. Byron tries to get my attention. I hope he's been keeping away from Ross. I doubt it, though. He's been feeling his own pressures. The rest of us are calming down, but he's still buzzing. Byron's walking circles in front of his locker. If he were on grass instead of concrete, he'd have worn a hole in the ground by now. I recognize this in him because it's been me, more times than I care to admit.

If these recruiters see any of us falter, it may screw the team as a whole. All I can think is: *I can't let anyone down. Not again.*

CHAPTER 20

Hey Viv,

It's funny. Between you, me, and Vin, I think the only thing we ever agreed on—besides how boring the TV mysteries Mom watches are or how bad Dad's jokes always are—is that peanut butter and chocolate are the best combination ever made. Most other times, I remember us disagreeing. For example, First Day of School Pancakes. Vin liked banana chocolate chip. I preferred chocolate chip—why ruin it with bananas? You were all about blueberry, also a favorite of Mom and Dad's. "A traditional fave," they used to say.

Usually, Mom and Dad used to default to your preference, because it was theirs too. Mostly, Mom said she wanted us to learn to share and compromise. She or Dad said it was no big deal, it was <u>one</u> breakfast. It's a silly example, but it seemed like some of us were compromising more than others.

When I was your age, my teacher told my class a story about the Incredible Shrinking Girl. The girl got smaller whenever she went unnoticed. If days or weeks went by where no one said her name or acknowledged her, she'd shrink and shrink until she was no bigger than a speck of dust. Then she'd disappear forever. "Poof," the teacher would say, blowing a pretend speck from the tip of a finger. One day, a prince—there's always a prince—almost stepped on her but caught himself. By then, she was only a couple inches tall; she'd been ignored for weeks, but the handsome prince—the prince is always handsome—noticed before his shoe squashed her whole body. When he asked her name, he had to bend down and put his ear low to the ground. She squeaked her name, then he repeated it, leading the girl to grow an inch. From then on, the prince always made sure to look down when he walked so he wouldn't flatten her, or anyone else. Each day, he made a point to find her and say her name. I never remember the name of the girl or the prince, but I remember the story clearly. It's not the best story for kids or anyone really, but it's one I can relate to. Especially now that I have so much time to think.

Here's the truth, Viv: I felt small. In photos I was always cheering you or Vin on, but not being cheered for. I am quiet and nervous and, like Callie says, bad at track. I stand out because I don't stand out, even in my family. And that made me feel small because I didn't know how to make my voice bigger.

When you hear your older brother tell you, "Don't be so dramatic all the time," or you overhear Mom and Dad say about you, "She just wants attention," or Gram and Gramps say, "She's a sensitive child compared to the others," it sounds like the problem—the common denominator—is you. That's when you shrink little by little over time.

So maybe when people thought it was cute whenever you stood on chairs commanding attention, or when Mom and Dad negotiated with you for what you wanted rather than dismissing you, it made me feel smaller.

I guess you could say I let myself be that girl in the story. And I thought maybe Pascal was the prince. There's no happily ever after for me, like there was for the girl and the prince. But when Pascal noticed me, without me having to say anything, it was kind of like I grew. Not necessarily into myself but into someone bigger than I was, if that makes sense.

Hopefully, this does make sense. What I'm trying to say as your big sister is: I hope no one ever made you feel like that. Even now, I'm finding my way to grow.

I'll write again, I promise,

Letta

CHAPTER 21

VINCE

Days since the decision: 29

My parents' room is the messiest I've ever seen it. Their sheets are spilled onto the floor rather than tucked into the bed. Their pajamas are balled up in the rumpled sheets. Clothes hang out of the hamper. An open laptop is balanced on a pillow. It's reminiscent of my room most of the time. Mom used to say they set the example we needed to follow: Keep things neat and tidy. I figure now my room can look like a cyclone came through it.

Since I was already upstairs, Mom asked me to bring down her slippers. Our Saturday afternoon is going to be spent watching the end of Letta's first Trial week with Randall present.

Mom's slippers peek out from under the bed. The laptop catches my eye, though. I listen for anyone coming, either my parents or good ole Randall. Only thing I hear is the faint murmur of voices downstairs.

The computer screen comes to life as soon as I tap a key. With a swipe of the trackpad, it goes straight to the page that was already up: an encyclopedia entry on the Trials. Another browser tab takes me to the overloaded inbox of Mr. and

Mrs. Chen-Samuels. Keeping the laptop on the bed, I crouch on the floor and get to scrolling. There are draft emails to Randall and saved recipes. There are lots of deals for the stores Mom loves getting her work clothes from, coupons from food delivery services, emails with the subject "Condolences," "With Sympathy," or "Sorry to Hear." And a message to the parents of students at Claremont High School, reminding them about parent-teacher night and alerting them of the upcoming district-wide drug tests.

Most of the messages are unread. Yet every email from Randall has been read and flagged. What's going on with the Trials is important, but—dang—a notice from school doesn't warrant a glance? My fingers stop above the keys, hesitant to move in case someone appears. It wouldn't hurt to check, right?

I scan Randall's emails until I spot TRIAL OUTCOMES. I search for the most important parts. It reads like a doctor's diagnosis: **The Offender appeared anxious and fidgety for the beginning portion of her Trial (Comprehension). Increased productivity burgeoned from day-to-day activities as determined from video stills (see attachment). Unclear if she's gained awareness of purpose for this method of rehabilitation.**

My fingers work quickly on the trackpad, but it's still more technical-word soup. "Parameters for upcoming Trials will be implemented once Mr. and Mrs. Chen-Samuels conclude a pass-or-fail option. The Offender will continue to be monitored by her counselor, with reports back to the Bureau. Victims will be updated as needed."

Updated as needed?

"Vince!" Mom's voice carries upstairs. "Have you found them yet?"

"On my way!"

I tear out of my parents' bedroom, then rush back for Mom's slippers before thundering downstairs to the living room.

"Here you go, Mom."

Mom and Dad are cuddled up on one side of the sectional. I stretch myself out on the L part farthest away from Randall. His emails talk about my sister like she's an experiment or something. And when it comes to every part of this—his involvement especially—I have questions.

"Are we all set?" Randall asks us. Tablet in hand, he's ready for business. In what's become his trademark metallic suit, he takes his place right in front of the TV and the Bureau seal.

"Let's get this party started," I say.

"Yes," my parents agree.

Randall taps his tablet, and the screen shines bright against his pale, waxy face.

"All right. Days one and two, there isn't much to report. Violetta became acclimated to her Trial. She worked diligently in the mortuary setting. However, yesterday, Friday, there was, well, a reaction."

Mom and Dad's voices are one when they ask, "What do you mean, 'a reaction'?"

"Apparently . . ." Randall stretches out the word as he scrolls through his report. "Ah, she came face-to-face with an element that may have triggered said reaction. Which, to an extent, is what we want."

Mom shakes her head so hard her bun unknots itself, black hair spilling around her shoulders. "Randall, please. *What type of reaction?* Is our daughter okay?"

Randall points his tablet to the screen like it's a remote. "You're welcome to watch yesterday's video to see for yourself."

The television provides a kind of room-wide view of where Letta is, reminding me of a security camera. Letta and some masked guy are in black-and-white, slightly grainy yet still visible. The two are frozen in whatever they're doing. At first, it all seems par for the morbid course: Each of them on either side of the room. The guy bent over a body, and Letta brushing powder on whoever she's working on.

"Is this—" Mom starts.

Randall interrupts. "I can fast-forward if that's all right." Another *tap tap* on the tablet and things speed up.

Letta goes to a new bed, and suddenly she's on the ground.

Mom runs to the screen so fast even slamming her thigh into the coffee table doesn't stop her. She presses a hand to Letta's figure, fingers spread over her masked face. "Stop! What was that?"

Randall rewinds. He pauses at Letta folding back a sheet to reveal a child. I join Mom at the screen. Letta practically leaps away, knocking over a couple trays. The masked guy ushers her back to her feet. She's gone for several minutes. When my sister returns, it's like she's a new person. She enters slowly.

She tugs the strings of her apron together, ties them tight, puts on another pair of gloves and mask from the boxes propped up near the door, and goes back to work. The whole time, she and the guy talk.

"Is working on bodies always this hard?" my sister asks.

"With these Trials? I've done worse," the guy responds.

Mom and I stay put. Dad joins us near the screen. We watch Letta put polish on the little girl's nails, taking her time with each finger. Holding her tenderly, like how I imagine she used to do Viv's nails. Violetta tucks the girl into her sheet before she starts on the next body. In the eeriest silence imaginable, we watch her make up a couple more people before the screen goes blank and we're welcomed to THE END, with the Bureau seal again.

"Like, seriously, what *was* that?" I step to Randall, wanting answers both for that display and his emails.

"Vincent, this isn't about you," he says. "This is about—"

"Cut the crap!"

Dad inserts himself between us, so he and I are face-to-face. His whole face crinkles up in disappointment. He's aged—so has Mom—over these past few weeks. It's enough to make me wish I could scoop the words back into my mouth. The way he says my name isn't a warning; it's a request. I can almost hear the "please" behind it. I take a seat on the couch and remind myself to breathe, like *really* breathe. Adult voices bounce around me. The stress is high, then again, when isn't it lately?

Mom joins me on the sectional. Her hands are soft as she

pats my arm, her attempt at making the hurt go away. But there's no getting rid of this.

"I think it's time to be done with this," my father says.

Randall once again centers himself in our home. Arms behind his back, he gives one of those authoritative looks at my parents like they must be joking. "Done with this Trial, or all of it?"

"I honestly don't know anymore," Mom says. "You told us this would help and in two minutes what I saw didn't seem to be helpful to our daughter."

"Well." Randall flips his tablet case open to swipe the screen. "Based on what I've seen and read in Violetta's reports from her counselor"—Randall scrolls some more, nodding at what he reads—"she's showing some signs of stress from her incarceration, which is expected." His tsks set me even more on edge. "Violetta's counselor has noted she won't speak too much about her state. However, she does maintain a journal of sorts—with her regrets, indicating remorse. What else? She's silent, keeps to herself. Is this enough for you to feel comfortable about moving on to the next Trial?"

"Can you talk like she's a person," I say, "and not a test subject, please?"

The way Mom keeps rubbing my arm, you'd think I was a sad-eyed collie in need of attention and not a ticked-off teenager. "Vince, please." To Randall, she asks, "You mean we don't know what she's taking in from this Trial? As in she could *not* understand the repercussions of what she did? If she's not talking, do we need to get her help outside of detention?"

"Mrs. Chen-Samuels, her silence isn't completely out of the ordinary. Your daughter is trying to get through the assignments given to her. That means she's doing what she's told. You mentioned she had a hard time doing that, did you not? Her previous pattern of behavior can lead to problems overall. *This* is how those potentially get fixed."

"Wait." Mom folds her legs to her chest, so she appears smaller than usual, child-like. She's not rocking back and forth, but she doesn't keep still as she tries to piece this all together. "She's remorseful. She's not drinking. She has a, what do you call it, monitored regimen, you said? When we spoke to other parents some said this type of rehabilitation put things in clear perspective for their child." Mom rattles off more Randall quotes, whatever she's learned from families like ours and pamphlets and the internet. *She's an encyclopedia of the Trials.*

"Mr. and Mrs. Chen-Samuels, I'm aware how difficult this may be. When we asked you if you felt Violetta was ready to come home after this accident, if you were prepared for her to return and rejoin society after manslaughter and underage drinking, you said 'no.' You said," and here he looks at that damn screen again, "you weren't equipped to help your daughter after such a crime. You said, and I quote, that you thought you knew Violetta, however, it appeared she had more issues than you could afford to handle on your own. And you said—"

"We know what we said for f—" Dad barks, sinking into the couch alongside Mom and me.

Ouch. I don't know what's worse, rehashing what my parents said about Letta or the fact that Randall had to recite their own feelings of failure right back at them in the static voice he says everything.

Randall finally lowers his tablet and flips the cover over it. "I'm here to help you through this. I imagine as a family it's not easy to see this play out in front of you."

From his sunken position, Dad's belly slightly pokes out from under his button-down work shirt and he fiddles with the edge of his collar. It's not just Mom who looks small on her end of the sectional, Dad does too. They're supposed to be the ones protecting us. Now I'm wondering who's protecting them, or any of us, these days?

Outside of constantly referring to his tablet every other second, Randall is arctic cool. He remains unbothered at every outburst. Between his stiffer than stiff stance, thin face and build, and shiny gray suit I could honestly mistake him for a robot.

"You don't know what this is like," Dad says, his voice quiet and firm at the same time. "You have no idea what it's like to lose a child and not know how to help the other one."

He's still in his work clothes, including dusty blue work pants from a day of moving from site to site checking electric connections.

"Annie, you saw how she reacted when she worked on that little girl's body. That child was almost Vivian's age. That had to affect her. This Trial broke through, even if she hasn't spoken about it, or about Viv."

None of us understand what it's like for Letta day after day in there. A glimpse at this video was too much for me. Maybe my anger is wearing off, or maybe this means I'm starting to forgive her. Could be weakness on my part. Honestly, I just want my family to be whole. And so far, it doesn't feel like the Trials are accomplishing that.

"She has to get what she did by now," I say. "She has to."

No one asked for it, but Randall adds his two cents. "I think the word you may be grasping for is 'stasis.' This does occur on occasion." Arms behind his back again, Randall forces his chest forward as if he's as important as he wants us to think he is. His shoes gleam; there's always a shine to those too. Everything about him is impeccable right down to the clean lines of his haircut. It's really irritating.

He takes one step, then another, toward all of us on the sectional. "She's being, as many inmates are—"

"Obedient," I finish for him.

"Yes. Obedience can mean less recidivism. However, it can also be a means to an end. It's evident what we want to ensure is that she understands everything she's done so she'll never do it again. That is why we have this system in place."

Dad's pacing around the sectional, bypassing Randall with each lap. Mom continues to rock herself. It scares me how much my parents look to this judicator for not just guidance— but for hope.

"And how can we get her to that place?" is Mom's question. "This isn't punishment. But what we saw . . . it wouldn't be what I wanted for Letta. If we're going to continue with a Trial, then we have to make sure it helps her. Can you do that?"

Randall almost seems giddy to reveal his tablet again.

"Absolutely. The Accountability Trial has proven to have very steady results. I could have this ready next week *if* you think Violetta has passed this Trial."

"Letta passed," Dad says. "But I want us to get more updates on these Trials. We also want to see the next Trial when it happens. Okay?" This is clearly not a request.

Randall appears unfazed by Dad's tone. "Whatever you say. You'll be kept abreast of what happens soon enough."

CHAPTER 22

VIOLETTA

Days in detention: 29

~~LHT~~ ~~LHT~~ ~~LHT~~ ~~LHT~~ ~~LHT~~ IIII

Technically, we have more freedom on weekends, which isn't saying much. Inmates are still led to breakfast, lunch, and dinner, and anywhere else they want to go around the facility. On these days I'm grateful for no classes, no Trials. Saturday's a day for extended recreation, and preparation for the mass of visitors driving in or dropped off by bus. It's also sentencing day, so Eve is back in line. This may be the day she gets an answer.

Petra and I used to go for a walk or try to do some art, or participate in an activity someone was specially brought to detention to teach us. Without her around, I decide to switch things up by sitting in one of the dayrooms any inmate can visit. The open space is nice for a change. The TV bolted to the wall is off, so the only sounds come from the girls sitting in pairs or solo at other tables that have checkerboards painted on them. A pile of board games are stacked near the entrance for us. Older types, with the rule cards missing, so most of us have no idea how to play them. Some girls just use the dice to bet on commissary items. Three girls are in the corner under the TV, already rolling dice against the wall. Their shouts reveal who's winning or losing.

It does feel the tiniest bit different to change the scenery. The floor-to-ceiling windows in this room are barred, like every window in this place. In the morning, the mist outside forms a blanket around the barbed wire and guard stations, almost hiding them. The world appears bigger. I may not be part of it right now, but staring outside reminds me I could be, soon.

A guard escorts more girls into the dayroom, including Serena. Her sleeves are rolled up by her shoulders, revealing more tattoos on her right arm. Flowers wind themselves up her biceps and under her shirt. I spot violets and marigolds along with the lilacs. The flowers stand out in the garden on her sandy, freckled skin. She catches me staring and saunters over.

"Noticing my ink again, I see."

"Sorry, didn't mean to stare," I say, trying unsuccessfully not to be awkward.

Serena pulls a chair over. She doesn't acknowledge any of the stares as she scrapes the chair along the floor. "You want a tattoo?"

"I recognize the flowers. Like the violets. I was named after them. My aunt's a florist. Also, I've heard tattoos hurt."

"Well, *yeah*. My mom gave me consent since I'm seventeen. She said there are worse things I could do than have a tattoo." Serena coughs out what I *think* is a laugh as she takes in the room. "Turns out she was right."

The skin of Serena's nose flakes off like she has a sunburn, but the rest of her face is flawless, and I'm jealous. Serena points her chin at my notebook and the golf pencils tucked inside. Eve used her commissary to get me new ones so my fingers don't ache from squeezing a nub. "You draw?"

"No, I write. Not like a writer. Just jotting things down. I don't know, whatever's on my mind. My counselor gave me the notebook. She said it'd be a good way for me to share my thoughts."

Just now I was writing about the bodies in the mortuary. I'd drawn a table of the people I dressed, sorted by the day I worked on them. I made note of almost everyone's name after my Trial. The last entry is the little girl; her name was Nora.

Without asking, Serena flips my notebook around to read it better. "What's this?" she asks, touching the Friday box.

Something in me panics from her directness. Serena is a cafeteria friend, someone Eve knows better than me, since they're in the same dorm. Now it's just the two of us. I immediately close my notebook, nearly catching her finger between the pages.

"It's just—"

"A hit list? Girl, that may not be the smartest thing to do in detention."

My pencils roll to the floor when I press the notebook to my chest as if it'll shield me. Serena throws her head back in a laugh and claps a few times. Apparently, I'm hilarious.

"I'm joking," she says. "But for real, what is it?"

"A list of people from my Trial. That I worked on," spills out of my mouth.

As if I'm the most interesting person in the world, Serena

lowers her head and her voice. "What do you mean, 'worked on'?" Her eyes are dark and focused on me. She almost hugs herself while she waits for my response.

My eyes dart around. A guard stands right outside the entrance. No one can hear, or cares to. One girl throwing dice says, "Damn it!"

"Comprehension. My Trial is to dress people for funerals. Do their makeup and put on clothes. I . . ." Unable to finish, I let my words hang in the air.

"Like in a funeral home?"

"Kind of, yeah."

Her tongue pokes into her cheek in contemplation. "Sounds messed-up," Serena finally declares.

"No, it's super fun," I say, making her laugh again.

"Mine is an Endurance Trial. I was told I need to see the root of the issue, or whatever, through actions." A suck of her teeth tells me exactly what she thinks of that.

Every time I hear the word *Endurance*, I think of Petra. Actually, I think of all the marks on Petra's arms. What my counselor and the Bureau say is part of rehabilitation but looks like punishment. It makes me scared for Serena.

"What do you do?"

"They have me working in an artillery factory. Before you ask, it sucks."

"Oh," is all I can say.

Serena tells me more. She doesn't stop talking when one of the girl's playing dice shouts, "Booyah," then does a little slide back and forth in celebration. "Give me my commissary!" the girl says to her group in the corner, all of them shaking their heads at the dice as if betrayed.

"I got next!" Serena calls over, then turns her attention back to me. "What was I saying? Right, artillery. It *blows*."

I can't explain why the more Serena talks, the more I relax until I rest the notebook on the table instead of holding it against me.

"They have us close to the machines making bullets. It's like serving in hell for real. You know how hot something has to be to melt metal?" She answers for me. "Practically a million degrees Fahrenheit. Almost burned my eyebrows off." As if making sure they're still there, her fingers tenderly touch her eyebrows, then her slightly burned nose. Her fingertips make their way back to her forehead, like she's checking for a fever from the heat of her Trial.

Miles doesn't want to talk much at our Trial. Petra is gone. Eve is always angry, understandably. And every time I see Counselor Susan, she wants me to talk instead of telling me what I want to know. It's kind of soothing to hear Serena be so open about her Trial.

I'm not scared to ask. I'm more nervous about Serena's response when I say, "Why are you making bullets?"

"Because someone died when I tried to steal from a pharmacy," Serena says so calmly I think I misheard her at first.

When I don't respond, Serena sucks her teeth before adding, "It was an accident. A friend needed some diabetes medication for their mom. Their insurance never covers it for some reason. They were desperate. Wasn't the first time someone I knew had an issue like that." Like me, Serena gets distracted by the designs on her arms; she rolls her sleeves down so they disappear from view.

"It also wasn't the first time I stole. My friend knew I was good at it. Despite this," she says, pointing at her pink locs, "I'm usually quick and don't draw attention. He swore he had an in at a pharmacy. Said he could get us inside after hours and all I'd have to do was snag the pills."

Sometimes reliving our crimes is its own punishment. Maybe that's why the Trials exist too, despite what Counselor Susan says. The constant reminder breaks you down. Serena is usually pretty upbeat, always eating when I see her in the cafeteria, and pretty chatty. She doesn't pause when she tells her story. Still, the more she talks about her friend, the harder her eyes become, almost darkening as she remembers what was taken from her.

"He was supposed to be lookout. *All* he had to do was let me know if someone was coming and we'd split. Turns out my dumbass *friend* had a gun. Word of advice, Letta: If there are bullets, it means intent to harm. If there aren't bullets, it means no intent and is a bit easier to explain before sentencing.

"I never carried a weapon, ever. I get the goods and get gone. The owner of the pharmacy lived above the store and heard us. Turns out, he had a condition. The guy turned on the lights and saw dumbass wave his gun around in a panic and ended up having a heart attack. And that's that."

And that's that. Those words make me wonder what pressure Serena may have been under, her friend too, to bring a gun.

My family isn't well-off, but we had enough. But maybe that's changed thanks to me too.

"So now I'm in a hotbox five days a week helping make bullets. The irony."

In Serena's own words, this is *a lot*. Serena, me, Eve, and Petra have people attached to our crimes, people we hurt or, worse, whose death we had a hand in. *Vehicular manslaughter* flashes in my mind. Serena produces parts of a weapon as a Trial while I have to face death during the week. Aside from the burn marks, I don't see any scars on Serena from her Trial; they may run even deeper for her knowing there's no erasing what's happened.

"I'm sorry," is all I can say. Because I am.

Serena stares off at the girls in the corner. Their game isn't as loud. By the way they chuck dice at the wall it's still high energy. Everything about Serena's usual glow is dulled, right down to the pink in her hair losing its luster. Elbows on the table, she traces the checkerboard pattern as if it's a maze she can find an escape route from. After more than a minute, she says, "So am I, Letta. So am I."

AFTER LUNCH, I'm taken to visit my counselor. Instead of telling me to go right in, the guard instructs me to take a seat in the hallway and wait my turn.

Counselor Susan attempts to keep her voice calm. But I can hear it get close to a shriek. With the guard on the other side of the door of the counselor area, I move my seat so I can see inside my counselor's office. Two women are in there. One is on her feet and quickly flips something off Counselor Susan's desk, which clatters to the ground. My counselor's face is the only one I can see, when she's not hidden by one of the visitors. The two women have long, flowing dark hair. I can only tell them apart by the colors they wear. The woman doing the most shouting is in head-to-toe military green, an almost fitting color for this place. The person on her left has on a red jacket and high heels.

The standing woman is on a roll. "You sent my daughter into a torture chamber for *months*! And you never told us she was in duress. Not once!"

"At any time Petra could've and should've informed you if she was upset," my counselor offers.

Petra! I lean over to see more of the room, but it doesn't look like Petra is with them at all.

"You shut your damn mouth! My daughter was being tormented by sociopaths *five days a week*, and you let it stand. Then you just casually shared this information with the Bureau, but not her family? What kind of shitty counselor are you?" The standing woman yells so much her voice sounds like it's going raw.

"My responsibility," Counselor Susan tries, but she's interrupted again by the woman in red chiming in that she will pray for my counselor's soul. She rises to get hold of the woman in green.

This is Petra's family, her mom and aunt or maybe sister? All that's visible is the backs of their heads, but I take in the power of their stances. How their anger makes them appear invincible. Counselor Susan must see it too, because she stays seated in place.

"You know who should've been aware of what was in this notebook?" the woman in green asks. She holds up the same type of composition book I have. "Us. Not the Bureau. Not the victims. *Her family.* And all those degrees on your wall don't mean shit because you failed my daughter. Do you understand me? You failed Petra."

The women march out. The woman in green, Petra's mom, looks exactly like Petra—from the natural rise of her cheeks, to the long chestnut hair curled at the ends, to the way she fills out her skirt and sweater. The notebook is rolled up like a weapon. Both women hold their heads high, not looking anywhere else, only forward.

I call out to them too late. My "Excuse me" is muted by the guard buzzing them out when they reach the barrier from the counselor station to the rest of the facility.

Does "failed" mean Petra still has to do her Trial? We're told our Trials are pass or fail. In here, our lives are about proving something to people we cannot see or speak to. I hadn't thought hard enough about when those people fail us inmates.

Saturdays are supposed to be the calm days. Today's been the total opposite. Minutes pass before I decide to enter the office. Behind her desk, Counselor Susan tries to compose herself by patting her cheeks and adjusting her blouse. She doesn't say anything to me. One of the visitor chairs is on its side, adding some chaos to the usual neatness of the room, along with the pens scattered on the floor. This is the only time my counselor has ever appeared imperfect. Maybe everything I've seen from her up until this moment has been a mask, one that's slowly sliding off, revealing what's underneath. There's a whole new feel to this room after seeing Petra's family that makes me fidget where I stand.

"Sorry for the delay, Violetta," she says, attempting to organize the folders piled on her desk.

"That was—"

Her voice is ice when she cuts me off. "That was none of your concern."

Things were bad enough already. Everything feels like a Trial: Waking up. Bathing at a scheduled time. Asking for maxi pads through a window. Dressing dead bodies. Talking about what I've done. Pretending I can handle it all. And now I'm wondering about the woman in front of me. The person who has seemed the most supportive, even through her lectures.

"I see you have your notebook," my counselor says, eyeing it. "May I?"

For the first time, I hesitate. Partially because of what just happened, the questions about my counselor swimming in my mind, and the fact that I'm not getting enough rest, and I wake up in a fog. I'm drifting along, not really thinking, only doing— mainly whatever someone else tells me to. I'm sure Counselor Susan wants me to do what I'm told as a way to distract us from what just happened. Something for her to write down about me instead of thumbing her pen.

My hesitation makes Counselor Susan push her lower lip

forward, bringing more attention to the mole on her upper lip. Her face is naked again, no makeup, not even lip gloss or lipstick. Sometimes I've wondered if the super-slicked-back hair, the perfect bun, her fitted suits—always a dark color, like navy or black—and her heels are her uniform. At the end of the day, does she actually let her hair down, put on a flowy dress or a sweatshirt, and eat ice cream out of the tub on the couch? Is her home as immaculate and bare as this office? Or is this how she wants us to see her so we don't get to know her?

Kind of how she only gets to see me in my detention uniform, my skin dry from crappy products, my hair growing out and frizzy, and bags forming under my eyes. Do I look like I deserve to be here because they've made me look that way? Did Petra? Counselor Susan and the guards are able to go home to their families, pets, and comfy beds, but not us.

"Is something else bothering you, Violetta? Something you'd like to talk about?"

"N-no. Here." I gently toss the notebook onto her desk. It plops right on top of her folder. *My* folder, I guess I should say. All the same stickies are there, with a few new ones.

My counselor goes through the notebook with purpose, as if she knows exactly what page she wants to read. It turns out to be the one with the tables of the dead I was working on this morning, all their names assigned to my Trial dates.

"What is this?"

I try to explain as I turn the fallen chair upright. "They're the people I made up for my Trial. Their names. I wanted to know their names because, um, well." *Am I rambling? It feels like*

I'm rambling. I can't take my eyes off where my counselor's pen lands when she slides it over the paper as she reads. She flips to a previous page. Her lips pucker while reading. Then comes the *click click click* of the pen. One of my feet crushes a pen as I take a seat. More are scattered around my feet and chair. I bend over to pick them up. I lightly place them on the edge of the desk, then take my seat.

"Um, is there a reason we're meeting today?" I say. "Is this about my Trial?" I grip the chair handle so hard the veins pop up on the back of my hands.

"Oh, well." She rests her pen and smiles at me. Her mask is back on. "We're actually here to discuss that too. A decision has been made. I'm happy to say you've passed the Comprehension phase of your Trial, Violetta."

"Are you serious?" I squeal. My fingers don't relax. I need to make sure this moment is real.

She puts down my notebook to open my folder, revealing a green sheet. "I certainly wouldn't lie about this," she says. A switch has been flipped—this is Counselor Susan from the other day, not the one from a few minutes ago.

It's like my grams said: When you're way down, there's always something to lift you up in the nick of time.

"You should be proud of yourself. This is a step forward."

"I am. Believe me, I am." This is the best feeling I've had since coming here, knowing my family saw me make progress. Everything I do is my promise to them.

"Your next Trial is Accountability. You'll be notified when it begins the day before."

And just like that, I'm back to the reality of this place. "So what does that mean for me today?"

"It means you should feel good knowing you're one step closer. I just hope you'll feel comfortable talking more to me."

"You mean about my Trial?"

"About anything."

"Anything?" I think on it, then ask, "Do you judge us for what we did?"

This makes her sit up straighter. "What? Oh, no. Not at all." Counselor Susan picks my notebook back up, and my heart jerks in my chest. "The work I do isn't about passing judgment. My job is to help you become the best possible version of yourself. Despite what people may think."

"Okay."

"Violetta, do you think the adults in your life are here to make everything horrible?"

I shrug, not wanting to admit that, yeah, sometimes I think that. But I know better than to say so. "It's not easy being a parent or a teacher, or"—I point at the frames of her diplomas for psychology and social work—"a counselor. I just think, sometimes, you're allowed to make mistakes that we're not."

"Really?" *Click.* She uses one hand to hold her place in my notebook and goes back to writing something in my folder with the other. "So that's what you think about what's happening?"

Her eagerness for a response shuts me up. A yawn comes at the right time. "I'd like to try and get in a nap, if that's okay."

She stops writing. "Of course. It was nice to talk to you, Violetta. I really hope we can have more talks."

"Yeah, sure," I say, standing up. I hold out my hand for my composition book. This time, my counselor pauses. Her eyes land on a page it seems she's not ready to stop reading, at least not yet. I yawn again to get her attention. Her grin is less real this time, but she returns the notebook.

At the door, I stop, hoping she may be able to answer this question.

"You said my next Trial is Accountability. If I pass, is that it? I mean . . ." I clear my throat, trying to find the right words. I don't want to bring myself down after passing the first Trial. "Will this be the one that gets me home?"

"Violetta"—she says my name slowly—"that all depends on you."

CHAPTER 23

VINCE

Days since the decision: 30

The drill is to run all the athletic teams hard before semis. After successful meets on Friday night, and the surprise drug test announcement, Coach bestowed us a break this Sunday. Pretty sure the day off is more for us to get our heads clear than anything else. I told Mom and Dad I had practice anyway. They said they didn't plan on going anywhere, so I could take my car. My parents have been pretty antsy about what's next for Violetta. Randall's name already came up too frequently for my taste, but these past two days it's almost nonstop about the next Trial. Whenever Mom's home she can be found bent over her laptop at all hours reading more on Trials and parenting "troubled teens," while Dad's been working overtime to cover bills they're late on. As soon as he gets home he goes straight to bed if he's not talking Trials, work, or overdue payments. Home is definitely not the funnest place on Earth at the moment.

Using some birthday money, I managed to get a new phone on the cheap, one with the most basic features on the family plan. I got up the nerve to text Levi. It was a simple one-word message: **Hi.** But it felt like the biggest olive branch. One that got slapped away by an auto-response saying he's working on photos all day—Levi's version of Do Not Disturb. If that wasn't a sign, I don't know what is.

All of the above equals me needing to get out of the house and get some air. At first, I was headed to the 24/7 Mart for my usual junk-food fix—I'd fill up on water too, maybe some nachos, should probably get some protein mix while I'm out. But I end up on the interstate, going eight miles out of Westbridge to the boonies. The part of Queens on the outskirts that's all stone and solitude. The signs take me closer and closer to a place I haven't been since Letta's sentencing.

I've been practicing what I'd say to Letta. Every opening from "How are you?" to "You look okay," to "Do you need anything?" sounds false, considering it's been a month since we last saw each other.

The Piedmont Facility is as awful as it was the first time I came here, for sentencing in March. The string of cars waiting to get in for visiting is a good avenue block long. Each one has to be checked. My car is probably twelfth in line. So I'm left sitting here, tapping the steering wheel, mind racing.

At sentencing, I wanted to get everything over with. All I could focus on was how angry and scared I was. This time, I take in all the surroundings: the seclusion, the guards stationed at every entry point with weapons secured to their hips, and the gleam of the guards' sunglasses even though it's cloudy this time of morning.

City buses have their own lane; one roars by us to a bus-stop sign in the parking lot to let visitors off. My car moves with the others at a snail's pace, inch by inch. By the time I get to the checkpoint, I'm offering my name and my license, and telling them I'm visiting the girls' facility.

There are no niceties, just a wave through to parking. There's sort of a maze of fences bordering the buildings. The sentencing building is closest to the parking lot. It's easier to get in and out without looking directly at how desolate the main facility is. Surrounding the detention center are endless curlicues of barbed wire atop every fence and more under every window or landing where someone has ever thought to jump for freedom. Farther off, on the side of all that brick, concrete, and wire, is a sad excuse for a track and a basketball court, from what I can make out. The middle of the field is patchy and less than half the size of Claremont High's. The court is concrete, with only a rusted baseboard, and a hoop with no net. The inmates wear pants and tops in colors reminding me of smashed peas as they shuffle along. Some are paired with guards with tasers.

I leave my car to join the visitors heading into the lobby for the detention center. Most of the people are older—parents probably. Maybe some are grandparents.

I hold open a glass door for a group of women and children shuffling in behind me. The kids pull at the adults' arms, trying to make a run back outside. Visitor rules are pasted outside the door as we enter, the paper curled at the edges. There are more don'ts than dos, including <u>DON'T</u> WEAR REVEALING CLOTHING—no V-necks or tanks. <u>DON'T</u> WEAR PERFUME, because it may agitate other inmates. <u>DON'T</u> BRING IN ANYTHING THAT ISN'T

REGULATION—nothing sharp. <u>DO</u> BUY FROM THE VENDING MACHINE IN THE WAITING AREA, but don't expect anything fancy. Okay, they didn't say that last part. I'll ask Letta if she needs anything, considering what we can't bring.

The line of people slows as some struggle with bags to be searched and scanned by guards. Pockets are emptied. Jackets are taken off and stuffed into trays. Guards open someone's Tupperware, and a couple bags people brought are tossed into a nearby garbage can. But when it's my turn, it's just little ole me. My ID, car keys, and some cash are all I have to offer.

The place smells like . . . nothing. Nothing at all. Like they can erase people's personal stench *and* their existence. Every wall is painted a dull blue, nothing like the sky on a good day. I stare ahead at what's keeping the people in front of me from moving, even a little. Behind me two little kids jump up and down, asking when they get to go inside. Shushes don't calm them. Do these kids realize where they are, or is this a regular outing for them?

By the time I get to the stack of trays, the guards don't acknowledge me, or anyone, really. Everything they do is on autopilot. Any jingle in pockets raises concern. Anything that doesn't fit in the basket for scanning gets dumped. And so on and so on. It's like going through airport security but there's not the pleasure of a flight to a far-off place on the horizon. Beyond security check there's another group of people waiting to be let into the main detention center. The crowd expands the more guards wave people through the metal detector until there's no longer a line, just a mass of folks waiting for the next barrier.

I hold my hands up like I'm waiting to be scanned at LaGuardia or JFK, but the guard monitoring whether people make the detector beep or not waves me to walk through. He's bulky enough to fill the frame of the detector. The type of guy I wouldn't mind on my lacrosse team but sure as hell wouldn't want to play against.

"No need for that, kid," he says to me.

I walk through expecting a literal green light; instead the light above my head beeps red.

"I'm gonna need to check you first. Protocol," the guard tells me.

I don't give an okay. This dude just twists me around and tugs me to the nearest wall away from the line of visitors waiting to be scanned and head inside. He presses against my back as he directs me to splay my hands against the wall. I'm an X once he kicks my legs open. His hands are on my waist, in my pockets, in my hair.

He turns me back around so fast I nearly trip over my own feet. His face is stone as he tugs my jacket down to my elbows. He squeezes my shoulders, biceps, wrists so hard I can still feel his grip as he makes his way lower, until he's crouching to pinch my thighs and calves.

"Shoes off," he orders.

"There's nothing in my—"

"This is not up for debate, kid. Shoes. *Off.*" Once again he doesn't wait for me to comply; he's already unlacing the sneaker on my left foot.

No no no. Every part of my body gets the jitters. I've resisted the urge to take anything to settle me down. But now, right now, it's more than that tickle of a craving; it's flat-out, nonstop want. A promise to erase this horrible moment and everything tied to it. I hate that being here to see Letta made that want real.

"Kid, you having some kind of attack or something?"

I don't answer fast enough, so he shouts at someone to call a medic.

"N-n-no," I insist. I slap hands away and push through the mob of visitors waiting for screening. Why did I think I could do this?

"I'm fine," I shout. Everyone in the room freezes. My neck snaps toward the exit. I'm rushing through the main door. I'm out of the gray building and under the gray skies. My left sneaker is loose on my foot, so I don't run so much as slide. I'm almost free. My heartbeat starts to slow as soon as I make it to my car.

But when I turn on the ignition, it doesn't kick. So I twist it again. Again. *Again.*

CHAPTER 24

VIOLETTA

Days in detention: 30

〣〣〣〣〣〣

Early April weather is confusing, especially today. It's super sunny, with a chill in the air, not hot but not cold. This time of the month means the Qingming festival is happening. My family is probably at the Flushing cemetery, honoring my grandparents' burial spots. And now my sister is part of that tradition. If I were there, I'd bring printouts of her favorite cartoon characters. We'd burn our paper offerings so she'd have them wherever she is.

My feelings sort of match the weather. I'm really glad to pass my first Trial after three days. That's luckier than anyone I know, Petra and Miles included. The whole time I've been outside, I've been walking circles around the basketball court and the girls tossing the ball against the backboard. I should be skipping happily, dancing, maybe even shouting that I passed. The sun hits me, giving me a boost and reminding me of the beauty of the day. Then I slip into the shade, and I'm submerged in the reality of how washed-out people look when they're dead. I'm reminded of death, my sister, my fault, Petra's struggles, Serena's crime, and that even passing a Trial is not an end for me or my time here.

A new set of girls exit the detention center and spill out around the blocked-off recreation area. Serena's never hard to spot thanks to her height and locs. Eve is right behind her. I jog across the court to meet them. As soon as I reach them, Eve breezes by me, already headed to the stretch of the track farthest away from the concrete court.

"Everything is such a waste of friggin' time here," Eve says. She spits on the ground like it did something to her. This is the first time I'm seeing her this weekend. And it's obvious another "no sentence" trip has her upset.

I haven't gotten to share my good news with her yet. Eve wasn't at lunch or dinner on Saturday. Now I know why. This is the reverse of me and Petra eight days ago: Petra was ecstatic about her news while I sat with my fate. Petra would be the first person I wanted to tell, if I knew where she was. Serena was kind about it. She gave me a high five at dinner last night, then asked the servers for an extra pudding cup for me, and herself. "Celebrating for two!" Serena exclaimed.

Eve's jacket is half-on, half-off. Her arms are in the sleeves, but it hangs off her shoulders. She charges ahead of Serena and me, letting off steam along the way. Her face is so tight with wrinkles on her brow and around her mouth, she looks like she's in physical pain.

I start to ask "Do you—" Serena shakes her head at me not to say anything about passing my Trial.

Eve keeps marching forward. "I don't want to talk about it." So we don't.

Our walks around the track are a gift. We get to breathe in the outdoors. As if we're part of society and allowed to take a break from our worries.

The gravel crunches underneath our detention-issued shoes, which slow me down. I'm hoping for thinner shoes when spring fully sets in. Better yet, I want to be home by then. Most of what we wear isn't fitted to us. Eve's jacket swallows her whole body. Mine is open so I don't overheat.

Eve stays several feet ahead, lost in her thoughts—or, really, her anger. I couldn't blame her after four weeks of no sentence.

After a full lap of complete silence, Eve opens up. "Met with my counselor this morning. She said I'm supposed to really be sentenced next week. The judicator is pushing the victims' parents to make a decision even though the girl is still incapacitated. I'm almost at the point where I say 'screw it' and go upstate. But . . ." Eve swipes at the air as though there's someone in front of her to take this out on. "I don't want to talk about it."

There are a bunch of similarities in how we're treated here. There are differences too. Serena arrived a week after Eve and got a Trial sentence the same day as me. Eve goes week after week, waiting, anticipating something, but nothing happens. It feels cruel. The waiting could be her Trial. Waiting is all we do here. Either to pass or fail, be sentenced or be forgiven. And the whole time, we walk around, shepherded from place to place, doing what we're told, hoping we'll be seen as people again. I wrote something like that in my notebook. I'm not sure if Counselor Susan saw it or not. It was as honest as I could be without having to actually say the words.

Serena tries again, "You *sure* you don't want to talk—"

"No!" Eve shouts back at us, never losing her stride. Hands still in her pockets, Serena shrugs in a *What can you do?* way.

Leaving Eve to her funk, Serena asks if I've heard anything else about Petra after what I mentioned to her at dinner last night. "I cannot believe Petra's family cursed out your counselor and trashed her office!" Her face brightens. "I would've *loved* to see that."

There was another night check after lights-out yesterday. I couldn't go back to sleep, because all I could hear was how angry Petra's mom was. My heart beat faster at the thought of my family coming to the facility if anything happened to me. What if no one came and they packed my things, or whatever was left of me? That's it for Violetta: a notebook, tiny pencils, and a couple bonnets. The only sign I existed in this place.

Eve not only slows down, she fully stops, and Serena almost bumps into her. "Why didn't you tell *me* this?" Eve says, sounding hurt.

"Girl, you've been pissed *all* day and said you didn't want to talk."

"This is different, though! You think I don't care about Petra?"

"You mean gossip," Serena clarifies.

"That too," Eve says without hesitation. "Back to Petra's mom. What happened?"

Serena starts walking, and me and Eve follow. They're an attentive audience, watching every gesture I make to try and reenact the moment. Serena jumps in to liven up the story. Her locs loosen from her ponytail when she jerks her head around and makes movements like she's flipping a table instead of tossing some pens.

Ultimately, Serena takes over, and I chime in with the actual details. "So her mom, I think, basically got all in the lady's face."

"Counselor Susan," I interrupt.

"Yeah, her. *All* in Counselor Susan's face and yells, 'My daughter wouldn't have tried to hurt herself if it weren't for you allowing them to torture her. How did you not know she was upset? What is your job?' And on and on and on. It was real 'Where's your manager?' energy. Right, Letta?"

"She didn't say all of that," I say, squeezing between Serena and Eve as they walk faster. I try to keep up with them and Serena's version of the story. "Her mom did say Counselor Susan should've told the family. She read Petra's notebook entries and told the Bureau."

"Whoa." Eve whistles. "That's messed-up."

"I know. Petra couldn't take it anymore. They had to have known that, right? Our counselors or anyone?"

"It's so hard to talk about it, you know? People outside don't understand. The adults sure don't." Eve kicks at the stones around us. "They try, but they don't."

It's true. Everyone expecting you to talk about being inside is like explaining a whole different world.

"Wish Petra talked more about it. Isn't that what you're supposed to do with your counselors?" Serena says. "My counselor always wants to hear what I'm thinking. It's annoying, but she's the only person who asks me how I'm doing in here."

Eve jerks her coat onto her shoulders so it's not sliding off her as much. She looks ready to storm off again. I don't think I've ever seen her smile in this place. The only time I see her braces is when she eats; most of the time her mouth is pinched as if she's sucking on a sour candy. "Don't get me started. Counselor meetings are guilt central. Nothing but reminders of why you're in here and what you're waiting for."

"Not everyone wants to talk," I say, thinking about my Comprehension Trial. How Miles and I barely spoke.

After a minute, Eve mutters, "Petra seemed happy those last days. Before—"

"She wasn't happy, though, not really. I know I'm not." It's not until I hear one set of crunching feet instead of three that I notice Serena and Eve stopped a few steps behind me. "What?" I ask.

They glance at each other before rushing to my side, squishing me between them. Serena hesitantly asks, "You're not gonna hurt yourself too, are you?"

My response is a little too loud. "No! Of course not!"

"You're sure?" Eve says. She peers at me so closely I see her brown eyes have flecks of green in them.

"I'm okay. I swear I'm okay." That seems to be enough for

them to believe me, so we keep moving. The murmur of electrified fences is our background noise.

I kind of laugh to myself, because it's these moments, brief and far between, that remind me what life is like. How simple it is. I don't feel the chill in the air anymore. I'm building a thin layer of sweat.

We've rounded the track at least five times. This time, I notice the parking lot in the distance. A bunch of cars are parked, and more are lined up waiting to enter. The buses for Piedmont visitors are gone. And the lot is filling up. Visiting hours begin soon. I'm hoping to hear from Callie about LeVaughn or tell her about the new Trial. It'd be easier to talk to her about it than anyone else. She'd have a lot of questions. Who on the outside wouldn't? But at least I know she doesn't think I'm a bad person who deserved to dress dead bodies.

A familiar roar breaks through my thoughts. I search the parking lot for the sound while Eve and Serena move ahead. The way it hacks and spits is the same as Vin's car, an old Ford Dad fixed up for him. I remember Vin trying to hide his disappointment. I caught it even though Mom and Dad didn't. That same night he got the car, I overheard him talking to Janice on the phone. "As much as I bust my ass to make them proud, I can't believe they couldn't pool more money." Janice told him to check himself. "I know," he said, "but come *on*. How much do I have to do to be noticed?" *Noticed?* I thought. I was so surprised to hear those words from him, of all people. Mom, Dad, *everyone* noticed Vin.

"I think that's my brother."

"What makes you think so?" Eve asks.

I'm already sprinting to the fence for a closer look. That's his car! I'm certain of it. Another choke of the engine echoes into the air. I can't believe he's here.

"It's him." I wave them over. "It's him!"

The fence bounces in my grip as Eve and Serena join me. I'm ready to run through the gates separating me from the world and my brother. I want to see his face, his walk—that Vincent strut—before I dash inside to prepare for his visit. My head fills with all the things I'll say. Tears sprout up too.

I haven't seen him since the video, and that wasn't him so much as a vision. But here he is. Tall runner's build, his black hair slicked into a wave, the way he stuffs one hand in his pocket and lets the other arm swing free. He's here. Instead of walking to the gate of entry, though, Vin lifts the hood of his car. His hand jerks in and out before he slams it back down.

"I can't believe it. I can't believe it!" I say.

But he's here. He wouldn't leave. He wouldn't come all this way just to leave.

His car roars awake, and he pulls out of the space and speeds off.

Eve and Serena try to hold me up when I fall to the ground, my fingers still wrapped around the fence, my cries loud enough to be heard by anyone near or far.

CHAPTER 25

VINCE

Days since the decision: 31

Track-and-field semis are in mid-April, meaning next week. It sounds close and far enough away that I don't have to freak out—yet. The team's looking nice, and Byron's been on good behavior today. I settle into the middle with Byron and Cameron. It's good for me to practice in each lane. I'm not a big fan of the outer lane, but I can make it work for whatever heat we're in.

The wind is fierce, so this'll be extra fun to push through. Byron's been complaining about it all day. Right now, it's only the 100-meter and 200-meter dash, then the relays. No hurdles, thank God. Also no recruiters in the stands. It's better that way. I'm still not entirely focused from my—well, let's call it what it is—spinelessness yesterday. As soon as I got home, I took a shower and washed my hair because I hated the feel of that guard's hands. If I couldn't handle that for a minute, let alone a few seconds, how is Letta handling all of it? How does Callie deal with it when she visits?

Cameron and Byron crouch on either side of me. Feet in starting blocks, they're all set.

Pow! We're off. Head down, I keep my arms in full swing. Gotta make sure my gait is steady the first few feet. Then I look up to the finish line. My heart is in my throat, and breathing comes in speedy huffs. I'm the first one past the finish.

"Good time, Vincent!" Coach calls from the sidelines. "But we know you can improve on that."

No trio of friends in the stands today, just Levi crouching to get the perfect shot, with his camera raised to his face. He responded late into the night with a **What's up?** Since I was on a roll with being cowardly, I texted back **Nothing. See you tomorrow,** and left it at that. Janice and Jorge said yearbook's keeping them busy. Levi's making sure to be at every meet to capture what he needs for our year-long memories. So I couldn't avoid him if I tried. The cheers aren't loud today, but I can tell Levi's pumped, even behind the camera; he's on his feet every time I come in first. Problem is, not far from Levi is Ross. Ross adds some clapping with the usual suspects.

These stands will be packed again in ten days, with parents, students, and definitely recruiters. I've counted how many scholarships are offered at the schools with the highest-ranked track teams. In the best case, there's eighteen spots; in the worst case, eight. I'm not sure how many schools will be around next week or past semis, but Coach made sure to let me know—they were coming for the team, sure, but really they were coming for me.

"Break your best time, and you'll be showered in offers. I guarantee it," he'd said to me in the locker room.

Just what I needed to hear.

Byron jogs to the bleachers. I'm wondering if he's meeting a personal fan, one of the guys he said he had a crush on from Algebra II, but it's Ross who approaches.

Crying out loud, Byron. I sprint to catch up. He can't be this dumb, not after the warning we got about testing.

Ross leans over the fencing. A breeze sends a whiff of his body spray my way, something like pine and money. As soon as I get to them, I'm pulling Byron away by the back of his tank.

"Hey, Vince," Ross says, his smile widening from the smirk he had just before.

"Hey. We're leaving. *Now*," I tell Ross. I ask Byron if he's stupid.

"I'm not, but thanks for thinking so highly of me." Byron wrenches himself out of my grip. "It's for after. My nerves. All this. I just need to know I have something for right after."

"You guys want to come by later?" Ross calls. "No pressure."

I do a couple high knees to let him know we're busy keeping our eyes on the prize. I'm not gonna lie, the temptation has been there this whole time. I was hoping Byron had stopped after our standings on Friday, now I'm not so sure. He's sweating up a storm, considering the weather. A 100-meter run isn't a cakewalk, but on a fifty-degree day with wind, it doesn't make sense how much his tank and shorts stick to his body. He's blushing all over, from his biceps to his forehead, and some pimples are glistening.

I pull him close enough that I can whisper in his ear. "Don't let this get to you. You're almost there, man. You're *so close*."

"It's too much. I . . . ." Whatever else he was gonna say is cut off by sniffles. "Dad's been laid off, again. I'm not *trying* to fuck up, but I need something to help."

Ross is still staring at us.

Damn it, Ross. Cinching his leather jacket tight, Ross settles back into his seat. Levi catches my eye, and now he's marching toward Ross. Levi's digital camera bumps against his chest with every step. I wouldn't bet on either of them in a fight. I've rarely seen Levi angry, plus Ross seems the fragile type.

Ross edges away from Levi and then rises to leave. Gotta admit, it's kind of hot to see Levi be forceful. No idea what he said but he's sending some bad juju at Ross's back.

I remember what Levi said the day I crashed on the hurdles. How he found a packet of capsules in between my car seats when we made out one time start of the school year. I'd hoped I was cool in that moment, tucking them away, stuttering my excuse that they were aspirin for headaches. Levi isn't an idiot, though. When he challenged me, I kept up the lie until he didn't ask again. I assumed he believed me.

Ten days. We can do this. I can concentrate on right now, right here. No point in bringing up this other junk from outside. It'll all tumble back to me at home. Next week, I'll break my record.

My personal pep talk gets interrupted by Mr. Nelson, who's hanging beside Coach at the benches. Nelson in his sweater vest, with his parted afro, definitely does not belong in this scene. I become more distracted when Mr. Nelson gestures my way. Did I miss something in debate or history?

Coach's hand is a visor to block the sun's glare, but I can tell he's looking in my direction too. His face is set, and not in the good, stern way that says *Good job, Vince.*

"Vincent!" Coach yells. He points to me, then the ground right in front of him.

I tell Byron to give me a minute.

"We got notice from your parents you'll be out tomorrow," Coach says.

The burning in my body is doused with terror. *Letta.* "What happened?"

Coach tilts his head at Nelson. "Your parents . . . What was it, Jim?"

"They said you won't be in at all tomorrow. Back on Wednesday," Mr. Nelson responds.

"Are you kidding me? This next week is crucial." I turn to Coach. "I can't miss more time if I'm gonna start, right?"

Coach begs off. "Not my call, Vincent. Family says you're not coming in. I can't get involved."

Byron's voice thunders beside me. "This is *bull*! Vince has been out several weeks already! He's okay." Byron whispers, "You're okay to come in, right?"

"Byron, you see I'm fine, don't you?" I gesture at my body like I'm disappearing. "Coach, what's this about?"

Coach and Nelson share a look. I hate when adults share looks.

"Byron, let's give Mr. Nelson and Vincent some space. I want to see your hundred again. Your technique was more off than usual."

Byron doesn't push it. He falls in with Coach back to the starting line.

As soon as they're out of earshot, Mr. Nelson says, "I hate these Trials, Vince. Always have."

Something in me sinks. A new hole widens. I feel it in my gut.

"Your sister's next Trial will be here tomorrow, with safety protocols in place. This is not why I got into teaching, Vince," Nelson says. He glances at my teammates huddled around Coach. Where I should be.

"Between you and me, our system is a crap show. I'm sorry your family is dealing with it. Especially Violetta. She's in my AP class too. Good kid. On my list to recommend for the Student Diplomacy Corps junior year. You and your sister, future ambassadors. You have it in you, you know."

I stand there, sun on my back, unsure what to do or say. Now I'm the one with a layer of sweat. I need to move. I need to run. My left leg shakes. I just got done telling Byron he can make it, but will I?

The sound of the starter pistol cracks the sky, sending my teammates racing, while Mr. Nelson continues his list. The wronged and the wrong. Those who did some jacked-up stuff, or not jacked up enough, as far as Nelson's concerned.

An itch in my thigh becomes a burn, a warmth creeping up my body. But I'm stuck here, listening instead of running. Hearing another adult tell me how they feel instead of checking how *I* feel.

My mind drifts to Ross's offering. The twitch in my leg intensifies, along with a throb behind my eyes. My body calmed down this past month, the worst of my withdrawal having passed, except during that episode at the cemetery. I gotta move. I gotta relax. I gotta take my mind off this.

There's a tug-of-war inside me. A push-pull situation where one half is mad at Letta. I silently simmer at what Mr. Nelson doesn't acknowledge. How people don't realize Viv lives in every corner of our home. I can't escape her in my own room, where I find evidence of my seven-year-old sister when she wasn't supposed to be there. One of her colored pencils was tucked between my computer screen and the dock for my laptop. Sometimes stray hairs of hers are on my clothes, super long and wavy.

"I don't know all the particulars, Vince. And I couldn't tell you even if I did." He whistles, then adds, "Poor girl."

The other half is the part of me that wants Letta back with us. Especially after escaping the place she now calls home and seeing a small portion of what Letta has to deal with.

The thrill of running seeps out of my body into the flattened grass I'm standing on. That rush I got on the track—to be with my teammates, to zone out, to help lead us to victory because everyone *expects* me to—is gone again, because of Violetta. Instead, it's replaced by the thing I'm trying to avoid and the person Levi chased away.

"My sister is dead," I tell Mr. Nelson.

"My God, Vince, why didn't you tell me?" he yells. "No one

said anything to us about that. She was supposed to be here tomorrow."

"Not Letta. Vivian. My baby sister. The one Violetta killed."

Mr. Nelson gets real quiet.

"I'm not saying Letta doesn't deserve to be pitied," I say. "She's been through a lot. Just maybe don't make a party out of it?" My tone drips with sarcasm, the thing Mr. Nelson dislikes the most. The ultimate sign of disrespect. This teeny bit of power I have over a teacher who may know more about my sister's Trials than I do—another thing that pisses me off—reminds me of that slight high I get from Ross's pills.

I swallow it down. I don't need the pills or Ross. I don't. But I've been standing too long. I can already feel the beginning of a knot in my quad.

"That was insensitive of me, Vince. I'm sorry."

Before I return to the starting line, I ask, "Is there anything you *can* tell me? Anything at all?"

"I wish I could. I honestly do. I've seen Trials before. Here and at my previous school." He clears his throat. "All I can say is, the system isn't as balanced as people like to think it is."

CHAPTER 26

VIOLETTA

Days in detention: 32

~~LHT LHT LHT LHT LHT LHT~~ II

My counselor and the guards in this van, and even a couple of the other inmates, have told me Accountability is one of the most popular Trials. This can't be a good thing.

Comprehension was one thing. Not that I could've predicted what it would be. My sister is probably buried by now. And maybe I needed to see that up close. If Miles had been up for talking more, I would've asked him how working at a morgue made sense for him. But if he's still there he's probably helping another inmate by now.

I'm the last girl in the vehicle. What I can't quite wrap my head around is why we are where we are: right in front of Claremont, my high school. I'm wearing the yellow inmate jumpsuit I'm given for Trials, with a long-sleeved white undershirt. The word CORRECTIONS is printed in big block letters on the back. I'm in the same oversized Velcro shoes, my hair is as good as it gets without decent curl product, and Petra's nail polish has chipped.

It's not like the first day of school. No one's outside, no one.

No security or teachers or stragglers. The clock on the dash says it's almost nine o'clock. So that means everyone is in first period.

I'm searching for some kind of trap. Is there a weird gym class I'm going to have to take, or some obstacle course? Do I have to go through the day like a student but in my detention gear, or something else? Only one way to find out.

"We're not going to rush you," the guard in the front seat says. "Sooner it starts, sooner it ends," she adds. "We can go back to holding. But—"

I stop her from saying the rest. "I'm not quitting. I . . . I need a few minutes."

Through the grating the driver's face looks fractured, almost like a photo made of color and wires. The driver fills the silence with what I need to know for this Trial. Unlike Comprehension, I might be facing people I know: classmates, teachers.

I'm here until I quit or they tell me it's over. Just like in detention I'll be escorted through my Trial. If I'm in danger—serious danger—school security is on high alert. The guards in this van will also circle back to come to my aid. My escort will explain the rest.

"Up to speed?" she asks.

"Open the door, please," I say.

"Alrighty, then. Also." She reaches for my wrists. "Gotta get this off." I flinch at the flick of her blade. "Please don't move."

The sky isn't dark, but clouds hide the sun. I catch sight of the gargoyles on the roof of the school's clock tower and shiver.

The wind that just blew past doesn't help. My butt is off the seat, my feet hit the ground, and I'm on the concrete leading to the front steps.

Everything in me is jittery, like my very first day of kindergarten. My arms were wrapped around my mom's neck. Every time she tried to put me down, I bounced back up, wearing her patience and probably the muscles in her neck.

"You have to let *go*, Letta. I can't carry you. You're too big."

I begged her not to leave.

My mom kissed me, carried me into school, and sat with me. She squatted in a child's chair while I focused on drawing, stories, and snacks. At some point, Mom was gone. I didn't see her again until the end of the day during pickup.

She'd laughed, squeezing me into a hug. "Now that wasn't so bad, was it?"

My mom isn't going to carry me inside today. This time, she's one of the people sending me in alone.

I'm through the doors, returning to a place I'd never been sure of myself, a place I felt invisible. I enter halls with no students. Sunshine-yellow lockers border either side of me; to my left are doors and an empty desk where security is supposed to be sitting. And not too far from the entrance is the big sports trophy case that's practically a shrine to Vin and the TRACK CHAMPIONS OF CLAREMONT HIGH. Multiple trophies gleam under the lights along with a framed photo of him holding up his first place medals for his solo efforts and the team relays. I'd been at each race to see my brother break through his competition in nanoseconds.

One full-color photo captures my brother, his hair wind-blown and all over the place. They caught him giving a thumbs-up at the stands, in the direction of where my family sat. I passed by this photo every day my first year. There was no getting away from Vin's legacy; I couldn't outrun it if I tried.

I choke back a sob thinking about him running away from the facility, and me. I'm glad I'm alone so no one can see me. It's almost a relief.

"Violetta?" Assistant Principal Orlando's reflection appears in the glass case. He's in his usual khakis, the best way to recognize him, along with his thick brown beard. He holds both hands in front of him, almost in prayer.

"I'm so sorry I didn't meet you outside. I thought . . . Well, never mind." He glances at his watch and mutters, "We need to get you to the auditorium."

"Auditorium? Is that where my Trial is?"

"It's—"

An announcement comes over the PA. The sound crackles before smoothing out in a steady hum.

"All freshman classes are to meet in the auditorium for a mandatory assembly. Teachers, please direct your students to the auditorium. Freshmen in free period are also expected to attend."

It's like clockwork. The quiet hallways overflow. A trickle of students turns into a full wave. I press myself up against the wall, with my back to the stream, hoping no one notices me, but they'll see my uniform and CORRECTIONS in solid block letters.

People filter past, including a couple of my classmates from history. One gasps an "Are you kidding me?" before AP Orlando warns, "Enough of that." They speed on, disappearing into the stairwell.

"Is that . . . Vince's sister?"

"The girl who killed her sister?"

"Is she even supposed to be here?"

I'm rooted in place. Faces are twisted in disgust or suspicion, jaws are almost on the ground, and mouths in the shape of slanted O's meet me everywhere I turn. There's no hiding.

I don't hear my name—just what I did or who I'm related to. I try to ignore the worst comments, but each one is a cut that exposes more flesh.

I cannot do this. How did I ever think I could do this?

I look down at my jumpsuit, the regulation outfit marking my crime. I know I can't cover my uniform, but it doesn't stop me from wrapping my arms around myself.

I try to block it all out, but every word seeps in. My shoes are heavy, so each step feels huge. Vin and Janice used to joke about freshmen being "fresh meat," and I thought everyone was sizing me up against my brother. I wasn't totally wrong about that. My teachers and my parents kept asking, "Why can't you be more like your brother?" Today is nothing like what I thought my first day of high school would be.

Entering the detention center and orientation had been a similar experience. You want to be invisible, because everything is overwhelming: to be locked up, called a delinquent, judged for what you did, not who you are. The day I arrived at Piedmont, my life became lines and escorts. We were on display for security as our bodies were searched. We were given a bag of toiletries and pointed in the direction of another line, this one to our cells. We marched to our corridors, seeing girls mash their cheeks against barriers to get a peek at the newbies. None of the inmates had commented, though. Not that I could recall.

AP Orlando's voice booms throughout the hallway. "Let's go, everyone! Move it, move it."

AP Orlando gently nudges me to walk with him. "Come on, Violetta."

Pushing through my classmates, I say, "Excuse me." There's a hitch in my voice and my walk.

The stares don't stop, but with the AP by my side, people don't say much, at least not that I hear. Teachers and students are all over the place. At the facility, we're shouted at if we're not directly behind one another. I'd almost forgotten about these small freedoms, the way people jostle one another and joke on their way from place to place, without someone leading the way.

AP Orlando and I make it to the auditorium in record time. People part for us, probably because they don't want to be near me.

"Let's go through the back to the stage," he says.

Stage?

"Mr. Orlando—"

"Violetta, there's a lot to explain in a short amount of time. How much—you know what, the detention staff rarely ever tells you what you need to know in these scenarios."

AP Orlando shuffles by and evades people and doesn't stop. I try to keep up with his pace and his words.

"Okay," he says. "Pardon me! You okay, Violetta?" He briefly looks to see where I am before continuing, "There'll be four separate presentations as part of your Trial. Parents were informed there'd be a detainee on sight so they could remove their children from the building if they felt uncomfortable, even though there are additional security stationed at all exits of the auditorium. Two officers will be backstage, just in case. *No one* is allowed to have their phones. All student devices have been confiscated for the day." We're on the main floor headed for the auditorium. Instead of going through with the crowd, he moves to the side so I can go in front of him down a passageway I've never seen before.

AP Orlando never stops talking as we move or whenever he opens a door for me. "However, this Trial will be recorded by the Bureau of Corrections for them to have on file for your parents to view or if anything happens. *Which it won't!*" he emphasizes. "And we're running a bit late. Again, I'm so sorry I didn't meet you out front. I was in with Bureau people—you know what, never mind."

He ushers me through another door so we can navigate the darkened backstage area. There's a hint of light from the main stage. Ropes for the curtains are tied to hooks, and set pieces in the shape of trees and benches for this year's school musical litter the floor.

Someone with a tool belt that clangs as he walks approaches us.

"All set, Dante. You ready?"

"We will be." AP Orlando taps my shoulder, an indication to move toward the light.

Everything goes in slow motion. I push through thick velvet curtains until I'm on the stage. My eyes gradually adjust to the brightness. The seats are being filled, person by person. I can't say I recognize too many people, since I hadn't been in school a full year. But I do know everyone in the front row.

Maybe I'm the only one, but I've considered Mr. Nelson an intimidating type of guy. Because of his height, his voice, plus the way he holds himself. Ramrod-straight, head held high, an eyebrow slightly quirked, as if he's waiting to be impressed, or disappointed. But the Mr. Nelson sitting up front with his class, my classmates, is deflated. Like he's carrying bad news. The sight causes every part of me to tingle, and I have to take a few steps back. What does he know that I don't?

Callie's is the first face I'm happy to find, until I see the shock written all over it with her mouth open so wide her jaw could also hit the ground. Everyone is ready for something. Their murmurs sound like the buzzing of cicadas. It's just me and AP Orlando on this stage, along with a chair right in the middle.

AP Orlando claps three times, his signal for things to get settled. "Everyone, the sooner we sit, the sooner we start."

More seats fill until only a few rows are left, far in the back.

Callie mouths at me, "What's going on?"

I mouth back, "Trial."

My best friend gasps. She lifts herself out of her seat like she's going to bum-rush the stage. I shake my head. This is what I have to do.

"Violetta, please take a seat."

I do as I'm told. I'm good at that by now. Knees locked together, I sit and wait. The tool guy reappears, and I overhear him say something about a video. I focus on a square of flickering light in the balcony. The projector room is open and in use.

AP Orlando taps the mic three times, another signal. Students settle down almost instantly.

"Good morning, faculty and students. While today's assembly isn't under ideal circumstances, I must convey that we're here first and foremost for our students. This means we impart knowledge as well as values. Today, one of our own returns."

"She's not one of ours!" someone shouts.

The "oohs" that follow ring throughout the auditorium.

"Settle. Down," AP Orlando commands, his voice almost at a growl.

Mr. Nelson shoots up, turning in the direction of the student's comment. "Let him finish!" His voice booms, silencing the student body even faster than AP Orlando could.

Clearing his throat, the AP begins again. "Today, we're here to learn from one's mistakes. We're present in this moment to recognize that bad things happen, in addition to dissecting *why* they happen. We're not here to pass judgment. However, we *are* here to provide understanding and recognize accountability. Violetta Chen-Samuels's wrongs will be addressed today by someone close to her."

"What?" I squeal.

AP Orlando ignores me.

I don't know if anyone can see me sweating, but it's clear the AP is. He wipes his brows between every other sentence. My armpits, palms, and thighs are damp and I'm afraid to move. I'm so tense my neck and shoulder muscles strain.

"We're in this room for Violetta to recognize and be held accountable for an incredibly unfortunate decision, one that had monumental consequences."

Callie's eyes are orbs. She's silently panicking, which isn't helping. Callie's finger points at me, then at her. Translation: *Focus on me.*

"To begin, we'll hear from someone who knew her well during the first few months of the school year. Pascal Thomas, please come out."

The minute I hear Pascal's name, I grab the seat of my chair for dear life to keep myself upright.

Pascal walks out slowly without his usual confidence. He looks like he did the night everything happened: curled hair down to his ears, flawless golden skin, and his dimples showing, not from a smile but from how hard he's swallowing. What makes my stomach clench with guilt is that I want his attention. I want him to look my way, to say things will be okay. There's been no letter from him in a week, and now here he is. About to say . . . something about me, or us.

Pascal faces forward, taking in the auditorium. It's the most serious I've ever seen him, no smirk or swagger or snark. When he speaks, his tone is clear, filling up the whole room, and I almost cry because I've missed his voice.

"I was so upset, like heartbroken, when I heard about Violetta's accident. Everybody here probably knows Violetta and I dated most of this year. What you all don't know is I was with Violetta the night her sister died. And I'm going to tell you about it."

I don't have to steady myself anymore. His words paralyze me.

The house lights have dimmed, and scenes from my dream flash in front of me, like a movie reel playing above the audience. And only Pascal and I are illuminated.

CHAPTER 27

VINCE

Days since the decision: 32

Mom and Dad prepare to watch Letta's latest Trial like it's opening night at the movies. There are *snacks* on the end tables.

At least my parents' wardrobe doesn't look like they just rolled out of bed. Mom's in a floral house dress and Dad's wearing clean jeans and a polo. Dad's kept up shaving, though his grays peek out in his sideburns. Add to that the whole first floor is cleaner. Recycling's taken out and shoes aren't piled on top of each other. Even the living room tables are cleared of magazines, newspapers, and dust to make way for tortilla chips and popcorn. All in all, I call this progress. I'm off to the side in the recliner, where I fit in the dent Dad's made over the years.

Randall's here, complete with his trusty tablet. He explains that this being a Trial in a public setting means more advanced preparation for others' safety, "And the offender's safety too, of course." *Of course.* Parents signed off on kids being present or taking them out for the day, and the Bureau promised my sister would be guarded.

I recall Mr. Nelson saying he's seen Trials before. Turns out the Bureau of Detention Services has this all on lock. At the start of the school day my classmates were searched for phones or any recording devices. Electronics had to be locked in classrooms for the duration of the day until Letta leaves school premises. The moment Randall says "searched," my skin tingles like something's crawling on me. My mind shoots back to the guard at detention, my arms and legs splayed, me not having a lot of choice. Another reason I'm not totally upset I'm at home right now.

"As we always do with Trials or any type of service or public activity, we have to ensure that the incarcerated will not be a threat to others."

Mom scoffs at that last part. "Our daughter isn't a threat."

Randall's response is enough to shut us all up. "If that were the case with any offender, then I'd be out of a job. The TV will—"

Dad cuts him off, his frustration seeping out. "We understand, Randall. Please leave us be."

Thankfully, Randall exits without another word. And we're left with the anxiety of whatever's about to appear on our television. Nowadays the living room isn't a spot to lounge or binge shows or glance at happier times in the string of photos on the fireplace mantel. Photos capture my sisters when they were toddlers in their Easter outfits, us at Rockaway Beach holding up cups of shaved ice. There's Ma and Pa Chen or all of us bunched together in a photo from Aunt Mae and Sonali's wedding. All these decorations of a happier time get ruined when I see the Bureau's seal on the mounted TV screen.

The picture slowly fades in and we see students streaming into, yup, that's my school's auditorium. Scooting up in my seat, I recognize the guy at the podium.

"That's the assistant principal."

"Mr. Orlando?" Mom asks.

What the AP says is vague—vague enough that we don't completely understand what this Trial is. Letta's sitting smack in the middle of the stage, in front of what looks to be a big chunk of the school. Being the center of attention like this is not my sister's thing. That's one of the biggest differences between us.

So I'm forced to ask, "What is this assembly about?"

Aunt Mae's head pops in from the hallway. "Anybody home?"

We practically shoot out of our skin.

Aunt Mae's afro is wrapped up in a translucent purple scarf that almost matches her top. She smiles, showing off her snaggletooth, while holding up a bouquet of yellow and pink flowers she most likely freshly cut from her shop.

"Thought I'd stop by . . . Vince, shouldn't you be at school? You sick?"

Dad's half up, half sitting like he's confused on what to focus on between his sister and the television. "Mae, what are you doing here?"

He tries to block her view of the TV by keeping her out the living room, but she easily glides around him. Aunt Mae's not only packing flowers. Her other hand holds a paper bag of what

I assume is food. Extended family has kept us well fed; without them, we'd only have the delivery Mom keeps ordering.

"I brought some vegetarian lasagna. If you don't want to eat it tonight, you can always freeze it."

Mom rises to take the food. She tries to usher Aunt Mae into the kitchen with her, but my aunt is all questions and she barely budges. Peeking over Dad's shoulder, she asks, "Is this one of those new teen dramas?"

Dad's and my attention snaps back to the TV. What's on the screen now raises my temperature a few degrees. That smug bastard Pascal is at the podium, instead of Assistant Principal Orlando. Actually, he doesn't appear smug. He looks kind of sad. Pascal nods at my sister. That small gesture makes me want to rip the flat-screen off the wall.

"What the hell is Pascal doing there?" I shout at the screen like it'll answer me. If Randall were here, he'd be the one I'm yelling at.

Dad's literally scratching his head at this revelation. "Pascal? *That's* Pascal? Are—are they rounding up Letta's friends from school?"

"Letta?" Aunt Mae asks. Once my sister comes into view, the bouquet hits the floor, and my aunt's next question comes out as a screech. "What *is* this?"

"Letta's Trial," I say, since no one else will.

Giving up, Dad points to the couch. "You may as well sit, Mae."

Mom's back from the kitchen. The minute she sees what we all do, her jaw drops right along with the rest of us. In a daze she scoops up the flowers, clutching them like a baby, and takes a seat next to Dad on the sectional. Dad updates her on the Pascal appearance. The way my parents are reacting to this and last week's Trials reminds me how much is and isn't in their control. We're all experiencing this together with Letta, only we can't be there to help her. *We* did this to her.

Pascal being onstage makes no sense. Until he says, "What you all don't know is I was with Violetta the night her sister died."

Oh shit.

Dad rubs his face like he wants to tear skin, and Mom covers her mouth, waiting for the worst. Meanwhile, Aunt Mae evil-eyes them both.

What he's about to say is going to be damning for Letta. But will it also be for us? Letta was grounded after giving attitude and missing curfews. It was supposed to be just her and Viv. Definitely no dudes. Which means Pascal may be even more responsible than I thought.

The camera zooms out enough for us to see them both, Letta's every move observable while Pascal speaks about her. I don't know if I can keep listening to this.

"The last night I saw Violetta, she wanted to have sex. Was pretty adamant about it, in fact." As the gasps of students echo from the TV, I swallow my own shock.

Dad keeps molding his face, and Mom slaps the flowers onto the coffee table so hard pastel petals fall to the rug. My parents slide in closer, leaning forward, a mirror image of each other.

He continues. Pascal's not reading from a paper or prompter.

It's like he's focusing on a point. That's how Mr. Nelson instructs us in debate. If we have stage fright or can't handle all eyes on us, find something—a bug on the wall or the top of someone's head—and focus.

"She took me upstairs, and she had some wine. A whole thing was planned. I mean, *she* invited *me* over. Her little sister was downstairs." He rolls his shoulders. "She asked her to stay put so we could, ahem."

Mom's off the couch in a second, ready to stab someone with the stems of the bouquet. "She *what?*"

"Annie . . ." Dad tries, and fails, to grab her before she stalks to the screen.

"This is not the daughter we raised. That is not *my* daughter, Albert!"

"Last time I checked, we didn't get to choose our children," Aunt Mae offers.

"Oh, shut up, Mae!" Outside of the night we came home from the hospital, this is the angriest I've heard Mom. "Why are you still here anyway? To butt in as usual? You want to blame us too?"

"No one's blaming anyone!" Aunt Mae says. "She's a teenager. Teenagers have sex. Vince has probably had sex."

Please, God, don't bring me into this.

"We're talking about Violetta." Mom looks like she wants to erupt, complete with cheeks and forehead flushing. Every part of her vibrates and she clutches Aunt Mae's bouquet so hard more petals fall like confetti. This is one of the times I'm thankful Letta isn't here to feel anyone's wrath. Behind bars almost sounds safer at the moment. "Violetta left our baby girl downstairs, *alone*, to get drunk and have sex with that boy-band-looking kid. She was already punished, then she ignored our direct orders and look what happened!"

The Letta in the hospital after the accident was just as remorseful as the Letta in her video plea. Every sob was accompanied by an "ow," because of the bruising from the crash. Her sorrys were wet and gargled, but she never mentioned anything, or anyone else, beyond her regret that night. I held her hand gently because she looked so fragile in her hospital bed. I was scared I'd break bones. But I was so pissed at her. Even then, smelling the bitterness of her breath, I should've known Pascal was involved because of those two other times I caught her tipsy.

"Did you set this up for her?" Aunt Mae coming with the tough questions.

"Christ. Everyone be quiet and sit down!" Dad thunders. "This is the first we're seeing a full Trial or hearing about Pascal. This is news to us and we need to see this moment through." Dad turns to his sister, who, from her vantage point, is looking down at all of us. The rest of us are watching Letta while she listens to Pascal. "Mae, if you want to stay, you will have to shush, *please*."

With a huff, Mom stalks back to the couch and plops down next to Dad.

My butt is on the edge of my seat. Letta looks as frozen as

she did at sentencing. She's clutching the seat of her chair, staring forward, but every so often her head turns, just a little, at something Pascal says.

Pascal continues his side of the story: "Violetta is a very pretty girl. Not always confident, but she could be fun. Was up for anything."

"Including drunk driving and murder?" someone shouts from the audience.

I wasn't cringing before, but I am now.

Pascal stumbles at the comment, glances at my sister, who flinches. If that's what they're saying about her, *to* her, while she's there, what *aren't* we hearing?

"I was asked to speak here today. I don't know, maybe as a warning for others. But mostly to say that I regret that night. I don't regret our laughs or our time together. Not most of it. But seeing the result . . . was too big a price to pay. For anyone. Thanks for listening." That last part, he says to my sister. Pascal hustles off the stage so fast you'd think he was expecting stones to be thrown his way.

AP Orlando returns to the podium, coughing into his fist like he can't find the right thing to say after Pascal's speech. He finally manages, "Next, we'll show a larger presentation on the pitfalls of drinking and driving. After the video, you'll head to your next-period class. We'll need you to clear out soon so the sophomore group can come in."

Whoa, this is a whole PSA situation, and Letta is the prime example. This is *not* going to get better, only worse.

CHAPTER 28

VIOLETTA

Days in detention: 32

~~IIII~~ ~~IIII~~ ~~IIII~~ ~~IIII~~ ~~IIII~~ ~~IIII~~ II

Students put on their backpacks as soon as the bell rings, sending them to their next class. Their seats flip and their footsteps thunder through the auditorium as they exit. Freshmen out, sophomores in. Juniors after that. Then the seniors.

Pascal's words pierce through me. Not what he said to everyone here—well, not everything. What he said to me, in private, that night.

You want me, right?

I should've never messed with a freshman.

Of course he wouldn't admit he was the one pushing for sex or that he usually encouraged drinking alcohol. Maybe part of the Accountability Trial is to paint me in a desperate light: *Here's Violetta Chen-Samuels. She's the type of girl to do whatever a guy wants and look how that turned out.*

The video they played after Pascal spoke was pretty generic. Nothing specific to me, but enough to make anyone view me as a prime example of what not to do. Photos of people, including children smiling and cheerful, until it's revealed they'd been killed by drunk driving. Images appeared of cars with crumpled fronts and hanging bumpers post-accident. An explanation of how drinking messes up your insides; they made sure to show pictures of a liver before and after alcohol. I'm a cautionary tale, complete with my inmate uniform showing I'm guilty of all of it.

"Hey!" Callie's at the tip of the stage.

AP Orlando is off directing school security to make sure everyone goes where they're supposed to. I'm unsure if I could or should move, so I stay put and only offer a weak "Hi."

"That was kinda awful."

"Kinda?"

Callie makes a pillow out of her arms on the edge of the stage. She blows some brown and emerald strands out of her eyes. "Okay," she admits, "I won't lie to you. That was pretty messed-up."

"Yup." Every time I fold or unfold my arms, I can feel and hear the wetness in my armpits. I'll probably be completely drenched by the time the seniors get here.

The sophomores enter, some laugh, others point at me. All this attention.

The last time I was on this stage, Callie was with me, and so were five other freshmen. "Honor roll!" AP Orlando had announced to applause. Each grade's recipients went up to receive our certificates. My brother was in the audience. When it was the juniors' turn, the cheers were loudest for Vin. He'd made honor roll three years in a row, without fail. When we first sat down for that assembly and AP Orlando stepped to the podium, I was nervous, wondering if I'd made it. I'd been turning in assignments that weren't my best. The time I got a 70 on a chemistry test, I almost fainted at my desk. But my chem teacher gave me extra credit. She said, "I'll allow it this one time, for Vince's sister." Being Vince the Great's sister let me slip a little, so I took advantage when I could. The first few months of school, I was up later than usual, texting with Pascal. Him asking me to show him sexy photos, and me hesitating each time.

C'mon Letta. Give me something to think about.

I typed what I thought might sound hot. As soon as I did, I tapped the back button until those words vanished. **I want you. I want to kiss you. We could cuddle.**

Cuddle? he replied with a smirk emoji. **Are you naked when we cuddle? Could I see?**

Naked? Did he want photos of my butt out, lips pouty, back arched? I tried on each pose like a new outfit, and none fit or felt right, just like the bra I bought for our special night. It was too much, left me too exposed. But I tried, I said that, yes, I'd be naked. But I couldn't send a photo. Maybe another time?

Promise? he asked.

Yeah! I told him, thinking maybe that'd be enough. Immediately after, I said I had to go to bed, that it was getting late.

I'll be dreaming about you.

None of that was said to the freshman class. Pascal rushed through his speech and conveniently left out how he pressured me. All of what he said is more ammo for my own punishment. And all I can do is sit with the sting of what everyone has to say about me.

"Letta!" Callie calls.

"Sorry, what?"

"I'll be in the back."

"You don't have to stay. It'll probably get worse with people who don't know me."

"I'm not here to watch people be mean to you, Letta. I'm here *for* you. So you know someone out there cares."

I force a smile when all I want to do is cry.

The tap of the mic startles me. Callie blows me a kiss before fading into the crowd.

I adjust my top and, mentally, adjust myself for the latest round of my Trial.

AP Orlando repeats the exact same thing he said to the freshman class for the sophomores. It's not as quiet this time. Pockets of discussion break out. I don't need to hear what they're saying to know what they're saying.

I feel it before it lands. A can makes a perfect arch into the air, floating out of a sea of darkness. It's open, and the liquid inside trickles out before fully splashing, right near my feet onstage. The bottom half of my pants are sprayed with soda, grape and sticky-sweet. It leaves a strong smell of fake juice, a smell I've sort of missed. The can swivels toward my shoes, oozing more soda until there's a fizzy purple pool in front of me. Oohs and laughter come from the audience. I don't move. I just hope I won't smell like soda for the rest of the day.

"Who threw that?" AP Orlando screams. He's in front of the podium, searching into the shadows for the culprit. "Security!"

"You deserve worse!" is screamed back. Maybe that's the

thrower, or someone else. I knew they were thinking the worst of me.

I decide to focus on the projector room. School security pound their boots up and down the aisles until I hear a kid saying, "I didn't want to listen to this stupid assembly anyway." The kid is pushed through the doors.

AP Orlando demands quiet and respect. "There'll be no throwing of *anything*. Do you all understand me?" His voice is the loudest I've ever heard it. Usually, he's the nice and gentle administrator. The one who remembers almost every student's name and encourages us to visit his office. Now, he's speaking through clenched teeth. "The next thing thrown means suspension. No questions asked. Do you hear me!"

He gets mumbles in response.

"I *said*, do you *hear* me?"

"Yes," they chorus.

AP Orlando says someone will come in after to clean up the soda. He says it more to me than to the students watching. "I'm sorry, Violetta. You didn't deserve that."

Didn't I?

After more warnings from the AP, Pascal returns, this time refusing to give me a glance. He moves swiftly to the podium, again without the slight swagger and confidence in his walk. His words are similar, but this time he adds that I seemed "smart but not clear on how high school works." That got some laughs I didn't appreciate. The whole time he speaks, the soda puddle in front of me grows as liquid leaks slowly from the can. Pascal's story is all about my desire to get us drunk. He still doesn't mention any of the small pressures building from September through February. He doesn't mention tilting wine to my lips to drink that night and other nights.

What he says right before he leaves sets off a burn in my stomach that heats up my whole body: "The thoughtless actions of that night were too big a price to pay."

I've been sitting here taking a pummeling, everyone speaking about me but not *to* me. Before AP Orlando can take back the mic, I ask, "If this is about accountability, do I get to speak for myself?"

"I, uh, oh . . . Um." AP Orlando's head twists, from the audience to me to whoever is or isn't behind the curtains.

"Yeah! I wanna hear from her!"

I try to hide the smile forming at hearing Callie's support.

"What's the party girl got to say?" someone says, to a smattering of chuckles.

AP Orlando shields his eyes. Maybe he's searching for backup or a signal for what to do next. I'm not sure. With the projector room all lit up, I'm wondering who would have asked Pascal to be part of this Trial. Is someone in there instructing him or orchestrating this whole day? My family is the one who chose this Trial for me. I'm accountable to them, not Pascal, not the people sitting here watching me at this very moment. If Comprehension was about me understanding the end result, then Accountability could be about me standing up for myself. Next group is juniors and my brother will be in the audience. If he couldn't face me this weekend, at least he can hear me in person and not on a screen.

Approaching the podium, I wipe my face, then rub my hands on my pants. The dampness leaves a streak on my thighs. Maybe I'm the only one who hears my shoes squeak thanks to the soda. The assistant principal shuffles off to the side to give me space, but he doesn't leave the stage.

"This whole school is going to hear a version of what happened the night my sister died. And I'm not saying what Pascal is saying is a total lie. But it's not the *whole* truth."

"Go, Letta!"

"*Quiet*," a teacher tells Callie.

"Yes, Pascal and I were dating. And, yes, we were . . . planning to hook up that night. I wanted to, or I thought I did. But I couldn't. And he knew I couldn't." An itch starts in my elbow that I need to scratch. It doesn't go away, but I don't stop speaking. If anything, the itch gives me something to focus on so I can say what I need to. "Before that night, he asked me to . . . you know. I wasn't ready yet. I want to be clear: I don't regret not being ready."

"Your body, your choice, girl!" someone says.

It's awkward, and I'm unsure why I do it, but a hold up a fist in solidarity, since I can't see who spoke.

"I regret *so, so* many things. Including dating Pascal and inviting him over that night." This incites some unexpected laughter. "I regret drinking. I so regret the driving after drinking. I regret thinking I needed to be someone I wasn't. And"—I choke on the next words, because I can't say it enough, and I'm not sure if saying it right now, in front of the whole sophomore class, will make a difference—"I *really, really* regret my sister being in the car with me. That was not supposed to happen. Everything that night, God, a month ago now, was *not* supposed to happen."

I'm super glad I can't see anyone in the darkened auditorium.

"If I'm an example of what not to do, then I guess it's about being honest about my regrets." I have nothing else left in me, or to say. The itch is gone. Talking in front of people this long is a triumph. "Um, that's all," I add before I retreat backstage.

AP Orlando, Pascal, and an officer meet me behind the curtain.

"Am I in trouble?"

For the first time today, the assistant principal offers me a real smile. "Violetta, that was a very brave thing to do. I hope your parents get to see what we did today," he says. AP Orlando gives me a wink before he heads toward the light of the stage. We overhear him introduce the anti-drunk-driving video.

Pascal's eyes follow AP Orlando. His cool is deflated. The flutter of want I had seeing him was washed away the minute he lied about me onstage. His skin isn't as bright and his curls look crusty, not soft.

Pascal glances at the officer nearby and lowers his voice. "Letta, we should talk about this. Did you get my let—"

"*Talk?* Are you— You humiliated me up there! Did you enjoy that?" Same as in my dream, he gets cloudy. But I'm not drunk. My mind isn't fuzzy. I am crying. My head's pounding, and I smell like sugar.

"Violetta . . . I didn't ask to be part of this. If you let me explain . . ."

Every time I've dreamed of the night that changed everything, I wished I could push *him* away instead of the other way around. Now, I want to release all the pain of what they're making me sit through today. When you're in a cell alone, you don't get to think about anything else except for what you have to do to get through the day. No one hesitates to remind you of the choices you've made and what's been taken from you. For two more periods, I have to sit and be judged—if I'm lucky, silently—by my peers. And here's Pascal, the same person he was the last time I saw him.

As upset as I am, I can't blame him for my sister's death. This is my Trial, not his.

"You come near me again, I will kick you in the place it'll hurt most. Do you understand?" I don't give him the opportunity to respond. Instead, I walk back to the chair onstage and my fate for the rest of the day.

CHAPTER 29

VINCE

Days since the decision: 32

Letta went from being a statue to speaking for herself for the next three classes. *Like a boss.* Each time Pascal came out—*Pascal,* I crack my knuckles at the thought of him—Letta followed up to claim her part in it *and* to name him for the douchebag he is. Pascal did sound a bit different after Letta mentioned he pressured her. He had to take on *some* responsibility.

As grateful as I was for Callie staying to pump Letta up each period, I wish I could've protected my sister. In a never-ending tense silence, my parents, Aunt Mae, and I watched Letta finish speaking, then get guided out of the auditorium by AP Orlando.

Once Letta was back in the van, our screen went dark. We stayed put. All of us unsure how to begin processing what had happened. Each of us probably saw something different, but if the goal was for Letta to admit what she did while also making sure that douchebag didn't totally gaslight her, I think she passed with flying colors.

The bowls are empty, meaning the snacks are all gone—

hello, panic-eating on my part—and Randall has returned, with his tablet tucked under his arm like a weapon. At first, he seems surprised to see Aunt Mae here. But the evil-eye she sent Mom and Dad earlier is no match for the *Who the hell are you?* energy she gives Randall now.

"This is a matter for the family," Randall starts and is immediately shushed.

Aunt Mae crosses her legs, shifts her whole body, because she is not one to be trifled with, and declares, "I *am* family."

"All right, then. Mr. and Mrs. Chen-Samuels, do you have a verdict?" His casual air does not match our intensity. I try to relax my face after biting my lips dry. It was hard seeing people Letta knows, people *I* know, observe her like some sort of experiment in humiliation. We heard at least one person each period call her a murderer or a drunk or a shitty sister.

"That. Was. Horrible," Dad says. He's a collapsed lump on the sectional to the point his round face looks flattened too.

"Did it garner the response you feel would allow you to pass her?" our judicator asks. "Or will there be another Accountability Trial to set up?"

"Randall, we'll need to think on this . . . after everything we've heard." Mom scratches at her hair so hard it's like she wants to rid herself of the worst parts of what we saw.

"The day of the accident we came home and saw all the mess, I was enraged but— *Oh my goodness* and she asked me for money to buy clothes, was this all for . . ." She keeps stopping herself mid-sentence as another possible scenario enters her mind that she needs to vocalize.

Aunt Mae can't get a word in. By now Dad's plain given up. I'm watching all this as helplessly as I watched Letta's Trial.

Mom morphs from a volcano to a tornado gathering every fact from the Trial and what's happened this past month in her path. "I cannot believe"—is a whisper immediately transformed to a fireball meant to ignite the room—"that rico-suave-looking boy pressured her into sex! My daughter is an honor roll student who should never let a boy get in the way of common sense."

My mom has obviously not been a teenager in a very long time.

"Annie," Dad begins.

Mom's on a roll, though, complete with pacing. As short as my mom is at five feet, she's made our living room her own track with how many times she circles Randall. He's basically part of the background now, as Mom rattles off a list of what Letta is and what she isn't.

It's Randall who ultimately gets things back on track, I think. "There was a statute established for this Trial, Mrs. Chen-Samuels."

"Meaning?" Aunt Mae asks my question for me.

"Meaning this Trial is about accountability for one's actions. The offender was held accountable, and she also decided to speak to what occurred. The point of Mr. Pascal Thomas being part of this Trial was for a full account of what took place to be laid bare. It's evident everyone present was not aware of the extent of what happened before the accident." Trusty tablet back in hand, Randall gets to swiping. His eyes scan what's in front of him. "Your daughter had written about Mr. Thomas and their relationship in a journal provided to her counselor. Let's see . . ." More swiping. "This journal has been a suitable frame of reference for the counselor to keep track. And . . ." He looks up at us with some assurance. "This has helped us to prepare the Trials you've designated."

Mom's face has gotten paler. Her lips have been mashed up in confusion and calculation the whole time Randall's been speaking. Dad remains a deflated beanbag on the sectional, his whole body folded in on itself. Aunt Mae searches all our faces for signs of life. To be honest, we're all empty and pissed and on edge. I'm still processing that I have to face people tomorrow at school, including Pascal.

"We need to think about this, Randall." Dad's voice is low but steady, a welcome surprise. "Can you please give us some space?"

"Of course. We can revisit this conversation tomorrow or another day." Randall starts to leave but he halts, keeping his body bone straight, and adds, "If you're unhappy or uncertain about how she did today, may I remind you of the option for a third type of Trial stipulated. You mentioned Endurance. Endurance Trials tend to run longer than others, depending on the setup."

What I love most about Aunt Mae is how she gives off serious *We're done here* vibes to people, particularly people she doesn't like. She's escorting Randall out like he doesn't know the way. It'd be awesome if she could also give him a swift kick for good measure. We're polite people, though.

"Okay, so that accountant-looking guy is not someone I

would trust with the fate of my child," she declares when he's gone.

Dad sighs his sister's name. "Come on. Not now."

"Not *now?*" Hands on hips. *Oh, it's happening.* "I just saw my niece slut-shamed at school by some skeezy teenage boy, whom I never liked, by the way."

Mom agrees. "Neither did we, Mae."

"But you let her date him."

"*Let?* We're not about to hog-tie our children to a . . . I don't know what." Mom snaps her fingers for some help.

"Chair?" I offer.

"Thank you, Vince."

Aunt Mae slides in right next to my dad. He's in the middle of a high-emotions sandwich with his sister and Mom on either side.

What keeps rolling through my mind is, *I should've been there.* I should've been there to protect Letta from Pascal before and today.

"Far be it from me to act holier than thou as a stepmother to two young girls. I know this is different. We're not talking about a four- and six-year-old. We're talking about Violetta. That"—we all stare at the blank flat-screen—"was not discipline."

Dad's grunting as he gets up. Checking the bowls on either side of the couch for nacho crumbs or stray caramel corn, he says, "Who said the Trials were about discipline? It's rehabilitation. This isn't a spanking or a time-out. This is life-and-death stakes now, Mae. We can't make light of that."

If you look super close, you'll see everything Dad and Aunt Mae share. Stubbornness is the most obvious trait, but it's also their sharp noses, the patch of moles near their right ears, even the deep wrinkle between their eyebrows when they're thinking real hard, like they are now. Aunt Mae is older. She loves to tell stories about how she kicked Dad's butt, then kicked anyone else's butt who tried to mess with him. She may want to kick all our butts right now. If that's the case, she doesn't show it. She takes Dad's hand. Her thumb rubs his knuckle, like a secret language between siblings. I don't think I ever had that secret language with Viv—or Letta, for that matter. And these days, it's like I'm an only child—one sister in a cell of the state's making and the other underground.

"Mae, we're trying here. Trying and it feels like we're failing. But for now, I'm going to ask you to leave. We'll see you later."

"Al—"

"Please, Mae. I keep having to hear from everyone and anyone what they think my wife and I should do for our daughter. There's too many pots in the kitchen. And today was just . . . too damn much."

"Cooks in the kitchen," Mom corrects.

"Yeah, that works too," Dad admits, rubbing the back of his neck.

I expect Aunt Mae to have her rebuttal at the ready. Surprisingly, she gathers herself to leave. She hugs us all and gives me a kiss on the head. "You okay, Vince?" I'm surprised by the question. It's been weeks since Mom and Dad have asked.

"I'm okay."

"You're lying," she says. "This is why I bring you pound cake."

"Cake is always welcome, no matter what's going on."

She gives me another kiss, and off she goes. It's just the three of us again—or, really, my parents, with me as an afterthought.

Mom wraps Dad's arms around her, making a blanket out of him.

"I wish she'd told us all this. I wish . . ." Mom says. "I know you want to see her succeed too."

Dad tightens his hold on her and they're both all tears when he says into her hair, "We're going to get this family back together, you hear me?" I'm sure for Dad his promise sounds like one he can keep.

At this point, though, I think we all know this isn't true.

CHAPTER 30
VIOLETTA

Days in detention: 32

~~卌 卌 卌 卌 卌 卌~~ II

As soon as I'm back from my Trial, I ask to go to the bathroom for a shower. The guard's kind enough not to shout for me after fifteen minutes pass. This is as close as it gets to washing away my Accountability Trial. With Comprehension, it was the smell, the acidic scent I swore I carried with me each day I left the morgue. Today, it's the soda staining my pants, yes. But mostly, it's the looks, it's what was said, it's knowing deep down what people thought.

The one thing I'm thankful for is that my Trial wasn't a full school day at Claremont. I got to leave in the middle of sixth period. Only a few students hanging out in the parking lot saw guards put the zip ties back on me before I got in the van. Some stared as the van drove away. One girl waved. Another gave me the finger.

My fingertips are pruned; the water's now lukewarm, veering toward cold. The coral nail polish is barely visible on my nails. I exit the bathroom feeling a little better, a little more human. My clean jumpsuit sticks to me in a different way now.

Since I missed lunch, the guard brings a tray to my cell so

I can scarf food down before mandatory afternoon classes. I barely pay attention to what we're being taught. The whole time my teacher talks, I'm back in the halls of Claremont—the students are probably at the tail end of their day right now. Callie and I would be in AP English Literature, trying to figure out the symbolism in whatever book we were assigned. Here in detention, at these cruddy plastic tables and chairs, the girls and I write in worn workbooks. The math here is something I've already learned. I'm able to speed through it while other girls keep working, leaving me more time to think about my day and what got me here.

Once class ends, guards take us back to our corridors to settle in before dinner. When we pass the mailroom, I ask if I can check if I received anything. I'm probably punishing myself again, but it's been a few days since Aunt Mae's last letter. Maybe she sent me more conditioner or, better yet, shea butter.

"Chen-Samuels. Inmate number 965829," I tell the woman behind the grate. In return, she slides me three letters, envelopes cleanly cut open.

I'll wait until I get to my cell to read them. I see one is from Gram and Gramps. Another is from Pascal—the first one I've received in over a week. Part of me wants to rip his to shreds, then flush it down the toilet, but I'm curious after today. The third letter's return address is a PO box in Brooklyn, no name. *Weird.* Most of my family is in Queens; some live out of the state.

Guess I'll have to open it and see. But the moment we step

back into my dorm, the other guard at the security station informs me I have a visitor.

The day of a Trial?

Vin comes to mind. So does him speeding away from the facility. Maybe it's him. Maybe he was at school during my Trial and needs to see me. The thought locks me in place.

"If you don't want to see the visitor, I can tell them so," the guard says.

"N-no, I'll see them," I say, stuffing the unknown sender's letter back in the envelope.

Callie is all smiles when I enter visitation. I'm mostly relieved and only a little disappointed it's her. As much as I keep wanting my family to visit, seeing Callie waiting for me is the more welcome option. The room is quiet this Tuesday. It's only us, the guards, the half-full vending machines, plus a bunch of empty tables and chairs.

Callie digs into her shirt like she has an itch. She dares the nearest guard to look while she adjusts her bra straps. He averts his eyes. When she's done, she cups her palms under the table. Something light lands in my lap.

"Told you I'd come through with some moisturizer action," she whispers.

I whisper, "Thanks," as I hold a small plastic tube. Such a tiny thing from the outside makes me feel a little less like a prisoner. "You could've mailed it. Less risky."

"I wanted to see you! I'm sorry it's been a while. It's midterms. My parents want me to prep for PSATs, which is dumb, because they're a *practice* test. We're getting ready for the spring concerts and I moved up a chair in my section. Mom's been driving me around so much already it's hard to ask her to come out here too." She blows upward so her bangs fly a little. "Anyhoo, how are you after today?"

"How do I look?" I ask.

"You want me to lie to you?"

"Not this time."

I count to ten and tuck the moisturizer into an envelope so a guard won't see it. If they did, they might not let Callie visit again. I can't have my one lifeline taken away from me.

Finally, she says, "Really tired. Beat-down tired. Which makes sense."

"Yeah."

"You did great, though! When you said Pascal was a jerk, I was practically screaming, until the teachers told me not to."

Three periods in a row, Callie was told to pipe down by a teacher, a new one each time. It warmed me up knowing she was there. By the time the juniors arrived, I was scared Vin was in the audience too, not that I could see him. But other voices joined Callie's. Janice, warning someone to shut their mouth after I was called a murderer. Levi, saying he was proud of me. But none of them were my brother.

"Do you know if Vin saw?"

My best friend plays with the cross on her bracelet. That's a no.

"I don't think he was at school today. But Pascal was pretty much laughed at. Not by everyone, though." She rolls her eyes. "Monique and his friends stood by him."

I plop Pascal's letter on the table. "Look what I got."

My best friend doesn't wait for me to respond. She's already unfolding it.

"'Dear Jolie.'" She sticks out her tongue. "'Writing to say "hey" and also I guess to apologize.'" Callie is gagging now. "He's the worst."

"Callie, focus."

"Sorry. *Ahem.* 'I don't know what to say exactly. I hope you'll understand why I'm doing what I'm about to do. I hope you get this letter before your Trial. Maybe you won't. I don't know how mail works there. You and my grandparents in Montreal are the only people I ever write to.'"

Callie wrinkles her nose as she reads the next line. "'The Corrections people asked me to be part of your Trial—' Oh no . . ."

"Repeat that."

"Oh no . . ."

"What Pascal wrote, Callie," I snap.

She lowers her voice. "Don't bite my head off, Letta."

"Sorry, just . . ." Instead of waiting for her to go on, I snatch the letter from Callie.

Dear Jolie:

    Writing to say "hey" and also I guess to apologize.

    I don't know what to say exactly. I hope you'll

understand why I'm doing what I'm about to do. I hope you get this letter before your Trial. Maybe you won't. I don't know how mail works there. You and my grandparents in Montreal are the only people I ever write to.

Here it is: The Corrections people asked me to be part of your Trial. Some guy came to my house. He and my parents were waiting for me one day. I was cornered, Letta. I didn't want to. The guy—he could use some serious sun—said you told them I was with you the night of the accident. He said you told your counselor inside you had regrets or something like that with me. There was other stuff too. I don't want to make this a long letter, because my mom says my handwriting is terrible. Point is, we'll see each other soon. Just know I'm sorry about what I'll say. I'm already on thin ice with my parents. They can't know I was drinking too. I figure you're already inside, right? So why should the two of us get in trouble?

Also, I'm sorry about everything else. From the way they made it sound, I was pushy. You didn't have to do anything we did, you know. You always seemed like you were having fun. And you never said anything. Why didn't you say anything?

I have to stop reading.

Why didn't you say anything? Why should the two of us get in trouble? You told your counselor inside. I was cornered, Letta. I didn't want to. This is basically what he said onstage in front of class after class. Why didn't I say anything about the alcohol burning down my throat? Why didn't I go with Callie when she asked if I was ready to leave a party while I sat on Pascal's lap? I stayed, saying I was too tired to move, but really I was afraid I'd stumble, showing I wasn't ready to handle the beer I'd drunk.

Whenever I went shopping with my mom, I tried on jeans, tops, bras, to see what would fit. That's how my first year of high school felt. Me being with Pascal was me seeing if our relationship was a fit, if any of it made sense. The night everything changed, I chased him because I wanted us to fit, even when we didn't.

My forehead lands on the table. The moment of coolness from skin meeting metal doesn't relax me. I don't know how to answer his questions. But, more importantly, I want to know why Counselor Susan told him and the Bureau what I said. Does that mean my parents know what I wrote down too? From what Petra's family said, Counselor Susan didn't tell them about Petra's hard days, so maybe she didn't tell my family about mine. But do they know now? Did they see what happened to me? Was that what they planned?

My breath moistens the tabletop when I tell Callie I'm exhausted.

There's a soft pat to my head. Kind of a *There, there* gesture. "I'm so sorry, Letta," she says.

It's started to rain outside, not too heavy. When it does get heavy, the rain pounds on everything metal, creating its own kind of thunder. Callie and I sit quietly for a while until she can't take it anymore. She tells me about the rest of the day. How more people were on my side than those who weren't.

"Or maybe they kept their mouths shut," she adds, "because they know I'd punch them in the face."

"You wouldn't punch them," I tell her. Callie's a band geek. She wouldn't know how to throw a punch. Then again, she may have a mean arm with her violin.

"It's true. I'm a lover, not a fighter. But I'd try. I got your back. Next time I see Pascal, I'm gonna make him hurt."

"I told him I would kick him in the balls if he ever talked to me again."

This earns me a slow clap from my best friend. "Good, he deserves it. Jerk. Jerkwad. Mayor of Jerktown."

"I get it."

"I'm not done. Jerkceratops. Jerk McJerkerton."

"Thanks."

"Letta, I was just as scared as you were about starting high school. And if someone I really liked was treating me nice, I probably would've done whatever to keep him treating me like that. My mom says we learn our worth and then we make better choices. That's why she wanted to make sure I was there for you today. She could've taken me out but she didn't."

Tears form. I crinkle the letters in my hand; her and her mom's kindness is more than I deserve. "Callie . . ."

"I know Viv dying isn't *just* a mistake. I know it's awful to have to live with. But you have to live with it, Letta. It could've happened to anyone. Oh!" Callie sits up like she's been hit by the lightning starting outside. "That reminds me. The LeVaughn kid. You wanted me to look him up?"

Now I perk up too. No email and internet make the days go even slower here.

"Turns out that kid was sentenced to twenty years in prison! He was only thirteen when his accident happened. Did you know that?"

"Yes, yes. What did you find out?"

"He died about twenty years ago, when he was eighteen. He, uh"—thunder cracks the air before Callie finishes—"died by suicide."

"How?" I croak out.

Callie hesitates at first. "Uh" is every other word as she explains, or tries to, that he was found in his cell, bedsheets around his neck.

Petra was covered in sheets when she was taken away. I don't know what she did, or tried to do, but this isn't a coincidence. It's what can happen. It's what *has* happened.

"There wasn't too much more available. Quotes in articles said he was a 'model inmate,' he liked to go to church, and he worked in the mess hall. They called cafeterias 'mess halls' back in the day. Did you know that?"

I shake my head more at hearing who LeVaughn was than at Callie's question. If he was doing okay inside, why did he take his life?

"Did the articles say anything else? About his family?"

"His mom blamed the court system. Said it was super biased and he deserved a second chance because he was so young. She said she regretted not doing more to get him help after he was sentenced. Sounded like the family got fractured from all that, which . . ." She pauses. "You know."

"Yeah." Grams and Gramps's latest letter probably offers prayers or asks if I'm okay, and that's it. Aunt Mae wishes me well. But I hear from no one else. If LeVaughn's family didn't forgive him then, do they forgive him now that he's gone? Is that what it takes?

"That's all?" It's more a plea to Callie to tell me anything that may give me something to cling to.

"That was everything I could find. His family did have a nice service for him, from what I read. Lots of people showed up. A state congressman even said LeVaughn's death proved that the system wasn't working."

"You know, that's not the whole story," I tell Callie. "A friend of mine in here hurt herself."

"Is she okay?"

"I don't know. I really, really hope so."

Callie slides the envelope for Pascal's letter to me. "Unless you want me to burn it."

"No," I say. I need to go to Counselor Susan about this. I need answers.

"Time's up!" security says.

Callie is quick to swallow me up in a hug. "You kicked ass today. I'm proud to be your best friend."

As soon as she's gone, I wish I could've said something just as kind to her.

The moment I hear the guard's boots move away from my

cell, I check the moisturizer and see it's one of my favorites. "Thank you, Callie!" I say out loud. Callie has left me with two things: a path to better skin and more questions about what these Trials are supposed to do to "help" us be better. Shaking the other letters out of my pillowcase, I make small piles: one for my grandparents, one for Aunt Mae, the other for Pascal. My grandparents' latest letter is on the usual blue paper with GOD BLESS at the top. As expected, Grams's written, *Get Better.*

The letter from Brooklyn makes me forget all the rest. There's no name on the envelope, just the PO box. The letter is written on yellow notepad paper. And the first words are *Pretty Little Violet.*

Only one person called me that. I scan front and back for a name, and almost cry when I see my hopes confirmed.

It's signed: *Love, Petra.*

CHAPTER 31

VINCE

Days since the decision: 33

The phrase *if looks could kill* is a good one, because if they could, most of my classmates would be on another plane. I stalk into school Wednesday morning, ready to take names after Letta's Trial.

Ethan from lacrosse is in my face with a raised hand, looking for a high five. I'm pretty sure I turn his ass to stone the way he freezes up from my glare. Other teammates start to approach me before slithering off, like I've morphed into a shark about to attack. Good. Screw them for how they treated my sister yesterday. They turn their faces to talk with friends about how they can't wait for the meets later this week. Like I should be happy they want to see me on the field.

Because I'm consistent, I haven't responded to anyone's texts. Janice is the only one to seek me out first period. "All I'm going to ask is how you're doing. That's it."

"I honestly don't know, Jan."

"Okay." Janice gives me the type of hug I didn't know I needed. The kind where she rubs my back and I almost feel like things will be all right. "Find us at lunch, okay?"

Five periods later, it's lunch. I don't have much of an appetite, but I head to our table outside, where Janice, Byron, and Jorge are chatting it up.

Jorge is usually dressed to impress, but today I notice they and Janice are dressed up more than usual. Jorge's hair is shorn on the sides, with a nice bump. On top of that, their nails are newly done in a blush tone that matches their skin.

I ask, "Don't y'all look purty?"

"Yearbook staff photos. Levi is taking them after school today."

"Yup!" Janice says, mimicking taking a photo with her fingers. Her braids are tied up in a crown around her head with little gold ornaments between the strands. The wraparound dress she wears is royal blue, the best kind of color for her darker skin. Byron, like me, is in a tracksuit and T-shirt. Easier to get in and out of uniform for practice.

Jorge asks me how I am, in the sympathetic way they ask everything nowadays, even "How's the weather?"

"I'm all right."

"Yesterday . . ." they say. "Yeah, I definitely don't have a follow up for 'Yesterday,' except I think Violetta was ballsy for standing up for herself. Not that balls define bravery, but you know what I mean."

Janice agrees. Byron is noticeably quiet. Uncharacteristic for him. He's focused on his soda can like it's the most interesting thing in the world. I keep my anger down until I see the can. Whoever threw soda at Letta was probably suspended, from what AP Orlando said yesterday. Even so, I'd like to rip whoever tossed it a new one.

Breathe, Vince. Breathe.

Jorge unscrews their canister and takes a sip. "Vin, are you sure you're okay?"

"I'm here, aren't I?" That probably sounded defensive, but I'm not in the mood to perform for people today. Not even my friends.

"Yes, I see. But, uh, did you know what was happening? Was that like an actual Trial?"

Janice says Jorge's name in warning.

"What?" They turn to Janice, almost shocked. "I love Vin like a brother, but can we be up-front, super duper honest right now?"

"Might as well," I say.

Byron's finally turned his attention to our conversation. He's wearing his team jacket and seems, for once this season, not jittery. Maybe that means he's not on anything. Maybe something scared him straight, like seeing my sister onstage as an example for everyone to judge.

Jorge leans in, ready to say their piece. "The Trials are a barbaric way to try and impose values on people who have broken the law. It's ridiculous. Like a hamster in a hamster wheel." This is followed by an "Ow!" Since they're next to Jan, she's either pinched or punched Jorge. Having been on the receiving end of some of Janice's hits, I can confirm they do indeed sting.

"I am not saying this is Vin's fault," Jorge adds. "*However*, that was jacked up, and y'all know it was jacked up."

"What's jacked up?" Levi asks, arriving at the worst time.

He sits next to me, already unwrapping his sandwich. He takes one good look at our faces and says to himself, "Right. Sorry I asked."

"While I'm all for not censoring conversation among friends, I do think," Janice says, solely to Jorge, "that in the interest of respecting what others are going through, perhaps we should not discuss our personal thoughts on the matter?"

"This is why you should be in debate," Levi says through a mouthful of sandwich. "You talk like you're running for office."

"I *am* class vice president."

Jorge adopts Jan's eyeroll. "Yeah, we know, girl. You're as busy as Vin over here. But you are not going to silence me when I say that I can love my friend *and* be opposed to a system that is created to punish Black and Brown folks, like our dear adopted little sister Violetta." Jorge gives Jan "the look," full-on raised bushy eyebrow and pursed lips, letting her know they're not backing down. They *both* should be in debate.

Byron's voice breaks through the silence. "I mean, Letta did kill somebody, right?"

Want to shut down an argument among friends, or anybody? Mention someone's dead sister. That'll halt any and all conversation immediately.

Jan gets to massaging her head like she's questioning sitting with, and maybe being friends with, us. "Christsake."

"Shit, Vince, I didn't mean it like that," Byron tries. "I—I—"

"Should keep your mouth shut," Janice encourages through the whitest teeth I've seen since Ross's. Honestly, I don't know how she does it with all the soda we drink.

"It's fine," I tell Byron even though it's not. None of this is fine. None of this will ever be fine, and now I know my friends also think my family sucks for what's happening to Letta. Thing is, I couldn't explain it if I wanted to. As much as Jorge and Janice and Levi ask "How are you?" As much as I *want* people to care, I wouldn't know how to respond.

Even though it may not be true, I tell my friends I'll be back. I head inside to the cafeteria. A group of kids bang through the doors, almost hitting me. I do a double take, seeing Callie's with them.

"Hey, Callie," I call.

Callie stops searching for my voice once I hold up a hand to get her attention. She sizes me up before she marches on, head purposely turned away from me so all I see is the back of her head and the green streaks in her straightened locks. She's been the one looking out for Letta. Shouting support each period while missing her own classes. It physically hurts to know I couldn't do that and had to watch it all on TV like a reality show. Except, hello—one starring *my* family.

"Callie. *Callie.* Damn, can you wait a minute?" I catch up to her before she gets in the lunch line. "Jeez. I wanted to talk to you."

"Not today, Vincent." She stalks off without getting a tray, heading right back to the lunchroom doors to leave.

Vincent? She has never called me that.

I start to reach for her arm but restrain myself, not wanting to be that guy.

"Callie!" I yell before lowering my voice. "How . . . how was she?"

"How *was* she? Oh. My. God." Callie's full lips sputter at me. Her backpack is slung over a shoulder and she hooks a thumb under a strap like she's ready to hit me with it. "How could you do that to her? She's your sister!"

"It wasn't me. The Bureau—"

"Stop acting like you're innocent. You're the one who delivered the verdict. You're part of this! What's next for her, huh? Make her walk on hot coals? Are you gonna make her dig a grave with her fingers? What?" She pushes me. "What?" Another push. *"What?"* Each blow lands harder than the one before, smack-dab in my chest. Each time, the charms on her bracelet makes the teeniest jingle. She's much stronger than I give her credit for.

"What you're doing is not okay!" she yells at me, her tan face splotchy with anger. Callie's hazel eyes pierce me with pure hate, so much so I swear I see a tinge of red in them. She's on the verge of tears.

"Jesus, Callie. This is intense for everyone."

"No, it's not, Vincent. Stop saying that. Stop saying that like Letta isn't suffering!"

What she says scares me, because she—and apparently my friends—see something I never saw in myself: cruelty. My delayed response gains a "hmph" from Callie like she pities me as she walks away.

As if everything else today weren't already enough, Coach

appears. Never without a cap, Coach's hat pretty much matches his beard and the fire Callie sent my way. "Vincent, where's Byron?"

"Oh, uh." I weakly lift my arm to point to the court my friends are sitting in.

"Good. Round up whoever you can find here on the track team. Spread the word, and meet at the nurse's office. The other coaches are rounding up their groups too."

"What is this about, Coach?"

"Testing, Vincent. Testing starts now."

"As in *now* now?"

"Surprise," is all Coach says before knocking through the double doors in search of my teammates.

"Positive," the nurse says. This isn't the good kind of positive.

"How?" is all that comes out.

I mean, seriously: *How?* I haven't taken anything in over a month! Just a few minutes ago, I peed in a cup marked 2345—pretty easy to remember—then handed it to a nurse. I was ready to be done with the anxiety, with how wound-up the whole team's been, particularly Byron, who annoyed me with the number of questions he asked within a five-minute span. All of us were lined up like we were in elementary school, tapping our feet, making jokes that weren't funny, to ward off the nerves. I should've heard a confirmation that I'm good to go. But, no. Instead, this woman, whose lips are slanted in that judgy way, says, "Positive."

"I've been cl— I don't . . . I didn't touch anything. I swear I haven't."

"You can go take another test. You need water?"

Tears prick my eyes. I can't even win for losing. Even when I do good, it's not good enough.

"Screw this." I kick my chair backward.

"Mr. Chen-Samuels," she scolds, but it doesn't matter. None of this matters. The nurse shuffles away, clutching my results.

I bolt down two flight of stairs, my teammates' voices trailing me. I need to get out of here. I pick up speed down stairwell after stairwell until I'm at the main doors.

Security doesn't bat an eye when I show my school ID noting it's my lunch period.

I don't think, I just move. Moving is what's going to get me a scholarship and the hell out of here. Out of this city. Out of my duplex. Just out. The only thing I can't outrun is my mind. Then again, I know a way to do that. My fingers fumble for my keys; once I do find them I'm so frantic they fall under a wheel.

"Ahhhhhhh!" I scream into the air, finally free to let out the rage bubbling over from the minute I stepped through Claremont's doors this morning to hearing the word "Positive."

"Whoa there. Need anger management?"

Smoke curls out of Ross's mouth. His head is angled out his Mustang's window as he watches me. We're separated by a couple cars, asphalt, and some awkwardness.

"How's life?" he asks, opening his door. He spews smoke, then puts his vape pen in his pocket.

"I needed a break. From everyone."

Ross smiles. Damn, he has perfect teeth. I almost want to ask how much his parents paid for that too. Whenever I catch Ross he's usually alone and—this is the first time I've thought on it—maybe that's the last thing he wants. As much as I've been asking people to leave me be, I've craved my parents' attention, like it used to be, and more than that Levi and me going back to how it used to be.

"I got a lot going on right now."

Ross stays seated in his car, door open. "I've seen."

"You've been watching me?"

"Not in a creepy way. More . . ." He tilts his chin to the air, his features appearing sharper in profile. "More like admiration."

"I am not one to be admired," I tell him, bending down.

"What are you doing?"

"Dropped my keys."

"Oh," he says, getting out of the car. In a minute he's kneeling beside me with a hand sweeping the ground.

Half his head is under my car when he says, "I see you on the field and off. There's something about you. But it's gotta be rough with your sisters. And the testing."

"When I lied, everyone thought I was doing everything right. Now that I'm telling the truth about not using, suddenly I'm guilty."

"Not following. Got it!" He jingles my key ring at me as if he's saved the day, wiping his hands on his pants.

It's weird to see him even the tiniest bit disheveled. Everything about him is about maintenance. He's always clean-shaven. The leather jacket is gone, but he's in a fitted shirt and acid-washed designer jeans, ones now marked with a dust print from where he wiped his palms. I honestly don't know how his sneakers stay sparkling white compared to every stain known to man on my running shoes and the holes in my jeans—some deliberate, most accidental.

"Apparently, I tested positive just now."

"No way," he says, offering me a vape. I decline.

"Yeah, I know!" Now that I can unlock my door, I slam my door once, twice, three times. It doesn't make me feel better, but it gives me something to do.

"But you're not guilty."

"Maybe I *am*," I tell him.

"Guilty of what, though? It can't be pills. You've been avoiding me for weeks."

"Obviously not successfully."

The ring of the bell, even outdoors, surprises me. I can't think about what's next. Everything is crumbling apart. And Ross could be a pretty good escape route.

I will him to ask so I don't have to. And he does: "Wanna get out of here?"

CHAPTER 32
VIOLETTA

Days in detention: 33

~~卌~~ ~~卌~~ ~~卌~~ ~~卌~~ ~~卌~~ ~~卌~~ |||

Pretty Little Violet,

I miss you so much! My wish is you don't get this letter, 'cause you'll be at home, where you belong, Trials all done. ☺

First, I'm okay. Second, you probably want to know what happened.

Well, that last day I saw you at breakfast, I had asked Counselor Susan, "Why isn't my life worth defending as much as the guy who tried to rape me?" She said, "You're here to tell your story. He's still incapacitated and can't tell his. How fair is that, Petra?"

Lemme tell you, every conversation with her was like a tug-of-war. She wanted me to feel bad for what I did, and I kept asking her if she cared how I felt. That Endurance Trial in a field? That was torture. Pure torture. And no one cared.

I know what we did is not at all the same. Mine was an act of self-defense, though people don't always believe me. And yours was an accident. I didn't want to switch

From my Trial to a full-time cell upstate. I know violence isn't okay, but protecting myself wasn't wrong. I don't think I'm the one who deserved to fight for forgiveness. I deserved to be heard.

Day after day, week after week, for nine months, this guy's family was successful where their son failed by taking something from me. When they reversed their decision, it felt like this would happen again and again.

I couldn't go back to that Trial after tasting freedom, so I declined continuing. Once I was back in my cell, I just wanted it done. I'm glad someone found me, though. I'm glad they sent me to this hospital and I got to see my family.

Oh, and I'm officially forgiven! ☺ Thanks to my mom, who never shuts up—you see where I get it from, LOL—everyone agreed it was best for me to go someplace to rest and heal.

The food isn't any better at this hospital. But I do get to use a computer for 30 minutes a day, just for email and some approved sites. We watch TV. We have art therapy. I get to speak to someone who doesn't guilt trip me. Things look and feel different here. The hospital is all white, with a few blue streaks here and there. It's still another place you don't forget you're in. We have a schedule, but we also have some freedom, and security doesn't have to take us everywhere all the time. We're also not allowed anything sharp. (But I do get real pencils and not tiny ones!)

Oh no. ☹ I'm running out of space already. I guess I write as much as I talk, huh? LOL. I'll write you again. I promise! Last thing: Please don't let anyone make you feel lower than low. It's a scary place to be when there's nothing around you except a sludge you can't dig yourself out of. You're a beautiful person, Violetta. I know your family loves you. And I hope you love yourself as much as you deserve. She may not believe it, but Counselor Susan was right about one thing: We're more than our worst mistakes. You're your sister's legacy now. Don't throw that away.

Love,
Petra

THE GUARDS HAVE cut the nightly checks down to twice a week, but the night after my Accountability Trial, they appeared. The flashlight and banging on my door plus the pounding rain made it hard to sleep. Really, it was Petra's letter that kept me up. When I wake up in the morning, my body is dense. I'm in a fog. I drift along, not really thinking but doing.

The morning after my Accountability Trial, Counselor Susan beckons me to her office. I grab my notebook. I read through it after I read and re-read Petra's letter. Pascal's too. I had to know exactly what I wrote about Pascal for him to be part of my Trial.

My counselor's desk is back to its organized state. Pens in

their cup, folders aligned, her computer screen turned toward her and away from me. I take a seat, notebook in my lap.

"I'm sorry we couldn't meet yesterday after your Trial. I had to leave early. That's why I wanted to check in first thing today. How are you feeling?"

How am I feeling? The notebook practically burns in my lap. Damning me for being as honest as I was able to be in those pages. "I was humiliated by my ex-boyfriend. Someone threw soda at me. Some people called me a murderer. And I'm pretty sure most of my school agrees."

"Oh, Violetta. I'm so sorry."

"You're not sorry, are you? You saw what happened to me. You said after my first Trial you watched the video. So you saw it, didn't you?"

Counselor Susan's lips are pressed together. For a change she has on shiny lip gloss. "These meetings are for us to talk things out. For me to hear how *you* feel."

"*You* told them. My parents. Detention Services. *Pascal.*" I throw my notebook at her desk. Counselor Susan scrambles out of her chair before it lands on her folder. Or should I say *my* folder. There's no one else around; it's just her and me until she calls a guard. If I get out of hand, will that be what's next? Me taken back to my cell in restraints, the same as in my Trials? Or maybe she'll tell the Bureau and they'll tell my parents to make my next Accountability Trial that much harder.

"Violetta Chen-Samuels, *please* do not do that. You can't make sudden moves like that. We don't know—"

"What I'm capable of? I already killed my baby sister, so maybe I can hurt you too? Is that what you think of me? Is that why you lied to me? Is that why you dismissed Petra—because she didn't deserve to be heard?"

My counselor closes her eyes. Her glossed lips move, but no words come out. With her hand on her heart, her chest rises and falls three times before she opens her eyes again to sit. She adjusts her black and gray striped blazer, tucks her feet one under the other, and folds her hands on top of her desk. She's a model of composure, while I want to leap out of my chair to rip every paper in sight, right down to any verdict she has for me.

There's so much information in my head—from Callie's most recent visit, to my counselor's Trial presentation, to Petra and Pascal's letters. I practically memorized Petra's. Yes, her forgiveness is official, but look what it took for her to get it. LeVaughn didn't have the option of someplace else, an outlet or help. As fair as this is all supposed to be, really none of it is.

Grams's recent letter to me said that "Life isn't fair" and that the most important thing was to live honestly. She asked me to sit with that. It's like Grams thinks I'm much older than I am. Based on how I'm treated in here, the staff may think the same, especially by the way Counselor Susan is looking at me. Waiting, watching.

"Why did you lie to me?" I say. "You said everything here was confidential."

"I said you could trust me not to say anything to others. But I do have to share information with the Bureau of Detention

Services. They need to know how best to create a fitting Trial or sentence."

I don't budge when Counselor Susan offers me the notebook. Instead, I ask, "So everyone knows what's in there? My family. The Bureau."

"That's as far as it goes, Violetta. I don't share any information with anyone who doesn't require it. This is part of your rehabilitation. I am not a psychiatrist. I am a counselor. And my responsibility is to each individual inmate as well as to the state. My responsibility is in the interest of justice."

"Liar," I spit out.

"I'm sorry you feel that way." Returning to the person she was earlier, rigid and unwavering, the same counselor who told me Petra's family was not my concern, she asks if there's anything else I'd like to discuss about my Trial.

Anger isn't the only thing running through me now. There's also pain. Pascal hurt me. Counselor Susan hurt me. And my family . . . I'm not sure. Deep down maybe none of them realize it. Actually, from the blank look and cold stare from Counselor Susan, I'm sure *she* doesn't. But all of them are. And that's the worst part.

Maybe this is also part of the Trials. Me feeling the pain I caused others so much it forces me to sit with a simmering hatred that may be more for myself than for those around me. I'm not sure of anything anymore. But I won't tell Counselor Susan how I feel. I can't afford for it to be used against me if my Accountability Trial continues.

"Did I pass?" I ask.

"I'm sorry to say I haven't heard back about that. When I hear from the judicator working with your parents, I'll let you know. All I know is they've decided to pause this Trial and consider what they may have seen or been told about yesterday."

"So . . . that means?"

"It means we wait. If they choose to continue your Accountability Trial, it may come in another format or be similar to what you did. If you pass or fail Accountability, then we wait to hear about the option of a third Trial. And—"

"What did you just say?"

"About what exactly?" She says this as if she didn't drop a bomb on my life, even though it's already in ruins.

"A *third* Trial?"

Counselor Susan sits back with the most pitying expression you can imagine. "Violetta"—she says my name so I hear every syllable—"after sentencing, you knew there was the option of a third Trial."

It's like rewinding a movie where all the scenes run backward with no sound until I reach the exact moment I'm searching for. I replay every memory in the past thirty-three days, searching for those words. Like I said, time moves differently here. A little over a week ago, "an option for a third, final Trial" pops out. I was so frightened about my first Trial, I must've forgotten the rest of what she said.

"So this isn't over." Like Eve, I'm in limbo now. Waiting for a Trial I may or may not pass, with the possibility of another right around the corner. Miles has had four Trials. Petra had *one* for nine months. Serena is in for who knows how long.

I notice my counselor has straightened the one tilted diploma frame. I want to tilt it back, to make something, anything, in this office less than perfect. "I'm just supposed to sit here and wait?"

"I'm afraid so. This may be over sooner rather than later, Violetta."

Of course, I don't believe her.

CHAPTER 33

VINCE

Days since the decision: 33

I keep to a corner. Ross is sprawled on his four-poster bed—a gigantic one, might I add. Matches the whole feel of his home: the bigger, the better. This thing takes up most of his bedroom. My phone's buzzed a few times—texts from Byron and Levi, calls from another number I don't recognize. I ignore them all and finally switch it off.

"You're practically on an island all by yourself," Ross says.

"I like to think of myself as a peninsula."

His laugh is fast and rough. Every time we were together, before I went clean, I was usually on something, so my senses were dulled. Right now, there's a craving, but not for him. Mainly I want to be close to someone who won't judge me or ask questions, and Ross will have to do. I go to lie beside him and decide to go for it. Our faces collide, noses first.

We're not in sync so he tries again. At first, his lips are like a suction cup. I pull away, and he puts his arm around my waist.

"I've been wanting this a long time." He kisses me again, this time with tongue. Sad thing is, I don't feel anything. Okay, that's a lie. I feel stirrings, the tiniest sparks. It's not like with Levi, where electricity flashes from my mouth to my calves, where I lose myself in the whole thing. I try harder: Press myself against Ross, wrap my arms around him. Feel the firmness of his chest against mine. He lifts up my shirt. Goose bumps erupt where his skin grazes mine before he pulls away.

"Hey," he breathes.

I don't stop. I press my hands on either side of his head. His cheeks are smooth to the touch. He smells like he just showered in something spicy. I need him to shut up and kiss me. *Keep kissing me so I don't have to think, Ross.*

"Hey," he says more forcefully mid-kiss.

His whole face is want, from the O of his mouth to the way his eyes—*Damn, how blue are his eyes?*—soften the more he stares at me.

Ross sighs in the same loud way that he laughs. "It's only when people want something." He picks at his comforter.

"Want what?" Sliding off the bed, I slouch against his wall, faking chill.

Ross rolls on his side, all supermodel-pinup pose, resting on his elbows. His dirty-blond hair sticks out a bit on the sides, from where I clutched his head. Dude stares at me the same way he always does when he says, "You're not really interested in me, are you?"

"I mean . . ."

He pouts. "Don't lie. I can tell."

"There's a lot going on, Ross. What do you want from me?"

"I think the question is: What do you want from me? People only want things from Ross, after all." He unveils a tiny Ziploc from under his pillow and flaps it, like he's signaling a dog with a treat. "You want a toke?"

I reach for the one he offers, but he's playful, pulls his hand away. "Warning time."

"Now a warning?"

"This isn't run-of-the-mill stuff. This is laced and it's no joke. You'll be mellowed out in seconds. But you gotta hang here until you get rest. Okay?"

I stare at the tightly rolled paper in his hand. I really should go. Turn tail and run, like I did when I tried to visit Letta. Bolt to prove I'm not that kid who tested positive for anything. I could head back to school and fight for my place on the team. As I think about things, I start to slump: more to prove, more to do, more of a show. And isn't this who I am? Today's test certainly said it was.

Eyes still on the joint, I tell Ross, "Light it."

You DISAPPEAR; IT's the point. Stars flash and pop all around you.

I sit down, or I'm already sitting down. Something is near me. Something tickles my skin. A kind of electricity or static. But it isn't painful. My body is both a feather *and* lead.

It's dark too. Wait. I open an eye. It's daytime. Light slices through blinds, the lines blur. That's weird. I smile at the light show.

Next thing I see is Ross's face hovering over mine.

I move my lips. I'm fairly sure to say, "Hey."

"How'd we get here?" I say.

He answers. "You said, 'Yes.'"

Ross seems thrilled. He puts his hand on my chest, but I don't feel him put it there.

"I'm not used to chasing, Vince."

I'm not used to being caught.

He says something else, but I'm tuned out. I disappear.

"Hey."

What?

He clears his throat. "Something . . . wrong?"

I'm. High. As. A fucking. Kite.

"I mean, I know it works fast . . ." Ross's words fade.

Now everything's getting *really* fuzzy. "Where'd you go, Viv? Viv, where'd you go?"

"Vince?" There's snapping. There's shaking . . . is that me or the bed or the earth? Ross's voice is muffled, like he's speaking to me underwater, before the world fades away.

PART III

The Verdict

CHAPTER 34

VIOLETTA

Days in detention: 34

~~HHT HHT HHT HHT HHT HHT~~ IIII

Whenever I arrive at the cafeteria, I can tell who's worn out from almost a full week of Trials versus those anxious to hear news at sentencing on Saturday. This time of the week is when the bustling of the cafeteria fades and us inmates have been stripped down to nothing.

Several girls' heads are bent like drooping branches, whether they're in line or sitting to eat. Some stare into space. A few of the other girls from my afternoon class are scattered around, talking to one another or waiting to get their food.

I move through the food line. The same stuff is plopped on each tray: peas and carrots, mashed potatoes, a slab of meat, a small carton of juice, and an apple. The whole room smells like boiled potatoes, which doesn't give me much of an appetite. Tray in hand, I wander through the space, past the gated windows, to the long tables with benches arranged in tight rows. I take a seat by myself to eat food that tastes like paste.

I miss Serena battling for what's on my tray and Petra laughing, offering her what she doesn't want. Being with other people gives me a chance to not think as much about the outside because the inside is more real. There are less people here for me to disappoint, and the other inmates don't judge because we all have things we're not proud of. This is what I cling to now that I'm in limbo.

Everything about my life is piling up: Possibly three Trials, not two. An ex-boyfriend telling the school about our last night together. My brother coming to visit me, only to run away. My family possibly hearing everything about the night of the accident. My counselor telling Corrections what I'd written in my notebook, so that it could be used to punish me. I lower my spork. I shove the tray away.

More girls line up along the wall for dinner. Serena and Eve are at the end. Eve's arms are crossed, meaning she's upset. Serena calls out to me.

I lean over my food, another drooping branch. *I don't want to be like this.* I repeat those words to myself while inmates dump their trays and disappear out the cafeteria doors.

Eve and Serena take a seat. Serena doesn't pick at my abandoned tray. Eve chews loudly, her mouth wide open, so I can see the mush in her mouth. Her perpetual scowl makes everything on her face look smaller from the squint of her eyes to the tightness of her mouth.

While Eve sulks and eats, Serena and I talk about anything *but* our Trials. My two Trials took four days total, but Serena's been in her Trial for a couple weeks. Up close I can see more skin chapping along Serena's nose, peeling away freckles, and how her left eyebrow looks shorter than the right. Outside of what she told me during our day in the game room, she's not too shaken by what she's doing: creating tools meant to hurt, when she didn't mean to hurt anyone. Between bites, she taps her spork against her tray. The sound draws me to the grill marks on her hands, ones that remind me of barbecues. From what I can see of Serena's arms there are no other scars. Serena sits up straight and chews her food eagerly. *How,* I want to ask, *are you able to appear like you can handle all this?*

I haven't heard back from Counselor Susan since I saw her yesterday, when she acted like she was doing me a favor, not stabbing me in the back. I left her office so upset I had to ask to be let outside for a walk, even though I hadn't eaten breakfast. The guard saw how stiff my body was, my fingers flexed like I was ready to throw something, maybe even a punch. I got to breathe in the air; it and the ground were damp from the rain. I took in everything around me, and I realized that as long as I'm in this place, I will never be seen as anything other than the girl who killed her sister. *Manslaughter. Murderer. Violetta.*

"Petra wrote to me," I tell Serena and Eve.

"Whoa! She's alive!" Serena covers her mouth for a quick burp. "Sorry, that came out wrong. But she is alive if she's writing to you."

"Yeah, she's at a hospital in Brooklyn. She's getting the help she couldn't get here in detention."

"Good on Petra! Probably getting better food too. Speaking of . . ." Serena's spork taps my tray.

"It's yours," I tell her.

"*Nice*. What else she say?"

I sum up the letter as best as I can, glad to share it. Eve looks off into the void, still smacking her lips, while Serena eagerly listens to everything I'm saying.

"Cool, cool. So she's good."

"I don't know if 'good' is the right word. But she's not dealing with finding a needle in a haystack."

"You mean thornbushes," Serena says.

"Yeah, it was a figure of speech."

"Gotcha."

"I'm sure her family gave those victims hell. That Trial was just straight-up evil. Oh." Serena's shoulders go up and down in quick succession, almost like she's holding in a laugh. "Hiccups. Dunno what's going on with me today." Serena digs back into my food but hands me the apple. I take it and offer a smile.

After several long minutes of all of us in our heads, Eve says, "I heard today."

"Heard what?" I ask until it hits me. "Oh . . . But it's Thursday."

"Yeah, that's what *I* said, but my counselor told me they finally came to a decision after being pressured by the judicator."

I don't need to ask. Good news isn't the kind you keep to yourself.

"Two years," Eve says.

"Two years . . ."

Eve throws her spork onto her tray. Bits of mush fly. "Two

years in detention upstate. No Trials. No forgiveness. I'm going to state detention for what they're calling online bullying." Every sentence sounds like it takes so much effort. "Two years of my life. Gone. They made me wait over a *month* for that decision."

"I've heard about girls getting ten or more. Or that kid that the Trials was started because of," Serena says, looking to me for help.

"LeVaughn Harrison," I say, feeling the full weight of his name, now that I know how he died.

"Yeah, him," Serena says. "Two years might fly by."

"How are you going to tell me the time will fly by? I don't want it to *fly by*." Eve's fists press into either side of her head as if she wants to keep everything out. And I don't blame her.

"Eve," I say. "I know—"

"No, you don't *know*, Letta," she cries. When our eyes meet, I can see how much this has taken out of her. Her face isn't a smooth brown like when we first arrived. Her eyebrows are thicker. Her straight hair's grown past her ears and is frayed at the edges, kind of like mine. The pinch of her face is permanent on her after weeks of indecision. None of us are the same.

"I've been jerked around waiting for an answer, and then I get *this*? I'm sixteen, and I have to finish high school in detention for something that wasn't even my fault. I didn't make that girl do anything. All I did was share what everyone else already knew."

As much as I feel for Eve, what she says frightens me. Some

of what she's said takes me back to Pascal. How he wouldn't admit that his actions influenced my own. I really hope Eve doesn't believe this when it comes to bullying.

"Do you, um, at least feel a little better knowing now?"

Eve stares daggers at me. "Better?"

Nope, that didn't help either.

"You know," Serena says through a mouthful of peas and carrots, "I'm hella upset to be here and about my Trial. Especially because it was Dumbass's fault, not mine."

"Is that his name?" I ask.

"It is from now on. Eve, sometimes we have to come to terms with what we did in whatever way we can. Especially when we hurt people. If we can't change it, we work through it." Serena sounds exactly like Miles. "And we hope they see us trying. Someone died because of me. So let me take these licks and hope they don't totally kick my ass."

Eve picks her spork back up. Using the tines to dig food out of her braces, she shakes her head at us as if we're the ones to be pitied. "You"—she gestures to Serena—"are an idiot. And you," Eve says to me, "you got these Trials, and you're sitting here trying to prove something to your family. Well, guess what? It'll never be enough! Just like for Petra it wasn't, or anyone in here. I don't deserve to be here."

"And we do?" I know better than to push, but why not? I've had a rough few days. Whether she believes she did or not, whether Pascal believes he did or not, they have *harmed* people. I don't think Eve is a bad person. But at least I'm not trying to hide what I did or make others pay for it. I have to know I can move on from this moment.

"*I* didn't kill my sister," Eve says.

"O-*kay*," Serena says. "That is harsh."

"She's right, Serena. But at least I admit the pain I caused." I take my apple, and I don't say goodbye.

CHAPTER 35

VINCE

Days in detention: 3

///

Chalk. That's what's in my mouth. Water would be a blessing. But all I taste is a gravelly bitterness I want to wash out.

Everything is dark; then my eyes adjust.

What exactly happened? I'm dressed in an off-green top and pants, and I'm . . . in a cell. I lurch from my cot, because this has to be a mistake. I hold my head and count, while gathering the courage and strength to stand up.

Desk. Bed. Thick door. Cement walls and a floor to match.

I am screwed. This last thought sends me right back to lying down.

My body isn't featherweight. It's not heavy either. I am me, but it's like I'm hollow. At least this means the effect of whatever Ross gave me is gone, physically at least.

Damn it, Ross.

There's a bandage on the back of my hand that pulls tight when I curl my fingers. It doesn't hurt, though. I definitely don't remember having this at Ross's. My stomach rumbles. I think about a beef patty cut open, with a slice of cheese melting inside. The thought doesn't make me want to vomit, which I guess is a good sign.

Where am I? Maybe this is a holding cell, and my parents are on the way to pick me up. Though, if my parents *are* on the way, I might want to stay in here indefinitely.

I wait for the swimming in my head to settle before I try standing again. I sink my fist into the pillow, imagining the hurt in Mom's face. First Viv, then Letta, now me. My barred window is pretty tiny; it's basically the size of my head. The only other light is a flickering fluorescent bulb above the sink. Otherwise, it's just me and the slick walls.

The door creaks open, and I'm face-to-face with a man in a security uniform.

"Chen-Samuels?"

I search around as if to say, *Who else?*

"It's time for you to meet with your counselor."

"Counselor? Where am I? Rehab?"

"You've been charged," he says, starting to count on his fingers, "and drug tested while you were being treated. Sentencing will be next."

"Sentencing? For what exactly?" I regret asking, because I think I know what's coming. Violetta's charge was immediate from the state since she didn't deny what she'd done and the evidence was damning as ever. Sentencing took a few weeks for my parents to decide because of Viv's funeral and, you know, life in general sucking after that accident. The guard doesn't wait for me to pummel him with more questions. As soon as my mouth opens he stops me with:

"Your counselor will inform you. Right now, this is your cell. We couldn't fully register you until your parents were aware, and"—the veins in his neck throb the moment he swallows— "you were conscious and controllable."

"Controllable?"

He stands back to let me out. But there are too many questions to ask: How long have I been here? Did I hurt someone? Where is Ross? Am I in the same boat as Letta or worse? Why the hell can't I remember anything beyond being in Ross's bedroom?

The guard sees my uncertainty and says, "Your counselor can answer any questions. You'll be fine. People generally don't get hurt in here."

He waits. The first step out of my cell reveals many more on one floor in an enclosed area where you can hear every sound, from the other guys in uniform talking to the *brrr* of a door opening near a glass booth where two guards sit. Everything, and I mean everything, is pretty much barred, with criss-crossed metal on windows, cell doors—any door, really. Tables and chairs are bolted to the ground, the walls are bluish gray, and pipes run along the walls in every corner. *Crap.*

There's a stopgap every thirty paces—I keep count. The guard leading the way swipes his card against every door. Finally, we get to an office, like AP Orlando's, except smaller and way more cluttered. There's a man with a fierce comb-over and a thick mustache sitting behind the desk, but it's the stacks of folders lining the walls, threatening to tip over, that I focus on. The guard motions for me to sit, but I don't see where. The folders and papers take up every surface in this place, including the chairs.

"Oh, you can move those," the man sitting behind the desk tells me. Towers of more tabbed folders bookend him. "Vincent?"

"Yeah."

"Welcome. Maybe that's the wrong word."

My throat is sandpaper, but I manage, "I wouldn't say it's the right word."

"Are you all right?" He flips open what I guess is my file, scans it, nods to himself. "You want water?"

I'd like to swim in it, please. "That'd be nice."

He picks up a phone to make the request.

"Do you know what charges were brought against you, Vincent? They say you were semicoherent when you were found and charged in the hospital."

"Hospital?"

"You were in Roswell Allen's home when you showed an adverse reaction to a chemical substance. You were taken in, your stomach pumped. After several hours of an IV drip, you were brought up on charges."

Explains the bandage. I don't recall too much. I remember being at Ross's, and I kinda remember someone yelling at me to wake up. Seems like a lifetime ago. So many things this year feel like they happened in another time, to another person.

The same guard who brought me here returns with a paper cup. "Thanks," I say.

I try not to glug the water, but some dribbles down my chin. I breathe deeper.

The counselor is hunched over. Every so often, he smooths the left side of his hair like it's threatening to fly away, which some of it is. "It's been fifty-five hours since you were taken into the hospital. We'll have to get you something solid to eat." He smiles. I don't smile back. His lips pucker, like he's about to say something but then decides against it.

"So, I've been passed out for over two days?"

"Yes, Vincent."

"Time flies when you're not having fun."

"I'm glad you recognize what you went through wasn't fun."

"Definitely not, sir."

"No need for 'sir.' I'm your counselor during your time here and leading up to sentencing. We're here to provide support to young offenders."

Young offenders. I'm an *offender.*

"Shall I read the charges?"

"Might as well keep the party going."

"You were charged with illegal drug use and possession. And dispensing illegal substances."

I'm on my feet. "Dispensing? As in selling?"

"Yes." He clucks his tongue as his finger slides down a document. He repeats the three charges.

"Bullshit. I admit to using. The only reason I took it was because of Ross. We were in his house. The whole school knows he deals. Not me. Ross doesn't hide it. What are *his* charges?"

"I . . ." He pauses. "I'm not at liberty to tell you someone else's charges. Since Mr. Allen doesn't have any charges pending, I can tell you that. He admitted to using, and because you were in his home, his parents' home, *they* pressed charges for possession and dispensing an illegal substance to Mr. Allen on their premises. Mr. Allen's charge of use was dismissed with probation since the only other pills found on the premises were prescriptions."

"You're saying Ross isn't in here?"

"That's what I'm saying, Vincent. You, on the other hand, are. And we—"

The paper cup goes flat in my grip. "He's the reason I'm in here!"

"Did he make you go to his home?"

"No, but—"

"Did he physically force you to take drugs?"

"No."

"Did you say no when he offered you the substance?"

The counselor searches his file for more details, flattening his hair every other sentence. Everything he asks or says bounces off me and hits the ground. It's all *blah blah blah* until he drops another bomb.

"You willingly went with Mr. Allen after you were told of a false positive at your school?"

Record scratch. "Can you repeat that, please?"

"Yes." His finger lands on a part of the page he's been reading. "You had a false positive. Apparently, the cup used for your sample was contaminated. The nurse has been put on notice."

"Why didn't anyone tell me?"

"Let's see." And there he goes again with the index finger, finding the answer. "A few calls were made to your phone to notify you. Your parents were contacted. They answered. You didn't. And, well, we know what occurred after that. Don't we, Vincent?"

Crap. Crap. And more crap.

"Do you need some air, some more water?"

"I need to get out of here."

"That's what we'll be working toward, Vincent."

"No, I mean I need my family."

He's scribbling away like I'm making some momentous declaration. I tamp down my rage. Last thing I need out the gate, now that I have a record, is to be labeled a "problem."

"Is there a way to see my parents?"

"Absolutely. They have been wanting to see you. You're allowed visitors on a restricted guest list. But first, we have to prepare you for what comes next. You will not see those prosecuting you at any point. Only during the video—"

I stop him cold. "Sir, I already know what comes next."

CHAPTER 36

Hey Viv,

Thirteen. That was the age Mom & Dad said I could look after you by myself. You were five. The first time I babysat you, all of us were at Fresh Meadows Park for Aunt Mae and Sonali's engagement barbecue. God, it was so humid that day. All we wanted was ice cream and shade. Luckily, because the ice cream wouldn't last in the coolers, we got to eat that first while everyone made burgers, hot dogs, and veggie skewers.

Vin got recruited on the spot for a touch football game when someone saw him toss a rogue ball that landed in our picnic area. That's how it always is for Vin, noticed without trying. Sonali's kids were tiny and occupied themselves by driving their toy cars on the nearby path. That left you and me. I spotted a handball court tucked underneath a bunch of trees, which felt like a great place to shelter from the heat temporarily. The people playing handball were so serious. Some of them screamed as they helped someone off the ground or ran to catch one of the blue balls before it rolled out of the court.

One guy with stringy black hair that stuck to his neck asked if we wanted to take a seat to watch them play. You remember, he called us "little ladies." The players had fold-out chairs and mini grills, and they passed around chilled cans of soda and beer. The groups playing owned the courts. The minute I settled into a seat, you got into my lap. I could still smell the butter-pecan ice cream on you, since you'd rubbed some of it off your hands onto your I'M THE BABY T-shirt.

I could never run as fast as Vin or kick my legs high, like you could for karate. Watching from the sidelines was what I was used to. One of the girls playing handball wiped her face with the bottom of her tee before asking if I wanted to join: girls against boys. I told her I wasn't any good at the same time you squirmed out of my lap, urging me to go ahead.

The girl's arms, shoulders, and neck were sun-kissed, probably from playing as hard as everyone else around her. She tossed a ball our way that you caught. You gave it a half-hearted throw so it bounced close to the ground. The girl beckoned me over again, insisted there was nothing to it. "Kinda like tennis, but with your hands," she'd said.

My knees wobbled as I made my way to her corner of the court. Their beer and power-drink bottles were lined against the fence along with other spectators. I stuttered that I hadn't played before. The girl kept telling me not to worry, it wasn't a competition. This was all supposed to be fun. From what I'd seen, it never seemed like "fun." Not by how the crowds roared at Vin's track team or how his teammates growled at each other on the lacrosse field, or how the only time I heard Dad and Mom curse was when they watched our local teams bomb. All around me felt intense from the sound of the ball meeting wall, then hand, then wall again, all those grunting noises and speedy movements.

The girl held out the ball in her gloved palm. You came closer to sit on the exposed roots of a tree right behind us. The girl explained the rules. She hit first, then the person on the other team, then me (or her), then the other team, whoever was closest to the ball. The other team got the point when someone missed the ball. Before I could say I got it, she screamed, "Play to eleven," then gestured to where I should stand.

I missed the first ball, the next one, and the next one. We lost the first round, with the girl carrying us to eight points. This confirmed I sucked at pretty much everything sporty. Why try? But the girl bounced the ball at me, told me to serve for the next game. That's when I got the hang of it. My eye sized up the ball enough to actually smack it with my palm. It hurt, every time. It was also kind of thrilling. I moved closer to the wall, then farther from it. The girl would go up court so I could go down court. As we played, all we heard was the thwack of the ball and the sounds we made trying to get to it, whether we ran or dove. The girl jumped on her toes between hits. Her eyes never left the blue ball whizzing by or at us. At 10-10, I felt the rush. I wanted to help us win. One of the guys served, then shuffled back, and the ball came right at me. I stepped to the side, using my left hand, not my right, but I arched too much, sending the ball behind me instead of in front of me. Within a second, I heard your cries.

Everything, and I mean everything, stopped. Your head was lowered but I could see you holding your face. When you let us see the welt, there was a group sound of sucking in air. We could see the red mound forming with smudges of dirt on the edge of your cheek, right by your right ear. I thought there was blood, but thankfully there wasn't. That's how red your face was.

I rushed you back to Mom & Dad. I was more scared that you were hurt than I was of getting in trouble. The handball girl and the other guys offered to come with us. I told them it was fine. I was your big sister.

Our family wasn't that far. Everyone heard us before they saw us. You clung to me, your legs wrapped tight around my waist so you wouldn't slip, crying and screaming my name. Even Vin stopped midgame to help carry you. Mom & Dad surrounded you. Mom tried to see your face while Sonali got whatever ice was left from the cooler to press against the swelling, which only made you cry more.

I should've known better. I was supposed to look after you. "How could you have let this happen?" was yelled at me. "You're the big sister and you should know better. The first time we give you responsibility with her and <u>this</u> is what happens?" Your sniffles lessened after a bit, but I could tell you were angry with me.

I wished the day had ended better. But I was glad you were okay. A welt would be there for a few days as a constant reminder to everyone of how I'd failed.

On the ride home, Mom & Dad mellowed out. Vin playfully pinched me like usual. But you fell asleep, snuggling under my arm. I figured it was because you needed rest, not because you cared who you were close to. But when we started to unload the car, you insisted I help you go to bed.

That night, the bump ballooned to look like you had mumps on one side of your face. It was a mishmash of reddish purple. I couldn't stop staring at it while we read a story. "Today was so fun!" you said to me before I said good night. Whenever someone brought up the day, you'd say the best parts were ice cream and handball. How good the ice cream was and how fun the game looked. As if you'd forgotten about the ball hitting you. As if the only thing that mattered was seeing the fun being had, rather than being part of it. That day wasn't ruined for you by me or anyone else.

All this got me wondering: Is that what forgiveness is? Is it forgetting and moving on? Is it doing whatever

*it takes to hear "I forgive you"? Is the word "sorry"
ever enough? So much has me thinking these last 37
days. Including the fact that I should start forgiving
myself too.*

*Love you always,
Your Big Sister Letta*

UNDER THE MATTRESS, my fingers find the edges of paper until I've gathered all the letters I've saved. I sort through every one. Thirty-seven days in detention, almost five weeks. Today will be the first day I'll have something to send. I go downstairs to dorm security to request an escort to the mailroom. Petra didn't just leave me pencils, she reminded me I deserve more.

I make sure to respond to Petra, Grams and Gramps, and Aunt Mae. The letters to my grandparents and my aunt are short. Really short. Mainly, *I'm sorry* and *Thank you for writing to me, for loving me.* My response to Petra is harder. A lot of *I'm glad you're okay or getting to okay.* And *I wish you'd had the support here that you deserve.* I told her that no matter what, I would write her again or, even better, come visit if that was okay. The last thing I mail is a bundle of letters for my family. These are the most honest letters I've written. I fold the batch into an envelope, including the one I wrote just this morning, and I stick another note for my parents and brother right on top.

My family may not get these for a couple days, or more. Either way, they'll know where I stand.

CHAPTER 37

VINCE

Days in detention: 4

||||

There's a lot to remember after my meetings with the counselor. The word *regulated* comes up a lot. *Prescheduled* too. The boys' side of the detention center is separated from the girls' side by a good couple miles of land. I don't get to do things out of a *designated*—that's another word they use a lot here—rotation each day. If I need something, then say something. Don't expect too much, though.

I've been here for four days; conscious for two. I keep patting my back pocket, expecting the bulge of my phone. I get up thinking I'll go to my computer or head downstairs to get something to eat, some juice or water. In the middle of the night, I smack right into the door and into the reality of being a prisoner. Like Letta. I thought I'd want to punch something regularly at first. Instead, an eerie calm has come over me.

I try to only take a piss in the toilet in my cell. I can't open my window, meaning the air doesn't circulate, so I can't stop sweating now that it's warming up outside. My head and body sink into the pillow and mattress. None of this is home.

Morning classes are a breeze. I'm done with the school assignments and zone out pretty regularly when the instructor speaks. The classroom is also stuffy as hell with barely any air, so I'm glad to take the option to go outdoors whenever possible. I scope out where everyone else is, then head the opposite way. This week, I've hit the track outside. Once I choose a lane, I imagine the *crack* of the gun and the sharp cut of Coach's voice. In my mind, I'm at school, on the field, where I take a knee and—bam, I'm off. Every step feels like freedom until I hear the guard's whistle telling us recreation is over.

I haven't seen Mom and Dad. I know they've come by, because I've been told they met with folks—judicators for Ross's family, my counselor, whoever else advises them. I remember some of the protocol with Letta. Different yet the same. Next for me is sentencing to hear how Ross's family wants to proceed. That could take a week, could take more. I suspect Mom and Dad are ticked to the point they want to disown me. It's what I've long expected, what I fought against, a fear to end all fears. The big *D*: disappointment.

All this runs through my mind when I go to lunch after my latest class. Most of the guys in the cafeteria hunch over their tray as if someone is about to snatch it. If this place is anything, it's consistent; the decoration theme is prison chic. Get a color that makes you think of nothing—gray or bluish gray or puke green—and use it top to bottom, from the domino floors to the painted walls to the speckled tables.

Food acquired, I find an almost-empty table. My body mimics those around me. No need to call attention to myself. In a place like this, with this many people, I'm sure everyone can sense someone new. Or they can sense weakness and uncertainty. Eating is a way to bond, but it's also a way to hide. The last thing I need is to become recognizable in a place like this.

I spend too many minutes pushing applesauce and way-too-soggy vegetables around the partitions of my tray. The seats fill at my table, until there's only one or two separating me from the nearest guy. He's bulky in a way that makes me imagine him going full-on Hulk here, flipping tables, maybe even people.

I glance at him for all of a second, which was a dumb move on my part. Complete newbie behavior, because he latches on to it as though he's looking for *something* to be ticked off about.

"See something you like?" he asks with an undercurrent of a growl. His arms flex, popping blue veins through translucent skin.

I know better than to answer, because no matter what I say—considering I don't know this guy—it could be taken who knows which way. This could go south super quick. So I don't utter a word. Like Grams says, if you don't have anything nice to say . . .

He rotates my way so the width of his massive body is on display as well as the muscles bulging through his prison uniform. I know I'm outmatched. "Say something?" he says.

My pulse quickens, like when I pace around the track during practice, the warm-up before the sprint. I go to school, or I did, with guys like this. Sometimes they're kittens, and other times they're panthers.

Things go quiet around the table despite the rowdy bustle of the room. Security, a guard at each door, are too far away for my liking. They're looking the opposite direction: out in the hallway, as folks enter, instead of inside, at those of us eating.

"You gonna answer me or not?" He has a buzz cut and a thick neck. He pushes the one thing between us, a plastic chair, to the side, and the screech of it hits my nerves. He leans over and knocks my tray across the table. I wasn't gonna eat much of what was left, though I would've liked the option.

Maybe this is a pissing contest, and he needs to take a leak around my feet to mark his territory. Could be something bigger, or none of the above. I listen to my gut, though. I offer a half nod and get up. As I pass him, I hold my breath the whole while.

The dude shoves me. If he'd put more weight behind it, he could've knocked me over. "What are you going to do, pretty boy?"

The logic in me fades for a second. Irritated and pumped, I say, "Oh, you think I'm pretty? Thanks."

That's all it takes before his fist connects with my cheek and I'm laid out on the ground.

WHENEVER I TOUCH my sore cheek, I'm certain my decision to remain in my cell for the past twenty-four hours is a good one. Nurse said I was fine—nothing broken, no blood. The guards grabbed the guy to put him in solitary for a couple days, as a warning. Not that I asked for that. It was humiliating enough to be punched, to be here at all. I deserve it. All of it. I'll stay put in my cell and, from now on, curled up in bed, quiet.

A guard raps a stick against my open door.

"Visitor," he announces.

It's 228 steps total from my cell to the visiting area. Security stops, punches in a few numbers, and the door slides open.

Breathe.

"Clock starts once you sit down," the guard says.

Levi stands in the nearly empty waiting room. Like the one I never made it to for Letta.

Levi practically bests my time on the field when he gathers me in his arms. Being held by him reminds me of home. My tears aren't dribbles; they're waves. I can barely see when we take our seats.

"You're okay?" he asks, motioning at the bruise. He's jacketless and in a T-shirt. His arms folded on the table show off a rope of muscles around his biceps. Not only are they nice to look at, but his guns would've been really helpful in the cafeteria the other day.

"Depends what you mean by 'okay.'"

"You're not dead, so that's a plus, I guess," he says, wringing his hands, all nervous energy.

"Alive as I'll ever be."

He hesitates, reaching for my face, maybe waiting for me to pull away, which I don't. "Did this happen . . . in here?"

"I don't want to talk about it," I say. "But . . . I'm glad you're here."

"You're *glad* to see me? I didn't think I'd hear those words again. Being behind bars has changed you, man."

"I guess. It's been almost a week. And I remember only half of that week."

His face crumples. I wish I could offer him something uplifting.

"I'm just glad to see you." Levi dips his head so I can see the part in his high-top. When his eyes meet mine, they're red around the rims. Levi doesn't get angry often, but when he does it's like a force of nature, destroying everything in its wake. Dude is vibrating now. And if his skin weren't as dark as my parents' polished mahogany, I'd swear his face is changing colors.

"I'll kill Ross."

"No, Le—"

Slam! He slaps the table and is up, his chair knocked to its side, in two seconds flat.

"Problem?" my guard says at the same time Levi shouts, "Kill him!"

The guard approaches, a hand at his belt.

My hands shoot into the air signaling there's nothing to see here. "No, nothing. Just . . . getting out the anger. Better out than in, right? He doesn't mean what he's saying."

Still holding his belt, the guard walks backward slowly, returning to his spot at the door.

I shout-whisper to Levi, "I don't think this is the place you wanna say that. Ross chokes on a french fry, and you'll be a suspect." I'm not trying to be funny, more like I'm trying to take his mind off of this.

Levi rubs his face as hard as my dad does and takes the kind of big-ass breath I've been urging myself to take every day. He picks up his chair and apologizes to the guard.

"He could've killed you, Vin. You could be dead. Just thinking about it—" Something between a hiccup and a choking sound comes out. "Just so you know, a bunch of us got other students to talk to AP Orlando about Ross. Him dealing. Folks using. He's the reason several people on the sports teams tested positive."

Yeah, I was one of them. Even a false positive doesn't take away the guilt of what I did. Sure, the dispensing charge will be gone, but what about using? That I did on my own.

"Levi, you shouldn't try to fix this for me. I'm guilty. Maybe not for all of what my counselor told me. But for some of it, definitely."

"You're joking, right? Ross goes free. The athletes who tested positive get suspension, or expulsion. But you're *here*. How is that fair?"

"Dude." I want to take his face in my hands, so that he can see, like really see me. "Of all the times I choose to joke, this is not it."

"It's his fault you're here!" Realizing his mistake in raising his voice again, Levi mutters apologies. "Sorry, sorry."

"You sound like I did my first, uh, conscious day here."

For the first time in a while, I stare at Levi head-on, no

looking away. As cute as he is, there's a slight messiness to him. For one, his T-shirt has a hole near the collar, plus his collar is stretched out, looser on one side of his neck than the other. His high-top hasn't been fully picked out, for another. There's no camera around his neck, which he couldn't bring in here anyways, but it is his trademark. He constantly looked at me through that lens. It was scary—really scary—and a relief to be seen so closely like that. When he found the pills in my car, I thought maybe I could be open with him, of all people. Maybe I could let him in. Then he broke my heart and I shut down, pulled back, ran—because I'm good at all those things, apparently. Seeing him clear as day is like watching something imperfect yet so beautiful it hurts, because you don't ever want to look away.

"I'm angry." Squeezing my eyes shut, I try to erase the image of that night and the hurt. "I'm always so angry and scared, Levi. And I'm tired. I'm tired of pretending I can handle it all." I'm shaking so hard I'm inconsolable. This isn't withdrawal from whatever I took. It's full-on shame rocking me from my core.

"Vin," he begins. We splay our arms and hands on the table. His thumb inches near mine. "I didn't mean to hurt you. Really. I just wasn't ready to be in a relationship with someone hiding so much." He shrugs. "But I can't lose my friend, man. I can't lose you at all."

All I can do is grin, barely. If I say anything right now, it'll come out whiny or desperate. Like, *What is so wrong with me that we can't try to make it work?* At the same time, I know what he means. I'm in here because of what I was hiding. And the Levi in front of me right now? He's a mess partially because of me.

"There'll always be love between us. I know that," I admit, because it's true.

He looks hopeful. I think I even see a smile starting. "Yeah? As a friend, as your boy, I'm here for you always." His words do and don't fix things.

"How did everything go so wrong?"

"We're almost eighteen, Vin. We're supposed to let people down." He laughs. "That's almost a requirement of being a teenager."

Time is precious in here when you have a visitor. Even though Levi's my first, I know I don't have much more time with him. "Tell me what else is up in the world."

"Beyond us getting Ross's ass held accountable, not much. I mean, you know semis happened, and . . ."

Crap. I did and didn't forget about semis.

"Did we . . ."

Levi scrunches his face up like he's about to dole out bad news, and just as quickly morphs to a toothy grin. Byron came through in the clutch, which does and doesn't surprise me. Mainly because if *I* was positive—inaccurately, I know—how much time did *he* spend dry?

"I'm happy for him," I say. "Byron needed this. Like for real needed this."

From there, I decide to unload, because why not? I tell Levi about Letta's Trials beyond the one at school, the pressures, how much shame my family felt, my parents especially because of the accident. Swear to God, I feel lighter the more I speak to him. I've been holding all this in for weeks. And, worse, I've been angry at Levi for just as long. Him and Janice were my go-tos, more so Levi, because you can rely on him to be a steady listener. Even now, his head bobs to everything I say, like he's jamming to my words.

"Vin," he says, "just be honest about what *you* want. Be real. Your parents will listen to you."

"Hmph," I say, tracing the scratches of dates and numbers in the table with my finger. "They haven't so far. They didn't when I was home."

"Did you try? Like *really* try? Because what I just heard was a lot of vulnerability and fear."

I hate that he has a point. "Levi . . ."

"Vin." He shoots me that lopsided grin that totally melts me. "Be honest. When have you ever not gone after something?"

My answer is a grin just as big. We stay like this, quiet, until it's time to go.

CHAPTER 38
VIOLETTA

Days in detention: 38

~~HHT HHT HHT HHT HHT HHT HHT~~ III

My days have been emptier without a Trial. What fills them beyond my routine is the anxiety of what's next. Accountability Part 2, or something even worse? Back to my high school, or somewhere else to be judged? Counselor Susan hasn't summoned me to her office since I confronted her about my notebook and found out my Trial verdict was paused. I also haven't requested to go. I don't want to see her, because she'll either lie or keep me in the dark about what I deserve to know. So, the days move like the first three weeks. The difference is I'm lonelier without Petra.

It's Monday, and school begins at one thirty. We have an hour for lunch first. The girls in my corridor who also have mandatory afternoon classes line up by the dorm exit, four of us total. I'm happy to see Serena in the cafeteria. Since her Trial is in the afternoon, she sometimes takes a super quick lunch. She points to a seat across from her. I give her a thumbs-up, thankful to have someone to sit with at the start of a new week. After lunch, I'll daydream in class for almost four hours, thinking about the letters I sent. Wondering if I'll get a response or not. Scared that I won't.

Up close, Serena is made up too fancy for detention. Her skin is back to that freckled-beige radiance from the first day I met her; her nose is smoother too, with only a couple rough patches at the tip. Plus, she's wearing orange lip gloss and her baby hairs are tiny black swirls around her forehead and ears, while her pink locs fall around her face.

"What's the occasion?" I ask.

"Your girl just passed her Trial!" she exclaims.

"Really?"

Serena's singed fingertips wrap around her milk carton as she holds it up expectedly. I pick mine up for a cheers. "Yes, really! That shit was *horrible*."

"Congrats! So this means—"

"I'm gone end of the week. One and done." Our uniforms don't have collars. This doesn't stop Serena from pretending to pop hers. "The store owner decided a few weeks was enough punishment for me in that artillery hellhole. Dumbass, though, well"—she twists her glossy lips in mock pain—"I hear he's going to be in the heat for a while."

"But, remember, it's not punishment." I try to match the stony softness of Counselor Susan's voice. If I could, I'd top off my imitation by gelling my coils back so I'd look like her too. "This is *rehabilitation*."

Milk squirts out of Serena's nose she laughs so hard. With every laugh, the flower tattoos pulse on her neck.

"You still waiting?" she asks me.

"Just call me Limbo."

"That joke is not as funny as you think it is."

I raise my carton to her in agreement, then take a big sip. Chocolate milk would be so nice to have. Even in high school, the option between regular and chocolate milk was a small thing to get excited about with Callie.

"Can I join you?" Milk almost comes out of *my* nose when I look up to see Eve, tray in hand. For once, Eve doesn't look miserable—at least her face doesn't. It's more vacant; maybe *resigned* is the right word. Usually, her forehead is all crinkled in a forever frown and her arms are crossed, if she isn't holding anything. Right now, her dark skin is practically as smooth as Serena's, but the wear of this place is right there in the darker circles around her eyes and the red lines in them. She must be cold or about to head outside before class, because she has her gray Corrections jacket on.

"Have at it," Serena says. Eve sits next to her.

"Know what'd be nice? Chocolate milk," Serena says, as if reading my mind. "Or, even better, chocolate syrup. I could just squeeze it all over my food."

"Gross," Eve mutters.

"Don't hate," Serena says.

"That's a good idea, actually," I say. "I may get that first day I'm out." *If* I get out of here.

"You know what I'm gonna get as soon as I'm out?" Serena says. "Burgers. Big ole greasy burgers with everything on them, and those super soft sesame-seed buns. Like in those songs you hear on TV. Oh man, don't get me started." Serena pokes at her plate, the reality of our lunch draining her enthusiasm.

"I'd want scallion pancakes." My stomach growls with each word. "Superhot and crispy, with homemade dipping sauce."

The rest of the cafeteria fills up with girls—those returning from their Trials and those prepping for them. That was me, or will be me again. Did I look as drained as the ones trying to eat and failing? Or was I like the ones barely blinking, then suddenly shaking themselves awake as if from a deep sleep? I wasn't like the ones holding back tears or wiping their faces while searching to see if anyone's looking. It's like everyone's a type here.

"Chicken and waffles," says Eve. Which sounds amazing right about now. "There's a great spot in Harlem that makes them, above One Twenty-Fifth," she says.

"Harlem is another place I'm gonna hit up once I'm outta here." The more Serena talks about her impending freedom, the more singsongy her voice gets. She can't sit still, and I can't blame her. She reminds me of Petra, a bundle of energy you couldn't try to contain. Serena deserves this joy, but . . .

Eve tries to be happy for her. I can see her trying to keep her shoulders up, rather than curve her body like the rest of us.

"You got a growing list of what you're *gonna* do," Eve says.

"No need to get ready if you stay ready," Serena says, all smiles.

"Well, I'm getting ready to go." Eve hasn't been here ten

minutes, but she's cleared her tray clean. And that's saying something, considering the quality of the food here.

"I got a van to catch," she says.

Oh. I glance at her jacket. "It's today?"

"It's today. Ladies, it's been real . . . crappy." Eve forces a smile, showing what's left of her lunch in her braces. For the first time, I realize I have never seen Eve smile with her teeth, not once. It feels like there's a constant role reversal with people I know. Petra forgiven and me in Trials, then Petra not forgiven and me passing my first Trial. Now Eve's got her answer, two years upstate, while I'm the one waiting. It's not fair how things keep changing for us.

"I'll miss you most of all," Serena tells Eve. She jumps up for a hug.

At first, Eve is rigid about it, same as she's been the whole time I've known her in here. Then I see it. The slow melting of the rocky exterior to reveal the Eve I don't think we ever got a chance to know. The same Eve who hugged me when I watched my brother leave without visiting. I know she's been upset and hasn't been treated fairly. And I realize it wouldn't be fair for me to hold a grudge against someone in a lot of pain. What good would that do either of us?

"I'm gonna miss you, Eve," I tell her. "We came in together and I was hoping we'd leave together."

"Yeah, well, maybe you can write me?" She unzips her jacket a little. She's hoarding gifts: a new composition note-book folded against her stomach and a couple colored golf pencils. "My new address is on the front cover. No pressure, though."

I take them, grateful for the small presents she and Petra have given me, since I haven't been able to give them to myself. "You know," I say, "I've gotten into the habit of not just writing but sending letters. So, yeah, I can do that."

"What about me?" Serena whines.

"To you, I've left the greatest gift of all. Candy." She leaves a couple packs of wrapped chocolates on the table.

"Oh. My. God. Yes!" Serena almost falls out of her seat as she grabs at Eve's present. "You get a chocolate bar, and you get a chocolate bar, and *you* get a chocolate bar," she says, pointing candy to random girls around the cafeteria. All of whom ignore her.

"Enjoy the sugar rush."

Clutching her treasures, Serena promises she will. "I will do you proud. I'll be bouncing off the walls by dinnertime."

Knowing Serena, that is not an empty promise.

"All right, then." Eve takes her tray. It feels momentous and sad. I'm going to come to dinner tonight expecting to see her. Breakfast too. You don't forget people who've been by your side in detention.

"Hope to never see y'all where I'm going. So be good." She winks at me. "You got this."

At least I get to see Eve leave on her own two feet. But, just like with Petra, it's not a happy exit. It's not on her terms. It's not an end to what began in here. Something passes on to the rest of us when the people you're close to go. With Petra, I held the fear of her losing an unwinnable battle. With Eve, it's like I inherited the indecision that weighed on her every day. Serena gets to finish her week, with candy, and I sit here waiting. As alone as ever.

CHAPTER 39

VINCE

Days in detention: 9

||||| ||||

Dead man walking, sort of. I'm not exactly ready to see Mom or Dad right now, but it is what it is. Our meeting is a private consult, not a visit, like with Levi. Meaning we get our own room; maybe they have news for me. If what Levi said is true, the news could be that Ross's parents are seeing how foul their son really is. Could be I'll be here a long while.

It's Friday, and sentencing is usually held on Saturdays. My counselor said I'd be told beforehand if I had to go to a sentence review. He also mentioned I'd be given the option to make a video to plead my case beforehand. Déjà vu is happening all around me.

The private meeting rooms aren't necessarily nicer than the visiting room in detention. There's no vending machines. And this room has smaller windows, with a crisscross of bars, a rusty water fountain, plus the same metal chairs and tables you can find anywhere else around the detention facility. There's nowhere that's comforting in this place. And, with my guard escort stationed right outside the door, nowhere to hide either.

Mom, Dad, and Randall are huddled up near the barred

windows until they see me. My parents are out of their comfy home gear. Mom's hair is trimmed to reach her shoulders. She's got makeup on—a hint of blush to brighten her milky cheeks—so she looks a bit more alive, less sad. She's also added some eyeliner to make her brown eyes pop. Dad's fully shaven from head to chin. He's even wearing trousers and a button-down shirt that smooths out his belly.

As soon as she sees me, Mom rushes at me like Levi did. Dad isn't far behind. Together, we make a Vince sandwich, and I'm glad no one is forced to let go. It's all so overwhelming I start crying again. Levi earlier this week, my parents today. I'm a mess.

Mom forces me to look at her. She and Dad both grimace.

"I'm okay," I say before they have a chance to ask about the mark on my cheek. Here come the waterworks again. A hell of a lot of them too. "I'm sorry."

"It's okay, Vince," Dad tries to assure me, but his voice is breaking too. "Everything will be okay. We're talking to Roswell's parents. I can't stand them, but your mother is making headway. She's always been the nicer one."

"Sometimes I'm nice. Most times I'm awful," Mom says, laughing through her own tears.

"I wasn't selling anything. I swear. The test at school—"

I almost forget how short my mom is until she buries her face into my chest as she shushes me with another hug. "It's okay. You're a good kid. This is all a mistake."

"Besides," Dad says, "you have some great friends. Levi, Janice, and Jorge started a campaign to get Roswell expelled for selling drugs. This *whole* time a student was on grounds selling, and not *one* teacher knew? Unbelievable."

"Well, his parents are huge donors to the school." Mom practically coughs out "huge donors."

Before all this, I was actually starting to feel sorry for Ross. He had it all and, at the same time, didn't have much. Yet with a simple donation, his parents can get him out of any mess, while mine have to struggle to make sure I know the value of hard work. How much was a good work ethic hammered into me? Shoot, that's the stress that led me and Byron to Ross in the first place.

Dad squeezes my shoulder. Up close and tears aside, Dad looks how he did in the before, like he could handle anything and everything. He towers over me by a foot, no more hunch. If you line up him, me, and Mom, we'd look like those dolls where you open one and find smaller ones right inside.

"We know you tested clean and they gave you the wrong results. We know you. People slip up every once in a while. We understand." He clears his throat on the last sentence to steady his voice.

Randall watches us by the window, wearing one of his usual silvery suits. He's the odd piece in this supposedly warm-fuzzy family moment.

"It wasn't . . . Well, not all of it was a mistake," I manage. I don't want to let go of them or for them to let go of me. But it is time for a hard conversation. Like trying-to-break-through-granite hard. I pull away from my parents, needing them to hear me. For the first time in I don't know how long, they look ready to listen. They also look really worried. Dad's wide forehead is as wrinkled as the back of his bald head. Mom's hand covers her mouth, prepared to be shocked or amazed, and not in a good way.

"What does that mean?" Dad asks.

All kinds of guilt rumbles through me. How do I tell them the truth?

I take a seat while they stay standing. So I have to look up at them as I explain that, yeah, the test was a mistake. Me being at Ross's and almost overdosing was a *big* mistake. However, this wasn't the first time Golden Boy Vince took something he wasn't supposed to. Nine days ago wasn't the first time I needed to escape and used something way more dangerous than red licorice to do so.

Dad shuffles to the table so he's close enough to grip my hands. His touch is gentle, not that forceful kind like when I was a kid and he'd have to drag me across the street because I was trying to run off. His hands are dry, my palms are damp, and we both need to hold on to something, someone. He asks, "Be honest. Is it something we did? Or didn't do?"

Putting everything out there with Levi was and wasn't easier. I need to dig deep right now.

I stutter before saying, "It's been really hard, Dad. I didn't want to mess things up, and now I've messed everything up." No semis or championships. No track scholarship. No freedom, possibly. Just me in here with snot running out of my nose, sputtering "Sorry" over and over. If I could see myself, I'll bet I'd look and sound like Letta did in her video. See what I mean about déjà vu?

I can feel how scared my dad is when he squeezes my hand harder, he won't let go. "This whole family's been breaking apart, and we didn't even notice, Annie."

More tears slide down Mom's face. She digs into her bag to pull out a wad of tissues and wipes her eyes along with the eyeliner, leaving a streak of black near her scalp. "We'll get through this together. We will. After this is all sorted out with Vince, and Letta straightens out, everything will be better." The whole time she's dabbing her face, Mom promises this as if it's something she can make a reality.

We're not the same. Nothing will ever be the same. I try to say it, but it doesn't come out. It can't, because all the hurt needs to be spewed out first. Along with all the shame, hiding, guilt.

My parents sit on the other side of the table. The three of us don't hide our sorrow. It's good, though, right? To have this moment to be honest. Intimidating too. It's like detention strips everything away. No, detention is *exactly* that. I have nothing but this uniform labeling me a juvenile delinquent and this fading bruise from someone wanting to stand their ground. There's nothing left of Golden Boy Vince here, so the weight of being him, as heavy as it was, is gone. I wouldn't say *lighter* is the best word to describe how I'm feeling. But being able to admit I haven't been perfect, that I *never was* perfect, means I don't feel like an imposter. I get to just . . . be. What a concept.

Mom and Dad catch me up a bit more. Aunt Mae and

Sonali, Grams and Gramps, some extended cousins, and even the neighbors continue to check in on them.

Mom's voice goes all deep and serious when she says, "Don't think you'll be driving all around when you're out of here. You are grounded."

"*If* I get out of here."

"Hey!" Dad says. "No 'if.' *When*. You're getting out of here. All our kids are getting out of detention."

"Albert . . ." Mom starts, but Dad assures her with a tight smile that it'll be fine.

"What if—"

This time Dad cuts her off with a tilt of his head and a blank stare. Something's up. My parents have been married long enough to have a shorthand. If it's not with their eyes, it's with small but noticeable movements. Mom untying and retying her hair in a ponytail usually translates to *We'll discuss this later.* Dad digging a pinky in his ear is one of the first signs of his frustration on a given topic. The "look" thing is always a shared secret between them. *Always.*

"Well, if you are all caught up, it's almost time to head to the facility," Randall announces, reminding me he's been here this whole time. I got a whole forty-five minutes with my parents, which feels like forever and an instant.

"You mean leave the facility," I say.

"Leave *this* facility," Randall corrects.

It clicks immediately. *Letta.*

"What happened to my sister?"

And there they go. Mom and Dad do the thing I hate, where

they have a one-on-one convo with only their eyes. "We're going to see her."

I repeat myself. "Did something happen to her?" I almost say, *What did you do?*

"She's . . . fine." The way Dad stretches out *fine* is impressive, considering how short the word is.

"Meaning she's not fine?" I ask.

"She's refusing to continue her Trials," Randall says. This is the only time I'm glad to hear him talk and tell me what my parents won't.

I consider what this means, or could mean.

"Could she come home? Can she be done with these stupid Trials?"

Randall flinches at my last question, like I personally offended him. From what I've seen, these Trials aren't helping Letta. They're punishing her. So, yeah, I think they're dumb. If I got sentenced to one, what would it be? Making pills? Cleaning up after people in recovery? Cleaning Ross's family's house?

"That's what we need to talk to her about. She didn't tell us. She won't—"

"Mr. and Mrs. Chen-Samuels," Randall says, not even hiding his annoyance, "you have eight more minutes to confer with Vincent. Considering he's incarcerated himself, I don't think there's a need to confer with him on what your decision is for the offender."

"Randall! My sister's name is Violetta Chen-Samuels, *not* 'the offender.'" Man, it feels good to shout at him. It feels even better that he shuts up. Randall straightening his tie is the only sign of him faltering from being Mr. Robot.

I ask my parents if they can take me with them. "I can go, right? I'm on the visitation list at the girls' facility."

Randall begins to open his mouth. I assume to say he doesn't think it's wise. Dad gives a nice Aunt Mae impression when he holds a hand up, warding off any interruption from the man in silver.

"If it's possible, I want to go." It sucks that only now that Letta and I are in matching detention jumpsuits I find the courage to see her. But maybe her seeing me will . . . I dunno. Not make her feel better, but maybe let her know she's not alone in this. Not anymore.

Mom and Dad don't do the eye convo with each other this time. I have their full attention. I try not to seem too pitiful, though that's hard to do. I give a little pout, make my eyes even sadder, though they're plenty sad—believe me. I've barely shaved in here, so I have patches of hair around and under my chin along with an unimpressive fade of a mustache. Maybe that, my ashy skin, and my dry waves are enough for them to think, *Dang, let's at least get this kid out for a bit of air.*

A couple minutes that feel like hours pass before Dad says, "Let's go see your sister."

Randall struts past us to bang on the door for the guard outside. "I'll see what can be arranged."

Randall speaks to my counselor, who speaks to the warden on duty, who checks with whoever he reports to. My counselor tells the warden me getting the opportunity to see family might be helpful for my morale. Then someone, I forget who at this point, has to speak to someone else at the girls' facility to see if me visiting is okay. It's a good hour before they come to an arrangement. What's arranged is: While my parents and Randall can walk with an escort, I have to be taken in a van, cuffed. And I have to remain cuffed the whole time we're in the girls' detention center.

The boys' and girls' facilities aren't that far apart. If there weren't all these fences, I could run it in a couple minutes, entrance to entrance. Instead, they shuffle me into a black Corrections van that zigs and zags through a maze of fencing topped with barbed wire. The van barely hits a stride getting from one checkpoint to another. I'm cuffed in the back, behind a grate separating me from the two guards up front. Because we're on grounds and I'm not considered a flight risk, the guard tells me "this time" they won't use foot shackles on me too. I try to drum a beat to keep my hands from cramping, but one of the guards warns me to sit still. I'm practically bound in a cage; what do they think I'll do?

After being in boys' detention, the girls' facility feels smaller to me, which is saying something when your home has been a ten-by-ten cell for nine days. Once we're all through, my parents and I and—can't forget the metallic man with fiery hair—Randall are steered to another private meeting room to meet my sister. This one has a long rectangular metal table and several chairs on either side. The room reminds me of the interrogation ones you see on cop shows. Everything in it is draped in a kind of shadow. The one window doesn't provide much, if any, sun and the lighting flickers every few minutes, making it dimmer, then brighter, then dim again.

With my wrists still cinched tight, the guard urges me to sit while my parents are allowed to stand.

A few minutes later, my sister is brought in. It's almost funny that Letta and I are both in detention jumpsuits, kind of like wearing matching Halloween outfits. Hers is gray, and mine's a pale green. Her hair is longer than when we saw her at her last Trial, though the bags under her eyes are puffier, aging her. Her forehead crinkles in the same way Dad's does when he's nervous or surprised. She stops at the doorframe, taking us all in. One hand clutches her opposite arm like she has a scratch, but I know, really, it's because she's figuring out what to say or do. It's how she stood behind the podium when she spoke for herself at her Trial. It's so good to see that familiar part of my sister up close. I'd hug her if I could. Sadly, these ties aren't very forgiving.

Letta's staring at us bug-eyed, maybe even relieved. Mom and Dad stare at her too. It's like we're frozen in time, waiting for someone to tell us what's next.

CHAPTER 40

VIOLETTA

Days in detention: 42

~~卌 卌 卌 卌 卌 卌 卌 卌 II~~

Yesterday, I found out my parents wanted to see me. I didn't believe Counselor Susan when she told me. She had to repeat herself before it sank in.

"Victims talking to offenders mid-Trials isn't usually part of protocol," Counselor Susan said with a *click click click* of her pen. "However, your parents said they wanted to hear you out about not continuing with your Trials before making a decision. So we're allowing it. That is, if you want to speak with them as well."

Counselor Susan got new chairs for visitors—plastic with no cushion, with hard arms and a hard seat, that take me a while to get comfortable in. I had nothing to pick at, nothing to distract me. I was finally getting a chance to talk to my parents. I'd get to explain myself without a video, not through my counselor's notes or someone else diagnosing me, and not on a scribbled piece of paper sent through the mail. Face-to-face. *Isn't that what I wanted?*

"Yes," I replied to my counselor, "I would like to see my parents."

"I didn't know you wanted to stop your Trials, Violetta."

I told her, "What I want doesn't seem to be something you care about."

"I'm sorry you feel that way." Another *click* ended the conversation.

The note on top of the letters I sent to my family was short and sweet: *Please look up LeVaughn Harrison. I'm done proving myself.* I hoped they'd understand I didn't only mean I was done with the Trials. I am also done being what others expected. I need to figure out how to be me.

It's not just my parents in this meeting room when I walk in.

"Please sit," says a tall, lanky man in a suit. He appears frustrated as he adjusts his green checkered tie. It stands out against the gray he wears, the same color that's painted all around us, though his suit is a cleaner, brighter gray that glistens.

"Sit next to me, Letta," my brother says.

Without a word, I sit myself in a chair beside Vin. My family resembles a picture or a movie still. Every so often, the lights brighten, then fade, then brighten, as if someone's playing with a switch in a horror movie. I never expected to see my brother here like this, in a jumpsuit that matches mine. It isn't right seeing him in zip ties, with his body bent into submission. His hair has grown and flops to one side. His rich brown skin matches mine except for a greenish-yellow bump on his cheek.

I want to be mad at him for leaving when he had the chance to see me. I wish I could be upset he did the video sentencing me to the Trials. I want to feel so many things about him, only I can't summon up any of that anger. I want to picture the Vin next to me as the brother who helped me study for my learner's permit, who taught me how to be less scared of the road and more confident in my turns. But the guy sitting next to me glares at the ties binding his hands to his lap. And he seems broken. Is this how I look to my family?

Two guards are also in the room with us. One stands behind my parents, and the other, who brought me in, stands behind Vin and me.

The last time I saw my parents was in the hospital. They were a wreck then. Seems as though not much has changed now. Dad offers the saddest of smiles while mashing his hands together as if he were molding clay. Mom keeps wiping her nose with a frayed tissue and has a smudge of eyeliner near her left eye. The way we're seated, it's as if it's me and Vin against them, but I know better. It's me, and then there's everyone else.

The man in the suit stands at the head of the table, so we can all see him. "Mr. and Mrs. Chen-Samuels requested a meeting with Violetta Chen-Samuels"—the man glances at my brother—"whose Accountability Trial was suspended due to the family emergency of Vincent Chen-Samuels's accidental overdose and impending, or current, incarceration for drug use, dispensing drugs—"

"He did not sell drugs," Mom announces.

"All I'm doing is stating the charges, Mrs. Chen-Samuels." The man continues. "And being in possession of illegal substances."

"Thanks for repeating all that, Randall," Vin snaps.

What I'm hearing has to be a mistake. It just has to be. "You're in here because of drugs?"

My brother tucks his tied hands between his legs as if he can shrink himself. I know that feeling.

So it's true. "But why?" I ask.

The man talks over us. "As Vincent Chen-Samuels awaits sentencing, we were informed in a letter that Miss Chen-Samuels wanted to discontinue her Trials before a decision had been reached. Hence"—he presents the room with a flourish of his hands—"today's meeting. Vincent Chen-Samuels is a late addition. Are you all right with Vincent remaining in this meeting, Miss Chen-Samuels?"

I've heard our last name so many times I've lost track of who he's speaking to until the man raps his knuckles on Vin's and my side of the table.

"Me? Yeah, yes. I'm fine with my brother being here."

"Duly noted," the man says. Every word out of his mouth sounds mechanical. Nothing he says has any feeling. And maybe that makes sense considering how pale he is, the life drained out of him right down to how he speaks. If this is the man who's been guiding my parents and helping with my Trials, I can see why they've been the way they've been.

The man, Randall, looks to my parents to start. I certainly have no idea what to say. So we wait. We wait until Mom puts her purse on the table between us. It's her baby-blue one. She usually saves this purse for holidays, because it holds a lot. If anyone needed anything and Mom was carrying the wide blue bag with the metal latch, what you needed was in there. She wipes her nose again, leaving a small trail of tissue above her lip. She opens her handbag to reveal the envelope I sent to them earlier this week. Even though the ink is blurry from water spots, I can see the stamp for the Piedmont Facility on the front. The envelope is already rumpled, but my mom takes great care to pull out the ragged-edged papers inside. Still, no one says anything. As if Mom is opening a present and we're waiting to see if she likes it. But I don't want my parents to *like* my letters; I need them to understand.

Mom lifts up a piece of paper. I can see my handwriting in capital letters and hard strokes.

"You asked us . . ." Mom clears her throat and starts again. "You asked us to look up LeVaughn Harrison. And we did."

Dad scoots up in his seat, no more slouching. "We ended up going through a big ole internet hole to find out more about him. I barely remembered that case. It happened when I was your age, Letta."

"We were both teenagers," Mom reminds him.

"One day, the world worked one way. And the next, it worked another. I didn't think about why that was. To be honest, I didn't care. Once I turned eighteen, all that mattered was what I wanted in the world." My dad almost laughs, whether at himself at that age or something else, I can't tell.

"LeVaughn took his life. Are you saying you want to hurt yourself, Letta?" This is the hardest and clearest Mom has looked at me since before the hospital. Was this what Petra's family asked her when she was taken away, if she had wanted to hurt herself or meant to?

"No, I don't want to hurt myself," I tell them. "That's not what I was trying to say with that. My neighbor, another girl"—I feel myself begin to break—"she hurt herself. She was my friend."

"Oh, Letta," Mom says. She doesn't reach for me, but she does hold the letters closer to her chest.

"She's okay, I think. But she was so tired. And then I found out about LeVaughn and how he accidentally caused someone's death too. But no one believed him, or not enough people believed him, and he's dead!" I didn't expect it to come out like this, but there's no turning back now. "I'm not saying I don't need to be accountable for what I did. I just don't think I should be put on a stage to prove it. How could you do that to me? How could you bring Pascal into this to humiliate me?"

"Now, now . . . that wasn't us, Letta. Please know that. We only chose the categories. We didn't know—"

"But what happened when you did know?"

Vin attempts to comfort me, but the ties on his hands prevent him. Defeated, he sits back, tells me to "Find my zen."

"*You* find it," I tell my brother.

My brother tilts himself toward Randall, since he can't really point. "That Trial was because of Judicator Roboto over here."

"Letta, I know you're upset," Dad begins. "But we needed time to figure things out. And then we got a call about our son in the hospital. How do you think that made us feel? We almost lost our goddamn minds. We're here now to figure this all out."

"Figure it out *after* I've done Trials? Why not before? Why couldn't you talk to me *before* you sentenced me?"

"Letta, you killed your sister!" The booming voice that comes from my mom shocks us all into silence.

Six weeks ago, the Violetta who heard that would've shattered to pieces. The Violetta sitting in front of my family now—what's left of my family—has heard it too many times for it to hit me in the same way.

Of course it hurts; it'll always hurt. At this very moment, my chest tightens and my breath comes in smaller bursts, knowing I don't get to wake up from the nightmare of my sister's death. I've kept trying to explain why it happened, explain how it happened, explain that I'm sorry—and I am. I wish I could figure out how to make things better. Not go away, just become better. From the fire in their eyes, my parents may see their daughter as a murderer. And maybe LeVaughn's family couldn't see past what he did either. Maybe they never visited him, or maybe they visited him all the time. But if no one allowed him to be more than the death of his cousin, how could he live with himself?

"Do you know if LeVaughn's family wrote about him after he died?" I ask.

"Some did. Yes," Dad answers.

"What did they say?"

"That he was a kid who deserved better than what he got."

My letters to Viv were the only time I could be honest. It

was the closest I've felt to being me in months. The pages of the notebook Counselor Susan inspected were filled with every negative thought I had about myself, reminding me I was a horrible person, daughter, and sister. But that isn't all there is to me. The bad is part of me, yes, but it's not everything.

That's what Petra told me before she hurt herself. For nine months, she was only an offender scratched by thorns of all sizes. Nothing more, nothing less. It didn't seem like she got to be her. Ever. So who are we when we're not our mistakes? Does LeVaughn Harrison get to be a person or a sacrifice or an example? That's what I want my parents to think about. LeVaughn and I aren't the same, yet from where I sit we share a lot in common.

"I didn't think about what I wrote," I tell my parents now. "All I did was put pencil to paper, so my thoughts could flow along with the memories. It helped me feel a little closer to Vivian. She was all I had in here."

Mom's fingers tremble as she puts one letter, then another, then another, on the table. She lays them out like wallpaper for us to decide on. Each letter has my heart in it, along with my regret, but there's also something good. A nice memory I got to recall with my sister and me.

"Not everything has to be horrible," I whisper to no one and everyone in the room.

Vin places his bound wrists on a letter, sliding it closer to read. Mom taps the envelope, and Dad buries his face in his hands, a pose I'm familiar with because I do the same most days.

The man, Randall, coughs—for our attention, it seems. "We

only have a few more minutes. It needs to be decided if Violetta will be sentenced to time in upstate corrections or not. Vincent needs to get back to his facility. Per the agreement."

My father's request is muffled through his hands, but we can all hear him. "Can you give us a minute, Randall?"

"How long exactly, Mr.—"

"When it comes to *my family*, I'm at liberty to ask for all the time I want. Aren't I, Randall?" Teddy Bear Dad is nowhere in sight. The Dad whose eyes bore into this tall, rigid man is the Dad who would protect his family at all costs. For weeks, he probably thought he had to protect them from me.

"Fine. I'll be right outside." The man walks out as stiff as he sounds, his arms clinging to his sides, every part of him tightly wound.

"Not gonna lie," Vin says, craning his neck to the door closing behind Randall. "It's great to see him go."

"You don't like him?" I ask.

"'Like' is a very strong word, Letta. And no—no, I don't."

Scooting over, my brother tries to maneuver his way closer to me. It's a challenge in zip ties, but he manages to hold his chair seat and shuffle a few inches at the same time. I don't know if I can touch him or my parents. It doesn't matter that we're close together, finally in one room after more than a month. Everyone is so far away. Even me.

"These letters are really sweet, Letta. Like really. Viv . . ." Vin doesn't finish, so I try to for him.

"She would've said I worry too much."

"*Yup!* She would've said, 'Chill out and eat some ice cream. You'll feel better.'"

We all erupt in laughter. I catch one of the guards behind my parents cracking a smile too.

"Viv hated being punished," Mom says. New tears roll down her face, breaking through the blush on her cheeks.

"Sending someone to their room isn't punishment, FYI," Vin offers. "You sent us to our rooms, but we still had Wi-Fi. I made it work." This sets us laughing even more. It doesn't take long, though, before the cries of laughter turn back to grief. My sister isn't here. Her memories bring warmth and sadness all wrapped in one.

All the words and hurt and tears fight to come out of me at the same time. "I'm so, so sorry Viv is dead. I never meant to hurt her. I love her *so* much. And I'm terrified you'll never love me ever again. That—that's why you gave me the Trials." I stutter the rest. "D-do you want to send me upstate?" If they do, I'll get to see Eve sooner than I thought.

"Oh, sweetheart." Mom sits on top of the table and pulls me close. "You know," she says, "I'm not good with losing what I love. And when I was pregnant with you, I almost lost you. For a while, I'm sorry to say"—her breath catches in my hair, her words in my scalp—"I was so mad at you for scaring me like that. I didn't want to think I'd lose my little girl. Then you grew up, and I guess to protect you . . . I never allowed you to be you. I wanted you to be what I needed you to be, because I thought it'd keep you safe."

"By the time you have your third kid, you let them bounce off the walls," Dad says. "But you and Vin were, are, precious. So was Viv. But obviously . . ." Dad clucks his tongue once, twice, like he's counting a regret each time. "Obviously, we weren't listening hard enough. Were we, Annie?"

Mom doesn't respond. Her lips press against my forehead as she makes me a promise. "We're sorry too, Letta. We'll figure this out together. We'll find a way."

I clutch at my mother's waist so tightly the guards are going to have to pull me from her. This is what I needed the night of the accident. Not to be sent away or recited a list of crimes. I needed someone to say we'd figure out what's next.

CHAPTER 41

VIOLETTA

Days free: 22

The humidity outside and the threat of an oncoming storm fogs up the windows of my brother's car, so Vin has to take his time driving. I stretch my arms and legs, still trying to get comfortable being back on the outside. It's May and I've been home for three weeks. Some parts about being home feel good, other parts of being out aren't easy, like sitting in the passenger seat, the last place Viv sat. Vin said I couldn't be in the back: "I'm not your taxi. Get up here." I started to have a panic attack being this close to the driver's seat. As I tried to take in heaping gulps of air, I told my brother that I never want to drive again. Vin calmed me down. He checked his phone to see what buses could get us where we needed to be if I didn't want to ride shotgun. But this is one of those first steps I've been taking every day since I was forgiven, even though I'm not sure if I've fully forgiven myself yet.

This is also one of the few times we get to be together in Vin's car. He's grounded for a month with some leeway for important things like weekend finals, going to the occasional meet to support his team, and helping Grams and Gramps get to appointments. Today, Mom and Dad said we could make this special trip together because I said it was time.

I suck up the view. There are no bars or fences, no barriers getting from place to place; there's no guards telling me where to go; there are no ties around my wrists whenever I get in a vehicle, and nobody checks me when I come back inside. And, most importantly, no Trials. I adjust my bra strap, a real bra again, so it isn't showing, since my black dress is sleeveless. This is going to be rough. But at least I get to be me.

Vin settles us into a parking space in the lot. "You ready?" he asks. "Okay, not a great question. But if we can survive family therapy—"

"Ha! Would you call all our crying and yelling 'survival'?"

Vin says, "Of the fittest. We're lucky there's nothing sharp in that room."

"The table," I point out.

Vin shuts off the car. The engine roars once more before puttering out. "Too heavy to lift unless you're a comic book superhero."

"Maybe I am and I've been hiding my powers. Hmm?"

It's really nice to see my brother's smile take up his whole face. "You are definitely stronger than I gave you credit for," he says. He pulls me in for a hug, but my seat belt gets in the way. I swallow hard at how different things would be right now if Viv had worn hers.

For the past two weeks, two times a week, we've had family therapy. Though we haven't had a family dinner together since

Vin and I came back home. The food is there—Mom's slowly gotten back into cooking—but we end up scattered around the duplex. Either we eat in our bedrooms or the living room. Our therapist says this will also take time. We are planning a trip after school ends. Just the four of us, to be together to try and make new memories as a family. We're not sure where yet. But I want to go somewhere I can be outside as much as possible. Our therapist also says grief is never-ending. The *never-ending* part is what scares me most, but I don't want to forget; I want to move forward.

Vin kisses the top of my head. "We can take as much time as you need, Letta. No one is going anywhere . . . Ouch, that was kind of a gross thing to say."

"I know what you meant." What we have is the good kind of quiet, sort of. One where we don't have to say anything. Vin wasn't in detention as long as me but it affected him. Going from "Vince the Great" to "troubled youth" will do that to you.

"You know," I say, wanting to acknowledge how hard it was for him too. "I never blamed you for trying to be perfect."

"That's good, because I had plenty of blame for the both of us." My brother's smile disappears, and his chin trembles. It's my turn to try and comfort him with a hug.

"I'm serious, Vin. You had so much going on. I'm sorry I always thought it was easy for you."

"You know what's funny? Not ha-ha funny . . ." He wipes the tears flowing down his chin. "I did like doing most of that stuff. I liked running and just kicking ass on the lacrosse field."

He punches the button on the glove compartment. It explodes with car registration papers, mints, wadded tissues, Band-Aids, a jockstrap, and an empty water bottle.

"Been looking for that," he says, picking the jockstrap off the floor between my feet.

I hand over a tissue.

"I enjoyed the games and the field for what they were. It was the *not* winning that I couldn't handle. Losing wasn't an option, and I hated it. Plus, it wasn't only Mom and Dad. My teammates, Coach, recruiters—everybody expected the best results. Nothing less." He shrugs it off before looking at me again.

I wish a hug could erase all of the pain, for both of us. It's suddenly cold and hot at the same time, like his air conditioner is only half working.

"I get it now," I tell him. "Or at least I see how it affected you."

"Just because I felt the pressure doesn't mean I shouldn't have looked out for you too. A good brother would've protected you from feeling like you had to . . . I dunno, be as good as me, I guess? I just . . . I didn't know how to speak up, Letta. Some days . . ."

"Yeah," I whisper because he doesn't have to explain. I know exactly what he means. My last days in detention, it was so much easier to write everything down than to speak it out loud.

Would it ever get easier for me to speak? Maybe. That's something we're working on in family therapy. And what I'm trying to figure out in my virtual classes. I've missed so much of the school year that online makeup courses are the only way to stay in my grade. While my brother prepares to regain his spot in track this summer, I'm going to test to see if I can still be a sophomore next year. My parents aren't sure if I'll stay at Claremont or go somewhere else to try and start new.

"You have time to decide," our therapist says. She's a really nice Korean American lady who wears colorful bead necklaces, new ones each session, and speaks so warmly you want to sit and listen to her all day. Plus her office has decorations, some drawings from kids she's helped and some photos of landscapes. She and her office are a welcome change from Counselor Susan and nowhere near as severe as that Randall guy.

Vin and I collect everything that landed on my seat and around my feet, stuffing items back into the glove compartment. Then we sit again, not a word between us.

"Okay," I finally say. "Let's go."

Aunt Mae agreed about things taking time. She took me to the community garden to plant a yellow rosebush in Viv's honor. Yellow roses mean joy and affection. That's Viv in a nutshell. Some of the buds were blooming, so I cut a few to bring with me and Vin today.

Before I open the door, I catch my reflection in the rearview mirror and see all of me. Not a wreck. Not with my hair all over the place or hacked shorter than I want. Not in an assigned ash-gray uniform or with zip ties around my wrists. I smell like home, not the facility or the dead. I see my dad's forehead scrunched up and my eyes that aren't as red or as haunted as they used to be. It's me in pieces, yet I'm whole. It's time to face what I've done. I need to apologize to the person who deserves it most.

I pause, with one leg out of the car, one foot on the pavement. Vin parked right next to a sign etched in gold lettering pointing us to the entrance of St. Andrew's Cemetery.

Vin says, "Seriously, if you aren't ready, it's okay."

I'll never be ready. But I need to do this. Vin gets the flowers from his back seat. He hands me the rosebuds and holds on to the peonies he brought. I made sure to clip the thorns off the roses before we brought them today. While we were planting Viv's special rosebush, I asked Aunt Mae what would be the best flowers to give someone who hates roses. She suggested tulips, then she helped me make a bouquet of tulips and daisies to send to Brooklyn. Petra told me she could receive flowers at her hospital. And at some point, when she's feeling up for it, she wants me to come visit. I hope that's sooner rather than later. But I remembered our therapist's words and repeated them in a letter to Petra: *Take your time. No worries.*

My brother and I walk arm in arm through the gate to the cemetery and past all kinds of headstones. Some are so huge I think they're sculptures of actual people. It's a short walk that feels miles long.

"Hers is coming up right along with Pa and Ma Chen," Vin whispers into my ear.

I grip my brother's hand tight.

It's not a shock when my grandparents' headstones come into view. We visit them a few times a year on their birthdays,

Qingming, and their wedding anniversary. It's the new one next to theirs, half the size, with rounded edges and a picture of my little sister, front tooth missing from her grin. I'm pretty sure that was Viv's last school photo. A bunch of flowers are spread around their gravesites. Most of them look new. Some are potted, and others have been laid on Viv's headstone with rocks, to keep the stems in place.

It hits me that this is the final resting place of my little sister. At home, her bedroom door is closed, a sign that we should keep out. My first days back, it felt like Viv was away seeing family or on a summer-camp trip. Sometimes, I expected to hear her bounding up and down the stairs, announcing she was awake or hungry or bored and asking who wanted to play a game.

Seeing her birth date and her death date scratched into stone makes this so much harder.

"She's really gone," I say. Vin's eyes are glassy with tears, and that's all I need for my own to appear. "I'm sorry, Viv," I choke out. "I'm really sorry. I hope, wherever you are, you can forgive me and that you're telling horrible jokes to people who laugh at them."

Vin gives me a sad smile. "What happened to the turtle that crossed— *Splat!*"

"At first"—I sniffle—"I didn't get that one."

"Neither did I. Viv was ahead of her time."

My knees buckle, and my brother grabs me to keep me upright. "I feel horrible, Vin!" I moan into his shirt. "There's no *un*feeling this. No wonder no one can forgive me."

I wrap my arms around him. He smells like soap but more fragrant, like cologne.

"You know I love you, right?" he says, holding me tight, not letting go.

"Yeah." I start to feel a little better, a little more at home in his arms. "But it's always nice to hear."

AUTHOR'S NOTE

First and foremost, I wrote a book about a family.

But the idea for this novel started as most do, with a question: What if victims of (alleged) crimes decided the fate of those who committed them?

From there, more questions arose: What if the victim was your own family? What if your crime was an accident? What does impartiality look like when those directly affected decide instead of judges or juries?

Ultimately, I came to the question that nagged me in every draft: What does *forgiveness* look like?

Numerous organizations and individuals make justice advocacy and prison abolition their life's work because our system is irrevocably broken. So broken that people can be incarcerated for decades when their perceived guilt was more convenient than the actuality of their innocence. Where prisons isolate, dehumanize, and fail to offer adequate living conditions or medical care, let alone provide services to rehabilitate. When, during the height of the COVID-19 pandemic, a judge deemed a fifteen-year-old Black girl in mental distress in need of "zero tolerance" for missing probation (i.e., being unable to do her homework due to depression) and thus sentenced to juvenile detention. Strip away the courts, the judges, and the juries— remove the current bureaucracy—and the question became: Would things be more fair if victims of said crimes could decide the fate of those shown to be guilty? Would we be more empathetic or forgiving? Would the structure itself still find ways to sustain *Us vs. Them* or insist that some teenagers deserve to be tried as adults and receive "zero tolerance"? Depends on a bunch of factors, doesn't it?

In the United States, Black youth continually outnumber white youth in juvenile detention.[1] (This is the same case with Black adults compared to white adults who are incarcerated.)[2] The system functions to irrationally interrogate and criminalize BIPOC youth and needs to come under continual mass scrutiny. This sobering reality is one that is touched upon in this book, yet it wasn't the sole basis for *Forgive Me Not*'s creation.

So, yes, I had an idea, but I wrote a book about a family.

Violetta and Vincent Chen-Samuels appeared as clearly as if I'd known them for years. And for years I'd get to know them even better as I grew into myself and became more aware of my ignorance, U.S. history, and the depths of what this story really needed.

I wrote and revised the bulk of *Forgive Me Not* while living a few blocks from the Queens County Criminal Court. Attached

---

1   National Association of Criminal Defense Lawyers: nacdl.org/Content/Race-and-Juvenile-Justice

2   Prison Policy Initiative: prisonpolicy.org/research/race_and_ethnicity/

to the main criminal court is men's detention. At any time of day, people exit the holding area with only the clothes on their back and they carry a paper scribbled with whatever they were arrested for. Every day, I walk past this place where I see families or friends gathered on the corner of Queens Boulevard and 83rd Avenue waiting for loved ones. I hear the rumble of the corrections bus that zooms by or I stare at the abundance of barbed wire looping around every window of the detention center. Walking or biking by every day made me think of the revolving door of people entering these buildings who are fighting to be seen as people first and not as "offenders."

I had questions, and for me at least, the best way to process those questions was through writing, as well as learning. I wanted to know how Violetta and Vincent would get through one of the hardest moments of their respective lives. Would Violetta be seen as a teenager who, unfortunately, made a deadly mistake? Would her family, let alone others, view her as anything more than "the girl who killed her sister"? Could she ever forgive herself?

It may go without saying that since this is a work of fiction, I took various liberties to fit the rules of the world I constructed, a world that is and isn't a mirror of the one we live in right now. In cases throughout this book, I use words like *inmate*, which is considered dehumanizing, to reflect the current (and problematic) vocabulary used about individuals who are incarcerated.[3]

---

3   Formerly Incarcerated College Graduates Network: ficgn.org/
    how-we-work; *The Hill*: thehill.com/blogs/congress-blog/
    politics/451099-language-matters-for-justice-reform

I hope reading *Forgive Me Not* provokes a different way of thinking about incarceration and leads to questions about the practices currently in place. I also hope when you finish this novel you remember that it's a book about a family. A family in pain, a family who loves, a family who errs and works through what forgiveness is for themselves and others.

Thank you for reading.

ACKNOWLEDGMENTS

The saying "It takes a village" applies to books too! *Forgive Me Not* wouldn't be in the shape it is without some strong critique and much cheerleading. My first thanks goes to the very early readers of some *rough* first pages: Amy Christine Parker, Jenny Peterson, Nicole Settle, and Jessica Valeske.

I'm also extremely grateful to:

- Sera Rivers, for regularly showing her enthusiasm for the initial pages to the final product, and for being a great friend for a decade plus.
- Essie Brew-Hammond, Elizabeth Johnson, Erika Lo, Benedict Nguyen, Vivian Nixon, and Jon Reyes, for additional insights that strengthened this work from character to clarification of space and stakes.
- Those who took the time to provide kind words about *Forgive Me Not*: Brendan Kiely, Randy Ribay, and Renée Watson. As writers I deeply respect, the fact that these pages resonated with you means the world to me.

- The extended Nancy Paulsen Books team, including Caitlin Tutterow and Nancy Paulsen, and everyone at Penguin Young Readers and Putnam BFYR who has touched and advocated for this book—and especially Cindy Howle, who was especially generous in her time to ensure these pages were clean. Everyone's role and every department is crucial to the whole bookmaking ecosystem. Thank you all so much!

- Cover artist Michael Machira Mwangi for rendering Violetta so beautifully. And photographer Gaby Deimeke for having a great eye and taking excellent headshots.

- The Highlights Foundation and Baldwin for the Arts for providing me time and solitude to get closer to the finish line on this book.

- Alex Gino, for lending me space, and a kind ear, as I worked through how to revise this book as well as start the next one.

Now, this book *really* wouldn't be where it is without two people in particular. Editor extraordinaire Stacey Barney! The detailed editorial letters she provided were critical in pushing this book to be the best it could be. (Stacey, you are known for your letters!) The moment you meet an editor as thoughtful as Stacey, it's intimidating and welcomed, because you know you're going to come out the other side a significantly stronger writer—if not without some stress-eating during revision stage. She dug into every line, questioned areas that needed to be questioned, and loved these characters the way they deserved—especially Violetta. And agent superhero Jenni Ferrari-Adler helped shepherd this book to acquisitions and has looked out for me from the time she first saw *Forgive Me Not* to this very day. Jenni, you are one of the most caring and respected agents in the field. I am truly humbled to have been gifted the opportunity to work with you and Stacey. You two are a Type-A writer's dream. 😊

Last, but certainly not least, because these acknowledgments are getting to be chapter-length, I am who I am because of the Black women who raised me, so many of whom are/were lifelong readers. They instilled a love of words in me at a young age and always, *always*, encouraged me to pursue storytelling. Even when I was writing some really funky pieces and emo poems. My aunt Glennie got me my first writers' magazine subscriptions; my aunt Debbie (God rest her beautiful soul) was always super supportive of my stories and laughed when they weren't actually funny; my aunt Vida gifted many notebooks, pencils, and other items to me in my early years; my grandmother Louise (we miss you terribly) always told me how important education and literacy is for Black people; and my mom, Viola, constantly fulfilled my need for more and more books (and other things) even when money was tighter than tight.

And, of course, deep gratitude to all educators, librarians, booksellers, and readers. You're essential and so valued.